SFBC 50th
ANNIVERSARY COLLECTION

# The Iron Dragon's Daughter

# Other Books by Michael Swanwick

*Bones of the Earth*
*Tales of Old Earth*
*Puck Aleshire's Abecedary*
*Cigar Box Faust and Other Miniatures*
*Griffin's Egg*
*In the Drift*
*Jack Faust*
*A Geography of Unknown Lands*
*Gravity's Angels*
*Stations of the Tide*
*Vacuum Flowers*

SFBC 50th
ANNIVERSARY COLLECTION

# THE IRON DRAGON'S DAUGHTER

*Michael Swanwick*

FANTASY
39

*FOR TESS KISSINGER AND BOB WALTERS*
*who didn't suspect I was stealing part of their story*

# ACKNOWLEDGMENTS

The author is grateful to Greg Frost for his encouragement and suggestions and for spotting the significance of the shadow-boy, Bob and Tess for dirt on insurgencies and rich relations, Susan Duggan for help navigating Penn, Dr. David Van Dyke for the p–chem here misapplied and for electric pickles as well, Gardner and Susan for football yobboes, Janet Kagan for help with French neologisms, Dafydd ab Hugh for Celtic words left on the cutting room floor, Gail Roberts for Dickens references, Elizabeth Willey for funding the University's carillon and one of its bathrooms, Lucia St. Clair Robson for the Gordon Riots and the Half-Crown Chuck Office, and Sean for his many insights. Health insurance and emotional support were provided by the M.C. Porter Endowment for the Arts.

# ACKNOWLEDGMENTS

# — ONE —

The changeling's decision to steal a dragon and escape was born, though she did not know it then, the night the children met to plot the death of their supervisor.

She had lived in the steam dragon plant for as long as she could remember. Each dawn she was marched with the other indentured minors from their dormitory in Building 5 to the cafeteria for a breakfast she barely had time to choke down before work. Usually she was then sent to the cylinder machine shop for polishing labor, but other times she was assigned to Building 12, where the black iron bodies were inspected and oiled before being sent to the erection shop for final assembly. The abdominal tunnels were too small for an adult. It was her duty to crawl within them to swab out and then grease those dark passages. She worked until sunset and sometimes later if there was a particularly important dragon under contract.

Her name was Jane.

The worst assignments were in the foundries, which were hellish in summer even before the molds were poured and waves of heat slammed from the cupolas like a fist, and miserable in winter, when snow blew through the broken windows and a gray slush covered the work floor. The knockers and hogmen who labored there were swart, hairy creatures who never spoke, blackened and muscular things with evil red eyes and intelligences charred down to their irreducible cinders by decades-long exposure to magickal fires and cold iron. Jane feared them even more than she feared the molten metals they poured and the brute machines they operated.

She'd returned from the orange foundry one twilit evening too sick to eat, wrapped her thin blanket tight about her, and fallen immediately asleep. Her dreams were all in a jumble. In them she was polishing, polishing, while walls slammed down and floors shot up like the pistons of a gigantic engine. She fled from them under her dormitory bed, crawling into the secret place behind the wallboards where she had, when younger, hidden from Rooster's petty cruelties. But at the thought of him, Rooster was there, laughing meanly and waving a three-legged toad in her face. He chased her through underground caverns, among the stars, through boiler rooms and machine shops.

The images stabilized. She was running and skipping through a world of green lawns and enormous spaces, a strangely familiar place she knew must be Home. This was a dream she had often. In it, there were people who cared for her and gave her all the food she wanted. Her clothes were clean and new, and nobody expected her to put in twelve hours daily at the workbench. She owned toys.

But then as it always did, the dream darkened. She was skipping rope at the center of a vast expanse of grass when some inner sense alerted her to an intrusive presence. Bland white houses surrounded her, and yet the conviction that some malevolent intelligence was studying her increased. There were evil forces hiding beneath the sod, clustered behind every tree, crouching under the rocks. She let the rope fall to her feet, looked about wonderingly, and cried a name she could not remember.

The sky ripped apart.

"Wake up, you slattern!" Rooster hissed urgently. "We coven tonight. We've got to decide what to do about Stilt."

Jane jolted awake, heart racing. In the confusion of first waking, she felt glad to have escaped her dream, and sorry to have lost it. Rooster's eyes were two cold gleams of moonlight afloat in the night. He knelt on her bed, bony knees pressing against her. His breath smelled of elm bark and leaf mold intermingled. "Would you mind moving? You're poking into my ribs."

Rooster grinned and pinched her arm.

She shoved him away. Still, she was glad to see him. They'd established a prickly sort of friendship, and Jane had come to understand that beneath the swagger and thoughtlessness, Rooster was actually quite nice. "What do we have to decide about Stilt?"

"That's what we're going to talk about, stupid!"

"I'm tired," Jane grumbled. "I put in a long day, and I'm in no mood for your hijinks. If you won't tell me, I'm going back to sleep."

His face whitened and he balled his fist. "What is this—mutiny? I'm the leader here. You'll do what I say, when I say, because I say it. Got that?"

Jane and Rooster matched stares for an instant. He was a mongrel fey, the sort of creature who a century ago would have lived wild in the woods, emerging occasionally to tip over a milkmaid's stool or loosen the stitching on bags of milled flour so they'd burst open when flung over a shoulder. His kind were shallow, perhaps, but quick to malice and tough as rats. He worked as a scrap iron boy, and nobody doubted he would survive his indenture.

At last Jane ducked her head. It wasn't worth it to defy him.

When she looked up, he was gone to rouse the others. Clutching the blanket about her like a cloak, Jane followed. There was a quiet scuffling of feet and paws, and quick exhalations of breath as the children gathered in the center of the room.

Dimity produced a stolen candle stub and wedged it in the widest part of a crack between two warped floorboards. They all knelt about it in a circle. Rooster muttered a word beneath his breath and a spark leaped from his fingertip to the wick.

A flame danced atop the candle. It drew all eyes inward and cast leaping phantasms on the walls, like some two-dimensioned *Walpurgisnacht*. Twenty-three lesser flames danced in their irises. That was all dozen of them, assuming that the shadow-boy lurked somewhere nearby, sliding away from most of the light and absorbing the rest so thoroughly that not a single photon escaped to betray his location.

In a solemn, self-important voice, Rooster said: "Blugg must die." He drew a gooly-doll from his jerkin. It was a misshapen little thing, clumsily sewn, with two large buttons for eyes and a straight gash of charcoal for a mouth. But there was the stench of power to it, and at its sight several of the younger children closed their eyes in sympathetic hatred. "Skizzlecraw has the crone's-blood. She made this." Beside him, Skizzlecraw nodded unhappily. The gooly-doll had been her closely guarded treasure, and the Lady only knew how Rooster had talked her out of it. He brandished it over the candle. "We've said the prayers and spilt the blood. All we need do now is sew some touch of Blugg inside the stomach and throw it into a furnace."

"That's murder!" Jane said, shocked.

Thistle snickered.

"I mean it! And not only is it wrong, but it's a stupid idea as well." Thistle was a shifter, as was Stilt himself, and like all shifters she was something of a lack-wit. Jane had learned long ago that the only way to silence Thistle was to challenge her directly. "What good would it do? Even if it worked—which I doubt—there'd be an investigation afterwards. And if by some miracle we weren't discovered, they'd still only replace Blugg with somebody every bit as bad. So what's the point of killing him?"

That should have silenced them. But to Jane's surprise, a chorus of angry whispers rose up like cricket song.

"He works us too hard!"

"He *beats* me!"

"I hate that rotten Old Stinky!"

"Kill him," the shadow-boy said in a trembling voice from directly behind her left shoulder. "Kill the big dumb fuck!" She whirled about and he wasn't there.

"Be still!" Casting a scornful look at Jane, Rooster said, "We have to kill Blugg. There is no alternative. Come forward, Stilt."

Stilt scooched a little closer. His legs were so long that when he sat down his knees were higher than his head. He slipped a foot out of his buskin and unselfconsciously scratched himself behind an ear.

"Bend your neck."

The scrawny young shifter obeyed. Rooster shoved the head farther down with one hand, and with the other pushed aside the lank, ditchwater hair. "Look—pinfeathers!" He yanked up Stilt's head again, and waggled the sharp, foot-long nose to show how it had calcified. "And his toes are turning to talons—see for yourselves."

The children pushed and shoved at one another in their anxiety to see. Stilt blinked, but suffered their pokes and prods with dim stoicism. Finally, Dimity sniffed and said, "So what?"

"He's coming of age, that's so what. Look at his nose! His eyes! Before the next Maiden's Moon, the change will be upon him. And then, and then . . ." Rooster paused dramatically.

"Then?" the shadow-boy prompted in a papery, night-breeze of a voice. He was somewhere behind Thistle now.

"Then he'll be able to fly!" Rooster said triumphantly. "He'll be able to fly over the walls to freedom, and never come back."

Freedom! Jane thought. She rocked back on her heels, and imagined Stilt flapping off clumsily into a bronze-green autumn sky. Her thoughts soared with him, over the walls and razor wire and into the air, the factory buildings and marshaling yards dwindling below, as he flew higher than the billowing exhaust from the smokestacks, into the deepening sky, higher than Dame Moon herself. And never, oh never, to return!

It was impossible, of course. Only the dragons and their half-human engineers ever left the plant by air. All others, workers and management alike, were held in by the walls and, at the gates, by security guards and the hulking cast-iron Time Clock. And yet at that instant she felt something take hold within her, a kind of impossible hunger. She knew now that the idea, if nothing more, of freedom was possible, and that established, the desire to be free herself was impossible to deny.

Down at the base of her hindbrain, something stirred and looked about with dark interest. She experienced a moment's dizzy nausea, a removal into some lightless claustrophobic realm, and then she was once again deep in the maw of the steam dragon plant, in the little dormitory room on the second floor of Building 5, wedged between a pattern storeroom and the sand shed, with dusty wooden beams and a tar paper roof between her and the sky.

"So he'll get to fly away," Dimity said sourly. Her tail lashed back and forth discontentedly. "So what? Are we supposed to kill Blugg as a going-away present?"

Rooster punched her on the shoulder for insubordination. "Dolt! Pimple! Douchebag! You think Blugg hasn't noticed? You think he isn't planning to make an offering to the Goddess, so she'll keep the change away?"

Nobody else said anything, so reluctantly Jane asked, "What kind of offering?"

He grabbed his crotch with one hand, formed a sickle with the other, and then made a slicing gesture with the sickle. His hand fell away. He raised an eyebrow. "Get it?"

She didn't really, but Jane knew better than to admit that. Blushing, she said, "Oh."

"Okay, now, I've been studying Blugg. On black foundry days, he goes to his office at noon, where he can watch us through the window in his door, and cuts his big, ugly nails. He uses this humongous great knife, and cuts them down into an ashtray. When he's done, he balls them up in a paper napkin and tosses it into the foundry fires, so they can't be used against him.

"Next time, though, I'm going to create a disturbance. Then Jane will slip into his office and steal one or two parings. No more," he said, looking sternly at her, "or he'll notice."

"Me?" Jane squeaked. "Why me?"

"Don't be thick. He's got his door protected from the likes of the rest of us. But you—you're of the other blood. His wards and hexes won't stop *you*."

"Well, thanks heaps," Jane said. "But I won't do it. It's wrong, and I've already told you why." Some of the smaller children moved toward her threateningly. She folded her arms. "I don't care what you guys say or do, you can't make me. Find somebody else to do your dirty work!"

"Aw, c'mon. Think of how grateful we'd all be." Rooster got up on one knee, laid a hand across his heart, and reached out yearningly. He waggled his eyebrows comically. "I'll be your swain forever."

"No!"

Stilt was having trouble following what they were saying. In his kind this was an early sign of impending maturity. Brow furrowed, he turned to Rooster and haltingly said, "I . . . can't fly?"

Rooster turned his head to the side and spat on the floor in disgust. "Not unless Jane changes her mind."

Stilt began to cry.

His sobs began almost silently, but quickly grew louder. He threw back his head, and howled in misery. Horrified, the children tumbled over one another to reach him and stifle his cries with their hands and bodies. His tears muffled, then ceased.

For a long, breathless moment they waited to hear if Blugg had been roused. They listened for his heavy tread coming up the stairs, the angry creaking of old wood, felt for the stale aura of violence and barely suppressed anger that he pushed before him. Even Rooster look frightened.

But there came no sound other than the snort of cyborg hounds on patrol, the clang and rustle of dragons in the yards stirring restlessly in their chains, and the distant subaudible chime of midnight bells celebrating some faraway sylvan revelry. Blugg still slept.

They relaxed.

What a shivering, starveling batch they were! Jane felt a pity for them all that did not exclude herself. A kind of strength hardly distinguishable from desperation entered her then and filled her with resolve, as though she were nothing more than an empty mold whose limbs and torso had been suddenly poured through with molten iron. She burned with purpose. In that instant she realized that if she were ever to be free, she must be tough and ruthless. Her childish weaknesses would have to be left behind. Inwardly she swore, on her very soul, that she would do whatever it took, anything, however frightening, however vile, however wrong.

"All right," she said. "I'll do it."

"Good." Without so much as a nod of thanks, Rooster began elaborating his plot, assigning every child a part to play. When he was done, he muttered a word and made a short, chopping pass with his hand over the candle. The flame guttered out.

Any one of them could've extinguished it with the slightest puff of breath. But that wouldn't have been as satisfying.

---

The black foundry was the second largest work space in all the plant. Here the iron was poured to make the invulnerable bodies and lesser magick-proofed parts of the great dragons. Concrete pits held the green sand, silt mixes, and loam molds. Cranes moved slowly on overhead beams, and the October sunlight slanted down through airborne dust laboriously churned by gigantic ventilating fans.

At noon an old lake hag came by with the lunch cart, and Jane received a plastic-wrapped sandwich and a cup of lukewarm grapefruit juice for her portion. She left her chamois gloves at the workbench, and carried her food to a warm, dusty niche beside a wood frame bin filled with iron scrap, a jumble of claws, scales, and cogwheels.

Jane set the paper cup by her side, and smoothed her coarse brown skirt comfortably over her knees. Closing her eyes, she pretended she was in a high-elven cloud palace. The lords and ladies sat about a long table, all marble and white lace, presided over by slim tapers in silver sticks. The ladies had names like Fata Elspeth and Fata Morgaine, and spoke in mellifluous polysyllables. Their laughter was like little bells and they called her Fata Jayne. An elven prince urged a bowl of sorbet dainties on her. There was romance in his eyes. Dwarven slaves heaped the floor with cut flowers in place of rushes.

She took a bite of sandwich, and chewed it slowly to make it last. Crouched in the arch of the window was her very own aquilohippus, jeweled saddle on its back, and anxious to fly. Its glance was fierce and its beak as sharp as razors. Nobody but she dared ride it, but to her it was very gentle and sweet. Its name was—

Somebody stomped on her foot.

"Oh!" Jane scrambled to her feet, knocking over her juice, and saw that Rooster had just passed her, a bag of scrap slung over his shoulder—he was on the second lunch shift, and still working. "Heads up, dipshit! It's almost time!" he growled from the corner of his mouth. Then, to take the sting off his words, he smiled and winked. But it was a wan and unconvincing smile. If she hadn't known better, she'd've thought him afraid.

Then he was gone.

Her peaceful mood was shattered, Briefly, she had forgotten Rooster's wild plan. Now it came back to her, and with it the certainty that it would never work. She would be caught and punished, and there was nothing she could do about it. She had given her word.

The wall of the foundry farthest from the cupolas held a run of narrow offices for shop-level supervisors. Jane shoved her sandwich into the pocket of her work apron, and peered around the edge of the bin. She could see Blugg's office and within it Blugg seated at his desk, cigar in mouth, slowly leafing through a glossy magazine.

Blugg was fat and burly, with heavy jowls and a low brow. He had wispy flyaway hair, which was thinning and which he never tended, and a curling pair of ram's horns of which he was inordinately vain. For special occasions he had them lacquered and varnished, and once a year, on Samhain, he would gild the tips. Traces of gold remained in the whorls and ridges for weeks after.

"Hsst!"

Jane turned. The shadow-boy was standing in the niche she had just vacated, a ragged figure dim and difficult to see even at high noon. "Rooster sent me," he said. "I'm supposed to keep lookout for you." She could not make out the expression on his face, but his voice trembled.

She felt awful now, and afraid. "I can't," she said. She didn't have the nerve to go ahead with it. "I just—"

A roar shattered the midday calm. Suddenly everyone was running, throwing down tools, scuttling out onto the work floor and climbing up on the molds to see what was going on. They were all rushing toward the cupolas. Something was happening there. Jane stared into the swirl of figures, unable to make sense of all the noise and motion. Then suddenly everything snapped into place.

Rooster, laughing insanely, was pissing on a hammer giant's foot.

The hammer giant screamed in fury. It was the Sand Slinger himself, the biggest creature in all the plant, that Rooster had decided to pick on. This was typical Rooster shrewdness, since the Sand Slinger was not only largest but had the slowest reaction time of all the giants. But it was still a madly dangerous thing to do.

Now at last the Sand Slinger thought to raise its foot up from the stream of urine and bring it down upon its minuscule antagonist. The floor shook with the impact.

Rooster darted aside, jeering.

The giant moved its head from side to side in baffled rage. Brow knitted, it stared down at the three-ton maul lying atop its anvil. A cunning expression blossomed on its coarse face, and it reached an enormous hand for the hammer.

"Now!" The shadow-boy anxiously pointed to Blugg's office. It was empty. The door had been left slammed wide, open and unguarded.

*Crash.* The hammer slammed down where Rooster had been.

Running, stooping, Jane scuttled across those enormous empty spaces separating her from Blugg's office. She was aghast at her own daring, and terrified she would be caught. Behind her, the hammer slammed down again. The soles of her feet tingled with the vibrations. Then she was in the office. She stepped immediately to the side, where the wall would hide her, and straightened up to get her bearings.

*Crash.* The hammer fell a third time. People were yelling, running, screaming.

The office was close and cluttered. Technical manuals lay on the floor in heaps. The trash basket overflowed with litter. Water-stained plans for wyverns obsolete decades ago hung on the walls, along with thumbtacked production schedules gone brown at the edges, and a SAFETY FIRST poster showing a cartoon hand holding index finger upward, a ribbon tied in a bow just beneath the second knuckle.

The sole bit of color came from a supplier's calendar with a picture of naked mermaids, fat as sea cows, lolling on the rocks. Jane stared at those pink acres of marshmallow-soft flesh for a frozen instant, as if the image were a window into an alien and threatening universe. Then she shook her head clear and darted to the desk.

The pressed metal ashtray was exactly where it ought to be. A cigar smoldered on its lip, still damp at one end. Gingerly, she took the smelly thing between thumb and forefinger and held it aside. Hurry! she thought. In among the ashes were what looked to be seven crescent moons carved from yellowed ivory. She picked out two, put down the cigar, and whirled to go.

But then a speck of green caught her eye, and she glanced down in the wastebasket. One corner of a book peeked out from the trash. For no reason that she could think of, she brushed the papers aside to see what it was. Then she saw and caught her breath.

A grimoire!

It was a thick volume in a pebbled green vinyl cover, with the company logo on the front and beneath that a title she could not read in raised gold-edged lettering. Three chrome bolts held in the pages so they could be easily removed and updated. Jane gaped, then came to her senses. Grimoires were valuable beyond imagining, so rare that each was numbered and registered in the front offices. It was impossible that one should end up here, in Blugg's office, much less that it would then be thrown away as worthless.

Still . . . it wouldn't hurt just to touch it.

She touched it, and a numinous sense of *essence* flowed up her arm. In a way unlike anything she had ever felt before the volume spoke to her. It was real! Beyond any doubt or possibility of delusion, the book was a true grimoire. Here, within her grasp, was real magick: recipes for hellfire and vengeance, secrets capable of leveling cities, the technologies of invisibility and ecstatic cruelty, power enough to raise the dead and harrow Hell itself.

For a long, timeless instant she communed with the grimoire, letting it suffuse and possess her. At last its whispered promises faded and were still.

She dug it out of the papers.

It was too big to carry in one hand. Jane stuck the stolen nail parings in her mouth, where she could hold them between lip and gum, and seized the book with both hands.

At that instant there was a long, shrill whistle. She turned, and there in the doorway stood the shadow-boy, held back by the fetish-bundles nailed to the jamb, urging her out with anxious sweeps of his arm. Beyond, she saw that the Sand Slinger had been brought under control. Rooster was held captive by one of the hogmen. The spectators were breaking up, some into small knots to discuss what they'd seen, others turning away, returning to their jobs.

Cradling the book in her arms, she ran from the room. It weighed a ton, and she staggered under its weight. But she wasn't going to give it up. It was hers now.

The shadow-boy stood in open daylight, as close to visible as he ever came. "What took you so long?" he whispered fearfully. "He'll be coming soon."

"Here." She thrust the book at him. "Take this back to the dormitory, quick, and hide it under my blanket." When he didn't move, she snapped, "There's no time for questions. Just do it!"

In a voice close to tears, the shadow-boy said, "But what about my lunch?" His head turned yearningly to where the lake hag leaned over her cart, staring slack-jawed at the aftermath of Rooster's fight. She had yet to begin her second swing through the factory.

"You can have mine." Jane dredged her somewhat flattened sandwich from her apron pocket, and slapped it down atop the grimoire. "Now go!"

An indistinct motion that might have been a shrug, and the shadow-boy was gone. Jane did not see him leave. It was as if he had simply dissolved into the gloom and ceased to be.

She raised a hand to her mouth to spit out the stolen nail parings, and simultaneously saw Blugg all the way across the foundry, squinting straight at her. Jane stood in an exquisite paralysis of exposure.

Then Rooster darted free of the hogman and shouted something up at the giant. With a roar of outrage, the Sand Slinger seized the first weapon that came to hand, and *hurled* it.

Lightning flashed.

The afterimage of the molten iron that splayed from the flung ladle burned across Jane's eyes. Voices rose in a babble of fear, laced through with urgently shouted orders. High above them all, Rooster screamed an agonized scream.

In the confusion, Jane made good her escape. She was back at her bench in a minute, hastily pulling on her gloves. Maybe Blugg hadn't really seen her. Maybe he'd forgotten her in all the excitement.

"Did you get them?" Smidgeon whispered. For a second Jane couldn't imagine what she was talking about. Then she remembered, nodded, and spat out the stolen nail parings into her hand. Smidgeon took them and passed them down the line to Lumpbockle, who palmed them off to Little Dick, and from there Jane lost track. She scooped some emery powder into the palm of her glove. Back to work. That was the safest course.

To the far side of the factory, Rooster's still body was being carted away. Leather-helmeted spriggans ran about, dousing small fires the molten metal had started. Water sizzled and gushed into steam. A scorched smell filled the air.

Over it all rumbled the Sand Slinger's laughter, like thunder.

Blugg descended upon the workbench, face black with rage. He slammed his hand on the table so hard the emery trays jumped. "Stand up, damn you!" he shouted. "Stand when I'm talking to you!"

They scrambled to their feet.

"You vile little pieces of shit. You worthless, miserable . . ." He didn't seem able to compose his thoughts. "Who put Rooster up to this? That's what I want to know. Who? Eh?" He seized Smidgeon in one enormous hand and hauled the wretched creature struggling off her feet. "Tell me!" He twisted her ear until she whimpered.

"I-I think he did it himself, sir. He's always been a wild one."

"Bah!" Blugg contemptuously flung Smidgeon down, and turned on Jane. His face swelled up before her, as large and awful as the moon. Jane could smell his sweat, not the fine, clean astringency of a Rooster or a shadow-boy, but the strong, sour smell of an adult male. She smelled his breath, too, sweet with corruption. He had yellow little stumps of teeth, black where the gums drew away from them. A bit of rotten meat caught between two of his teeth mesmerized Jane. She could not look away.

"You—" he began. Then, shaking his head bullishly, he drew back and addressed them all: "You think you can ruin my career, don't you?"

They were too fearful to speak.

"Well, I have news for you! I'm not some dickless wonder you can fuck over anytime you feel like. You make things hard on me, and I'll make things hard on you. I'll make things harder on you than you could ever imagine!"

He bent over, turning sideways, and pointed to his own rump. "When you make trouble, Management is going to land on me right *here*, get that? And if they land on me *here*, I'm going to land on you *here* too." Every time he said *here*, he waggled his backside and jabbed his forefinger at it; it would have been funny, if it weren't so frightening. "Do you read me?"

They stood trembling and silent before him.

"I said: Do you read me!"

"*Yes, sir!*"

For a long time Blugg glared at them, motionless, silent, unblinking. A muscle in the back of Jane's left leg began to tremble with the effort of standing still. She was sure he was going to ask what she was doing in his office. Despair welled up within her, a force so overwhelming that once it started to leak from her eyes she knew it would fill the room and drown them all.

"You . . . little . . . vermin," he said at last. "There's nothing I'd like better than to strangle each and every one of you with my bare hands. I could do it, too—don't think you'd be missed! You eat like pigs and then spend half the day sitting on your thumbs." He walked down the line looking them each in the eye. When he came to Jane she again thought he would ask why she had invaded his office, but he did not.

"All right," he said at last, "line up by height, and out the east door double ti—where's the shadow-boy?"

"Here, sir," the shadow-boy said meekly. Jane started. She hadn't realized he was standing beside her.

Blugg rocked slowly on his heels, sweeping his gaze up and down the workbench, savoring their fear. Then he snapped, "all right, double time out—I've some special work duty for you little shits. Now!"

They were quick-marched, Blugg cursing them every step of the way, out the east door, past the loading docks, and around the steam hammer works. A brace of loaders were parked in front of the orange smithy, so they took a detour through the old file works building, which had begun long ago as a covered yardway connecting the planing shed to the machine shop and then been expanded and still later, after the new file works building was dedicated, renovated into a clutch of utility rooms.

Blugg had still not said anything of Jane's being in his office. She was beginning to dare hope that all that had happened had driven it from his mind.

"You!" He grabbed Jane by her collar, half-choking her, and kicked open a door. "Wait in here. If you're not here when I return, you know what'll happen to you."

He flung her inside and slammed the door.

The hurrying footsteps of the children faded away, and all was still.

# —◆— TWO —◆—

The room was empty. One wall was all windows from waist-high to the ceiling, panes painted over in a motley, unplanned pattern of gray and dull blue to reduce environmental distraction and promote worker efficiency. Pale light shone through them, wintery weak and shadowless. Thin cracks where the paint had contracted by the edges of the sash bars shone painfully bright.

Beneath the windows a long lab bench was cluttered with testing equipment. Three oscilloscopes shivered liquidly, square-cornered sine waves slowly creeping across their screens. White smocks had been hastily hung over wall pegs or left draped atop high wooden stools, as if the low-level technomancers who ordinarily worked here had been suddenly driven away by some industrial disaster. To the far side of the room, a new-model dragon's eyeball, as tall as she was, peered from a testing box. *Click*. It swiveled to look at her.

Jane shivered miserably. She tried to picture what punishment Blugg would inflict on her for her crime, and could not. Whatever it was, it would be bad. She walked slowly across the room and then back again, the sound of her footsteps bouncing from the high ceiling. The dragon's eye tracked her progress.

Was Rooster dead? His plan had turned out even worse than she had anticipated. She had expected that he would escape unscathed while she herself would be caught and subjected to a punishment both swift and dreadful. This was worse, far worse, on both counts.

Time passed, and Blugg did not return. Nor did the techs who surely worked here. At first she awaited them with fear, knowing they would not accept her explanation of what she was doing in their work space. Then, from sheer boredom, she began to look forward to the confrontation. Later, she despaired of it. Finally, she arrived at indifference. Let them come or not; she did not care. She was a creature of pure perception, a passive observer of the coarse feel of the metallic grit dusting the workbench, of the oxidized rubber smell of the voltmeters, and the fine sheen of the smoothly worn grain on the seats of the stools. Without her, these things would cease to exist, fading silently and gratefully into nothingness.

By excruciatingly slow degrees the windows dimmed and the room cooled. Just before darkness, someone walked by in the hallway, flicking switches. Row upon row of fluorescent tubes winked on overhead.

Jane's stomach ached. She felt miserable in a way that was beyond tears. Her insides cramped. For the umpteenth time she walked into the center of the room, the dragon's eye following her every step. She had no idea what time it was, but she was certain she had missed supper.

The door slammed open.

Blugg entered, looking weary and distracted. His gray work shirt was damp under the armpits, and the sleeves were rolled halfway up his woolly forearms. The dragon's eye flicked toward him.

"What were you doing in my office?" Oddly, Blugg did not look at Jane. Instead, he frowned down at a small filigree-capped crystal that hung from his hand on a loop of thread.

"I was only . . ."

All of its own volition, Jane's hand rose to her mouth. Her lips pursed involuntarily. It was the exact same gesture she had been making when Blugg saw her in front of his office. Horrified, she whipped her hand down and hid it behind her back.

Blugg stared at her in a bug-eyed, unblinking way for a moment. A slow smile grew on his face. "You little minx. You were going through my trash."

"No!" she cried. "I didn't take anything, really I didn't."

Blugg slid the crystal back in its plastic case and stuffed it into his shirt pocket. He reached forward and seized her chin.

His smile grew dreamier, and more frighteningly distant. He turned her head from side to side, studying her face. "Mmmmm." He ran his gaze down the front of her work apron, as though appraising her strength. His nostrils flared. "Rummaging through my trash basket, were you? Looking for orange peels and bits of sandwich crust. Well, why not? A healthy appetite is a good thing in a youngster."

This was more terrifying than threats would have been, for it made no sense at all. Jane stared up at Blugg uncomprehendingly.

He laid his hands on her shoulders, turned her around slowly. "You've been working for me how long? Why, it's been years, hasn't it? How time has flown. You're getting to be a big little girl, aren't you. Perhaps it's time you were promoted. I'm going to put in for a Clerk-Messenger Three. How would you like that?"

"Sir?"

"Don't sir me! It's a simple enough question." He looked at her oddly, then sniffed the air again. "Pfaugh! You're bleeding. Why haven't you kept yourself clean?"

"Bleeding?" she said blankly.

Blugg pointed down at her leg with a fat, blunt finger. "There."

Jane looked down. There was *blood* trickling down her calf. She could feel it now, itching all the way down from her thigh.

This final indignity broke her delicately maintained control. The sudden, sorcerous appearance of blood from some previously unsuspected wound ruptured the membrane holding back all her fear and apprehension. She began to cry.

"Oh, shit." Blugg made a face. "Why does all this crap always happen to me?" Disgusted, he waved her to the door. "Go on! Go straight to the nurse's station, and do whatever she tells you."

<hr>

"Congratulations," the nurse said. "You're a woman now."

The nurse was a sour old creature with piggy eyes, a pointed nose, and two donkey's ears. She showed Jane how to fold a sanitary napkin, and what to do with it. Then she delivered a memorized lecture on personal hygiene, gave her two aspirins and sent her back to the dormitory.

Rooster was there already. He lay delirious upon his bed, head swathed in bandages. "He's going to lose his left eye," Dimity said. "That's *if* he lives. They said if he doesn't die tonight, he'll probably be okay."

Jane timidly touched Rooster's shoulder, though she could scarcely bear doing so. His skin was pale as wax, and cold. "Fly the friendly skies," he mumbled, lost in some faraway delirium. "Join the Pepsi generation."

Jane snatched her hand away from him, as if scorched.

"I'm taking care of him. So don't you interfere." Dimity smoothed the blanket down fussily. There was a defiant edge to her voice. When she was done, she leaned back, hands on hips, waiting for Jane to challenge her. Then, when Jane did not, she smiled meanly. "Time for you to go to bed. Isn't it?"

Jane nodded and went to her corner.

The grimoire was waiting for her. The shadow-boy had left it under her folded blanket as instructed. She undressed slowly, managing to spread out the blanket and slip beneath without exposing the book. When she put her arms around it, she experienced a tingling sensation, like a low-voltage electrical current running through her. It made her feel strange.

That night, it seemed to take forever for the children to fall asleep. Rooster groaned and cried and babbled in his sleep, and his pain terrified them. Some of the smaller creatures crept from their own cots to huddle with their friends. Even the oldest among them occasionally sighed or turned over on their sides to face away from his suffering.

At long last, though, only Jane remained awake.

Silently, she slipped from her covers and under the bed. She pried up the broken board and squeezed into the narrow space between the dormitory room and the sand shed wall. It was dark there and dusty, but not close, for neither wall reached quite to the ceiling. A tiny draft found her and, naked, she shivered. It was not quite cold enough, though, to force her back for her dress. She groped blindly behind her for the grimoire, and pulled it in after her.

Rooster groaned. In a high, lucid voice he said, "Two all-beef patties, special sauce, lettuce, cheese . . ." Jane found herself unable to breathe. ". . . and a sesame seed bun." It was too awful, his lonely voice speaking to no one in the emptiness of the night. "Teflon." She grasped the broken board with her hand and swung it to. With it closed, she could no longer hear him.

Settling herself down on her heels, she placed the grimoire on her lap and opened it. The pages were black and lightless, but the letters shone coolly, silvery to the eye and slick to the touch. She found that when she concentrated hard on them, a whispery sense of meaning filled her, though she could not quite capture the significance of each word. This was a table of compression ratios, and here was a section on machining tolerances for the cylinders. She lingered briefly over the calibration settings for the crystals, then flipped ahead, trusting to her fingertips to convey to her the essence of what they skimmed, skipping and leaping ahead until she came to what she wanted.

It was the chapter that told how to actually operate a dragon.

Until that instant, she had not known what she intended. Now, though, running her hands over and over the schematics with their cryptic symbols for capacitors and potentiometers and resistors and grounds, dipping her head so she could caress the printed dials and circuits with her cheek, breathing deep the ink and coated-paper smell that emanated from each page, it seemed to her that she had been born intending to someday steal a dragon.

The space between walls was so tight it pinched her shoulders. She did not notice. Her head was full of fast black dragons. What had been invisible to her, because ubiquitous, now stood revealed. She heard them scream supersonic across the sky, fueled by wrath and gasoline. She felt the gravitational pull of them, the super-heated backwash of their passing. And she saw herself riding one away, away, away.

First, though, she would have to master the grimoire. She would have to learn how the dragons were operated.

For hours Jane pored over the book, gently touching and internalizing the chapter sigil by sigil. She finished her first reading of it in time for breakfast. She crawled out of the wall just as the wake-up whistle blew, and was marched off to eat, yawning, bone weary and happy.

The next night, for the first time, she heard the dragon speak to her.

<hr />

Three days later Jane, Dimity, and Thistle were taken to the machine shop. The regular work spaces were all claimed, and after some argument with the shop supervisor Blugg took a box of machine wheels under his arm and led them upstairs. A balcony-level string of rooms ran completely around the building there. It was junk space, but Blugg found a place for them between a wooden stairway and the brick chimney-top of an industrial alembic. They were given a rickety wood bench at a window ledge, and told to wipe the wheels clean of grease.

Then Blugg left.

The window had long ago been painted over, glass and all, with white or green or gray paint—it was hard to guess which now—and there was a gap of at least a foot between the upper sash and the top of the frame, glued permanently open. Chill air poured down on them. A brown enameled kerosene heater wedged under the stairway strained to offset the cold.

"Trade places with me," Dimity said, as soon as Blugg was gone. "Thistle and I want to be closer to the heater."

Jane almost refused. But Dimity was always complaining about the cold; it was possible she felt it more. And Thistle was smiling in rather a mean way. It was probably best to give in to them on this one.

She stood, walked to the far side of the bench, and sat down again without saying a word.

The cogwheels were the size of silver pennies but much thinner, with fine teeth that prickled when touched edge-on. The grease on them was an almost translucent brown, and had hardened so that it did not come off easily. They worked industriously, knowing that Blugg would pop up to look in on them regularly.

But the inspections never came. Hours passed. Blugg seemed to have forgotten them completely.

Jane stared sightlessly ahead as she worked, her thoughts on the grimoire and on the dragon's voice she was still not entirely sure that she heard speaking to her at night. She dreamed of gleaming ebon flanks and smooth, streamlined surfaces, of strength and endurance wedded to ruthless speed. She imagined her hand on the throttle, with all that fearsome power under her control.

Beside her, Dimity sighed.

The silvery-dull sunlight streaming in over the top of the window was suddenly divided by the fluttering shadow of wings. Dimity looked up and eagerly cried, "Toad eggs!"

"Toad eggs?" Thistle said dimly. "Eww. Whatever are you talking about?"

"Up there, under the roof. That's where they've built their nests." Dimity climbed up on the ledge and stood on tiptoe. She stretched an arm out the window as far as it would go, her tail twitching impatiently. There were several muddy blobs on the undersides of the eaves. "Damn! I can't quite . . ."

"There won't be any eggs," Jane pointed out. "Nothing lays eggs in the autumn."

"Toads do. It's not like the spring clutch; it doesn't hatch. They store them away for the winter, so they'll have something to eat during the Axe Moon." She looked down, a strange smile twisting her wide mouth. "Jaaane! Climb out there, and fetch me in some eggs."

"I'm no climber! Why don't you get Smidgeon or Little Dick or . . ."

"They're not here." She exchanged glances with Thistle, and before Jane could react, the shifter had seized her and thrust her up alongside Dimity. The young feys were both preternaturally strong. Laughing, they stuck her out the window and shoved. The box of cogwheels was kicked over, and little metal wheels went spinning and rolling away. "Out you go, my lovely!" Dimity sang.

Jane clutched wildly at the frame. Cold wind blew in her face, forcing tears to her eyes. Across a cinder-paved courtyard, Building 6 reeled up at her, dark clouds scudding above. Below and to one side, she saw the tar paper roof of a utility shack, dotted with bits of brick and old soda bottles. It was at least a thirty-foot drop.

"Oh, holy Mother!" Jane gasped. Desperately, she struggled to pull herself back in.

But tough, merciless hands pried her fingers free. With a jar, she was pushed out into the void. Flailing, afraid she would throw up, she squeezed her eyes shut tight and grabbed for the window frame. Her weight rested atop the upper sash now. Only her legs were inside.

"Don't wriggle, you'll make us drop you."

She had hold of the frame again. Brittle flakes of paint crunched under her fingertips. She pulled herself flat against the building, brick scratching her cheek. The sweet, pungent smell of toad droppings filled her nostrils. The outside top of the frame was white with them. It was cold out here, too. She shivered convulsively. "Oh, please let me in," she babbled, "sweet Dimity, I'll do anything you ask me, I'll be your best friend, only—"

"Here." A hand shot out with a plastic bag in it. "Fill this up, and you can come back in again." One of Jane's shoes had fallen off and now she felt Thistle peel her sock back. A sharp fingertip drew itself up the center of her foot, paused, then waggled at the softest part of her flesh. "Stop that tickling! If she falls, I won't get any eggs." The hand moved impatiently up and down. "Take the bag."

Jane obeyed. She took a long, deep breath, and opened her eyes. Her head and stomach were so dizzy-sick that it took her a moment to realize that she was staring up at the underside of the eaves. There must be twenty nests up there, warty and bulging things with a hole to one side, like ill-made jars.

The toads had scattered when she first emerged from the window. They fluttered in agitation not far off, their black-feathered wings beating hysterically. They were loathsome things, the miscegenated get of jackdaws upon their lustful batrachian dams, and like their sires they were notorious thieves. Their nests were ordinarily kept cleared away from the roofs because they had a fondness for shiny objects and, unlike most wild things, had little or no fear of fire. They had been known to torch buildings by filching lit cigarettes and carrying them back to their nests. They were a terrible hazard.

Trembling, she stretched out a hand. The nest was just out of reach. Unhappily, she knew that Dimity would never accept that as an excuse. Taking a long, steadying breath, she forced herself to lean back over empty air. With the arm clutching the window fully extended she could easily reach the nearest nest. She squeezed her hand into the opening.

The inside of the nest was lined with fine black down, silkily soft to her touch. She probed to the back of the nest, and found a clutch of sticky warm eggs. She scooped them out and straightened at the waist, returning to the window. Awkwardly she opened the bag and dropped the eggs within. They slid to the bottom in a mass.

She hadn't gotten all the eggs. She leaned back again to scoop up those she had missed. This time, she only got a half-handful, along with two bits of aluminum foil, a shard of broken glass, and a chromed hex nut. These last she let drop to the distant ground.

Second nest. She dredged out the eggs quickly. Just as she was withdrawing her hand, the wind whipped up, sending a blast of icy air right through her clothing. She knew better than to look down, but the sudden swirl of air made her feel especially vertiginous. She wanted to cry, from fear and frustration, but dared not.

If she started crying now, she might never stop.

This nest had, in addition to the eggs, several more bits of foil and a jagged strip of copper sheeting gone green that made her think for a horrified instant that something had stung her, when she jabbed her hand against the point. "The bag is almost half-full!" she cried. "Can I come back in again?"

"Not enough."

"But I can't reach any more. Really I can't."

Dimity's face appeared in the window opening. Her grip on Jane's legs slipped a bit, and Jane cried out in fear. Dimity squinted judiciously. "That one there." She pointed. "You can reach it."

Jane's fingers ached. She was not sure her strength would hold out. The underside of the eaves crawled in her vision from her staring so hard, but when she closed her eyes all the world seemed to flip over, and she had to open them quickly or lose her balance.

She forced herself to stretch out as far as she could.

Her hand would not quite reach. "Dimity—" she began tremblingly.

"Eggs!"

There was only one way. Jane squirmed a little higher up on the window, so that her weight now rested halfway down her thighs. She stretched so far she could hear her bones creak.

Again her hand slipped into a nest. She felt the downy warmth and then the slippery stickiness within. She curved her hand and scooped out the eggs.

But the toads were beginning to regain their courage. They croaked and kawed at her, and made short, threatening swoops. One flew almost in her face, and when she threw up an elbow to protect herself, it bounced off her forearm with a solid, slimy thump. Jane's stomach lurched in revulsion.

"Hold my legs tight," she whispered, not at all sure she could be heard, but unable to speak any louder. She straightened at the waist.

Then she was back at the window. Grasping, she hugged it to her.

For a long time she was unable to move. When she had somewhat recovered herself, she tremblingly opened the bag and dropped in her final handful of eggs. Something red gleamed within. She stuck in two fingers to fish it out.

It was a ruby.

The ruby was half as long as her thumb, hexagonal in cross section, and flat on both silvered ends, an industrial crystal used in occult information systems for the storage and processing of data. Smaller than a pencil stub, it was probably worth more than Jane herself was.

The problem was that she dared not bring it in with the eggs, or Dimity, her avarice excited, would send her out again to look for more. She'd return it to the nest if she dared, but her strength and nerve both were shot. If she dropped it and it were later found, Dimity would hear and figure out what had happened.

The top of the window ledge was white with droppings. She stuck the crystal in among them, and said, "Let me in. I've got your eggs."

———⊸◉⊶———

Dimity snatched the bag from Jane's hand, even before she could climb wobblingly down from the ledge and collapse on the bench. "Good little Janie, *nice* little Janie-poo," she gloated, sliding her hand deep into the bag, and dumping a great gelatinous mass in Thistle's eagerly cupped palms. She placed an egg into her mouth and closed her eyes in ecstasy as it popped. She shoveled in more.

The cogwheels were all over the floor. Wearily, Jane righted the box and began picking them up. "Dimity," she said at last. "Why do you hate me?"

Dimity smiled an eggy smile. Thistle opened her mouth wide to show its inside yellow with yolk. Bits of shell clung to her lips. "Want some? After all, you fetched them."

Tears welled up in Jane's eyes. "I never did anything to you. Why are you like this to me?"

Thistle's cheeks were bulging with eggs. Dimity swallowed hers down, then turned the plastic bag inside out and began licking it. "I hear you're going to be Blugg's messenger," she said.

"Blugg's little pet is more like it," Thistle spat. "That's what you are, aren't you, Missy?"

"No, I'm not!"

"You know what he really wants, don't you?" Dimity thrust an arm up Thistle's skirt, and Thistle rolled her eyes in mock ecstasy. "He wants you to be his familiar."

Jane shook her head. "I don't know what that means."

"He wants to poke his wig-wag into your cunny."

"But that doesn't make any sense!" she wailed. "Why would he want—?"

Dimity's eyes turned the hard flat red of two garnets. "Don't act so innocent with *me!* I hear you creeping out of bed at night, crawling into the wall so you can stick your fingers up your rabbit-hole."

"No. Really."

"Oh! No, of course. You wouldn't do anything like thaa-at. Hotsy-totsy Little Miss Changeling. Think we're so special, do we? Just you wait until Blugg sticks his thing in your heinie-hole, let's see you put on your airs then!"

Thistle began to skip and dance about Jane, lifting her skirts up above her waist and waggling her skinny little behind. "Heinie-hole, heinie-hole," she sang. "Heinie-heinie-heinie-hole."

"Just keep this in mind, girlie-girl." The fey grabbed her by the collar, bunched it together, and lifted her painfully off the ground. "I give the orders here. What I say goes, messenger or not, familiar or not. You obey me. Got that?"

"Yes, Dimity," she said helplessly.

"He'll want to put it in your mouth too," Thistle smirked.

———◆———

Rooster lay abed for a week before he lapsed long enough into consciousness to get caught up. When his resources were at ebb, he lay motionless, struggling to breathe, each gasp of air rough and anguished. Sometimes he cried. Other times, snatches of glossolalic nonsense floated out of him. "The proletarians have nothing to lose but their chains," he said. "Lucky Strike Means Fine Tobacco."

Every night Jane waited until the others were asleep and crept into the wall to commune with the grimoire. When she had read herself into a trance, half exhaustion and half rapture, the dragon's voice would speak from the back of her skull. It told her they were both prisoners. It said their destinies were linked, and spoke of the freedom that would be theirs when they two flew off together, describing endless mountain chains with cold, high lakes, southern archipelagoes twisting like lizards, and high aeries niched among the autumn stars. She stayed, listening, inside the wall for as long as possible, emerging only when she was in danger of nodding off and being discovered missing at roll call the next morning. She didn't know if the dragon's voice were real or fantasy, and she didn't care.

She was under a compulsion.

It was always startling, when she emerged, to find Rooster still in his bed, she'd have forgotten him so thoroughly. He seemed an alien thing, slick with sweat, shining like an insect caught midway through metamorphosis. The pus that stained the edges of his bandages was faintly luminescent, like corpsefire, and he emitted an odd odor.

Jane's guilt was overwhelming. She ought to tend to him, she knew, wipe away his sweat, change his bandages, do what she could to ease his pain. But he repulsed her, even more than the foreign demons who worked in Section A as woodcarvers and joiners did, who were rumored to be cannibals and coprophages. She could not bring herself to go near him.

⚊⚊━◉━⚊⚊

One evening the children came tromping back to the dormitory to find Rooster awake and waiting for them. He had propped himself up weakly against the headboard. At the sight of them he twisted his mouth into what he must have thought looked like a grin. "Back so early? Now in my day, we had to put in a full day's work, we did. These young people today, I don't know."

The children clustered timidly by the door.

"Well, come on. There's no reason to stand back like that. It's me!"

They edged uncomfortably closer.

"Well. So how'd it go? Is Blugg dead?"

Nobody answered.

Now Rooster looked concerned. "Didn't the gooly-doll work?"

Dimity cleared her throat. "We haven't tried it yet," she admitted.

"You pussies." Rooster's face had the gently luminous quality of the flesh of some fey mushroom from the deep woods. The bandages were all crusty, for they hadn't been changed in days. His eyelids sank almost closed, then opened again. "Why not?"

"Dimity said—" Stilt began.

"—that we should wait on you," Jane said hastily. Dimity favored her with a quick glance that said as clear as words: Don't think that will get you any favors. Her tail switched twice. "So we'd be certain to do it properly."

"That's all right, then." Rooster was not a subtle creature and had caught none of the undercurrents of the exchange. "That's not half so bad as I'd expected." He nodded to Stilt. "You hear that? We look after your interests, old buddy."

Stilt nodded and bobbed his head, eagerly, grotesquely happy, perfectly secure in his friend's ability to protect him. In the face of such faith, Jane had no choice but to admit to herself that she no longer believed in Rooster's plan. They were only children. Their simple magicks wouldn't touch a grown-up like Blugg. Management must provide wards against such attacks as part of their benefits package; otherwise, overseers would be dropping dead every day. Most likely he wouldn't even notice he had been attacked. She felt cold and stiff.

"Get the candle, we'll do the thing now," Rooster said. Then, when Dimity did not immediately respond, "Come on, you cow! Get a fucking move on!"

Grudgingly, the young hulder complied. She paused just long enough after wedging the candle between floorboards to make it seem she expected Rooster to charm it alight, thus emphasizing his weakness, then struck a lucifer match.

Sulfur spat and flared.

"Where's the gooly-doll?" Rooster asked.

Shamefaced, Skizzlecraw produced it. Rooster ran a thumb over the stomach to feel the sharp tips of the horn slivers poking through, then handed it to Stilt. "You do it," he said.

Automatically, Stilt glanced toward Dimity for her okay.

Dimity tightened her lips, nodded.

"Hush," Rooster commanded.

They were still. Outside could be heard overlay upon overlay of distant machine noise, friendly rumblings, groanings, and poundings. Directly beneath them, they could hear the regular creak-creak-creak, almost inaudible, of a rocker. Blugg was whistling the Elf King's Tune, varying the speed and lilt of it as the rocker sped up and slowed down.

"Now!" Rooster whispered.

Stilt shoved the doll into the flame.

It had been stitched from old nylons, and the cloth bubbled and blackened as the fire touched it. A horrid stench filled the air. Then the cotton stuffing went up with a small roar, and Stilt dropped the thing with a startled cry. He cringed back, sucking on his hand.

The instant the flames touched the doll's belly, Jane's mouth went numb. She gasped. Her tongue felt swollen and prickly, as if it had been brushed by stinging nettles. Of course! There were still trace amounts of her saliva on the nail parings. A blind fraction of the curse was working on her.

Maybe they could kill Blugg after all.

Skizzlecraw began to cry. But Rooster ignored her. Hellfire malice dancing in his eyes, he sat bolt upright in his bed, fists clenched and head thrown back. "Yes!" he cried. "Yes! Die, damn you, die!" And while Smidgeon and Little Dick frantically beat out the flames to keep them from spreading, he laughed in triumph.

At that instant, there came a pounding on the ceiling of the room below, and Blugg bellowed, "What's that you brats are up to? By the Mother, I'm coming up there, and I'm bringing the strap!"

They fell silent.

A minute later, they heard his heavy tread coming up the stairs, and the lighter, more sprightly sound of leather tapping thigh.

Rooster's face was stricken. As one, the children looked away from him, to Dimity. Who lashed out an arm and commanded, " 'Neath blankets, all! Nimble-foot!" They scurried for their beds, hoping against hope to be spared the general punishment, Jane among them. But she noticed that Thistle was smirking with satisfaction.

Dimity was their leader now.

# — THREE —

Everybody blamed Jane.

Immediately after the doll's sacrifice, Jane came down with a light fever. Stilt stopped speaking altogether for three days. Skizzlecraw's hands and face blotched up with a rash. She turned sullen as well, but that was so in keeping with her prior character that it was little remarked by the other children. It was obvious to all that the curse was puissant, and an explanation was needed for why Blugg had not been hurt by it.

Dimity told them all, and Thistle backed her up, that Jane had lost her nerve in Blugg's office and come out without the nail parings. In her weakened state, Jane did a poor job of defending herself. And the shadow-boy was so bewildered and confused by the argument that he was of no help whatsoever.

Rooster knew the truth, of course; he had felt the parings with his own fingers. But he said nothing. After his moment of triumph, he had suffered a physical relapse and fallen back into silence and dead-eyed suspicion. So Jane was left totally friendless.

Her isolation was heightened by the new position Blugg had secured for her. Jane had to wear a Day-Glo orange vest to mark her as a messenger. It had two panels, front and back, that fit over her head, and was cinched at the waist by four ties of black plasticized cloth. She felt awkward wearing it, and exposed.

The work was easy, but unfamiliar. For her training period she trailed after Blugg as he made his rounds, and kept her mouth shut. "This is the meter house," he'd grunt, or "Here's where you get the emery powder, small bags only, and be sure to keep the yellow copy of the order slip." Jane was astonished to discover how much less Blugg had to do than his charges; his work seemed to her an aimless wandering process that consisted largely of long, incomprehensible conversations half-business and half-gossip. Sometimes he played dominoes with a squattie man in Purchasing, the two of them hunched motionless over a plank, peering suspiciously at each other and cheating when they could.

"Wash your face," he told her one lunch break. "Your hands too, and scrub under the nails. You have to make a good impression."

"Why?" she asked.

"Never you mind why! What business is it of yours why? You just do as you're told." Blugg followed her into the lavatory, and stood over her as she washed, making sure she lathered up with the brown soap, and at one point rubbing out a stain on the side of her ear with his own spittle.

They walked through a cold drizzle to a small office near the main gate. Blugg knocked, and they entered.

Inside, an elegantly lean elf-wife dressed in black sat smoking a cigarette and staring out the window. She turned her head when they entered, all powder and high cheekbones. Without any particular emphasis she said, "Is this she?"

"It's her," Blugg agreed.

The elf-wife stood. She was a good head and a half taller than Blugg. Heels clicking briskly, she strode to Jane and pinched her chin between thumb and forefinger. She turned Jane's head one way, then the other, frowning critically.

"She's an obedient thing," Blugg said wheedlingly. "Does exactly what she's told, snap of your fingers, doesn't have to be spoken to twice."

Jane stared up into the elf-wife's eyes. They were cold things, like gray chips of ice, and the flesh around them broke into complex structures of wrinkles, hinting at years and decades that had not been visible from across the room. Jane had a sudden vision of the flesh as nothing more than a thin mask stretched over the woman's skull.

Recognition of a kind sparked in those lusterless eyes. "Are you afraid of me?"

Jane shook her head fearfully.

"You should be." The elf-wife's breath smelled of candied sweets and nicotine. Two long pearls dangled from her ears, half as long as her forefinger, and carved into blunt-headed serpentine shapes. Her fingertips tightened on Jane's chin, until tears involuntarily filled her eyes.

At last those fingers freed Jane. "I'll give it some thought," she said. She waved a hand toward the door. "You may leave."

Outside, Blugg was in an inexplicably gleeful mood. "Do you know who that was?" he all but chortled. Not waiting for an answer, he said, "That was a Greenleaf. A Greenleaf!"

Jane forgot about the encounter almost immediately. It was but one odd incident out of many.

———◈———

It was not long before Rooster was back at work. The demons in the joinery shop made a little cart for him to use until he was strong enough to walk, and Jane and Stilt would lead the daily processions to and from work, each pulling at one handle of the cart.

One evening as they were marched back to the dormitory, they were stopped by the main gate while the shifts changed. They waited in the shadow of the monstrous black Time Clock while a flood of workers shambled, limped, and hopped by. The swing shift was letting out, and all the nonresident laborers were lined up before the Time Clock. They punched their cards, kissed the Goddess stone, and trudged off.

Stilt stared yearningly through the gate. Visible beyond were only the parking lot and the dusty curve of an asphalt road, but he stared as if they were a vision of the Western Isles. Blugg came up behind him, and laid a hand on his shoulder.

Stilt looked up.

Blugg's wide mouth twisted into what might almost have been a smile. He plucked a tiny feather from the base of Stilt's neck and held it up to his squinting vision. "Haughhmm." He put the feather in his mouth and slowly, savoringly, let it melt on his tongue. "About time you were sent to the infirmary, innit?" he rumbled. "Jane! Remind me come morning to send this one to the Doc for—"

It was not at all certain that Stilt understood what was being said. But something within him broke. With a high, despairing cry, Stilt dropped the cart handle and ran.

Blugg swore and started to lumber after the boy. But fat as he was, he was no match for the small, lithe figure. Slack-jawed workers turned as Stilt darted by. Their motions were slow in contrast, like those of flies caught in sap already hardening toward amber. Jane clutched the sides of her skirt with both hands in an agony of dread.

"Don't do it, Stilt!" Rooster screamed. He sat bolt upright in his cart, face waxy and white. "Come back!"

But Stilt was beyond listening. Arms out to either side, he ran down the road. The creatures of the swing shift stood frozen, gaping dully after him. He ran past the Time Clock, and through the gate.

He was outside.

As he ran, his arms appeared to thicken and lift. His whole body was changing, in fact, his neck elongating, spine curving forward, legs atrophying as thin as pencils.

"He's growing older," one of the little ones whispered in flat astonishment.

"Stupid!" Dimity snapped. "What do you think a Time Clock is *for?*"

It was true. With every step away from the Time Clock, Stilt put on days, weeks, months. He was a child no more. He ran through his adolescent phase and coloration in no time at all. He was an adult now.

Then he was in the air and flying. For one wondrous instant, it was just as Jane had imagined it would be. He flapped his new wings wildly, straining upward, and surprised laughter fell from his mouth.

He was glorious.

The wall around the factory grounds hid him briefly as he rose. He reappeared overtop of the gate, headed east and dwindling. Then Stilt faltered, and lurched in the sky. His wild flappings grew weaker and less effective. His brown-and-russet coloring grayed. A feather drifted down from his wings. Then another. One after another, until they were as thick as flakes in a snowstorm.

Stilt fell.

On the way back to the dormitory, everyone was silent. Even Blugg, though white with rage, could find no words to express himself; he kept punching the air with impotent little jabs of his fist. Rooster's face was like stone.

———◦———

Crawling back into her bed that night, Jane was surprised to find Rooster waiting for her, back against the wall, legs folded beneath him. A flash of alarm as harsh as an electric shock seized her. But before she could say anything, he shivered spasmodically and in a dry, toneless whisper said, "Something bad is happening to you." He swayed. "Something . . . bad."

"Come on," she said, forcing solicitude into her voice. "You've got to get back to bed." She took his arm, shocked by how light he was, how little resistance he gave her, and led him to his own cot. Eased him down, and pulled up the blanket. Touching him was not so repulsive as she had thought it would be.

"No. You've got to . . ." For the first time he opened his eye. It had no white. The pupil had swollen larger than his lids, opening a black, lightless hole completely out of the universe. She released his arm in fear. "Stilt . . . wasn't . . . the only one growing up. I have the sight. Not much, but a touch of it."

He shuddered again. The *awen* was upon him, moving about under his skin, threatening to splinter his bones from within. His slender frame writhed with the force of it, like an engine under too much strain.

Mastering her fear, Jane climbed in under the blanket, letting it engulf them both in its tentlike folds. She hugged Rooster to her. His flesh was cold as a corpse.

"You were in my dreams," he croaked. "I saw you."

"Hush."

"I lost my best friend," he said. "Not you too." His voice was fading now. His head thrashed to one side, then the other, as if trying to capture a fugitive thought. "We have seen the light at the end of the tunnel. Whip inflation now. Good fences make good neighbors."

"Hush, hush." She held him close, sharing her warmth and refusing to listen until eventually, the *awen* left him. He lay panting and exhausted, gray-faced, cold, and sweating. Quietly, then, Jane stole back to her own bed.

———◆———

One day Jane was let off work early. Blugg took her back to his room, a typical troll's den of black oak furniture and awkward ceramics of sentimental scenes. Puck stealing apples. The abduction of Europa. He stood her in the center of the room and inhaled deeply, noisily. His piggish little eyes looked pleased.

"At least you're not bleeding." He gestured toward a half-open door. "There's a tub in the next room. And soap. Take your time cleaning yourself."

It was small and dark next door and smelled warmly of ammonia and body gas. There was a bar of creamy white soap that smelled of lilacs resting on the lip of a zinc trough. Jane undressed and, seizing the soap in both hands like a sword, stepped into the steamy water.

She bathed slowly, thinking of napalm cannons, canisters of elf-blight, and laser-guided ATS missiles. Contemplating the dragon's weapons systems made the voice stronger, strong enough that she could sense it, weak as a tickle, even when she wasn't physically touching the book.

She fell into a dreamlike trance, the water warm against her naked skin, the dragon's voice almost real, stroking the bar of floral soap slowly up and down her body. The wiring diagrams floated before her like a mandala.

The dragon seemed to be insisting that she not let Blugg touch her.

Jane didn't respond. She knew that the voice's admonitions, whether real or a projection of her own fears, were useless. Blugg would touch her as he wished. He was bigger than she, and would do whatever he wanted with her. It was the way things were.

Her silence brought up a burst of outrage, and she seemed to feel the dragon dwindling in the western sky and she herself left behind, a prisoner, alone and unchanging, stuck here forever. In that adrenal burst of anger were undercurrents of what could only have been fear.

Jane had been gently lathering the brush of downy hair that had recently sprouted between her legs. Now she released the soap, and it bobbed to the surface. She turned her head sideways to look at it, one eye underwater and one eye not. She pretended it was a boat, a galleon that would take her far, far away. The water rocked up and down in time with her breath. All the world seemed to float in her vision.

The floor creaked under approaching footsteps. She heard it as a chord of sound, the solider grumble and squeak coming from the ear out of the water and its watery twin from the one under. She felt Blugg's bulk at the back of her neck, and closed her eyes. The light dimmed as his shadow touched her.

"That's enough." She stared up into a crazily skewed smile. "Rinse yourself, dry yourself off, and get dressed. We've got a date at the Castle."

——— ◉ ———

The Castle was an anomalous brick mansion located just off the center of the plant grounds. Older than the factory buildings that had arisen to surround and intimidate it, it had all the stylishness of a biscuit box turned on its side. Its trim and brickwork were hidden under industrial grime and black stains reached down the walls like tear tracks from its eaves.

The thin elf-wife answered the door with a disapproving frown, and waved Jane inside. "You may return in two hours," she said, and shut the door in Blugg's face.

Wordlessly, she turned and walked away.

Jane had no choice but to follow.

The mansion was much larger inside than out. She was led down a narrow gallery in whose high dimness chandeliers hung like giant luminescent jellyfish, then up a set of stairs, and through a series of rooms. The house appointments were everywhere valuable but nowhere absolutely clean. The damask silk settees were frayed, and the lace curtains were brittle as old spiderwebs. The taint of cigarettes and furniture polish clung to the textured walls, echoing a thousand yesterdays that differed from each other not at all.

Through one doorway Jane saw a sitting room where all the furniture rested comfortably on the ceiling. Shelves of knick-knacks and oil portraits hung upside down on the walls, and through the windows a gray drizzle fell up. The elf-wife frowned. "Not for us," she said, and shut the door firmly.

At last they came to rest in an unused bedroom, the four-poster's ancient hangings beginning to rip at the rings, a night-stand candle gone gray with dust and canting genteelly to one side. From a closet shelf, the elf-wife lifted down a large cardboard box. Tissue paper crackled.

"Put this on." She held out a pink dress.

Jane obeyed, folding her work things carefully as she shed them. The elf-wife *tsk*ed when she saw Jane's underthings and from a dresser drawer removed better, made of silk. "These also."

The dress was shell pink, linen, with cap sleeves. It was smocked across the bodice with tiny pink flowers and green leaves embroidered onto the cloth. The smocking went down to the waist, and then the cloth fell straight to her knees. There was another circle of embroidered roses at the hem.

The elf-wife watched, frowning and smoking, as Jane dressed. "Youth is wasted on the young," she remarked at one point. But added no more.

The dress buttoned up the back with pearl buttons. By reaching around awkwardly, Jane was able to fasten almost all, but the final closure, a single pearl button at the back of her neck, defeated her.

"Oh, for Cernunos' sake," the elf-wife said. She briskly stepped forward, and buttoned the collar.

"You may look at yourself in the mirror."

Standing before the oval claw-footed mirror, Jane expected to see anything other than what she did see: Herself. The dress was tight in the bodice, and it made her hips look big. It was for a child far younger than she. But it made her look not younger, or even different really, but more emphatically, awkwardly herself. She raised a hand and her reflection reached up yearningly to touch her. Her hand stopped just short of the glass.

"Please, ma'am. What am I supposed to do?"

"That should be obvious enough soon." She opened the door. "This way."

Five minutes later, they entered a den. Logs blazed in a high-arched fireplace. Pillars to either side supported tiled vaulting for a triple ceiling. The walls held paintings and photographs in ormolu and cloisonné frames, trophy antlers, religious fetishes in such profusion that the eye could not grasp them, and shelves of books in autumnal leather colors. The floor, by contrast, was empty save for a chaise longue, a rocking chair, and a scattering of rugs.

An elf-laird sat in the cushioned rocking chair, not rocking. He was old beyond belief, browned and gnarled as a tree stump. He stared straight ahead of himself.

"Father, this is young Jane. She's come to play here this evening."

The old laird's eyes swiveled around, but other than that he did not move.

"You'll enjoy that, won't you? You've always been fond of children."

Jane would have curtsied had she known how. But apparently that was not required of her. She stood in the center of the room while the elf-wife retrieved a large wooden box from behind the chaise.

Still the laird did not react. Only his eyes were alive, and they betrayed nothing of what he thought.

"Excuse me, please, ma'am," Jane said. "But what's wrong with him?"

Stiffly, the elf-wife said, "There is nothing wrong with him. He is Baldwynn of Baldwynn. Of the Greenleaf-Baldwynns. You will respect him accordingly. You have been brought here to brighten his evenings. If you behave properly, you will be allowed to return here on a regular basis. Otherwise, you will not. Do I make myself clear?"

"Yes, ma'am."

"You may call me Mrs. Greenleaf."

"Yes, Mrs. Greenleaf."

The box of toys rested on the hearth rug. "Well," Mrs. Greenleaf said. "Play with them, child."

Uncertainly, Jane knelt by the box. She rummaged within. It contained a marvelous mix of things: A set of mymble-sticks with ivory and mother-of-pearl inlays. A small ferris wheel that really worked, with seats that swung down and all the signs of the Zodiac painted on its sides. A set of toy soldiers, with archers and mine sweepers, two full armies' worth, each with its own commanding wizard. A faerie bell that when shaken filled the mind with a soft chime, breathtaking when sounded and impossible to clearly remember an instant later. Jacks and a ball.

Mrs. Greenleaf had settled herself on the chaise longue. She unfolded a newspaper and began to read. Sometimes she would read an article aloud for the edification of her father.

For two hours, Jane played with the toys. It was nowhere near so much fun as might have been expected. She was constantly aware of the laird's presence, of his eyes boring through her back. Everything went into those eyes, and nothing came out. He had the unhealthiest aura she had ever felt, a powerful presence that felt dangerous, capricious, random. Now and then she would glance at his trousered legs, never higher, and his shiny polished wing tips. It was like being in the same room as an overloaded boiler, waiting to see if it was going to explode.

"Here's an interesting article. They're phasing out those old Neptune-class dreadnoughts, and converting the shipyards for missile ships. You own some of that stock, don't you?"

The Baldwynn sat in his chair, looking at nobody.

———◦◉◦———

It was night when she got back to the door, in her own clothes again and oddly relieved to be free of that stuffy room, its uncanny laird, and the drear comments of Mrs. Greenleaf. Blugg stood on the stoop, shivering from the cold. His glance was dark when Jane met it.

"You may bring her back again at the same time in two days," the elf-wife said. Then, formally, "You have our gratitude."

Jane had expected Blugg would beat her. At the very least he would cuff her ear, and then complain and berate her all the way back to the dormitory. But once again, he seemed strangely elated by Mrs. Greenleaf's words.

"Gratitude!" he said. "You have our gratitude! That's worth something, indeed it is."

They did not go straight back to the dormitory, but cut through the storage yard to the smith shop, so Blugg could stop to have a drink with a boiler imp who lived in an outmoded annealing oven there. The imp was a slight, whiskered creature who obviously admired Blugg's bulk and self-assurance. He brought out a jug, and two tumblers.

"Did it work out well?" he asked anxiously. "How did it go?"

"It was a fucking triumph," Blugg asserted. "I have her gratitude. Her personal gratitude, mind you, the gratitude of a Greenleaf."

They clicked glasses, and the imp begged for details.

The shop was empty and, save for the red glows of the banked furnaces and a single bare bulb dangling over the imp's oven, dark. Left to her own devices, Jane eased back into the shadows. She found a warm niche around the curve of the oven and settled in among the cinders. It had a pleasant coke-smoky smell.

Feeling weary and unambitious, Jane leaned back and thought about her dragon. She had spent the last week studying diagrams of its electrical systems, and now she visualized them entire, a network of bright silver lines hung in space against a velvet sky. It was possible to rotate the image in her mind, and watch the wires close, converge, and pass one another as they orbited first one axis and then another.

After a time, the sense of the dragon's presence grew strong within her. With it came a kind of nervous energy, a jumpy sort of strength that drove sleep away without necessarily making her feel any less weary.

There was a warmth to the dragon's presence, an almost smug satisfaction that she hadn't been touched. At the same time, there were unclean depths to it. The better she was coming to know it, the more Jane realized that, morally at least, the dragon was no better than Blugg or anyone else in the plant.

Still, they had common cause.

"He didn't want to," Jane whispered, uncertain she could be heard. Around to the other side of the oven, Blugg and the imp were laughing drunkenly. It was easy to distinguish between the mousy squeak and the deep, trollish rumble. "It wasn't anything I had any say over."

But the dragon's presence was affectionate and approving. A compulsion seized her then. Her feet became intolerably restless. She could not stay behind the stove one more second.

Silently, stealthily, she slipped away.

It was time she finally met the dragon.

# — FOUR —

Jane slipped out into the storage yard. The dragon's presence filled her head like a hand inside a puppet. It was cold outside, and the earth was black. A few bitter flakes of snow, the first of the winter, drifted down from a low sky.

Feeling horribly exposed, she made her way down the narrow corridor between the smith shop and the erecting shop and past the mountainous stacks of iron boilerplate stock to the marshaling yards.

On the far side of a hurricane fence, the dragons rustled and clanked in their chains. Jane crept by, making herself small and insignificant, afraid of the carnivorous machines and painfully aware of their bloody and disdainful thoughts. In the shadow of a propane tank storage shed, she climbed the fence and dropped down into the yard.

A dragon snorted, sending her scurrying away in terror, like a leaf before the wind.

The dragons did not deign to notice the little figure darting through their shadows; their appetites for destruction were larger than anything a morsel such as she could satisfy. Cinders crunching underfoot, she hurried past the great lordly engines to a disused and overgrown corner of the yard.

There, between a pile of creosoted timbers and a hillock of moldering ammunition crates, was the ruined hulk of a dragon. It was half-buried in brambles and dried grasses, hollyhock and Queen Mab's lace. Rust had eaten holes in its boiler plates. On its side in chipped, flaking numerals, was painted No. 7332.

Jane froze, trembling with dismay.

This couldn't be her dragon! "It's not even alive," she whispered. "It's *not*." But sick with disillusion she knew she was wrong. It lived, crippled and demented, nursing one last spark of life within its broken carcass and harboring hallucinations. And she had been caught by its madness, by its fantasies of escape.

She wanted to turn, flee, and never return. But a compulsion seized her then, and she could not control her body. Her legs walked her to the dragon's remains. Her arms reached for the ladder up its side. The rungs sounded underfoot as she climbed.

She stepped into the fire-gutted cabin, all rust and decay, and the door slammed behind her. Alone in the darkness, she smelled the mingled scents of burnt carbon and high-octane fuel. From the depths of the machine a hum arose. A faint vibration trembled the floor, and rode up her legs. The air was warm.

Slowly, as if some unseen hand were turning a rheostat, the instrument panels came on. A soft greenish light suffused the interior of the dragon.

The cabin was transformed.

What had been rust and carbonized plastic was now chromed steel, optical glass and ebony-smooth surfaces. The charred pillar in the center of the cabin revealed itself as the pilot's couch, dark crimson leather with cushioned armrests.

Jane slid into the chair. It adjusted to her weight, hugging her hips, rising to support her back. Everything was positioned exactly as the grimoire had said it would be. She ran her hands over the engine instrumentation. At the flick of a switch the cybernetics curled themselves about her. She seized the rubber grips at the ends of the armrests and gave them a quarter-turn. Twin needles slid painlessly into her wrists.

Camera wraparounds closed about Jane's eyes. She peered through the dragon's virtual imaging system into a spectrum wider than human vision, trebling high into the infrared and booming deep into the ultraviolet. The yards were tangled orange and silver lines of power, the brick walls of the shop building purple quartz cliffs. Overhead, the stars were pinpricks of red and orange and green.

Then she fell, without a shock, into the dragon's memories, and was flying low over Lyonesse on a napalm run. Pink clouds blossomed in her wake, billowing over saturated green rain forests. She felt the shudder of hypersonic acceleration, the laminar flow of air over wing surfaces as she made a tight roll to avoid the guns of an antidragon emplacement. The airwaves were alive with radio messages, screams of rage and triumph from her cousins and the passionless exchange of positionals by the pilots. Black specks appeared at the horizon, an enemy squadron scrambled to meet them. Gleefully, she turned to meet the challenge.

Jane was trembling with adrenaline and surrogate emotion. In what was almost a sob, she cried, "Who are you?"

*I am the spear that screams for blood.*

Armies clashed in a continent of permanent night. The dragon's mind encompassed them all, cold as a northern ocean and as vast. Jane was half-drowning in its dreams of violence. A snapshot flash of elven warriors on the ground, spears held high as they posed behind a mound of trophy heads. Their grins were electric, wide, ecstatic. A line of trolls burning like torches. A city by the sea swelling in her gunsights, its slim towers shattering into crystal shards and dust. Tears streamed down her cheeks, big and wet and warm.

She was soaring now, alone, above clouds that shone brighter than hundred-watt bulbs, the air as cold as ice and thinner than a dream. The dragon's lust for blood was hers, and she felt the appeal of it, the beauty of its cruel simplicity. "No! No, I mean— what is your name?"

Abruptly, she was dumped clear of the memories, and found herself sitting damp and exhausted in the control couch, wrists stinging as the needles withdrew. Through the wraparounds she saw a dragon crouched on the far side of the lot, one clawed forearm raised. It stared unblinking at the moon. A voice as harsh and cool as static from distant stars spoke over the headphone speakers in the wraparounds. "You may call me 7332."

Jane felt unclean. Relieved as she was to be free of the dragon's mind, she yearned to enter it again, to once again feel that keen freedom from doubt and hesitation. Staring at the dragon across the lot, she felt the urge to climb in it and fly away, fly away forever, never to return.

"And so you shall," 7332 promised.

"Can I really?" Suddenly Jane found that hard to imagine. "Outside you look so . . . rusted, broken."

"Stealth technology, little savior. If our masters knew I was yet functional, they'd finish the job they began when I was first brought here. I'm too dangerous for them to ignore."

Jane's fingers ran lightly over the panels, caressing the potentiometer knobs and stroking the rowed switches she had night after night memorized from the grimoire. To have them before her in actuality made her giddy with possibility.

"Can we leave now?" she asked.

A deep engine noise thrummed up from the engine and through Jane's entire body. 7332 was chuckling. "You have the grimoire, that's a start. With that and three keys, we can leave any-time."

"Three keys?"

"The first is a ruby with a chromium taint at its heart."

"I've seen that!" Jane said, startled. "I've—" She stopped. "Was that your doing?"

"You must pay heed. Our time is short. The ruby will enable my laser guidance system. That is the first key. The second is a small thing. It looks like a walnut, but is made of brass and is cool to the touch."

"I've seen that . . ." Jane said uncertainly.

"It is in the box of toys in the Baldwynn's study." Jane started. "You must bring it to me; it contains part of my memory. The third key we already have: You."

"Me?"

"You, O changeling. Why do you think the Tylwyth Teg stole you in the first place? To sweat and swelter in the factories? Not cost-effective! No, you are merely being held here until you are old enough to be used. Dragons, as you must know, are built of cold iron around a heart of black steel. We generate a magnetic force which is carcinogenic to the elf-lords and their underlings. They cannot pilot us themselves. A pilot needs mortal blood."

"Then . . . I'm to be a pilot?" It was a dazzling future, and for a second Jane was blinded by ambition and forgot about escape entirely.

7332 laughed, not kindly. "A human pilot? Impossible! Pilots must be trustworthy, loyal to the system, bound to it by blood and training. It is only the half-blooded who are ever licensed to fly dragons.

"No, you were brought here as a breeder."

It took her a moment to absorb his meaning. When she did, it was with the shock of a physical blow. They wanted her to be a brood mare! To grow children for them—half-elven children who would be taken away at birth to be raised as warriors. She burned with cold wrath. "Tell me your name," she said.

"I have given it already."

"That's just your serial number. I need your name to get your operational specifications." There were hundreds of models this creature might be; the grimoire's index went on forever. Without the master key, a serial number told her nothing. "I can't operate you without your op specs."

"No names."

"I *must!*"

A touch of anger entered that cold, staticky whisper. "Changeling, what do you take me for? I am great beyond your kind. Your place is to free me; in return, I will take you away. Do not aspire beyond yourself."

"I can't release your bonds without knowing your true name," Jane lied. "It says so in the grimoire!"

The lights went off.

Jane sat in the dark, amid the dying whines of servomechanisms withdrawing the cybernetics. The door slammed open.

The glamour was either renewed or lost, for in the cold moonlight the interior of 7332 was again blasted and lifeless. Jane stood, swiping at the flakes of burnt vinyl that clung to the back of her dress. "I'm not changing my mind!" she said defiantly. "You need my help. So if you want to be free again, you have to give me your name." She waited, but there was no response.

She left.

———◈———

Blugg had a plan. Jane had no notion what it might be, but the machinations of it kept her busy throughout the days that followed, scurrying from the spring shop to the scale house, from motion work to the bolt shop and then back again by way of the metaphysics lab. She was sent to the cylinder machine shop to reserve three days' time on the boring mills, then across to the tender shop to collect a sealed envelope from an old demoted engineer who had lost one eye and both his ears to some long ago corporate discipline. When she went to the chemical supplies room to see how much jellied bryony compound was on hand and not already spoken for, the supply clerk put down his wire rims and glared at her through pink-edged eyes. "Why does Blugg want to know?" he asked.

Jane shrugged uneasily. "He didn't tell me."

"He's bucking for a promotion—that much is clear. Everyone says he has the Baldwynn's sponsorship for this project. Everybody says it but nobody knows for sure. The lines of authority here are so vague that any lout with a roach in his cranium can—" He drew himself up abruptly. "Has he really got the ear of the Baldwynn? How could a nobody like Blugg find himself in that position? But if not, how would he dare? Just what is he up to?"

"I really don't know."

"You must know *some*thing." The clerk was brown as bark and so grotesquely thin his eyes stuck out to either side; he looked to be an assemblage of twigs, like the stick men that were hung from poles and set ablaze on Hogmanay night. Rattling his fingers at her, he said, "Underlings always know." What he must have thought an ingratiating grin split his face. "Creeping and sneaking about like mice, little whiskery noses into everything."

"No, really."

"Bullshit!" He slammed the counter. "It's something to do with Grimpke, isn't it? The earless old bastard in Section A?" He turned his head sideways, so one eye could peer down at her. "I thought so! Something to do with his famous leg-assembly, no doubt." He eased back, cackling. "Well, if *that's* what Blugg thinks is going to makc him Management's darling, you can tell him—You can tell him—" A crafty look came over his thin face. "No, don't say that. Tell him," he twisted about to peer over a shoulder at the ranks of barrels arrayed on steel-mesh shelving behind him, "tell him that we've only got half a barrel of the bryony and if he wants more, he'll need documentation from the boys in the labs."

As Jane left, she heard the supply clerk laughing behind her. "Grimpke! What a joke!"

———◈———

When next she crawled into the wall, Jane did not settle into the little nest she had made there. Leaving the grimoire below, she climbed up between the walls, searching out the braces and supports for places to set her bare feet. It was surprisingly easy. Carefully she climbed all the way up to the very top. There she followed the cool currents of air until she found their source, a trapdoor that had long ago provided access to the roof.

When she tried it, she found that it had been tarpapered over, and would not open. But it would not take any great effort for her to steal a knife.

———◈———

The next day, toward shift's end, Rooster approached her with a new plan of escape. They were in the midst of a seasonal production slowdown, and rather than take them back to the dormitory early, Blugg had given the children brooms and barrels of sweeping compound and set them to work cleaning the floors of the pattern shop.

It was all make-work. The floors were built of enormous oaken beams almost a century ago, so warped and ground away by generations of feet that the wood between the lines of grain was worn into deep ruts and cracks, forming inexhaustible wells of dirt and dust. No amount of sweeping would clean them.

But so long as the children made a pretense of working, Blugg stayed in the pattern-master's office and left them alone. Jane could see the cubby through the window-wall that ran the length of the building, just below the ceiling: a modest warren of desk spaces, all carpeted and clean, a calm and different world from the one in which she labored. Grimpke was up in the borrowed office with him. The two old ogres bent low and solemn over their production schedules.

"Look." Rooster shook a dustpan full of dirt and waxy crumbs of compound in Jane's face. "Where do you think this stuff goes?"

Jane pushed it away. "Back to the floor, soon enough."

"Very funny. No, listen. We dump it in those dustbins, right? Then later, there's a couple of pillywiggins haul them out and dump the trash in a dumpster, okay? Along with scraps and sawdust, packaging, canisters of chemical waste, and the like. Then a truck comes along and empties the dumpsters. Where do you think that truck goes?"

"The cafeteria."

"Chucklehead! It goes out through a service gateway in the east wall. Nowhere near the Time Clock—get it? Nowhere near the Time Clock."

"Get real. You want to climb into a trash truck's belly? Have you ever seen the teeth on those things? They're sharp as razors and bigger than you are. That thing gets you into its maw, and you're as good as dead."

"Are you sure of that?"

"No, of course I'm not sure. But it's not worth taking a chance on."

Rooster looked cunning. "Let's say the only way out is past the Clock, then. How do people get by it? With their punchcards, right? But suppose we could get hold of a couple of cards. If we could find some way to delay whoever normally used 'em, we could . . ."

"Include me out." Jane began sweeping vigorously away.

"Jane!" Rooster hurried after her. With a quick glance upward, he seized her arm and swung her into the shadow of a pillar. "Jane, why are you against me? All the others are on Dimity's side, except for you. And Dimity hates your guts. So whose side are you on? You have to choose."

"I'm not going to be on anybody's side anymore," she said. "Sides are stupid."

"What will it take?" he asked desperately. "What will it take to get you back on my side again?"

He wasn't going to stop pestering her until she agreed to be a part of his idiot schemes. Well, she had resolved to do whatever it took to get out of here. She might as well turn this to her advantage. "Okay, I'll tell you what. You go places I don't. Steal me a hex nut. A virgin nut, mind you. One that's never been used."

Mercurial as ever, Rooster leered and grabbed his crotch.

"I'm sick of putting up with your crude jokes too. Help me or don't, I don't much care which. But if you're not willing to do a little thing like this for me, I don't see why I should be expected to put myself out for you."

In a hurt tone, Rooster said, "Hey, what'd I ever do to you? Ain't I always been your friend?" He closed his good eye and put a finger alongside his nose. "If I help you, will you help me? With my plan?"

"Yeah, sure," Jane said. "Sure I will."

When he was gone, Jane wearily swept her way to the far dark end of the shop. It had been such a long day, and she still had to go to Mrs. Greenleaf's to play. She fervently hoped Blugg wouldn't get so caught up in his project that he'd leave her waiting in the Castle's foyer as he had the past three days running.

Dimity was waiting in the shadows for her, and seized her just below the shoulder.

"Ow!" Jane's poor arm was getting all bruised.

But Dimity only squeezed all the tighter. "What were you and Rooster talking about?"

"Nothing!" she cried.

Dimity stared at her long and hard, with eyes like two coiled snakes. Finally she released Jane and turned away. "Better be nothing."

———— ◉ ————

As the winter weeks progressed, Blugg's plans ripened toward fruition. Creatures in suits began dropping by to confer with him. He grew more expansive and dressed with greater care, adding a string tie to his work shirt and bathing three times a week. Over in the erecting shop in an unused assembly bay—closed for structural repairs that wouldn't be scheduled until the economic climate picked up—a prototype of Grimpke's leg-assembly was taking shape.

During one of her trips to Section A, Jane pocketed a scrap of green leather from the floor of the trim shop. She stole some heavy thread and a curved needle, and sacrificed some of her time with the grimoire to make Rooster an eyepatch. It was more work than she'd intended, and she was feeling peevish by the time it was done. But when she woke Rooster to give it to him, he was so touched and delighted by the present, she felt put to shame.

"This is *great!*" He sat up in bed and unwrapped the rag from his head, revealing for a hideous instant the ruin of his eye. Then he ducked his head, tugged on the band to adjust it, and when he straightened he was the old Rooster again. His smile went up farther on one side of his face than the other, as if trying to compensate for the lack of balance higher up. His forelocks fell over the strap in a swaggering, piratical sort of a way.

He hopped off the bed. "Where's a mirror?"

Jane shook her head, laughing silently, his joy was so infectious. Because of course there were no mirrors in the dormitory or anywhere near it. Industrial safety regulations forbade them.

Rooster tucked thumbs into armpits, making wingtips of his elbows, and stood on one leg. "Dimity better watch out for me now!"

Alarmed, Jane said, "Oh, don't pick a fight with her. Please don't."

"I didn't pick this fight."

"She's stronger than you are. Now."

"It's only the other kids that make her so strong. Without their faith in her, she's nothing. All that power will come flowing back to me as soon as I kill Blugg."

"You can't kill Blugg."

"Just watch me."

"Well, I'm not going to listen to any of this," Jane said. "I'm going to bed." And she did.

But she had an awful feeling her innocent gift had started something spinning out of control.

Jane was standing on call outside Blugg's office when Rooster sidled up with the hex nut he'd promised to steal. He favored her with a one-eyed wink and pressed it into her hand.

"Is it cherry?" she asked.

"Sure it is," Rooster said. "What do you take me for? Some kind of a hardware-fucker?"

"Don't be crude." Jane slipped the nut under her vest and into a pocket. She was getting to be a pretty good thief; the motions were all but automatic by now. To her surprise she found that she actively enjoyed stealing things. There was a dark, shivery thrill to putting herself in danger and yet eluding punishment.

———◆———

By the time Jane got back from the Castle that night, the other children were asleep. With practiced swiftness, she stripped off her smock, slipped under her bed, and lifted the loose board. Agile as a night ape, she scaled the inside of the wall.

The wind was a lash across Jane's flesh. She crouched low on the roof, blue-skinned with cold. But Dame Moon gave her strength to endure it. With all her will, she stared at the hex nut in her hand, focusing on the memorized specs: its dimensions, weight and shearing strength, the exact composition of its alloy.

Nothing happened.

She joggled it into the exact center of her palm, concentrating on the heft and feel of it, the pale gleam of moonlight on its faceted surface, the tight coil of the thread down its core. With an almost audible click, she felt her knowledge of it snap together into a perfect whole.

I know you, she thought. Fly.

It rose spinning in the air.

Jane felt content. Knowing the hex nut's nature gave her power over it. It had to do what she wanted. Similarly, she knew that for all the dragon's silence, 7332 needed her. Someday it would have to call her. She would be ready then. She would have all its specs down by heart. And when they left, she'd leave knowing the dragon's name.

In control.

"What are you doing up here?"

Jane spun around in horror. Rooster was climbing up through the trapdoor. He had a big shit-eating grin on his face and Jane, remembering her nudity, vainly tried to cover herself with her hands. "Don't look!"

"Too late. I've already seen everything." Rooster laughed. "You look like Glam herself, riding the roofs." He reached into the shadows behind him and brought out a blanket. Carelessly he draped it over her shoulders. "There. That ought to prove I'm on your side, after all."

"Oh. Sides again." Blushing, Jane tugged the blanket tight about her.

Rooster stood on tiptoe, straining an arm toward the moon, as if he thought he could pluck it down from the sky. He pulled himself so high and thin it seemed he were trying to make himself one with the wind. "Hey, nice view you got here." He squinted down at her. "Would it make you feel any better if I took my clothes off too?" He began unbuttoning his trousers.

"No!"

"Oh well." Rooster shrugged and rebuttoned himself. Then, abruptly, he dropped to his knees before her. "Jane, I've been thinking and thinking how to get you to like me again."

"I do like you, Rooster. You know that." Jane edged away from him and he followed her on his knees so that the distance between them remained unchanged.

"Yeah, but you won't help me. You say you will, but you don't really mean it. I mean, you know what I mean?"

She lowered her eyes. "Yeah."

Rooster's voice grew small, as if he were admitting to something shameful. Jane had to strain to make out his words. "So what I thought was maybe we should tell each other our true names."

"What?"

"You know. You tell me yours, and I'll tell you mine. That means you really trust somebody, because when they know your true name, they can kill you like *that!*" He snapped his fingers.

"Rooster, I'm human."

"So? I don't hold that against you." His expression was bruised, wounded. He was perfectly vulnerable to her now, even without her knowing his secret name. Jane's heart ached for him.

Gently, she said, "I don't have a true name."

"Shit." Rooster went to the very edge of the roof and for the longest time stared straight down at the faraway ground. Jane was seized with dread for him, but simultaneously feared to call out lest he should fall. Finally he put his arms out full-length to either side and spun around. He stalked toward her. "I'm going to tell you anyway."

"Rooster, no!"

"It's Tetigistus. That means needle." He folded his arms. His face had taken on an eerily peaceful cast, as if all his cares and worries had suddenly fallen away. Jane found herself almost envying him. "There. Now you can do anything you want with me."

"Rooster, I don't know what to say."

"Hey, you still haven't told me what you're doing up here." The hex nut had fallen from the air when Rooster first spoke. All this time she had been holding it clutched in one fist. Now Rooster unfolded her fingers and took the nut from her. "Ahhhh." He peered at her through the bore. "So that's what you wanted it for. You're learning how to use things' names against them."

Numbly, Jane nodded. "Yes, I . . . I found this grimoire, see—"

"Yeah, right, I stepped on it down at the bottom of the wall." Rooster's voice burned fierce with joy. "Oh, that's perfect. That means anything can be turned against Blugg! We can crush him under boiler stock, call down molten brass on him, fill his arteries with particulate lead."

"Rooster, why this fixation on Blugg? Give it up. Revenge isn't going help you escape."

"Oh, I don't care about escape."

"But you said—"

"Only because that's what you wanted. Since my sickness, since I lost my eye, the sight has been getting stronger within me every day. What do I care what side of the factory gates I'm on? Right here and now I can see worlds like nothing you've ever imagined. Things you don't have the words for. And sometimes I get premonitions." He frowned with unRoosterlike solemnity and said, "That's why I keep trying to warn you. You're caught in something, and the more you try to get loose, the more tangled you become." Then he laughed, Rooster again. "But now we're working together! First you'll help me kill Blugg, and then we'll lift his punchcard and you can walk out free. It's so simple it's beautiful."

Jane felt awful. Rooster's plans were not hers. There was no way 7332 was going to let her take Rooster along when she left. She could feel the dragon's presence even now, a saturating medium pervasive everywhere in the plant. Even here, weakened by the moonlight, its influence was yet tangible. She could feel the iron certainty of its revulsion in the back of her skull. "It won't work. It's just another of your childish fantasies."

"Don't be like that. You're just letting yourself get all caught up in the illusion of existence." He held out a hand. "Here, let me show you."

She took his hand. "Show me? How?"

"You know my name, don't you? Well, use it."

"Teti . . . Tetigistus," she said hesitantly. "Show me what you see."

---

They were walking down a dark winter sidewalk. Patches of unshoveled snow had been trodden down to black lumps, hard as rock and slippery as ice. Stone-and-glass buildings soared up out of sight. Lights were everywhere, lining the endless shop windows, twinkling in scrawny leafless trees, spelling out words in enormous letters in an alphabet strangely familiar but undecipherable to her. The streets were choked with machines that moved as if they were alive, but had no voices of their own, only the roar of their engines and the blare of horns.

"Where are we?" Jane asked wonderingly.

Rooster shook his head.

They walked on, among throngs of silent, shadowy people. Nobody spoke to them or jostled them. It was as if they were ghosts.

In a window they saw evergreen trees spangled with popcorn and foil and strings of gingerbread soldiers. Beneath the firs was heaped an ogre's hoard of toys, bears in harness beating small drums, machines that were glossy miniatures of those in the street, dolls in lace-trimmed taffeta, a stuffed giraffe half as large as life.

Jane had never seen anything or any place like this repository of alien wealth, but some resonant echo of the spirit told her that this place was in some way identical to or congruent with the world of her earliest memories, that time and place when she had been small and protected and happy.

She began to cry. "Rooster, take me home, please."

He turned to her in surprise and unthinkingly released her hand.

They were back on the factory roof again.

"There." Rooster kissed her on the cheek. "Now we trust each other completely," he said.

---

Time was getting short. Jane could feel the grinding vibration of events coming together as the machineries of fate moved them about. The next night, as she was making a pretense of playing with the toys, Jane closed her hand around the nugget of brass 7332 wanted. As a distraction she lifted a glory-hand free of the box, waving it back and forth as if she were playing sorceress. This made Mrs. Greenleaf happy, she knew, acting childish; the more childish she acted, the happier the old elf was.

Craftily, she turned her body to hide the theft, drawing the nugget close with a languid gesture of her hand, and secreting it among her clothes. Mrs. Greenleaf, busy with pencil and magazine, noticed nothing. Casually, though the Baldwynn never looked directly at anything, Jane glanced up at him to make sure he also was not watching.

She gasped.

The elf-laird was not in his chair. Where he had been now floated an egg of light. It pulsed gently. Pale colors played over its cold, featureless surface. She cringed away from the thing, irrationally afraid that it would leave the chair and come after her.

Mrs. Greenleaf looked up from her acrostics. "Jane," she said warningly. "Is there a problem?"

"No, Mrs. Greenleaf," Jane said hastily.

But Mrs. Greenleaf had already turned toward her father. Her mouth opened in a round little O and her eyes bulged as if she had been suddenly ensorcelled into a fish. Her distress was so comically extreme that Jane had to fight down the urge to giggle.

Magazines sliding from her lap, the old elf-wife stood. She seized Jane's hand in a grip that was thoughtlessly painful, and hauled her straightaway from the room.

Once the door was firmly shut, Mrs. Greenleaf turned to Jane, the skin on her face taut and white, her mouth a lipless slit. "You saw nothing tonight, do you understand?" She shook Jane's arm for emphasis. "Nothing!"

"No, ma'am."

"We are an old family, a respectable family, there has been no trace of scandal since—what are you looking at?"

"Nothing." Jane was afraid that the elf-wife would strike her. But instead, she was led directly to the dressing room, even though her time here was only half done. Her work clothes were returned to her, and her play dress and lacy underthings packed away once more in white paper. It was early still, at least an hour before Blugg was scheduled to pick her up, when she was deposited out on the front steps.

"I *don't* think it will be necessary for you to return tomorrow," Mrs. Greenleaf said firmly.

She closed the door.

Blugg was half an hour late picking her up. Jane awaited him in an agony of expectation. When he finally arrived, startled to find her standing outside instead of in the foyer as in times previously, he demanded to know why. Then, when she told him what Mrs. Greenleaf's last words had been, he threw back his head and howled. It was a terrible sound, compounded of pain and the misery of broken dreams.

When they got back to the dormitory, he beat her.

# ── ⬧ ── FIVE ── ⬧ ──

It was agony getting out of bed the next morning. Jane's side burned with pain. One leg buckled slightly when she put weight on it, giving her an odd, twisting limp. She had to spoon her gruel through the left side of her mouth; the right was swollen shut by a lump the size of an egg.

Blugg took one look at Jane and yanked the messenger's vest from her back. He tossed it to Dimity, who slipped it over her head and followed him off to his office with a triumphant little flip of her skirts.

To her humiliation and amazement, Jane discovered that losing the position actually hurt.

But Blugg's project did not collapse with the loss of the Baldwynn's supposed sponsorship. It had taken on its own momentum; too great a mass of ambitious middle-management types had invested their time and prestige in the enterprise to allow it to die.

Paradoxically, the project picked up speed with Mrs. Greenleaf's dismissal of Jane. The prototype, which had for weeks stood in unhasty incompletion in its assembly bay, was rapidly finished, tested, and packed with grease. Smidgeon, Creep, and Three-eyes spent an entire day polishing its surface until it shone like mirrors.

Nights, Rooster would crawl into the wall to pore over the grimoire. He insisted that Jane show him the chapter dealing with cam assemblies and went over all the diagrams again and again until he was sure he had identified the one the wizened old engineer Grimpke had used in the prototype.

"We don't have much time," he told Jane. "I was talking with

Hob—that's Hob the whitesmith's gaffer, not one-legged Hob—
and he said there's some lord high muckety-muck from the head
office coming down to look over the leg in five days. The inspector general from the office for applications assessment." He all but
sang the words; Rooster was inordinately fond of high-flown ti-
tles. "Word on the floor is that they had to pull a lot of strings to
get the I.G. down here, and now they're all running around like
Lady Corus, trying to get everything firmed up in time."

"Rooster, give up this folly," Jane whispered back. It was
cramped within the wall and even though she was fully clothed,
she felt embarrassed being squished up against Rooster this way.
"You can't possibly hope to turn his own assembly on Blugg."

"Sure I can." Rooster shivered from cold or joy, Jane could
not tell which. "Those titanium claws are going to twitch and
swivel and then they're going to close around that bollocky fat
bastard. Slowly, so he's got time to be afraid. And then . . . it'll be
great."

"Anyway, I don't see how you can expect to have all those figures memorized in five days. There must be seven pages!"

"I'll manage it," he said grimly.

He frowned over the numbers, face dim and almost unseeable
in the silvery runelight. Jane knew how hard what he was trying to
do could be. She had cranked down her own ambitions from total
mastery of her dragon to control of several key functions in its optical and processing systems. "I don't even believe you can read
the numbers."

"Sure I can."

"What's this say, then?" She jabbed a finger at the runes signi-
fying 3.2 ohms.

"Look, I don't need to *understand* the squiggles to memorize
them. I can see how they look every bit as well as you can. I'll just
memorize them as pictures."

It was an impossible task that Rooster had set for himself.
Jane left him there and went back to bed, grateful for the chance
to get some sleep and sure that Rooster would give it up after a
day's effort, two at most. She could return to her studies when
he did.

But he did not. That night and the next and the three after that,
Rooster crept into the wall and stayed till dawn communing with
the grimoire. Jane found herself resenting the time he spent there.
It was, after all, *her* book, and she had serious need of it. Rooster,

though, shrugged off all her hints, suggestions, and finally demands that they alternate nights studying the grimoire.

There was no talking to him. Rooster was obsessed.

———— ◉ ————

The night before the scheduled inspection, the children were all lined up at the tub room and given baths, even though it was the middle of the week. One at a time they were called in. Dimity oversaw the girls, wielding a stiff brush to catch any places they might have themselves missed, while Blugg watched with frank amusement.

The brush was wielded with particular vigor when it was Jane's turn in the zinc trough. Dimity seemed to be demonstrating something to Blugg, something Jane could not decipher. "Get those clothes off, you slut!" she shouted. "Show some motion."

Jane stared fixedly away from Blugg as she undressed, and climbed awkwardly into the tub. She was largely recovered from her beating, but the bruises still lingered, yellow and black around purple clouds, like bad weather just beneath the skin. The water was still warm, and thin oily streaks of soap floated on its gray surface.

"You've beshit yourself, you pig!"

"I have not!" Jane cried involuntarily.

"What's that, then?" Dimity thrust the scrub brush between Jane's legs, and scrubbed with hard, fast strokes, forcing tears to her eyes. "It's all up and down the crack of your ass." Jane splashed and floundered away, and Dimity followed her to the far end of the tub, scouring her bottom with the sharp nylon bristles.

"Here!" She threw a dirty washrag into Jane's face. "Wipe your face. It's filthy."

When Jane was getting dressed, she timidly glanced up and saw an odd look pass between Dimity and Blugg, enigmatic and yet conspiratorial, freighted with terrible meaning.

———— ◉ ————

An unhealthy smile came and went on Rooster's face at breakfast. His fingers trembled slightly, and his gaze was darting and distracted. Since he had started crawling into the wall at night, his face had grown even more sallow and drawn; a constant weariness hung about him now. But an unnatural energy underlay his exhaustion this morning, like an electrical current pushing his muscles toward spasm.

"Rooster?" Jane said quietly. Nobody else noticed the state he was in. They were all preoccupied by the nearing inspector general's visit. "You mustn't feel bad if things don't . . ." She couldn't bring herself to say it.

"This is the day." He flashed her a weird, scary grin. "You know something? Lately I've been hearing Stilt's voice again. Like he wasn't really dead, but hiding somewhere in the shadows, or maybe in the back of my skull, you know? Well, I think Stilt is going to like today. This one is going to be for him."

"Yes, but if—"

"Shhh!" He winked and laid a finger alongside of his nose, just as Dimity came slinking up to order them into marching formation for work. "How's it hanging, *Dim*ity?"

"You just better watch yourself." She grabbed his ear between thumb and forefinger and pinched. "If you fuck up today, your ass is grass, buster." Then she let go.

Rooster ducked his head and looked away and when she was just one too many steps distant to turn back without losing dignity, remarked to Jane, "Sounds just like Blugg, dunshe?"

Dimity stiffened, but kept on walking.

———※———

Dimity suffered a mishap on the way to work that morning, just as they were marching by the pitch yards. She was striding past Rooster, making sure the line was straight, when there was a sudden flurry of motion and Thistle lurched and fell against her. Caught unprepared, she was sent spilling to one side, headfirst into a bucket of hot tar. When she stood, sputtering, she looked like a golliwog, face black and hair glistening.

The children laughed.

"Shut up!" Dimity gasped. "Shut up, shut up, shut up!" Her mouth gaped comically. She furiously swiped at her eyes, trying to clean the tar away.

Blugg exploded. "Get out of here! You fucking stupid brat. Go straight to the tub room and get scrubbing! I want that shit off your face by noon if you have to take the skin with it."

"But it wasn't my fault!" Dimity wailed. "It was—"

"*Go!*" Blugg swung around and jabbed a thick finger at

Rooster. "You! Go to stores and get a messenger's vest. A brand new one, mind, the best they have! Cernunos knows, you're not much, but you'll have to do."

"Yes, sir, absolutely, sir." Rooster grabbed his forelock and tugged, bowing himself down low to hide the leer of triumph on his face.

———— ⟨○⟩ ————

That day felt longer than any Jane could remember. Though they got no work done at all—appearances mattered, so they couldn't handle grease or polish—the children were constantly being shuttled from work site to work site, broken into groups and urgently gathered together again, so that a jumpy sense of unease extended through the morning deep into the afternoon.

At last, late in the day, the inspector general arrived.

A wave of dread preceded the elf-lord through the plant. Not a kobold or korrigan, not a spunky, pillywiggin, nor lowliest dunter but knew the inspector general was coming. The air shivered in anticipation of his arrival. A glimmering light went just before him, causing all heads to turn, all work to stop, the instant before he turned a corner or entered a shop.

He appeared in the doorway.

Tall and majestic he was in an Italian suit and tufted silk tie. He wore a white hard hat. His face was square-jawed and handsome in a more than human way, and his hair and teeth were perfect. Two high-ranking Tylwyth Teg accompanied him, clipboards in hand, and a vulture-headed cost analyst from Accounting trailed in his wake.

Blugg stood straight and proud in a mixed welcoming line of upper and middle management. His face and horns were scrubbed so clean their surfaces were faintly translucent. Rooster stood by his side and a little behind, an accessory to his dignity. Old Grimpke was present as well, hunched over slightly and rubbing his hands with grinning nervousness. The prototype leg-and-claw mechanism was upended in the center of the room.

The workers had been lined up against the walls, arrayed by size and function, like so many tools on display. The children stood straight and scared against the wall behind their overseer. Dimity was to the far end of the line from Jane, her face red with suppressed anger. She'd had to cut off most of her hair to get rid of the tar, which gave her a plucked and lopsided look totally disqualifying her from standing in the welcoming line with Blugg.

Rooster twisted around in line to peer intently at first Dimity, then Jane. He flashed his shirt open and shut again, revealing a near-subliminal glimpse of a white cardboard rectangle pressed against his flesh.

It was Blugg's punchcard.

Jane could anticipate what Rooster was going to say so perfectly that when he silently mouthed the words she found she could read his lips.

Come with me, he said.

She shook her head.

He reached out as if to take her hand. We're small—the card will shelter us both.

She pulled her hand away. *No!*

He raised an eyebrow, and his one eye filled with cold inhuman light. Then he faced forward again, posture stiff and correct.

"What was that?" Little Dick whispered. "That white thing in Rooster's shirt?" And Smidgeon echoed, "Yeah, what?"

"Shut the fuck up!" Jane growled out of the corner of her mouth. An ogre in a white shirt looked back over his shoulder at them, and they all did their best to look innocent.

But she had seen. The steely glitter in Rooster's eye had nothing to do with him. It was dragon's light that shone there, the alien intelligence of 7332 acting within him. He had been taken over, and made into a tool, one that 7332 could use for its own inscrutable purposes.

Don't don't don't, she prayed in her head. Don't do it Rooster, don't let yourself be used like this, and to the dragon she prayed, don't make him do this, don't, and to the Goddess: don't. Stop time, stop motion, unmake the world, halt the sun in its circuit, don't let this go on.

Now that she was alerted to it, she could feel the dragon's influence everywhere about them, a pervasive fluid medium within which they all moved, like fish in a hostile ocean. She could tell from the rigid set of Rooster's back that he was staring at the prototype. Now, too late, she realized that the evenings spent with the grimoire had not been wasted time on Rooster's part; they had created an opening through which 7332 might move and influence him.

The plant manager shook hands with the inspector general, and introduced the comptroller. The elf-lord worked his way gracefully down the line, making firm eye contact and occasionally reinforcing his handshakes with a small laugh or a pat on the shoulder.

The ceremony proceeded with the deliberate pace of a ritual drama. At one point, Rooster surrendered a bound set of production figures to Blugg, who handed them to the elf-lord, who handed them to the senior of the two Tylwyth Teg, and thus to the junior and finally to the cost accountant, who tucked it under his arm without glancing at it. Creep yawned and was savagely elbowed by Dimity.

Finally the officials all turned to the prototype, as if noticing it for the first time. Grimpke unscrewed an access cap, opening up the leg to demonstrate the array of eccentric gears stacked down the core. "Verra important," he said. "'Swod magesutt work, yasee?" One of the upper management types winced, but the expression on the inspector general's face was encouraging, bland, smiling. Grimpke reached into the grease to show how tightly packed the gears were, and light glinted between his fingers.

He screamed.

Bright, actinic power flared from the center of the assembly. It swallowed up and engulfed those closest to it. Suits and faces dissolved in the light. A hard hat bounced on the floor and rolled away. Everything moved. Flames arose. All this in an instant of perfect silence.

Then the world shattered.

Warm air slammed into Jane's face and she staggered backward; it was like being knocked over with a pillow. Her ears were deafened, ringing. She felt split and divided, her vision fractured into too many images to accept at once: The Tylwyth Teg ablaze, running, falling. A lesser giant doubling over with hysterical, disbelieving laughter. Something tumbling through the air. Cinder blocks bursting, spraying gravel and chips of paint.

Hazy gray smoke filled the room, and the black stench of burning PCBs. Alarms wailed.

In the center of the geysering sparks, Blugg stood stricken. A pillar in a chaotic sea, he did not move, while the light passed beyond and through him. One arm slowly rose, as if there were a point he wanted to raise. Then he fell apart, crumbling into gray ash.

Dimity shrieked as a spray of slivers dotted a curve across her face, a graceful line that neatly avoided her lips, nose, and both eyes by coming within a hair of marring them all. Other children were leaping, dancing in quickstep pain, slapping at arms or sides.

But Jane was looking at none of them. She stared, as it seemed she must always have been staring from the beginning of time, at Rooster.

There was a gray enameled box bolted to the wall by the exit. It was a security device, one of the Time Clock's lesser daughters. Featureless and eyeless it was, but not blind. Nor without power.

Rooster's body, reduced and thin, like a piece of paper that, purpose served, has been wadded up and thrown down, lay across the doorway. A wisp of smoke curled up from his chest. Only she in all the room had seen the brighter-than-magnesium flare that had erupted from beneath his shirt as he passed the security device and crossed the threshold. It had come from Blugg's punchcard. She had seen the flare, his agonized arc as the brutal force punched through his body, heard his truncated cry of pain, like the short, sharp cry of a night-lark.

She stared at Rooster, and he was dead.

—————=◎=—————

The children had instinctively clustered together. Amid all the smoke and flames, the screams and shouted orders, Dimity said with gentle wonder, "Blugg's dead."

"And Rooster." The shadow-boy spoke from somewhere behind her. "They've gone to Spiral Castle together."

The strangeness of this, the improbability of two such fates being mingled, held them all silent for an instant. Finally Thistle asked, "What do we do now?"

She was looking straight at Dimity, pleadingly. But Dimity did not reply. The accident had frightened her as much as the others. She trembled, stunned and shaken, her face pale as snow and dotted with blood where the splinters had hit her. Some leader, Jane thought sourly.

A donkey-eared supervisor in torn white shirt staggered by, touching them each on the shoulder in passing, as though he would fall down without the handhold. "Stay here," he said. "There'll be a safety officer along any minute now. He'll want to interview you." He disappeared into the smoke.

Then the dragon was within Jane again, filling her with purpose and strength. "Form up!" she snapped. "Line up by size. Square off. Lead out!"

Meekly, they obeyed.

Jane marched them out of the shop and across the grounds.

Rescue forces were still converging on the erecting shop. Ambulances screamed. Flashing lights filled the night, and the stenches from the explosion. The loaders and trucks were all stirring restlessly in their stables, crying out with alarmed mechanical voices. The children walked through the chaos as if enchanted, protected by their purposeful air. Nobody stopped them.

Jane marched them, some—the littlest ones—still hacking and coughing, back to Building 5. There were quiet sobs and sniffs, and those were all right, but when Skizzlecraw threw back her head and began to wail, Jane whacked her a good one right on the ear. That shut her up.

At the dormitory stairs, Jane stepped aside and hustled them before her with snarls and shoves. As the last—it was Creep, of course—went by, she snagged the first aid kit from its hook just outside Blugg's door.

The first order of business was bandaging up wounds. Fortunately, few of the children had been injured by the explosion; the trauma was mostly from shock. When she came to clean up Dimity's face, the shifter broke out of her frozen apathy and cried, "My face! What am I going to look like?"

"A freak," Jane said, "if I don't tweeze these things out. Shut up and let me work."

She did as good a job as she could manage with the tools at hand. There were still a few black specks under Dimity's skin when she was done, but most likely they were nothing serious. She dosed the more hysterical of the children with morphine, and then she sent them all to bed.

Jane was their leader now.

But not, if she could help it, for long.

———※◎※———

When the children were all at last asleep, Jane climbed up to the roof to watch over the unfolding events. Smoke and sparks belched from the smokestacks, and rescue machines prowled restlessly about the grounds. The death of so important a figure as the inspector general had roused all the plant to action, whether productive or not.

Slowly, order reasserted itself. Thaumaturges emerged from the labs and walked through the grounds in orange environmental suits, scattering particulate radioisotopes from thuribles and censers and muttering incantations that stiffened the air with dread. In their wake, the ground was crisscrossed with ley lines glowing blue and red and yellow, like a wiring diagram gone mad, all overlapping circles and straight lines meeting at unlikely angles then separating again. It was impossible to see how they could expect to untangle the readings of magickal influence, and apparently they could not, for none of the lines was tracked back to No. 7332.

Jane watched for half the night from the rooftop, fearful the dragon would be unmasked. She was a small and pale pip on the black expanse of tar, and if anyone saw her, they must've taken her for a warehouse tutelary about her legitimate business.

When the moon had sunk low in the sky, 7332 finally called for her.

***

Calmly, Jane climbed down from the roof, gathered up grimoire, crystal, and nugget, and dressed. She let herself out of the dormitory with Blugg's key, stepping outside without a glance to either side, and headed for her dragon. She walked straight across the grounds, making no attempt to avoid detection. She was no longer afraid of the plant's security forces. That was 7332's job, not hers.

When she came to the marshaling yard, the great dragons crawled aside to let her pass. They were too proud to look directly, but more than one glanced sidelong at her, their expressions haughty and unreadable. Their navigation lights were bright strings of red, green, and white tracing the contours of their flanks.

Jane reached No. 7332 and climbed its side. She felt invisible.

Soft lights came on as she stepped into the cab. There would be no protective camouflage tonight. The door clanged shut behind her.

"You killed him," she said.

From the lightless depths of the machinery came a voice, superficially calm but with undertones of anticipation. "I had to distract the security forces from their normal business long enough to complete my preparations. You needn't mourn the spilling of a little elf blood."

For a second the response made no sense. Then Jane realized that 7332 thought she was talking about the inspector general. "I meant *Rooster!* You used him. You got him to steal Blugg's punchcard, knowing what would happen when he tried to use it. Just to cover your trail."

"The little one?" 7332 sounded puzzled. "There's nothing special about him. I can get you as many of his kind as you like." Gently, it urged her, "Sit. It's time we left this prison for freedom and the sky."

Numbly, Jane sat down in the chair, and let the servomechanisms wrap themselves around her. She clutched the black handgrips and gave the left-hand one a quarter-turn. Twin needles slid into her wrist. Vision swam and transformed, and she was looking through the dragon's eyes, feeling the cool winter breeze on its iron hide through its nervous system. She was no longer entirely Jane, but part of something much bigger than she alone could ever be. It felt good.

"Power up engine systems," she said.

"That's the spirit!" Fuel gurgled as electrical motors pumped it to the turbines. A high-pitched whine grew and grew until it filled the universe. If it hadn't been for the padded headphones, Jane would have been deafened.

"We're ready. Now insert the keys," 7332 said.

Jane flicked a line of switches off and on, checking that the navigational systems were operative. "That's not necessary," the dragon said testily. "All you need do is insert the keys."

Suddenly an inhuman voice howled. A second voice joined the first, and then a third as alarms went off all across the plant. Lesser, but more piercing voices bayed and yelped. The cyborg hounds. That could only mean that they had been discovered. With the turbines powered up, the tangled lines of force and influence leading back to source must be lit up like so many neon tubes.

"Quickly!" 7332 said. "We've been discovered."

The ruby crystal and the walnut were both in Jane's hip pocket; she was uncomfortably half-sitting on them. But she didn't move to take them out. "Tell me your name."

A troll from plant security appeared at the far end of the yard, flames in his eyes. He was followed by several more of his kind, black forms against a cold sky. They each held five or six cyborg hounds straining against titanium leashes.

"They're coming. We must leave now, or not at all."

"Your name," she insisted.

The cyborg hounds were released. They sped, baying, at the dragon. The first of them bounced against its side with a loud *clang* and sank diamond teeth into its side. Submerged as she was in 7332's sensorium, Jane felt the fangs meet in her own flesh. She cried out loud with pain.

Desperation finally entered 7332's voice. "If we don't leave now, they'll have us!" It kicked at the hound, sending it flying. But more were arriving, hot on its heels.

"That they will."

The hounds were leaping into the air to seize the dragon. 7332 twisted around to face them, almost throwing Jane out of her chair. Its turbines were screaming, and still it could not configure for flight. Shouts of anger and fierce commands came from the troll-ish warriors. 7332 damped down the circuits carrying sensation from its skin; Jane felt herself go numb all over in sympathetic identification. Still, the hounds were starting to do real damage.

*"The keys!"*

Jane waited. Half-submerged into the dragon as she was, and uncertain of her identity around the edges, of where she ended and it began, she was sure it must know that she was not bluffing. That without a name, without the control it would give her, they were going nowhere.

"Melanchthon, of the line of Melchesiach, of the line of Moloch!" the dragon cried. Its anguish rose about Jane like phantom flame. She felt her eyelashes singeing in his wrath, and knew down to her very core that it spoke the truth.

She flipped open the grimoire, riffled through the pages to the command codes and began to read: "Recurvor. Recusadora. Recusamor." The engines roared and shuddered. "Recussus. Redaccendo. Redactamos." Jane slapped the crystal into place. "Redadim. Redambules. Redamnavit." The dragon trembled with repressed power. She fitted the brass nugget into its receptor niche, and rotated the right-hand grip a quarter-turn forward. Now the needles were deep within both her wrists. "Now fly!"

"You'll burn in Hell for this humiliation!" 7332 promised. Remembered war atrocities flashed at the back of Jane's skull. "I'll feed you to the Teind with my own claws."

"Shut up and fly!"

They were moving. The tarmac grumbled under their weight as they picked up speed. The dragon's wings raised, deployed, caught at the air. Hounds fell away. Jane was laughing hysterically and so, to her surprise, was 7332.

He lifted.

Shuddering, they took flight. The factory walls moved toward them slowly, then quickly, and then flashed by underneath, alarm-ingly close. They were free of the plant altogether. Slowly, they gained height.

The last of the hellhounds lost its grip, and fell yapping to its death. A calm, unaccented elven voice spoke over the radio, from some faraway control tower: *You are violating industrial airspace. Surrender all autonomous functions immediately.*

Now Melanchthon screamed his battle cry over all frequen-cies, scrambling communications, jamming radar, scratching an ionized line high up into the stratosphere. Far below them, civil defense forces scrambled, flights of war-hardened creatures eager for another taste of combat clawing at the air, but too late.

Jane was laughing so hard now she was crying. She couldn't stop thinking of Rooster, couldn't drive the sight of his small, still body from her mind. Her emotions were so extreme, so chaotic, she could not tell which were hers and which the dragon's. It did not matter. What 7332 felt could be no more intense than what was happening inside her now. She was burning with joy.

They *soared.*

# — ◆ — SIX — ◆ —

Jane lived as a wood-may in a patch of scrub trees just beyond the landfill. She made her home within the cabin of what seemed to the rest of the world the rusting hulk of an ancient and wrecked dragon, half-buried in the loamy earth, with steel plates welded over the windows and pusher rods motionless.

She was a quiet creature, just coming of age, and a pretty one too, though she did not know that. The stench of cold iron hung about her from her choice of dwelling place, and she might normally have been expected to raise a fair amount of local comment. But she did not. The locals thought of her, when they thought of her at all, as a dull neighborhood institution, a nondescript fey who had lived in the area for as long as any of them could remember.

Such was the dragon's pervasive influence that only she and 7332 knew she was actually human and had lived there only a few short months.

Every weekday morning the school bell cast its glamour over the surrounding hills, calling the young to classes. They came running down the slopes and leaping over the streams, out from caves and the hollows of trees and suburban tract homes, impelled by powers greater than their own to gain an education.

Flinging open the door one morning, Jane discovered that spring had come to the land. The frozen ground had thawed and softened to mud, and a glorious earthy smell filled the air. The trees were still naked, black and budless, but the brown grasses looked hopeful, with tincts of fresh green glowing from the depths of each clump. A meryon struggled to haul a corroded zinc washer back to its nest.

A crocus had sprouted by the dragon's haunch. She hopped to the ground and squatted beside it, admiring, not touching. The petals were a delicate, almost translucent white. They had no scent, and trembled in the wind from her nostrils.

To her, this was freedom. So small a thing as being able to take a moment to admire a flower, the very uselessness of the act, was both token and reward for her, meat and drink for the spirit.

The bell sounded again, and the muscles in her calves jumped.

Convulsively, Jane stood. She slapped her wide-brimmed Morgan Calabrese hat onto her head and shoved both hands deep into the pockets of her loose trousers. Her windbreaker she left unzipped.

It was too fine a day to hurry. Forcibly resisting the tug of the bell at her heels, she ambled down the hill.

After a minute she began to whistle. She couldn't help it.

———— ◦(◉)◦ ————

Even when she arrived at the schoolyard and found it empty, doors shut and a solitary carrion-dog skulking across the soccer field, that warm sense of well-being stayed with Jane. She was going to the mall today—Ratsnickle had promised to show her how to jigger the change box on the shuttle bus. It wasn't until she actually stepped into the redbrick school building that her mood darkened. The hollowing echoes of those gray halls were a mumbling surf of misery. The fluorescent light fixtures hummed a jittery song.

In the depths of the building, the hideous creature that the Principal kept in his office screamed. Her stomach flipped over, as if somebody had scraped fingernails down her spine.

Hunching her shoulders slightly, Jane hurried to her homeroom.

Fat old Grunt puffed out his cheeks like a toad in display when she walked through the door. "Well! Miss—" A quick, almost imperceptible sidelong glance at the attendance roster he kept taped to his desktop. "—Alderberry, have you deigned to grace us with your presence? And only six minutes late? How charming! Perhaps you would care to share the source of your oh-so-fashionable tardiness with the rest of the class?"

Jane flushed and stared down at the floor. "I was looking at a flower," she mumbled.

Grunt put a hand to his ear and bent his knees out to either side, bobbing his round body lower. "What's that?"

"A flower!"

"Ohhhh, I see." His expression was so exaggeratedly solemn that scattered giggles arose here and there in the room. "Lost in the rhapsodic contemplation of our precious little floral friends, were you?" Now the entire class was laughing outright at her.

She could sense Grunt slipping around behind her, up on his toes, with that slithery, exaggerated bounce of a walk he employed when he was playing to the back rows. Grunt was proud of his histrionics, and often boasted to his pupils that they made him the most clearly memorable—and therefore best—teacher in all the district. "But my dear, sweet Miss Alderberry, don't you know that flowers are never fully enjoyed until they are—"

He was in back of her now, his breath sour over one shoulder, and she knew from having seen this same ritual enacted upon others, that he was dipping that sharp little chin of his down, down, until chin, smirk and all, disappeared entirely in fatty folds of neck and cheek, and his mouthless face was dominated by the vicious gray light glinting from the dusty twin disks of his spectacles. She knew what was coming, and knew too that if she didn't put up with it, she would be kept after school in retaliation and miss out entirely on going to the mall. Or, worse, she could be sent to the Principal's office, to learn firsthand what it was like to look a basilisk in the face. Jane squeezed her eyes tight with humiliation.

"—*plucked!*" He thrust his hand between her legs and snatched up at her crotch. With an involuntary chickenlike squawk, she clumsily leaped and twisted away. The class convulsed with mirth, all of them braying, snorting, snickering, laughing as if they had never seen him pull this joke before.

"Take your seat, Jane!" Grunt said sternly. "We have work to do, and no time to waste on your foolishness."

It was a long walk to the slow learners' row in the back of the room, where she and Ratsnickle both sat.

Jane had no friends in the class and thus to her they were largely indistinguishable, an anonymous field of feys and weirds. But even had she known them all, Ratsnickle would still have stood out among their malicious faces and wicked expressions. Two red little eyes peered madly from an uncombed thatch of hay, and a wise-guy grin cocked up one side of his mouth. His arms were too skinny and too long, at odds with his lumpish body; but once you accepted that, he had beautiful hands, fingers wondrously long and so fluidly jointed they could wrap twice around a Coke bottle.

He turned away when she sat down.

Jane felt an icy coldness tighten her face. Her hands gripped the sides of her desk so tightly the nails turned white. An alien resolve took hold within her. She waited until Grunt turned and bent to pick up the chalk. Then she straightened her back and flipped him the finger.

Only those kids nearest her saw. At their laughter, Grunt whirled. But Jane was prepared. Her hands were out of sight, and her expression was neither guilty nor innocent, but sullen and defensive in exactly the right proportions. Grunt turned back to the blackboard, baffled.

Ratsnickle swallowed back a guffaw. A lilac maid caught Jane's eye and smiled. Jane nodded back, ever so slightly, and opened her textbook.

She was learning.

---

At lunchtime, she hovered at the edge of the cafeteria, tray in hand, looking for an empty place. There was no point in sitting with dwarves, thumblings, or grigs, even if she could have fit into one of their chairs; they were all too clannish, each in their own way. Nor would it be wise to sit too close to a lamie, gwarchell, or kirk-grim. A corner seat would be good, preferably with another empty chair to serve as buffer from that table's cliques. She didn't want to seem presumptuous. Or a chair between two disparate groups; she could stare straight ahead of her then, and be ignored.

Finally, because there were no good alternatives, she took a place alongside Ratsnickle.

Ratsnickle was deep in conversation with a lanky fey named Peter of the Hillside. Jane shared a couple of classes with him. Peter was wearing acid-wash jeans and a denim jacket with the Wild Hunt's "Horns of Elfland Tour" logo painted on the back. He had a bad complexion and a good haircut. He looked up, not at her, when she sat, and addressed the air: "Who's the git?"

Jane stiffened.

"She's with me," Ratsnickle said. "Okay?"

Peter shrugged. "All the same to me."

Jane ate in silence, afraid to join in the conversation. It was all about machines—Peter was apparently a shop major—the psychology of wyverns, the aberrant behavior of a drill press that had been with the school for as long as anyone could remember and might have to be put to sleep. Jane listened in fascination. Her classes, where they touched on machinery at all, were purely theoretical; she envied the boys their hands-on experience.

When she gathered up her tray to leave, Ratsnickle offhandedly said, "Still on for this afternoon?"

She nodded yes, and fled.

———◈———

Because she lagged so far behind the rest of her class, Jane had to go to the pale man for two hours' tutoring every afternoon. The pale man was a tall, thin creature who wore beige chinos, a white shirt, and canvas deck shoes. His skin was as lifeless as his clothing, and his eyes deader yet.

As always, he did not look up when she entered. He sat motionless on a wooden chair, hands on knees, back to the chalkboard, staring straight ahead of him into nothingness.

"Hello? I was sent here for remedial?"

The pale man looked up. He nodded wanly. Unhastily, without emphasis, he picked up a book, opened it, paged forward a leaf, and then back one. "There are three stars in the heavens," he said, "moving about Jupiter, erratic sidereal bodies which establish a lesser zodiacal process for that wanderer in its mighty twelve-year progression about the sun."

Jane had to concentrate hard to catch the meaning of his words, so flatly were they delivered. If she didn't watch it, she'd find herself zoning out, thoughts drifting off into the empyrean as he droned on and on. The pale man would let her. He didn't care in the least. He was a forest creature, and exiled from his proper environment he had grown so enervated, thin, and attenuated that he seemed hardly to be there at all. There was a natural strength and vigor all other living things possessed that was lacking in him.

Without pausing in his lecture, he teased a limp cigarette from a softpack in his shirt pocket, straightened it between two fingers, stuck it in the corner of his mouth, and began patting down his pockets in search of a match.

She sighed to herself. Through the window the horizon was ragged with a wintery fringe of trees. She thought of Ratsnickle and the mall with yearning.

But she had made promises to 7332. Shelter, protection, and the food that through technological subterfuge he caused to be delivered twice weekly to the door were not free. The dragon needed an engineer if he were ever to be restored to full power; in her present ignorant state, she was useless to him. As Jane saw it, it was a fair deal, a conspiracy of equal needs. Tutoring sessions with the pale man were part of the price she had agreed to pay.

"Excuse me," she said hesitantly, "but what effect do these minor planets have on our behavior and fortunes? I mean, you know, astrological influence?"

He looked at her. "None."

"None at all?"

"No."

"But if the planets affect our fortunes—" She stumbled to a stop at the dispassionately scornful look on the pale man's face, the slow way he shook his head. "Surely you'll agree that the planets order and control our destinies?"

"They do not."

"Not at all?"

"No."

"Then what does? Control our destinies, I mean."

"The only external forces that have any influence on us are those we can see every day: the smile, the frown, the fist, the brick wall. What you call 'destiny' is merely a semantic fallacy, the attribution of purpose to blind causality. Insofar as any of us are compelled to resist the flow of random events, we are driven solely by internal drives and forces."

Jane seized on this last. "Then what you're saying is that our fate lies within us, right?"

He shook his head. "If so, it must be extremely small and impossibly distant. I would not suggest you put any reliance in such an insignificant entity."

An icy, nihilistic void seemed to unfold itself around Jane, stretching to infinity in all directions at once, a perfect sphere encompassing all the universe. It seemed unimaginable, this existence the pale man presented her with, unregulated, sourceless, without purpose or direction. And yet, he was so obviously beyond illusion, solace, or desire, she could not imagine him lying to her. Why would he bother? "But everyone I know believes in planetary influences."

"Yes. They do."

She waited, but he did not elaborate. "In introductory astrology they told us that each person has a tutelary star and that each star has its own mineral, color, and musical tone, and a plant as well that is a specific for the disease that is caused by that star's occultation."

"All untrue. The stars do not concern themselves in the least with us. Our total extinction would mean nothing to them."

"But why?" Jane cried. "If it's not true, why would they teach it to us?"

A dry fingertip tapped the page not impatiently but pedagogically. "All courses require textbooks, charts, and teaching aids. By the time the information codified as astrology was discredited and became obsolete, it had a constituency. Certain . . . personages benefit from the supply contracts."

The smell of chalk dust was harsh in Jane's nostrils, a statistical effluvium of dead molecules suspended in the still air and nothing more. She could taste it in her mouth. "But if what you're saying is so, then it's all meaningless. Isn't it? I mean, nothing means anything at all then, does it?"

"*Acu tetigisti*," the pale man said in his affectless voice. "You have touched it with a needle."

She shivered, as if a rat had run over her grave. Maybe it was just that the chance evocation of Rooster's true name brought back memories she did not want. But deep inside something small and true as a bell told Jane that it wasn't like that at all.

Something awful had just happened, and she had no idea what.

---

The mall was everything Jane had imagined it to be, and more. It rose from a gracefully bulldozed hilltop on white marble pillars, and was roofed over by a high, grassy dome. She passed nervously through a lot in which chrome horses snorted, pawed the tarmac, leaked oil. "Come on," Ratsnickle said disgustedly. "Don't be such a pussy." He led her through the gates of ivory at the main entrance.

Within, time did not exist.

Soft music filled the air, and subtly arrayed lights pleased the eye with an endless variety of shades and textures, rendering shadows edgeless, gleaming from brass bedsteads and joyously leaping away from the mirror balls that spun among the banners overhead. Jane felt ennobled just being there, one of a thousand gracious shoppers whose tastes all the soft interior world sought to please.

The air smelled of lilies, leather, and chocolate chip cookies.

"Don't dawdle, okay?" Ratsnickle said.

The mall contained a hundred perfect shops, each one a jewel box of treasures. Sound systems, cloth-of-gold gowns, emerald shoes: row upon row of identical riches filled the racks, wealth multiplied and repeated upon itself in such profusion the mind could not contain it. Standing in front of Der Zauberberg, her reflection in the plate glass window superimposed itself upon cut crystal goblets, ashtrays, decanters, paperweights, and bowls, each diamond-sharp facet throwing off flecks of rainbow, while behind her floated the rippled ghosts of nutmeg trees, fountains, and escalators. Jane's head swam for the sweet richness of it all.

Dazedly, she let Ratsnickle lead her into a boutique. It was called Eulenspiegel's.

"Stop gawking," he said testily. "Here." He yanked at her trousers and something fell heavily to the bottom of her pocket. "Look natural."

"What?" She froze and in a whisper asked, "What is it?"

"A wristwatch." Ratsnickle made a face. "Don't whisper like that, you'll draw attention to us."

Timidly, she let him lead her through several stores. Speaking in a perfectly normal voice, one that lapsed naturally into silence whenever someone drew too near, he lectured her on security procedures and the finer points of shoplifting. "Don't snatch any of the gold," he said before a jewelry store. "It's only for display; the real stuff is kept in a safe in the back. The crap in the windows is only good for a day. By the time you get it home, it'll have changed into dried leaves or a dead mouse. Pebbles maybe."

"Oh," she said.

Ratsnickle showed Jane where the antitheft charms were placed, in high unobtrusive corners of the shops, the ensorcelled mirrors through which a security ogre might be watching over the merchandise from a distance, the quickened silver brooches that would cry thief if removed from their cases. He certainly seemed to know his business.

She noticed, however, that he didn't hit Enchanté or Mother Holle Fashions or indeed any of the high-elven shops, but concentrated on the more proletarian and traffic-dense stores, places where their mere presence would not be enough to draw the baleful glare of security.

"Now it's your turn," he said.

"I couldn't!"

He ignored her. "That one right there—The Eildon Tree. Just be sure you don't touch any of those scarves in the back. They're protected. I felt it when we walked by; like a little electric shock." He gave her a shove. "I'll meetcha by the well."

Somehow, Jane found herself inside. She walked slowly between a rack of pushed-lime and cherry sweat suits and a countertop perfume display, then turned and carefully, wonderingly picked up a leaded-glass bottle of Merde du Temps from Ricci of Ys. It was a lovely thing, and fit perfectly in the palm of her hand.

"May I help you?" A hag materialized at her side, cheekbones aristocratically sharp, skin of a fashionably corpselike pallor. Her expression suggested that she rather doubted it.

"No!" Jane hastily returned the bottle to its table. "Just—just looking."

With an icy smile, the hag retreated slightly. Jane journeyed deeper into the store.

Wherever she went, though, she felt the hag's suspicious eyes at her back, like a physical force pushing her farther and farther to the rear of the shop, until she wound up at the very back, fingering a red-and-black scarf with a border of white skulls and four Celtic spirals on the fly. She looked up and saw for a wonder that the hag was distracted by a new customer and no longer looking her way. Hastily, she shoved the scarf inside her blouse.

It was only then that she remembered Ratsnickle's warning to avoid the scarves.

For an instant she expected lightning to strike her, guards to descend, a clawed hand to close upon her wrist. Then, glancing up into the corner of the ceiling, she recognized the bundle of bones and feathers there affixed. It was, with minor variations, exactly the same as the fetish bundle outside Blugg's doorway, which she had crossed to steal his nail parings on the day she had discovered the dragon's grimoire.

Her blood was human. The fetish was helpless against her.

Heart pounding, she made her way from the shop.

When she and Ratsnickle rendezvoused at a bench by the holy well at the far end of the mall, she had already gone to the ladies' room to draw out the scarf in privacy and reposition it. Standing on the well's mossy rim she twirled on her toes, momentarily as wild a creature as any of the girls in her homeroom. She made a fist and then, reaching through it, pulled the scarf from her sleeve and waved it in the air. "Do you like what I got?" she asked, and laughed at Ratsnickle's amazement.

"How did you do that?" he asked suspiciously.

"Oh," she said airily, "I have my ways." She licked her lips. "Let's do it again."

When Jane finally left, she had a handful of gimcracks stuffed into one trousers pocket and the scarf blowing from her neck. They had spent hours within the mall, and yet outside the afternoon was no later than when they had entered. Almost, she turned around and went right back in. But Ratsnickle wouldn't let her lift any more. Her enthusiasm for the sport unnerved him. She suspected he hadn't had as much experience at shoplifting as he'd led her to think.

But she knew she was going to come back on her own.

———— ))·(( ————

"I'm home!"

7332 did not answer. He never did. In all the time they had lived above the landfill, he had not spoken to her once. After their one wild and glorious flight the night of their escape from the factory grounds, he had gone completely to ground. "They will be looking for us," he had said. "Keep your promises, and there won't be any trouble." Since, he had lapsed into silence. 7332 had the uncanny patience of all iron-based saurians. Yet for all the months since she had last heard him speak, his presence still lay heavy at the back of her skull, like a lump of dirty ice that had outlived winter.

She laid out her books and began to study.

Outside, there was a soft thud and then the softer sound of wings laboring heavily to lift into the twilight. An owl, possibly, or a lesser harpy had found food for its young. Jane yanked a grab rod to open a cabin window. The sky was beautiful outside. Three low stars glinted in the dusk. A bead of red gleamed atop the water tank.

It was around this time of night she could sometimes glimpse the wolf-boys running single file over the landfill on their way to the park, and hear their howls, lonely and ecstatic. She longed to be one of their pack then, to wear a heavy leather jacket that creaked when she moved and shitkicker boots with short chromed chains across the back of their heels, to hang out at the arcade, bored and spoiling for a fight, listen to some hot music, maybe score a little taste of something illegal.

Often, she would stay up at the window into the small hours of the morning, waiting for them to come trotting by on their way home, bloody-muzzled and sleepy. Once, one of them, last in line, had turned to look at her. Their gazes had locked for an instant, and she had felt a wild urge to fling open her door and go running barefooted after him.

Jane knew better, though. Wolf-boys weren't safe.

So tonight as always she kept the door locked. After a while, she undid her scarf and smoothed it over her knee. It was pure silk, hand-dyed by dwarven artisans with the spirals arrayed as if radiant from a common center, so that they seemed to whirl one into the other. She reknotted it loosely about her neck, and turned it around so the triangular part hung down in front. "Did you see what I got? Pretty, isn't it?"

7332 did not respond.

"It's stolen."

Nothing.

"I went out to the mall with a boy, and he taught me how to steal things. I was good at it."

Still the dragon did not answer.

Every night, just before she slept, Jane spoke to 7332, meditating silently and with all her will, trying to communicate her needs to him. My shoes are wearing thin, she thought, I'll need new soon. And galoshes too. Money for schoolbooks, new jeans, a poster of Bryan Faust dressed in black leather with his Stratocaster slung low at the hip. Sometimes he listened; more often he did not. Now the cumulative effect of his indifference welled up within her and came boiling out in tears.

"Damn you! Why won't you answer me, you stupid fucker? Why?" She slammed an iron plate wall with her fist. "You know what? I don't believe you're even alive anymore. You only had the stuff for one flight left in you, and you used it up. You're nothing now but a hunk of iron. Maybe there's still some current in your electrical systems, some kind of dim awareness, but that's it. You've been lobotomized, you can't even speak. You're nothing! *Nada*. I ought to sell you for scrap."

No response.

Angrily, she swept her books from the pilot's couch. They slid down and scattered themselves across the Pnuk counterpane that covered her bedless mattress. Her possessions were meager, but even so the cabin was tiny enough that there was scarcely room enough for them.

She plonked down in the couch.

At a touch the navigational systems came alive. The wrap-around closed about her head, and she was once more looking through Melanchthon's eyes. He was staring fixedly at the ground. She raised up his gaze. Her vision now covered a full 360 degrees, over the landfill to one side of the scrub, and down a short, sharp slope on the other, where a sooty-bricked line of row houses showed their narrow backyards, all cinders and the rusting bones of bicycles and other dead machines. The graffiti on the garden walls shone in the dragon-sight like neon: ELVES GO WRACK! and DWARVES RULE O.K. with a pair of crossed hammers beneath it. In the human range of the spectrum, three windows flickered an uncanny television blue.

For a long instant she hung on the edge of the precipice, ready to invoke Melanchthon by name. The syllables hovered a fraction of a second away from her tongue. But at even this faintest thought of them, nausea rose up within Jane, a perceptual queasiness so strong she almost threw up. Something half-uncoiled inside her brain.

Her gaze unfocused and turned inward on the machine diagnostics, green lines unscrolling and multiplying upon themselves as if they had a life of their own. Schematicized, Melanchthon was a map of misery and disrepair, every break and gap where reconstruction was needed—lubricants, rewiring, replacement parts—glaringly obvious. There must have been a thousand such failures riddling the black iron body, and each one an obligation she had pledged her soul to heal.

The presence of the dragon welled up beneath her, all iron and cold, cold blood. She felt like an ant on a moving mountaintop. An aura of sickness emanated from him, blackening the air, and the realization struck her for the first time that in his present state Melanchthon was a cripple, and like any crippled creature, dangerous in proportion to his strength and former vigor.

Sanity returned to her, and with it, fear.

With hands gone suddenly cold, Jane slapped off the interactives. The dragon's presence died away.

It took her a while to pull herself together. When she did, she began to gather up her books. She was not going to invoke the dragon. Not tonight at any rate. Their next conversation would have to wait on a moment of far greater import.

The printed pages, however, were unreadable to her now. Seven times she went over one before realizing she had not the slightest notion which text she had opened. She let it slip from her fingers, and rolled over on her back, staring blankly at the iron ceiling of the cabin.

After a while she began to cry.

Her loneliness seemed overwhelming, now, her isolation complete. Jane felt her inferiority like a physical blow. In a world filled with enchantment, she was nothing but a changeling girl, nothing but a high school kid, nothing but a little thief.

# SEVEN

The material world is ultimately composed of primitive matter. No one has ever seen primitive matter, however, since it has only a potential existence until it is acted upon by form to create air, fire, water, and earth, and the near infinite number of elements that are admixtures of those four. Creation occurs in two exhalations. The Sun's heat acting upon the ocean causes a vaporous exhalation, which is both moist and cold, and its resultant compounds are therefore largely, but not entirely, composed of water and air. But when the Sun acts upon the land, there is a smoky exhalation, which is both hot and dry, and its compounds are mostly admixtures of earth and fire.

Jane loved alchemy. She was fascinated by the elegance of it. From formlessness by way of two operations arose the four basic elements and all things that derived from them. An oak tree stripped down to its components was made up entirely of these four in combination. You could prove this by taking a log from that tree and applying sufficient heat. The unraveling would begin with the expulsion of flames and hot jets of air—the first two elements. As it burned, tarry liquids would bubble from the cut end of the log—water. Then, when calcination was complete, a residue of ash would remain, and this last was the final element of earth.

"The smoky exhalation," said the pale man, "is masculine and the vaporous one feminine. Mercury is a womb in which embryonic metals can be gestated. This is why all the great alchemists are female."

*Female* Jane wrote in her notebook, and underlined it three times.

———

"I don't see why anybody would want to be wicker queen anyway," Jane said.

The others looked at her pityingly.

"For the glory," Hebog said. "She gets to cut classes, skip finals, date whosofuckingever she wants, and ride in a great big float while everybody looks up at her and cheers. She even gets to wear a stupid little tiara." He hawked up a gob of phlegm and spat it out. "What's so hard to understand about that?"

"Yes, but—"

"Oh, don't be tedious." Salome skinned a slim pink cigarette from her purse and lit up without offering the pack around. She was a musty-smelling girl of vague origins with a long skull, perpetually damp hair, and the unfortunate habit of biting her toenails in class. Jane didn't exactly like her, but it wasn't as if she had a great deal of choice whom she could hang with. "This topic is boring me to distraction, daawling. Let's talk about something else."

"Yeah." Ratsnickle took a casual swipe at Jane's head. "Change the record, dipshit."

"Hey, speak of the devil, here comes Peter," Hebog said. "Peter, my man! What's the word?" He was a red dwarf and like many of his kind his moods swung precipitously between surly fatalism and a puppyish eagerness to please that bordered on the grotesque.

"Yeah, hi." Peter of the Hillside nodded vaguely down at the dwarf, ignoring the others, and then, to her amazement, addressed Jane. "Listen, I hear you know how to lift tapes from that store down to the mall."

"Yes," said Jane. "I can do that."

"Well, could you tell me how? This rusalka chick I'm seeing, you know what they're like. She wants me to get her this one particular tape, you know, and I'm flat out of money."

"Jane never—" Hebog began.

She quelled him with a look. It was her own decision to make, after all. To prove it, she said, "Okay. I've got this little red leather purse, see. I carry it in my right hand with the flap unsnapped, so I can slide in a cassette with my left when nobody's looking." The others, Salome in particular, were listening with interest; normally she didn't share her methodology. Ratsnickle's eyes were narrow slits of concentration.

"But what about the security gate?"

"That's why a purse instead of just shoving the cassette into your pocket. I go to the gate and just as I'm starting through, I see a friend out in the mall, okay? So I've got to call out to her, right? So it's like: *Salome!*" She squealed the name as if amazed and delighted, going up on her toes and waving her purse-hand high to draw her friend's attention. A step carried her through the imaginary gate and she brought her hand down. "You see? The purse actually goes over the gate, not through, but it all happens so naturally that store security doesn't think twice."

Her friends laughed and clapped their hands. "She's got a million of 'em," Hebog said proudly.

"That's no good," Peter said. "That'll only work for a girl." He started to turn away. "Well, thanks anyway."

"Wait," Jane said. "What tape do you want?"

"The new Conjunction of Opposites album. It's called *Mythago.*"

"I'll get it for you. As a favor. Come see me tomorrow."

"Yeah?" He squinted, as if noticing her for the first time. "That's really nice of you."

When Peter was gone, Ratsnickle said, "Why did you go and tell him a thing like that?"

Jane didn't know why. She had acted on impulse. "He's kind of cute." She shrugged.

"She's sweet on him," Hebog said. "Talk about hopeless! That boy is doomed. You can see it written on his face."

"'As was prophesied Beneath the Mountain,'" Salome said mockingly, "'and y-carven in Runes ain spear's-haft deep even in its granite Heart.'"

"*Hey!*" Hebog clenched his fists and glared up at her. "That's not funny."

Ratsnickle stepped between the two and pushed them apart. "Shut up, Salome. You too, Hebog." He favored Jane with a withering look, as if it were somehow all her fault. "He's right, though. It's worse than hopeless. That rusalka bitch Peter's seeing, you know who she is?"

"No," said Jane.

The bell rang, signaling the end of recess. Salome threw down her cigarette. "Well, back to the mines."

"Fuck you too," Hebog said.

Jane caught up to Ratsnickle at the door, took his arm, and said, "Who?"

He smirked. "Gwenhidwy the Green. Oh, come on now, don't shake your head like that. You know Gwen. Yes you do—it's the wicker queen herself."

———◉———

Because she spent so much time in the mall, Jane aged more rapidly than the other girls in her class; it was possible to spend days on end within that glamourous domain and reemerge into a world no older than it was when she went in. Jane did a lot of schoolwork there. She was catching up in her studies, and only the predetermination by her teachers that she was stupid kept her from being promoted out of the pale man's tutoring sessions.

"What happens to the wicker queen?" she asked him that afternoon.

He stopped reading, looked directly at, through, beyond her. "You know what happens to the wicker queen."

"Yes, but why?"

"It's a tradition." He returned to the text. "Words which are transliterations from the Arabic via a metathetical process include 'Abric,' more accurately transcribed as *al-kibrit*, for sulphur; 'Al-chitram,' from *alqitran*, for pitch; 'Almagest,' or *al-majisti* for—"

"Why is it a tradition?"

"It just is."

"But why?"

The pale man sighed. It was a singularly passionless sigh, and yet the first ghost of emotion Jane had ever yet caught the pale man at, and as such shocking. He put the book aside. "There are things," he said, "which may be known, and these we study in order to gain in understanding and increase our power. Alchemy, metaphysics, and necromancy are such fields of knowledge, and on them and their sister sciences are based the whole of our industrial civilization. But there are other, darker things which will not yield to the intellect. The intent of the Goddess is neither known nor knowable. She makes us dance, male and female, in ever-converging gyres that bring us ultimately each to our own destiny, and that destiny is always the same and never escapable. She does not tell us why."

"You said there were no outside forces ordering our lives. That there was nothing but chance and random occurrence."

He shrugged.

"You did!"

"The Goddess is unknowable and her aims unfathomable, unpredictable, and ineluctable. They might as well be random. We live our brief lives in ignorance and then we die. That's all."

"But the rest of us just die sometime. The wicker queen dies this year!"

"Have you even listened to me?" With short, violent motions, he stabbed a fresh cigarette into his mouth and lit it, throwing the paper match away so that it bounced angrily from the chalkboard. "The Goddess wants blood. And what the Goddess wants, she shall have. One way or the other. If the occasional sacrifice averts her desire from us, why then it is a case of the greatest good for the greatest number."

"Yes, but—"

The pale man stood—it was the first time Jane had seen him stand—and strode to the window, tracing a fine blue line of tobacco smoke across the room. The panes were festooned with construction-paper flowers, priapi, eggs, taped up to welcome in the spring and already turning white at the edges. He stared through the streaked glass and the mesh grating, though there was nothing to be seen from here but the back of the gymnasium and the loading dock for the shop.

"I am not from here," he said. "But where I did come from, there was a young fool who loved not a wicker queen but an orend who was chosen to be the blood-maiden for a new housing project. She had hair like flame and skin as clear and unblemished as a lampshade.

"He was a scholar and wore a black robe. Like you, he thought that it was possible to outwit the Crow-god. So he made a simulacrum of his orend out of flowers. It was a brilliant piece of work. When the flower lass was burned she struggled and screamed most convincingly.

"Covertly they moved to a far city where he found work as a substitute teacher. He rented a room with money we—they—had saved. He bought a mattress and a television first, and then later an icebox, a couch, and a bed. They were reasonably happy.

"But a night came when the air was filled with owls and omens. The television set groaned and wept blood when they turned it on. There had been a fire in the housing project. Two hundred died. Her eyes turned a milky white then. Her hair lifted and sizzled with electricity. Oh Goddess, she cried, what have we done?

"He comforted her as best he could—but how good was that? The facts could not be changed. She should have burned. There was no denying her guilt. It festered and turned to a fever so hot within her that her skin blistered and flaked. I—he—would wake in the night to find the bedclothes smoking and about to ignite. It was necessary to keep a bucket of water close to hand at all times.

"Once I opened my eyes to a hideous blue light. She was an acetylene flare, hissing and spitting in the center of the room. In a panic I threw the blanket about her, smothering the flames. When she was herself again, I put her to bed. In the morning she would not speak to me. She wept and no tears came out. Only steam.

"Day after day, this went on. I cropped her hair short to prevent spontaneous combustion. I threw away all the matches so she could not eat them. I unplugged the appliances for fear of an electrical fire. Before I left for work each morning, I drenched the rugs and threw water on all the walls. Then I locked her in and pocketed the key.

"By that time her speech was barely intelligible. She sputtered and rattled like a teapot. Her skin had hardened and it crackled when she moved. She was more reptile than woman. Her eyes did not blink when she stared at me. Sometimes she was taken with the *awen* and would prophesize."

Jane could barely breathe. "What did she say?"

"You are too young."

The pale man was silent for so long then that Jane half-thought he would never speak again.

But when he did speak, his voice was normal once more, emotionless and flat. "One evening I came home and found she had put towels at the bottoms of the doors and windows, turned on the gas, and stuck her head in the oven. All my efforts had been for nothing. She had died, but not well.

"I bowed to the Crow-god then, and made my sacrifice to him." He shrugged. "Let me be frank. By then, it was a relief."

The pale man picked up his book and returned to the lesson. But Jane could not concentrate. Her mind was full of the vision of Gwenhidwy the Green, clad only in her beauty, swinging within a wicker cage hung over the fifty-yard line. The bleachers were full, and all the school assembled. She smelled the gasoline. Flames leapt up. Everyone roared.

Gwen was burning like a moth in a candle, and screaming too.

It was a vision that stayed with Jane through her classes and all the way home. The ground crunched underfoot where she crossed the landfill, rusty tin cans grinding against each other beneath the soil. She walked carefully, afraid of turning an ankle. Inside the dragon, she kicked a stack of underwear from the pilot's couch and patched herself into his sensorium.

"Hello," she whispered. "It's me again."

No response.

7332's vision was focused tightly on the ground. Jane started to raise it up and then, curious, returned it to the original settings. It took her a minute to figure out what he was up to.

He was watching the meryons.

Jane had never paid much attention to the six-legged folk. They were the smallest of all intelligent creatures, the remote descendants of pixies, reduced by the evolutionary processes of aeons to the stature of ants. Simplification had stripped them of passion, gallantry, honor, and ambition. Their wars were butchery. They had no literature or songs. They loved nothing but toil. She could not understand why 7332 would be watching them.

Tiny figures scuttled through the weeds, lugging scraps of metal thrice their size. Wisps of smoke from their underground forges rose here and there among the weeds, faint and blue. They'd be mistaken for ground haze at a distance.

A meryon trundled down an almost invisible trail pulling a wagon laden high with three chokecherries. Where a dirt bike had left a rut in the ground, two straws had been laid across it an axle's width apart to form a bridge. At the far end stood a minuscule amazon with a metal-tipped spear the length of a carpet needle. She waved the laborer past.

The carter pulled his load to the nozzle of a vacuum cleaner emerging from the dirt and disappeared within its maw. Jane blinked and in an instant of perceptual giddiness she realized that what looked like a scattering of trash beneath the trees was actually a well-ordered village. Here a pipe stem served as a fireplace for a buried hut with an egg carton roof and acorn-cap chimney pot. A coffee can half-sunken in the ground was a Quonset hut, within which were stabled a matched pair of field mice, broken to harness and available to haul the really big loads. Roads were being devised, widened, and camouflaged with plant cuttings. A rusting sadiron attached by a hundred threads to straining teams of June bugs served as a grader for the larger thoroughfares.

The meryons were everywhere in motion, tireless microengineers, wee masters of bricolage. A mayonnaise jar, shaded by three oak leaves stitched into a conical roof, held a reservoir of water, and a system of soda straws was being devised to pipe that water into every hidden house and den in the hamlet.

Jane was entranced.

She watched them until the light failed and there was naught to be seen but the occasional glowworm spark of a lantern carried in the invisible fist of a border guard and the ghostly light from a prototype methane gas production plant. For all their lack of individual complexity, meryon society taken as a whole was as intricate and inherently fascinating as a crystal pocketwatch.

Abruptly Jane looked up and realized that she was stiff and tired and still had homework to do. Well, she could afford to miss the occasional assignment; it wasn't as if any of them were expecting anything much from her.

Then she remembered that she had promised Peter she would lift the Conjunction of Opposites tape for him that night. "Shit!" There was still time to catch the shuttle to the mall, but only just. Anyway, she really didn't want to have to run to make the connection at this time of night, skip into the Cineplex for a quick nap so she wouldn't make any foolish mistakes, buzz the music store, cop a tin of something-or-other to kill her hunger, find a free bench and crack the books, then hurry back out to catch the Red Eye Express. It was too much work for just a casual promise.

In the end, though, that was what she did.

But she spent too long lingering in the mall's entranceway, where the time flow was half-normal and all the flyers for the good sales were posted. So when she emerged, she was just in time to see the red taillights of the last ride home fading down the road. Two miles she had to walk down the miracle mile, with steel behemoths blasting by so close they staggered her with their backwash. The brickyards and vacant lots were full of bright eyes and tiny cries. Something shifted in the shadows, and she was sure it was following her. Wolf-boys! she thought, terrified.

To make matters worse, Peter never showed up the next day. At lunch Jane made a few cautious inquiries and discovered that he was known for cutting classes. "That's Peter for you," a nisse said carelessly. "As fickle as they come. You have to love him for it."

———◆———

So it was that immediately after school Jane ventured out into the part of town beyond the landfill in search of Peter's digs, to give him the cassette and a good piece of her mind.

Peter lived in a declining commercial district. He had a dingy third-floor walk-up above a bankrupt discount stereo store. A length of wire stuck out where the buzzer had been but the lock on the door was busted anyway so Jane went on up. The stairway smelled of boiled linen and old paint. The linoleum in the hall before his flat was cracked and buckled. She knocked.

"Come in."

She opened the door.

He was lying pale in a rumpled bed, head back and naked. His ribs stuck out, and she could see one ash-gray nipple. A chance throw of the tangled sheets over one thigh hid his privates from sight. "Just set it down on the table," he said without opening his eyes. "Add two bucks for a tip and put it on my tab."

Jane stood there, not knowing what to say. Peter had a light fuzz of hair on his chest, with a fine line marching straight down the middle of his stomach. A black-and-white television set on a chair in one corner muttered to itself, video on, volume turned all the way down. "I . . . I don't think I'm the person you're expecting," she ventured at last.

Peter jerked up into a sitting position, and all in a panic grabbed at the sheet to wrap it about himself. Then he sank back down on the bed, all his energy expended. "Oh, right. The tape. Hey, I'm sorry, I—well, you can see I'm not exactly in shape for school."

"You look terrible," she told him.

"I feel terrible," he agreed.

A toilet flushed. Gwenhidwy the Green emerged from the bathroom, snapping her skirt together. She saw Jane and stopped. "Hello," she said pleasantly. "Who is this?"

"It's a friend from school," Peter said. "Jane Alderberry." His eyes were closed, their lids almost translucent. His lips were white.

Jane didn't know which amazed her more—that Peter would

call her his friend, or that he knew her name at all. She held out her little package. "I just came to bring this. It's yours. From Peter."

"How sweet." Gwen accepted the tape, admired it briefly, and made it disappear. She glided to Peter's side and, crouching by the bed, stroked his forehead. "Poor baby. Does this help?"

"Your hand is cool," he murmured. "So cool." He reached blindly to draw the fingers to his lips so he could kiss them.

Jane felt her heart go out to them. They were both so beautiful, so perfectly in love, so doomed. Her own life was tawdry, complicated, and inconsequential compared to theirs. She felt for them a sentiment so delicate and strong that it too could only be called love.

Suddenly Peter's eyes snapped open. "What time is it? Have we missed it? It must be coming on right about now."

"Hush." Gwen smiled. "I'm keeping track of the time." She went to the television set, put her hand on the volume control. "Just about now, in fact."

There was a talk show on. Everyone on it was tall and gracious, clothes accessorized, their hair and teeth and nails each as perfect as the other. Jane didn't watch much television; it was all elves and money, with maybe the occasional dwarf thrown in for relevance and contrast. The shows might as well be broadcast from another universe, one where nobody ever had body odor or crook-teeth or a dead mouse caught in their hair. They didn't have much to do with her own experience. "Well," she said awkwardly. "I guess I'll go now."

"No, stay!" Gwen cried. "It's my moment; we want you to share it too, don't we, Peter?"

"I want whatever you want. You know that."

"You see? Oh, I think there's still enough time to light up. Peter, where did you put the pipe?"

"On top of the dresser."

Gwen got out a long-stemmed pipe with a frowning meerschaum Toby bowl and dropped in a chunk of something black. "Hash," she explained. She sat down on the edge of the bed between Peter and Jane, lit a match and inhaled, drawing its flame down over the hashish. Without asking, she passed it to Jane.

The tip of the stem was still damp from Gwen's lips. Gingerly, Jane put it in her mouth. She inhaled deeply and her lungs filled with harsh, rasping smoke. She choked and coughed. Cloud upon cloud of smoke gushed out of her, impossible volumes filling the room, and still she could not stop coughing. She prayed she wouldn't disgrace herself by spilling the pipe.

Peter laughed. "Whoa! Hold it in, hold it in!"

But Gwen took away the pipe and pounded her on the back. "There, there," she said comfortingly. "Went down wrong, did it? Next time, don't draw in so much, you'll be fine."

"Yeah." The word buzzed and echoed in Jane's ears, reverberating deep into her skull where everything was sparks and swirling gray. For an instant she had no idea where she was or what she was doing, and to cover she said "Yeah," again, even though she was not at all clear on what she was agreeing to.

"It's on!" Gwen leaped up and turned up the sound on the TV.

⸻ ⸨◉⸩ ⸻

Afterward, Jane was unable to separate what happened on the screen from what happened in her head. It was a documentary on Gwenhidwy, of that she was sure, filled with lingering slomo shots of her long, green hair swirling when she turned her head first one way then the other, like a transient planetary ring around her smile. Stoned, the narration was impossible to follow. The music swelled up and down—or was this just Jane's perception of it?—peaking with demon synthesizer shrieks and bottoming into baroque spinnet.

Something was being said on voice-over.

"A *goddess?* Oh, la!" Gwen cried. Peter emerged from the bathroom, newly dressed and looking ten times healthier than before. He sat down by Gwen and leaned his head against her shoulder. Absently, she stroked his hair.

Looking back and forth from Gwen on the screen to Gwen on the bed, Jane could not decide which impressed her most. The television Gwen was more voluptuous, leaner, with crisper cheekbones and the kind of glossy beauty that took video technology to perfect. But the real Gwen was so much warmer, so vital and spontaneous, so . . . real.

Peter stared at the screen, hopeless with yearning. Jane tried to imagine what it would be like to have a boy look at her that way. It must feel very strange.

At that very moment Gwen's face, lips moist and parting, was superimposed over footage of last year's wicker queen twisting in the flames. Jane turned to her and forgetting her manners entirely asked, "How can you stand it?"

Gwen smiled, as if possessed of some great secret. "I have Peter," she said. "Hush now, this is the best part."

When the show ended, Jane must have said something, for Gwen looked enormously pleased. "Oh, let's not go overboard," she said. Feet sounded on the stairway and she flung open the door. "All *right!* The pizza's here."

It was late when Jane finally staggered down the stairs, still high and a little dizzy, her throat cottony and dry. The night air seemed velvety warm, soft and inviting. Gwen followed her to the door. They were going dancing later, Peter and Gwen. Gwen loved to dance.

"You'll come back and visit again, won't you?" Gwen's eyes were large and dark. There almost seemed to be—although there couldn't be, not really—a note of pleading in her voice.

Jane could refuse her nothing.

———— ◉ ————

The next morning everyone in the schoolyard was talking about Gwen's special. Jane was filled to bursting with her visit to Peter's flat. Seeing Gwen's show with Gwen herself was just about the coolest thing she had ever done in her life. But she didn't want to say anything about it until lunchtime. She wanted to keep it her own special secret for just a little while longer.

But then something happened that drove all thought of Gwen from her mind.

It was obvious that the day was going to be different as soon as Jane stepped into her homeroom. Strawwe the proctor sat perched on the edge of Grunt's desk, tense and thin-lipped. That meant a test at the very least.

Strawwe wore a tricorn hat, flat side frontwards, as his badge of office. His hair was pulled into a ponytail so tight he couldn't blink, and he was perpetually goggle-eyed as a result. He tapped his thigh with a steel-edged ruler once for each child who entered. When the last student was in, he nodded to Grunt.

After Grunt had called attendance, he cleared his throat. "The Three B's," he said. "The Three B's are your guide to scholastic excellence. The Three B's are your gold key to the doorway of the future. Now—all together—what are they?"

"Be-lieve," the class mumbled. "Be-have. Be Silent."

"What was that last?" He cupped a hand to his ear.

"Be Silent!"

"I caaaaaan't heeeeear you."

"BE SILENT!"

"Good." He put his fingertips together. "Now, class. Children. Dear, dear little children. We are privileged today—most privileged—to have a distinguished visitor coming here to visit us in our class from the Board of Industrial Corrections. Do you know who he is?"

Nobody said anything.

"That is correct. You do not know. You must wait for me to tell you."

Now Strawwe slipped from the desk and began silently gliding between the rows of students. It took an effort not to cringe when he appeared suddenly in the periphery of vision, or when the shadow of his ruler fell across Jane's knuckles, hesitated, hovered, and finally moved on. She didn't dare look at him as he passed. For such inattention, a sharp blow to the ear was the least of what she might expect.

A board creaked underfoot just as he reached the front rows, and a head covered with tight red curls turned reflexively at the sound.

*Whack.* The ruler slashed down, and Jane heard Hebog suck in his breath sharply. He didn't cry out, though. Dwarves were tough.

"Mis-ter Hebog. It appears you are a little *short*—" Grunt paused, to let a tiny smile blossom on his puffy lips. "—of attention today."

The tension broke and everyone roared with laughter, Jane included. Too late, she caught hold of herself and stopped. But even the other dwarves were laughing. Three of them were black dwarves, of course, but it was depressing even so.

When the laughter died down, Grunt said, "The Three Ins! Recite them!"

"In-dolence, In-solence, In-gratitude," they chanted dutifully.

"That is correct." A sense of Presence was building in the hall outside, an ominous pressure tinged with ozone, as if a storm cloud were gathering just over the horizon. "And when you are, despite my best efforts, indolent, insolent, and prone to ingratitude, you may then be required to answer to—" The proctor materialized by the door, opened it a crack, and nodded. "—the child catcher."

Strawwe flung open the door, and the child catcher stalked in.

———⊕———

He was an eerily handsome creature, artificially tanned, and wearing an imported silk suit. His strong hands were sheathed in black leather gloves. His hair was stiff and bristly—there must have been a touch of wolf in his blood—and his ears were aristocratically laminate. He smiled with square, even teeth. But he said nothing.

The class stirred uneasily.

Standing before the desk, the child catcher dominated vision. Grunt and Strawwe vanished in his presence. Above him the clock over the blackboard provided a secondary focus of attention, its disk the only curved line in a surround of right angles, the nervous once-a-second leap of its thin red hand the only movement in a universe where all motion had died long ago.

Now the child catcher took something from his pocket. It was a scrap of cloth, coarse and scratchy-looking, of a color somewhere between olive and brown. One black glove clenched it tight and raised it slowly to his long, lean nose. His eyes darted back and forth across the class.

Slowly, deeply, he inhaled.

Memory flooded Jane.

She was back in the dormitory in Building 5 of the steam dragon works. This was one of her earliest memories, and one that had always puzzled her. It was morning, and the forges were going full blast as they had for the past two weeks, their roar a constant in the background. She stood by her bed, folding her blanket. All the children were bustling about, preparing for Blugg's morning inspection and eager for breakfast.

Suddenly her vision blurred and doubled. Simultaneously she was standing here by the bed and sitting in the back row of what she did not then recognize as a classroom. Strangers were all about her. A tall, dark creature was staring at her from across the room, his eyes two pinpricks punched in reality.

Her hand froze on the blanket, its material coarse and scratchy, of a color somewhere between olive and brown. It seemed infused with some terrible significance. In all the world only it seemed truly real, an anchor to reality; if she let go of it, she would fall headlong into her vision and be lost forever.

Rooster punched her shoulder. "Yo, droopyhead. What's with you?"

She shrugged, and was back in the classroom. The child catcher was lowering the scrap of cloth from his nose and staring straight back at her. He raised a long arm, cuff links sliding smoothly into view, pointing toward the back row, and for the first time spoke.

"You. Young lady. Please stand."

Paralyzed with fear, Jane watched as the girl to her immediate left tremblingly stood. It was Salome.

The child catcher stared at her. One eyebrow rose quizzically, and his nostrils flared ever so slightly, as if there were something about the situation he did not entirely understand, but was sure he could puzzle out. He started to take a step forward.

Out of nowhere, somebody farted.

It was a horrifyingly drawn-out monster of a fart, one that brought all eyes to the front row. It smelled of methane and wild onions slathered over a base of boiled cabbage, with a nose-pinching tang of sulfur to give it depth. The air took on a distinctly greenish hue as it slowly expanded to fill the room. Several of the girls giggled nervously and clapped hands to mouths. The ruder feys held their noses.

"Mister Hebog!" Grunt cried, aghast.

Strawwe, returned to existence, had already reached the front row and yanked the struggling dwarf from his seat. Grunt seized the opposite arm and the two of them ran him full tilt at the blackboard. His skull hit the slate with a resounding crack, and a thin line zigzagged crazily away from the point of impact.

The child catcher watched it all with a politely detached smile.

Grunt stepped back, and Strawwe hauled the dwarf to his feet by the back of his collar. He held him so that Hebog stood on tiptoe, red-faced and choking. In a trice he had been whisked out the door, toward the detention hall.

Jane felt a soft touch on her wrist. She whirled, and no one was there.

At a frantic gesture from Ratsnickle, meanwhile, Salome had slipped back into her seat. It was exactly the sort of opportunity Ratsnickle would spot first, the chance to sit down and be forgotten. Salome appeared dazed. Softly, wonderingly, she said, "Hey. I didn't think he'd . . . Hey."

The child catcher cleared his throat. "Now where was I?" His shrewd eyes studied the last row, lingering this time on Jane. "Ah, yes."

Again, he drew the scrap of cloth from his pocket.

When he inhaled, Jane felt a shuddering wind blow through her insides. She shivered with cold and a strange sense of violation. The child catcher was still staring at her. His eyes narrowed.

Slowly the scrap of her old blanket came down from his nose.

The sounds and smells of the classroom faded away, like noise from a dying radio. Jane felt a panicky inability to catch her breath. The room was still and airless. Her classmates sat as motionless as so many brightly printed cut-out figures.

The child catcher turned to Grunt and took him between thumb and forefinger. He gave the pedant a shake, then laid him flat across his own desk.

Unhurriedly the child catcher went down each row, plucking the children from their seats and draping them across one arm. When the stack grew thick, he would return to the front of the room and set it down atop their teacher. He saved the back row for last, taking up everyone but Jane herself and carrying them to the front. Jane trembled and tried to avoid his eye. The last child to go was Ratsnickle, still smirking. The child catcher put Strawwe down atop him, bug-eyed and indignant.

He pulled a chair from back of the desk, and sat down.

"Come." The child catcher gestured to Jane. "Sit on my lap, and we'll talk."

Jane had no choice but to obey.

His legs were hard and bony under her; Jane felt awkward perched upon them. She stared at the back wall. One gloved hand squeezed and massaged her shoulder. "I have the power to seize you here and now and take you away by force. Do you doubt me?"

Jane shook her head, unable to speak.

"I am an agent of Law, Jane, and it is important that you understand and acknowledge my authority over you. A compact was made when you were small, a binding contract whose terms you have unlawfully tried to escape. You will say that this was your right because you had suffered an injustice, and that it was an injustice because it was not your signature on the deed of indenture." He shrugged. "But you were—you still are—a minor, and legally your signature would mean nothing. If an injustice exists, it is rooted too deeply in the past for you to do anything about it." He took her chin in his hand and turned her face to his. His eyebrows were dark and thorny. His eyes were as flat and calm as two mirrors.

"You can see that, can't you?"

Jane squirmed, but said nothing. He could kill her, he could send her back to the dragon works to labor forever. He could never make her agree it was right.

The child catcher sighed then, as if profoundly disappointed in her. "I come from the North. We hunt monkeys there with a wide-mouthed bottle and a stick. Do you know how that's done?"

"No," she squeaked.

"It's very amusing. We drop a single sweet cherry into the jar and then withdraw a distance. The monkey comes along. He sees the succulent in the jar, reaches within, and grasps it in his fist. But the jar is so shaped and sized that he cannot withdraw his hand when it is clenched. He could easily escape the jar by letting go of the cherry, but he wants that little treat too dearly. He cannot bring himself to let go. Even when the hunter approaches whistling and twirling the stick, he cannot bring himself to surrender his prize.

"So up comes the hunter and bashes his brains out with the stick."

The child catcher drew an ostrich-hide memorandum book from an inside jacket pocket. He handed her a piece of chalk. "Now, Jane, I want you to write in your very best hand the words I tell you. Write them in five even columns as straight and neat as you can." He waited until she was in place. "Recurvor," he said. "Recusable. Recusacao. Recusadora."

Jane was so frightened that she was halfway down the board before she recognized the words she was printing as the operational lock-codes for Moloch-class dragons.

Trying hard not to show she knew what they were, Jane printed out the words as he gave them. Maybe, she thought, they wouldn't work. The landfill was a good quarter-mile from the school after all.

When she reached the bottom, she looked at what she had made:

| | | | | |
|---|---|---|---|---|
| Recurvor | Recusable | Recusacao | Recusadora | Recusamor |
| Recusancy | Recusative | Recusaturi | Recusavel | Recuser |
| Recuserati | Recussion | Recussus | Recutio | Recutionis |
| Recutitos | Recutitum | Redaccao | Redaccendo | Redactadas |
| Redactamos | Redactaron | Redadim | Redadinar | Redambules |
| Redamnavit | Redendum | Redibitar | Redictor | Redivamat |
| Redocculla | Redoctar | Redoctamos | Redombulas | Redorradio |

"That's a good start," the child catcher said over her shoulder. His breath was sweet and tickled her ear. "Now take up the eraser."

His hand closed about hers and gently guided the eraser over the blackboard, like the planchette of a Ouija board. It glided above the surface, not touching, then abruptly dipped down to erase a word. Up and down the board their merged hands moved, seemingly at random, wiping out the lock-codes one at a time.

Finally the child catcher released her hand. "There," he said in a pleased voice.

| | | | |
|---|---|---|---|
| Recurvor | | Recusadora | Recusamor |
| | Recussus | | |
| | | Redaccendo | |
| Redactamos | Redadim | | Redambules |
| Redamnavit | | | |

The temperature in the room dropped. A tremendous sense of presence darkened the air, like an iron cloud passing before the sun. Voiceless words said, *What do you want?*

It was Melanchthon.

Jane tried to turn around, but could not. Her neck muscles seized up tight and unswiveling as if she were held in steel claws. Nor would her legs respond. She stared at the blackboard while the child catcher said, "Your name."

*What does it matter what my name is, little doggie?* The dragon sounded gentle, almost sad. *You can call me Death, if you wish. I killed your kind by the thousands in Avalon.*

The floor creaked as the child catcher walked to Grunt's desk, slid open the drawer and removed something. A second later, he held that something sharp and slim against her throat. It was Grunt's silver letter opener. "Did you want to discuss death?"

Paralyzed, Jane felt like an egg held in the grasp of two hands and contested for by each. Melanchthon's presence was overwhelming, like the gravitational tug of a mountain that had suddenly materialized in the schoolyard.

*Yes, let's. Tell me: Living I am worthless, until death gives me value. Dead, that value is gone. What am I?*

"A hostage." The child catcher removed the letter opener from Jane's throat. She felt a dreadful itch where its point had pricked her. "You like riddles, do you? Try this one: Johnny-a-locket hides in my pocket. Yet when he shouts, whole armies turn out."

*I do not think your beeper will work. My turn: See, see! What shall I see? A bow-wow's head where his feet should be.*

The forces holding Jane captive weakened, and she turned to see the child catcher grimly confronting an empty room. For all that the dragon's aura was everywhere, a cold reptilian unders-tench of malice, he was not physically present. He was waging this fight entirely by electronic countermeasure technology.

As quietly as she could, Jane edged sideways, toward the child catcher's blind spot, behind his head, between the blackboard and the desk.

A swirling formed about the child catcher, like swarms of gnats flying too fast for the eye to get a fix on them. A warping magnetic field, it spun about his head, but could not close upon it. "Idle threats!" he scoffed. "Did you think I would be sent up against a dragon without protection? You cannot decapitate me as easily as that."

Carefully he unfolded a pair of reading glasses and hooked them over his ears. He opened his memorandum book again, skipped over the page of locking codes and began to read. "The stuff of substance, the substance of thought . . ."

*No!*

"The matter of life, yet matter I'm not. A grain of me feeds you, live you never so long. A gram will destroy you, be you ever so strong!"

A howl filled the air, screaming up into the supersonic. Jane fell to her knees, clutching at her ears in pain. The sound was a steel needle through her skull. Her hands could not mute it. The dragon's presence faded, dwindled . . .

And was gone.

"There," said the child catcher. Shakily, Jane stood. She was directly behind him now, out of sight. She reached for the heavy stapler atop Grunt's desk. "Don't try it," the child catcher said casually. He folded his glasses up and carefully replaced them in his pocket. "Now, child, it's time you were put back where you belonged." He reached for her hand, unwillingly frozen just above the stapler.

Cold gusts of laughter filled the room. They grew and swelled until Jane felt like a cork bobbing on top of an ocean of scorn. *Stupid little puppy! One of the first things I did on arriving here was to ground my electrical systems. Your electromagnetic pulse weapon is useless.*

For the first time the child catcher looked startled. One hand jerked free of his trousers pocket, grabbing hastily for something in his jacket. "How . . . ?"

But the dragon had already begun his next riddle:

*Silent, unseen, small cousin of death,*
*Born this instant, closer than breath,*
*The killer of thought, assassin of dreams,*
*Memory's surgeon, the end of your schemes.*

"You're bluffing!" the child catcher cried. "I've studied your systems from top to bottom. There is no such weapon." The dragon's laughter gushed up afresh. "You have no such weapon. You have no such capability. If your riddle has an answer, then what is it?"

For a long, still instant, the dragon did not answer, savoring his triumph. Then the words came, so quietly they seemed to float in the air:

*An aneurism.*

Abruptly, Jane found herself back in her seat. She could breathe again. There was a normal stir and bustle in her ears; her classmates were back in their places. To the front of the room the child catcher looked puzzled. His gaze moved blindly back and forth over the back row, but did not connect with hers. He could no longer see her. The scrap of blanket fell unnoticed from his nerveless hand.

The dragon had won.

———◈———

When school let out, Jane was among the first out the door. She pushed outside and was free. The sky was wild and blue. A light breeze reached out and touched her gently, welcomingly.

The cherry trees were shedding their blossoms. A warm, gentle snow of petals swirled about her.

The other children were running and shouting, or slogging stolidly through the petal-storm, each according to their nature. The flower girls were in their element, moving graceful as ships under sail, while lesser sprites ran jeering circles about them and were ignored. Jane walked wonderingly through the cries and flurries of white, stunned by the perfect beauty of existence.

She was overwhelmed by a mingled sense of liberation, joy, and possibility. She was free and anything could happen. All she had been through, the years of forced labor in the steam dragon works, the petty persecutions of her teachers and classmates, the boredom and loneliness, the fact that she was still indebted to a dragon whose interests, today notwithstanding, were not hers—life was worth it.

This one moment paid for all.

# — EIGHT —

Over the summer the small civilization out back of the dragon grew and flourished. A behemoth laden down with coal got lost after taking an unscheduled detour, unwisely tried to make up time by cutting across the landfill, and ended up overturning. Only half its load was recovered. The other half enabled the meryons to industrialize. They had factories now, and the gaslights lining their streets like constellations of fireflies brought down to earth had been replaced by electrical lighting. At night their streets and boulevards were bright lines in a pattern as complex with hidden logic as an occult circuit diagram. By day a permanent gray haze clung to their territories. Their warriors carried rifles.

Summer classes were sparsely attended; students with full-time day jobs were excused for the season. Those who stayed knew that nothing they might learn mattered, since it would all be taught over again in the fall when their classmates returned. The days were drowsy and slow.

Jane welcomed the opportunity to catch up once and for all. She would have liked to get some more hands-on experience in the alchemy lab, but when she applied for extra time, the school secretary turned her down flat. So she worked on her math skills instead.

One afternoon Ratsnickle stopped her by the front door as she was leaving for the day. A granite wheel, higher than the tallest student, was set against the wall there to remind them of their duties, of the need to obey, of futility, and of their future. Leaning against it, he said, "I hear you're stealing things for Gwen these days."

"Yeah, so?" Jane had grown cautious of Ratsnickle. He'd been acting strange of late, wild and kind of crazy-aggressive.

"So what's the story? You going lezzie on us, or what?"

She hit him then, right in the chest, as hard as she could. "You bastard!" she cried. "You evil-minded, foulmouthed, repulsive . . . creature!"

Ratsnickle only laughed. "Touched a nerve, eh, Maggie?"

"Oh, shut up!"

"Listen, if you two ever decide you want to include a male in your little trysts—"

Blindly Jane stormed away and walked full tilt into Peter, who was coming up the steps.

"Whoa, careful there!" He steadied her, holding her at arm's length by the shoulders. "Hey, you look upset. What's wrong?"

"It's just—" She looked over her shoulder. Ratsnickle, typically enough, had disappeared. "I just—" She gathered herself together. "Where are you off to?"

"Shop. There's a destrier there I work on for extra credit sometimes."

Jane had homework to do, things to steal, a thousand housekeeping chores waiting for her. The school operated off of a central air-conditioning system, which meant that outlying areas like the shop never got much ventilation. This time of day, it must be like an oven in there. "Can I join you?"

"I guess."

Wordlessly they traced a crooked path through the empty halls. Peter didn't want to talk about Gwen when she wasn't around. Jane could respect that. So usually they talked about machines instead. "Who are you working on?" she asked at last.

"Ragwort. You know him?"

Jane shook her head. "What's he like?"

"Foul-mouthed, loud, kinda stupid." Peter shrugged. "Nice guy, though."

———◈———

The school shop was organized more eclectically than those Jane had grown up among. The absolute numbers of tools might be no more than those of a working shop, but the school had a far greater variety. Lathes, planes, and bench saws coexisted with soldering irons, electric grinders, sheet-metal equipment, even a welding bay. Everything had been fitted together with patchwork economy. Yellow lines on a scrupulously clean concrete floor separated the work areas from each other.

There were two work bays. One was empty. In the other, suspended from ratcheted hooks-and-chains was a pitted tin steed. Camouflaged chest panels had been removed to expose its innards. Two black spark plug cables dangled limply down the side. "Yo, old paint!" Peter said. "How's it hanging?"

Ragwort ponderously swung up his head and favored him with an enormous toothy smile. "Hung like a horse," he said happily. Peter had a wonderful way with machines. They responded to him with trust and sometimes even love. Ragwort had clearly been won over long ago.

"Glad to hear it." Peter stuck his head into the open barrel. "Jane, could you hand me a flashlight? And that ampmeter there on the workbench." She gave them to him, and he poked about, muttering. "Anybody locate that short in your electrical system yet?"

"Fuck no. You know what jerk-offs these shithead shop majors are."

"Hey, there's a lady in the room!"

"Aw, she ain't no prude." Ragwort tried to move his head to the side but, held in traction as he was, could not. One eye swiveled toward her on its gimbals. The other stared ahead sightlessly. "Are you, girlie?"

Jane had leaned back against the workbench and was fanning herself with her hat. Startled, she said, "No, fine! Really, it's okay."

"Yeah, well, *I* don't like it," Peter said. "Horns of Cernunos! Lookit what they did to your carburetor. Old paint, it's a flat-out miracle that you're still alive, you know that?"

"It's my engine block," Ragwort agreed melancholily. "The fucker's fucked. What the fuck—fuck it, that's what I say. Just fuck it."

Jane giggled.

"What did I say about that kind of language?" Peter emerged from the interior shaking his head. "Well, I give up. I've spent three days going over your wiring and I can't find that short anywhere. The only thing I can think to do is rip it all out and start over again."

"It won't hurt him, will it?" Jane asked anxiously.

"See, I told you girlie here was okay," Ragwort said. "Not like that prissy-ass little bitch you—"

Peter slammed a wrench against Ragwort's hood. "You talk like that and it *will* hurt. I'll make sure of it."

"I'll be good, boss." Ragwort winked at Jane. "Don't get a burr up your ass."

Peter got out a reel of wire, an adjustable wrench, and a pair of wire cutters. He winched Ragwort two handspans higher into the air. Several of the bolts holding on the belly panels had rusted. He gave them each a shot of graphite and hammered on their sides to loosen them up. Jane helped hold the panels while he worked out the last bolts; otherwise they would have warped.

"Who designed this mess?" Peter grumbled. "This wire loops right behind your exhaust system. I'm going to have to yank the muffler just to get at it." He was silent for a time, then said, "Ragwort, your exhaust system is in horrible shape."

"When I fart, birds fall from the sky."

"Terrific." Peter concentrated on his work for a while. When he spoke next, it was to Jane: "Hey, tell me something. How come all of a sudden everybody's calling you Maggie?"

"Ratsn—the guys gave me that nickname. It's short for Magpie."

A corroded length of pipe clattered to the floor. "I thought you were a wood-may."

"It's just a nickname. Because—you know—magpies are such good thieves."

"Oh yeah." Peter didn't approve of her stealing things. He thought that sooner or later she was sure to be caught. But having said so once, he wouldn't mention it again. Peter was good that way. "Well, I'll just stick with Jane, if that's okay with you."

Five minutes later, the muffler came down. Peter whistled, and motioned to Jane. "Come take a look." He poked at a bit of black wire. "See how gummy the insulation feels here?"

"Yeah?"

"We've got our culprit. Some idiot was replacing this section of wire and didn't want to bother welding another hanger to the underbody, see? So he just threaded the wire between the exhaust pipe and the bottom of the cabin and chocked it in with this." He tossed a scrap of wood in his hand. "So next time the engine's running hot, the pipe melts the insulation and the whole system shorts out. That's the straightforward part. But then, when the engine cools down again the insulation flows back over the wire and resolidifies, so the short doesn't exist anymore. That's why I couldn't locate it with the ampmeter. Pretty sneaky, huh?"

"Wow." Jane was seriously impressed. For all the time she'd spent around and inside machines, this was the first time it had ever occurred to her that working on them might be fun. That rebuilding a motor could be as intellectually engaging as the challenge of setting up and running an experiment in alchemy. "Peter, this is really something. It's flat-out wonderful."

"It only took him three days to locate too," Ragwort said. "What a fucking genius."

"Niceums horsey," Peter said. "How'd you like a sugar cube in your gas tank?"

"Aw, go piss up a rope."

———※———

It was a scorcher outside, but the mall was kept so cool that Jane was sorry she hadn't brought a sweater. The place was jammed with fugitives from the heat. They were recreational rather than serious shoppers, most of them. Their hands were empty and their eyes were clear.

Hebog, Salome, and Jane sat on a bench by the holy well watching the world flow by. "I saw Gwen the other day, at that supermarket opening," Salome remarked.

They were waiting for a hudkin who was in the market for a pair of white kid gloves. Jane had wrapped them in a plastic Tir na-n'Og Video bag and stashed it in a nearby trash receptacle. If the deal went through, they'd have enough for burgers and fries all around. If not, at least they wouldn't be stuck with the gloves.

"Yeah, she told me she had to do some ribbon-cutting," Jane said. "So?"

"So you should've seen this elf she was with. Tall, dark glasses, silk suit, manicured nails—the whole nine yards." Salome shook her hand, as if to cool off her fingertips. "Hot stuff. In strictest confidence, *mes cheris*, I would not mind having a piece of him myself."

"What are you saying? Gwen wouldn't be going out with some elf. She's Peter's girl."

"Bullshit," Hebog said. "I saw them after the ceremony when they didn't think anybody was looking, and he put his hand on her ass. She liked it too."

"They left together," Salome added.

"I'm sure you're—"

"Boogie at four o'clock," Hebog growled quietly. "And closing fast."

Jane twisted in her seat and saw Grunt, smiling broadly, bearing down on them. "Shit!" she hissed between her teeth.

"It's my darling, darling students! What an unexpected—nay, a delightful—surprise. Do you mind if I join you?"

They scooched apart and, turning, Grunt placed his fat bottom between Salome and Jane. He spread his arms to either side and hugged their shoulders, pulling them against him. Hebog sat at the end of the bench, scowling darkly.

"Now this is indeed a fortuitous encounter," Grunt said. "Yes, fortuitous indeed. You know, some children think of their teachers as purely locational phenomena. Educational apparati that disappear when the school day is done. Perhaps you believe that we retire to a line of freezers in the basement, eh? To awaken fresh and unspoiled in the morning." He laughed lightly. "Would that it were so easy. As your demiurge—and I assure you that insofar as you are concerned, I am nothing less—I am responsible not only for your mental growth but your spiritual and moral development as well. Your place and position in the larger world. My job does not end when you step out the door. Oh, no, no, no."

Jane tried to focus on what he was saying. But his armpits stank and his dust-frosted wire rims gleamed in rather a sinister manner whenever he turned her way. He was hard to follow.

"My every waking moment is spent focused on my students—yes, it is. I am constantly worrying about you. Let me give an example. Suppose that one of my children is not what she appears to be. Let us say that she is putting on a false front. Perhaps all her life is a sham and a deception. She is a fugitive from her rightful state, a horrid, nasty creature who does not belong in my nice class, where her mere presence threatens to corrupt her innocent, unsuspecting classmates."

He was staring straight at Jane. Something moved behind the milky disks of glass and in a flash of horror she realized that whatever it was that crawled about there, it was not his eyes. "When such a thing happens, it is my job to rip off the mask of lies. To strip away the robes, bras, and girdles of deceit. To leave truth standing naked! trembling! exposed! and helpless in the sight of all."

A thin, sour beeping arose from his wrist. Grunt looked down at his watch and touched a pip on its side. "Well. This has been pleasant, but I fear it's time I were on my way. Have fun, and remember: I have my eye on you." Through all his speech, his benevolent smile had never wavered.

For a long moment nobody spoke. Then Salome broke into tears. "He doesn't know a thing," she said frantically. "He doesn't know a thing. Even if he does, what the hell business is it of his, I'd like to know?"

"He's bluffing," Jane agreed. "I'm sure he's bluffing."

"Well," Hebog said, "looks like the hudkin's not gonna show." He sighed and dug into his pocket. "I've still got a little left from the white crosses I moved last week. My treat?"

"You're on," Jane said.

She had no idea what Salome and Hebog thought was going on, and unless she wanted them to know all about her past and origins, she was in no position to ask. But coming so soon upon the child catcher's visit, Grunt's speech could have only one possible meaning. She wondered could the dragon protect her from two searches? Six? Surely not a dozen. Half his batteries were shot—Jane had yanked the worst of them and tossed them out back for the meryons to scavenge—and his alternator was ready to go. There were limits to his power.

She couldn't focus on her own problems, though. Her mind jumped restlessly about, jerking wildly away from but always returning to the intolerable fact that Gwen was cheating on Peter.

━━━◦◉◦━━━

Not everybody was invited to Gwen's midsummer barbecue at the Little Tavern on the Green. It only seemed that way. Students mingled with townies, teachers with local celebrities, technical staff and overdressed administrators from the television station with elves in casual togs that cost as much as a gwarchell might earn in a month. They mingled and separated, like so many beads of oil of different viscosities, always regrouping down the lawn with their own kinds. Jane felt like a mouse in a maze. Timidly she moved between shifting groups of strangers, in search of someone she knew.

Trotter and Stinch came staggering in a four-legged walk across the greensward, arms about each other, shoulder pushing against shoulder. "Ratsnickle's looking for you," Stinch leered. Trotter smiled blissfully and said nothing.

"Oh, please!" Jane made a face. "Tell him you didn't see me. Tell him I'm not here. I'm not up to coping with him just now."

"I thought you two were friends. He told us you were close as close. Pals. Chumsy-wumsies." Trotter reached up to grab at the nub of Stinch's left horn and Stinch slapped the hand away. Their faces were gummy where they touched, as if they were melting together. "Said he made you—taught you everything you know, gave you a new name, molded you out of raw clay."

Trotter reached around Stinch's neck and into a bulging shirt pocket. "Wanna see something really neat?"

Coolly, Jane said, "I've seen that trick already. Stuffing a live frog in your mouth does *not* impress me."

"Speaking of Ratsnickle—" Stinch began.

"—here he comes now," Trotter finished for him.

Without looking, because if they weren't lying and she met Ratsnickle's eyes she would be caught, Jane scuttled around a nearby clump of partiers. Using them for cover, she fled.

Seconds later she ran across Hebog. He was one of a knot of uncomfortably overdressed dwarves that looked up angrily and dissolved on her approach. His face was flushed, his expression distraught. "Hello?" she said. "What's wrong?"

Hebog ignored the question. "You seen Salome?" he asked and not waiting for an answer: "Doesn't matter. She's not going to want to talk with me anyway. Not after what I did to her."

"What did you do?"

He clenched his fist. "Doesn't matter."

"Okay."

"I said it doesn't matter!"

"Okay, okay! I said okay, all right?"

"Yeah, well. If you see her tell her I was looking for her." He turned and stumped away.

Jane was still staring after him when a hand touched her elbow. She whirled. It was the pale man. A cigarette dangled from his mouth. He held an outsized cup of beer in one hand.

The pale man looked alarmingly out of place in short pants. His knees were knobby and fish belly white; the sunlight seemed loath to touch them. "I put in your application for scholarship aid through the school secretary," he said. "It won't do any good."

"What?" she said blankly.

He took her arm and strolled her toward the shaded side of the tavern. White-dressed waiters shot through its doors, trays in hand, trailing steam. "How much Grammar do you have?" he asked.

Jane shook her head. She had no idea what he was talking about.

"It's the queen of sciences," he said testily, speaking around his cigarette. "You really ought to—well, never mind. Let me put

it this way: There is a logic to the shapes of lives and relationships, and that logic is embedded in the stuff of existence. The
lover does not awake one morning convinced he would rather be
an engineer. The musician does not abandon her keyboard without
regrets. The CEO does not surrender wealth. Or if he does, he will
find it easier to give up everything, find a cave in the mountains
and become a philosopher than to simply downscale his life-style.
You see? We are all of us living stories that on some deep level
give us satisfaction. If we are unhappy with our stories, that is not
enough to free us from them. We must find other stories that flow
naturally from those we have been living."

"So you're saying . . . that I'm living a story in which I don't
get financial aid? Is that it?"

He shook his head. "It's not you. The secretary is living a story
in which she doesn't give you financial aid. It's a subtle distinction, but a crucial one. It gives you an out."

"What do I have to do?"

"You have to look at yourself through her eyes. She sees a
troublemaker, a dilatory student, someone with 'potential'—
whatever that might be—who is lazy, who will never apply herself, who neglects her studies, and on whom a scholarship would
be wasted."

"But I'm not like that!"

"What does that matter? In her story that's who you are, and in
her story your sort rarely changes. Occasionally, though, it happens. Your low qualities are channeled for low purposes. Strawwe
used to be just like you before he snitched on his friends."

"What? I wouldn't!"

The pale man had smoked his cigarette down to the filter. He
lit a new one from the coal, and ate the butt. "You'll have to weigh
the alternatives. On the one hand it's an unpleasant story to live.
Your former friends will despise you and they may even beat you.
You won't respect yourself. On the other hand, people you like
don't get scholarships. You can keep your own story or you can get
a doctorate in alchemy. But you can't do both.

"Think about it."

His speech done, the pale man looked away. Somebody
drifted between Jane and him. She took a step back. The masses
of partiers shifted, and without having moved he was gone. Jane
started after him, was shunted to one side by a waiter, and
ducked between two trolls. She found herself by the tavern's
front door. Not far away Grunt and Strawwe the proctor were

deep in conversation. Strawwe looked up and nudged Grunt. They both stared directly at her.

For an instant she stood frozen in their gaze. Then a strolling pair of Tylwyth Teg broke the circuit of vision, and she retreated into the tavern.

The foyer was high-roofed with wooden beams. Two folding tables had been covered with white paper and set up with shallow plastic glasses and bottles of wine set in tubs of ice. The steward was absent from his post. Nobody was looking. Jane poured herself a glass of red.

Then she noticed that somebody had left the door to the cloakroom open. She put down the glass and slipped inside. It was too hot for jackets, but a short line of purses sat dowdily on a shelf above the empty coatrack. She went through them almost reflexively— some coins, purple eye shadow, a Descartier watch—and stepped back into the foyer before the wine steward could return.

She picked up the glass and raised it toward her lips.

"No, dear." Gwen appeared at her side and firmly took the wineglass from her hand. Jane, flustered, began to apologize. But before she could manage a coherent word, Gwen said, "It's white wine with fish." She put the glass aside and poured a new one. Dipping the tip of her little finger, she flicked a drop onto the floor for the Goddess. "This is a white Caecuban. I think you'll like it. It's a little on the sweet side, and very crisp. Take a sip."

Jane took a miserly mouthful. She'd never had wine before. It tasted awful. She nodded. "Very nice."

"Isn't it? Come on, help me with the salmon. I'll show you how."

The grills stood at the center of the green. The tavern's barbecue chef stood aside for Gwen, and she accepted a pair of tongs from him.

After a quick look at the fish, Gwen laid down the tongs on the worktable and rolled up her sleeves. She cut a lime in half and squeezed its juice into a tub of softened butter. "Take this," she handed another to Jane, "and use the fine mesh of that grater to get the zest into the butter."

Clumsily Jane complied. Tiny flecks of green flew scattering into the tub. "Perfect!" Gwen took up a spoon and vigorously stirred them in. "These two on the end are almost finished." She took plates from a nearby stack, slid the salmon smoothly on, handed them to Jane. "Take a good gob of butter and dab it right on the center of each fish. Doesn't that look lovely?"

"Yes."

Gwen seized a brush and began basting the line of salmon with the lime butter they'd just made. Her enjoyment of this simple act was manifest. It was so like her to do this, as everything, with enthusiasm and pleasure. Jane felt dull and lumpish beside her.

"Gwen, dear." An expensive-looking elf with the pink-fleshed face of a purebred going to age, came up behind her and bent to kiss the side of her neck. Gwen raised her chin with pleasure. Jane felt her face freeze. "What a lovely dress."

"Do you like it?" The dress was long and white and flowing, with a green sash about the waist that set off her hair perfectly. Gwen lifted her skirt slightly to either side and twirled about to show it off. "My little sister gave me it. Have you met Jane?"

The elf took her hand, bowed low over it, and brushed her knuckles with his lips. It was such a courtly gesture that Jane had no idea what he was doing until it was done. "Enchanted."

"Yeah," Jane said. "Me too."

"Falcone is a theater designer," Gwen explained. "He did the bonfire at the edge of the green."

"The thing that looks like a wooden wedding cake, you mean?"

Falcone smiled in a way that indicated the bonfire was a trifle. "You have exquisite taste in dresses," he said. "Did you make it yourself?"

"Naw. I stole it from Eulenspiegel's down to the mall."

"You'll excuse us," Gwen said. She seized Jane's hand and hustled her away so fast Jane almost dislocated her arm. The barbecue chef, who had been waiting politely nearby, stood back to the grill.

Gwen took Jane aside to a bench in the shadow of the tavern and sat her down. Her eyes flashed. "All right. What is it?" She waited and then in a gentler voice said, "You can tell me. Whatever it is." Jane shook her head and Gwen took both her hands in her own. "Nothing's that bad. Give."

"It's you and . . . Peter."

"Ah."

"I don't understand how you can—" She was beginning to cry now. "—with other guys. I thought that you and Peter—" The tears overcame her then, and it was a while before she could manage, "I looked up to you guys! I thought you were perfect."

For a long time Gwen did not speak. When she finally did, her expression was somber. She was as serious as Jane had ever seen her. "Jane, you don't have the *right* to ask for an explanation. Do you see that? You haven't earned it. But because you're so dear to me, and because I love you, I'll give you one anyway. But I'm only going to tell you the once. Understand?"

Sniffling, she nodded.

"I cut a deal. I'm going to die on Samhain. In exchange for that I get to live as full and complete a life as anyone in the year before. I'm living that life right now. A big part of it is my relationship with you, my friends, my classmates, everyone who's gathered here. But love, physical love, is a major part of life too.

"Jane, I know you'll find this hard to accept, but you'll almost certainly have more than one lover in your life. Most women do. And each one of your lovers will provide you with different emotional and physical satisfactions. Each will give you something, however small, that the others can't. Should my share be less than yours? I enjoy my lovers—I won't pretend otherwise—but even if I didn't, they're still part of the deal. If I don't bring a full life to the wicker cage, the sacrifice can't go through, and I won't be accepted. I don't want that. I keep my promises."

"But Peter—"

"Peter knows everything. He might not be completely happy with some of my choices, but he understands. Peter is the bedrock of my existence. There's nobody else who could take his place, and he knows that too." She stroked Jane's hair. "Do you understand now?"

"No," Jane said. "But I'll take your word for it."

Spontaneously, Gwen hugged her. "I feel so much closer to you after this little talk. Isn't that funny? I feel as though you really were my baby sister." Then she began to giggle.

"What's so funny?"

"You. You were so jealous of Falcone."

"I don't see anything terribly funny about that."

"Falcone doesn't like girls, silly."

Gwen's laughter was high and silvery, and after a second, Jane's joined hers.

———⊸◉⊷———

She found Peter perched on a log at the bottom of the bonfire. Beside him was the straw Gwen which he was to fling atop the heap later in the evening, after she herself had hurled the torch that would set the entire structure ablaze. A minor lord of television stood nearby, blocking shots for the camera troll.

"Hey, Jane. I'd've thought you'd be with Gwen."

"She's autographing publicity photos now. Then she's going to lead the morris dancing."

Atop a distant stage a group of duppies were playing ska. They leaped and pranced in time to the music, skinny black creatures with dreadlocks and red eyes. "Well, that's Gwen. Did she show you her feet? We went out to the Pavilion last night and she danced so hard they blistered. She wouldn't stop, I begged her, she just laughed. I couldn't keep up. My knees were buckling, I was dying. It was as if somebody had shot fifty thousand volts right up her spine. She kept on dancing until her slippers fell apart. That's all she lives for."

"Excuse me." The television lord approached Jane. "Allow me to introduce myself. I am Avistaro. And you are—?"

"Who, me? I'm nobody. I'm just a friend of Peter's." Avistaro waited politely. "Jane," she said at last. "Jane Alderberry."

"Ah." He consulted his clipboard. "You don't belong in this shot, you know, Jane. No, no, I'm not asking you to leave, not just yet. But you should be aware that this conversation may have to be cut short." He smiled insincerely.

"I was talking with Gwen," Jane said quietly when Avistaro had turned away. "She told me you knew all about her and those other guys."

"I guess I do."

"Oh, Peter. How awful for you."

"It's worse for Gwen. She's going to die and I only have to lose—well. I don't see where I'm in any position to criticize her, you know?"

"You're so understanding of her."

"She's everything to me," Peter said simply. A yearning, faraway ache entered his voice. "The way I look at it, she's like the sun and I'm like the moon. She's so full of life it blinds you to look at her. I'm nothing without her. Whatever I am, it's but a pale reflection of her glory."

"Oh, that's super!" the television lord said. "Do you mind if we use it?" He turned to Jane. "Now I *will* have to ask you to leave, I'm afraid. No hard feelings, I hope?" He turned away without waiting for a response.

Peter smiled sadly and shrugged.

Jane would've like to find her way back to the tavern. She'd finished her wine and wanted another glass. She still didn't think much of the flavor, but it was something she believed she could acquire a taste for. But the shifting currents of the festivities kept shunting her from her goal. In a burst of gracious laughter, a group of elves broke up before her, a curtain parting to reveal the school secretary.

The secretary had rhinestone-studded harlequin glasses, a body like a stick, and a white head of hair that made her look like a dandelion gone to seed. Near her shoulder blades sprouted two chitinous brown stumps, the sad remnants of what in her youth must have been wings. Strawwe stood behind her, whispering in her ear.

Jane edged away from the pair but could not stop looking at them. They met her gaze unblinkingly. Eyes locked, she and they drifted apart until the crowds drew in to hide them from each other.

A sudden terror seized Jane. She was surrounded by enemies, caught in a closing web of plots and forces whose nature and source were obscure to her. She was mad to remain. Trembling, she was about to break and run for it when the crowds shifted again and she was steadied by the abrupt and unexpected appearance of a friend.

Salome was alone in the middle of an open stretch of lawn, whirling around and around. She danced lightly, casually; it was possible she wasn't even aware that she was doing it. Jane went up and touched her on the shoulder.

"Hebog's looking for you."

"Is he?" Salome said. "Really? Is he really?" She looked so happy that Jane half expected her to rise from the ground and float away.

"Are you on something?"

"What? Oh, don't be ridiculous."

"Then what's with you?"

"I am simply in a good mood. I hope there's nothing wrong with being in a good mood."

"It's just so unlike you."

"My dear young innocent," Salome said grandly. "You know how dearly I'd love to hang around and chew the fat, but I have things to do, places to be. *Noblesse oblige*, you know. Where did you say Hebog was when you saw him?"

She pointed and Salome was madly off. Jane was lowering her arm when the wake created by the young fey widened to disclose three figures, heads together: Feather, who taught applied astrology, Grunt, and the child catcher.

As had the others, they stopped talking when they saw her, and raised their eyes to catch hers. The child catcher nodded urbanely and crooked a beckoning finger.

She ran.

———◦◉◦———

The wheel turned. Gates opened and shut. A clear pathway appeared before her, and at its end stood Ratsnickle.

Caught, she walked to his side. He took her arm and together they went out of the green altogether and into the shady copse waiting quietly at its edge. A dirt path led them in and down. Leafy branches brushed against them.

When they were hidden within the green shadows, Ratsnickle released her arm. They faced each other. He stuck his thumbs into his belt. "Well?"

"Well, what?"

"You're with Peter, aren't you?"

"What, you mean at the bonfire? I guess so."

Ratsnickle's face twisted. "That bastard! He used to be my friend. Some friend. I trusted him, and then he goes and steals away my girl from me."

Jane was shocked. "What are you talking about? I was *never* your girl."

"So," Ratsnickle said. "That's the way it is, huh?" He edged closer to Jane, and she backed away. He came closer and she backed away some more. For a wild instant she thought this would go on and on until they had walked backwards entirely through the woods. Then the bole of a tree slammed up against her back. Ratsnickle chuckled humorlessly. "Okay. Now we settle accounts."

"I'll go get help," somebody whispered in Jane's ear. But when she looked quickly over her shoulder, there was nobody there. The words had come out of nowhere, so soft that she doubted their existence the instant they were spoken. A hallucination.

"Don't twist your head away like that. Look at me when I'm

talking to you." Ratsnickle grabbed a handful of Jane's blouse and pulled it toward him. It was linen and, afraid it would tear, Jane grabbed the cloth to either side of his fist, and moved with his motions. He swung her to and fro, like a terrier playing with a rat. It only seemed to enrage him the more.

"You bitch! You slut!" A tear raced down over one flushed cheek, was deflected by one corner of his grin. His eyes had almost disappeared in his distorted face.

Suddenly Jane realized she should be shouting for someone to rescue her. "Help!" she cried, too weakly. She felt immensely foolish, an actor shouting lines in a bad play. Her delivery didn't carry the weight of conviction. "Somebody help me!"

Ratsnickle let go of her blouse and punched her in the face.

It hurt. Her head bounced against the tree behind her and her hat went sliding away into the weeds. Twigs tugged at her hair. Legs tangling, she fell.

He's going to rape me, she thought flatly. Melanchthon will have to save me now. He made me promise no sex. I'm worthless to him if this happens.

But she felt no telltale trace of the dragon's presence. His attention was elsewhere. She tried to summon him, concentrating on his secret name, on his op codes, on what she could remember in her hysteria of his wiring diagrams. Hoping the distance was not too great, she silently screamed for him to come to her.

Nothing.

Ratsnickle was tugging at her belt. She seized it in both hands so he couldn't unbuckle it and he punched her again. In the stomach this time. That made one hand let go, but she managed to keep a furious grip with the other. He was trying to pry the fingers back. Wet, gloating sobs rose from the back of his throat. She clawed at his face. It was nothing but the indignity of event after event, as endless and inevitable as a nightmare.

"*Stop that!*"

Jane stared up, stunned, into the face of someone she'd never imagined she would ever be glad to see.

It was Grunt.

He reached down an enormous hand and hauled her to her feet. She tugged at her chinos, pulling them up, rebuckling the buckle. When she looked up again Ratsnickle had fled, crashing through the woods.

"You filthy child!" Grunt's lips were white with emotion. His tiny eyebrows made a comic vee over the expressionless disks of his glasses. He swung Jane onto the path, and grabbed her by the nape of her blouse. The cloth pressed against her breasts, dug painfully into her armpits. "You dirty little monster."

"But I didn't do anything!" Her face was beginning to swell; she could feel it. It wasn't possible Grunt could think she was a willing participant in what had happened. Not when she hurt the way she did. "It was Ratsnickle who—"

"Shut up!"

He quick-marched her through the crowds and into the tavern. She had a quick glimpse of the wine steward snoring in a chair and then Grunt had flung open a door and thrust her into the cloakroom. He slammed the door behind him. "Is this the way you repay me all my pains? You evil creature! Seducing honest boys with your nasty ways." He was beside himself with indignation. "I thought we knew all about you. But this—this!"

Suddenly he stopped and bent nearer. His nostrils flared. "And your breath reeks of alcohol!"

The lecture lasted forever. It was hard to endure because not only could she not speak up in her own defense but also, much like Ratsnickle had, he lost his temper anew any time she looked away. She could not track what he was saying. She followed each word so closely it became as hard and real as an object—a hammer, a ceramic mug, a painted rock—and she could make no other sense out of it.

At last Grunt ran out of steam. "Go!" He flung open the cloakroom door, and called after her, "We're watching you, young lady. Don't think we're not. Oh, no. Don't think any such thing."

Jane stumbled away.

Outside, it was the blue hour between afternoon and evening. Paper lanterns had been strung up but not yet lit. Jane didn't cry. She had that much control, anyway.

Jane's mind was a knot of confusion, with Ratsnickle and the child catcher all tangled up with Grunt and the voice in the woods. Everyone was angry at her; it was as if the outrage she felt had been turned against her. Her face ached, and her thoughts were all jumpy, uneven, disconnected. She could not go home in such a state. Melanchthon would greet her anger with silence and a nasty amusement. He'd gotten what he wanted, after all, without having to stick up for her. She could taste his humor in the back of her mouth, making her feel as though she were the butt of a smutty joke.

Everybody she knew was still at the barbecue. She couldn't enjoy the mall with her face like this. That left only one safe haven.

━━━━•◦●◦•━━━━

"Holy shit, girlie! Looks like you been in some kind of fight."

"You should see the other guy," she muttered. But in too low a voice, too darkly. She didn't have the self-possession to pull it off. "I just wanted to putty in some of these dents." She faked a smile. "You must've been a handsome thing when you were new."

Ragwort's eye swiveled apprehensively. "Whoa, you don't just smear on that crap without no preparation. You gotta grind away the rust first."

"So all right," she snapped. "That's what I'll do." She donned goggles and dust mask, and plugged in the electric grinder.

"Tell ya what, Sis. Not that I don't trust you or nothing, but how about you set up a mirror over on the workbench so I can watch what you're doing? I can talk you through it."

Jane hesitated, then nodded. She set up the mirror.

"Okay, the first thing you wanna do is find a spot where the rust ain't so bad. Up near the front flank, say."

Half an hour later, the left front fender was looking pretty good. Not perfect, but a few coats of paint to smooth things out, and it'd be fine. Jane felt a little better, too. Work could do that. There was nothing like a little directed action to fill up the mind, steady the nerves, drive away thought.

"Yo, girlie," Ragwort said. "Now that you got all that free-floating anxiety out of your system, I don't suppose you'd mind telling me just what's bugging you?"

"Oh, Ragwort. It's all too complicated and you don't even know the people involved."

"Like who?"

"Oh, gosh, like Ratsnickle, Grunt, the—"

"Don't know Grunt! Him and me, we're asshole buddies. Why, last year he come in the shop when I was telling some a my old war stories and he tried to say I was never no combat model. The little prick said I'd never seen action. I showed him some action all right. Stepped on his foot and broke three bones. He ain't been back since."

Jane stifled a laugh. "Really?"

"All together now, class." Ragwort managed a rough but iden-tifiable imitation of Grunt's voice. "The four fucks: Fucked-up, Fucked-over, Fucked-out, and just plain Fucked."

Jane laughed until she choked, and couldn't stop, even then. It poured out of her endlessly, as if all the pain and fear within had been converted to a river of laughter. "No, please!" she gasped.

"That's better," he said. "Dry them tears, girlie. Fuck 'em if they can't take a joke."

# NINE

"I've been doing some figuring," Jane said. "Do you know how much work it's going to take to completely restore you?"

The dragon did not answer. He was watching the meryons, as usual. Lines of tiny soldiers were marching off to battle. Derringer-sized cannons and other instruments of war were hauled by machines no larger than mice. Their tanks were marvels of miniaturization. Wisps of smoke arose from the temples.

"Years!"

No response.

"Decades!"

No response.

"Centuries!"

Silence.

She opened the grimoire and quoted: "Seventy-nine years of specialized labor go into each Moloch-class dragon. This does not include the armaments or surveillance and communication equipment, which are fitted to the mainframe after completion." Her voice went up slightly. "If the labor involved in crafting pretooled parts bought from outside vendors were factored into account, the total would be closer to eighty-six years." She slammed shut the grimoire. "Eighty-six years! I remember once Peter spent three days reworking the wiring on a horse he was trying to fix, and we're talking about something that probably only took ten minutes to install in the first place."

A cool breeze tumbled a poplar leaf through the cabin window. The leaf was yellow and shaped like a spearhead. The wind dropped it in Jane's lap. It seemed an omen, of what she did not know.

"You lied to me." The dragon's gaze was fixed on the streams of captives winding their way up the outsides of the temples. Priests waited on the top, invisible daggers in their hands. The temples formed a semicircle, all facing the dragon; from a certain perspective they looked like stylized geometric representations of his face. There was a sick interdependence between Melanchthon and the meryons; he gave them materials they required for their industries, and they in turn fed his monstrous need for diversion. "You made me promise I'd fix you, but that's not possible and you know it. You knew it then. Why did you make me promise something you knew couldn't be done?"

No answer.

She bolted out the doorway, leaving the hatch ajar. At the bottom of the ladder she hesitated to make certain there were no meryons underfoot. What had once been elementary courtesy was now a necessity. Their weaponry had advanced to the point where they were capable of killing her now, should she crush any of their number. Over her shoulder, she shouted, "I'm going to the mall."

As it turned out, she went to Peter's instead, to see Gwen.

＝━◈━＝

Gwen was not in a good mood. The campaign for next year's wicker queen officially began that morning. Five candidates had declared, and she approved of none of them. "Look at these grubby bitches!" She waved a fistful of handbills in the air. "Sleekit's running—am I supposed to take *her* seriously? She can't even keep her fingernails clean." She laughed bitterly. "I'm going to be torched by someone with five days' stubble on her legs. It would be funny if it weren't so pathetic."

"Oh, she'll grow into the role, whoever they choose." Peter picked up a flyer. "This one looks pretty cute." He winked at Jane. "I could go for her."

"You'll pay for that comment, Master Hillside," Gwen said ominously. She thrust a paper at Jane. "Did you ever see such makeup? She must slather it on with a butter knife."

Jane stared down into a face a million times more beautiful than her own would ever be. "It looks like a mask."

"Exactly! Peter, what are we sitting around here for? I don't want to be here. Let's go someplace, all three of us together."

"The clubs won't be open for hours."

"Who said it had to be a club? There's more to life than just dancing. Let's go to my place, Jane's never seen it, have you, Jane? I think she ought to see it, at least once. Come on, let's go."

Informed by some technological precognition, the limo was waiting at the curb when they hit the street. A black dwarf held the door open for them, then ascended to a box over the front boot and took up the reins. The interior was all gray plush with charcoal fittings. There was a built-in bar, but Jane didn't dare open it. Gwen stared moodily out the window the entire way.

Jane had never been in Gwen's penthouse before. Peter didn't like spending time there; it was where she entertained her gentleman friends. Round-eyed, Jane stared at the white grand piano, the slim vases of cut flowers, the enormous round water bed.

"Well? Try it out." After a second's hesitation Jane bounced down on the bed. Ripples fled, rebounded, lifted her like a boat. Gwen twisted her fingers in a sigil of power, and hidden motors began to revolve the bed. Another mystic sign and the sound system came on.

It was the single most luxurious thing Jane had ever encountered. You could lie flat on the white satin sheets and watch your image turning slowly in the mirrored ceiling, like a new constellation wheeling in the sky. The speakers were built into the frame: When Bloodaxe ripped into "Mama's Last Wish" from their *No Exit* album, the bass went right through your guts and made your stomach ache.

"This is wonderful!" she shouted.

"Yes, isn't it?" Gwen extended a hand and pulled her up. "Let me show you around." She spun about the room, opening doors. "Sauna's here, weight room here. This is the bathroom."

"What's that?"

"A bidet."

Reddening, Jane said, "Oh."

There was a Jacuzzi set in a faux-rock grotto. Orchids drooped from artfully natural niches and spider plants hung their babies down almost into the water. Colored lights spun at its bottom. There were closets crammed with impossible hoards of silks and synthetics. Gwen's dressing table had so many perfume bottles that an oppressive miasma hung over it. She lifted a sprayer from the clutter and let an infinitesimal touch of scent grace the side of her long neck. "I know it's awful of me to say so, but I can't help it—Isn't it all lovely?"

"Yeah, great," Peter said. He'd been silent ever since arriving.

He parted the drapes, made an eyeslit in the blinds with his fingers, let it snap shut. "Heck of a view."

"Oh, don't be like that!" Gwen drew open a drawer and from beneath a mist of lace underthings retrieved a small silver snuff-box. "A little pixie dust will pick you right up." She picked up an unframed oval mirror. They all sat down on the edge of the bed.

The mirror was like a mountain pool in her hands. Her reflection was a beautiful wraith, drowning in its depths. She chopped three lines of fairy powder, produced a straw, and inhaled one in three even, ladylike snorts. "Ahhhhh."

Peter took mirror and straw from her and did up the second line. He handed them on to Jane, who looked down at her fearful face. She took the straw, held it as Gwen had, inhaled.

A scattering of fine powder hit the back of her throat. Her eyes opened wide, and the world became very clear. It was as if a fever she hadn't known she suffered from had abruptly broken and dis-solved. She bent to snort up the rest.

"Watch out!" Gwen's hand darted forward to raise Jane's hair back and away from the dust. "Do you have any idea how much this shit costs?"

"Everything you've got," Peter muttered sullenly.

"Thank you, Mr. Sunshine." Gwen scowled and then, impul-sively, reached out and hugged him. With a mischievous smile, she said, "Did I ever tell you how Peter and I met?"

"Oh, she doesn't want to hear that."

"Yes, I do! Please!"

"Well. When I was young"—Peter held up two fingers; two years ago, she meant—"I lived in an absolute hovel. In a trailer camp, if you can imagine that, by the edge of a marsh. The mos-quitoes there were dreadful, and there were white apes that lived in the trees and would swoop down and snatch you up if you went out too late at night. They'd bite off your fingers and toes and the ears off your head. I knew a girl who lost her nose." She shud-dered graciously.

"I was so unhappy there. I had absolutely nothing worth own-ing. And then one day . . ." She fell silent. Her chin rose, and she stared into the distant past.

Energy crawled around inside Jane. It trembled her right leg, and raced her heart. It took an effort of will not to bounce up and down on the bed. Gwen's face was lovely in profile, so pure and focused. Jane leaned forward, eager to hear. "What happened?"

"Huh? Well, I suppose nothing happened. If by 'happened'

you mean some event or remark that pushed me over the edge." She tapped out some more pixie dust onto the mirror, bent over it again to chop it fine with a gold-plated razor blade. "But it all became too much. It was all of a sameness, you see. No one day was different from any other. It was all gray, gray, gray.

"So I went out into the marshes."

They paused to snort up some more dust.

"There was a little trail at the back of the trailer camp you could follow in. At the edges, it's all junk refrigerators and concrete rubble. You go past that, and there are all these little pools where they've dumped chemical wastes. Some of them have a kind of brown plastic crust, and others will try to ooze after you if you linger. Some are a beautiful, beautiful turquoise blue, and if you peer into them long enough, vapors rise from the water and you die. But if you go beyond them, you come to a place that's almost pristine. There are pools there where the black apples grow. They go down forever, into the heart of the earth."

"Black apples?"

"Yes. It took me an hour to get that far in, and I was all scratched and sweaty by then. But I found one of the pools. It was very quiet there, and the surface of the water was smooth as glass.

"I looked around to make sure nobody was looking and took off my stuff. This horrible flowered blouse and a pair of jeans that didn't even fit right. It's a funny thing. They were so cheap that when I stood there unclothed to the sun and wind, I felt beautiful."

"You *were* beautiful," Peter said earnestly.

"Isn't he sweet? But you're getting ahead of the story. So I gathered myself together, took a deep breath, and dove in. It was the single bravest thing I ever did in my life." Gwen put the mirror on her knees, tipped the snuffbox and tapped its side. Nothing came out. "Shit! Is this all there is? Peter! You were supposed to score some more for me." She flung it and the mirror aside. "I'm sick of this place. Let's go!"

"Where?" Peter asked.

"What the fuck do I care where? The clubs will be opening soon. We'll think of someplace, just let's go."

The limo was waiting. They got within, started down the streets. Gwen hammered on the roof with the flat of her hand. "Faster!" The dwarf obeyed. A twist of her hand and Green Man came on, their *Whitsuntide* album. She stared out the window.

"What happened then?" Jane asked. "After you dove into the pool?"

With a start, Gwen turned, frowning, to her. Then her mood shifted again, and she smiled. "I went down, down, down. At first the water was brown, like tea. But it turned black, fast, and then I couldn't see. I lost track of which way I was swimming, but it must have been down because I didn't return to the surface. My lungs hurt, and my ears—you can't imagine! It was like having nails driven through them.

"Little tendrils touched me, gently, like the fingers of a thousand small lovers. Then more insistently. They grew thicker and clung to my face and by now I was drowning, and even though that was what I wanted, I couldn't help struggling. But that only entangled me all the more firmly. I kicked and tore at the roots until I was shrouded in them, and could not move. It was then that something bumped against my mouth.

"It was soft, like an overripe plum, and about the size of my fist. It was a black apple, I realized that at once, one that had inexplicably grown much closer to the light than is normal. I thought to myself how sweet it would be to die with the taste of one in my mouth." Gwen reached out to stroke Peter's jeans. He shifted in his seat, parting his legs a bit, and she absently kneaded the inside of his thigh.

"I bit deep, and it was not sweet, no. It was bitter, so bitter. And good."

Peter closed his eyes and murmured, "We're almost to the good part."

"The roots released me and I ascended, oh, filled with energy, and the waters became brighter, brighter, brighter. The surface of the pool was a circle of light and then it shattered."

"What's a black apple?" Jane asked. She was ignored.

"I was standing on the edge of the pool when she burst out. It was the most fantastic thing anybody has ever seen. One second, nothing, and then this beautiful, naked—" He groped for words. "It was as if the sun had risen at midnight."

"But what were you doing in the marsh?"

"I was gathering leeches. For my apothecary class. So Gwen was a particularly good stroke of luck because she had hundreds—"

"Peter!"

"—of these enormous green and gold suckers hanging on her body. They were everywhere! On her breasts and face and legs and everything. It took us forever to get them all off."

"You bastard! You promised you'd never breathe a word about that."

"No, I didn't."

"I told you not to, and that's the same thing." She pounded on his chest, and then began tickling him under the rib cage. He collapsed helpless with laughter against the window. "Brute! Creature!" The limo careened through the angry streets. Jane, from her side of the seat, felt happy and a little embarrassed.

Gwen stopped tickling Peter. When he'd gathered himself together, she began sucking his fingertips, one by one, her mouth making little moist noises. "Tell me what you'd like." She peered intently into his eyes. "Tell me what you'd like to do."

Hopelessly, Peter said, "You know what I'd like. Just you and me—alone, together, forever."

Gwen eased back in her seat. "Yes," she said languidly. "Wouldn't that be lovely?"

Maybe it was the pixie dust, though its elation was long gone and had left in its wake a flat vacant buzz. Maybe the drug had a delayed effect on one's judgment. At any rate, Jane said, "Look. The sacrifice has to be voluntary, right? So what happens if you just say no? They'd have to use last year's runner-up, and then you and Peter can just go on with your lives. You could back to normal."

Gwen's eyes snapped. "I don't want to return to my *old* life," she cried. "I want *this* life to go on forever."

"But—"

"Oh, what do you know?" She flung herself back on the seat. "You don't know anything. You're just an ignorant little wood-may."

Stung, Jane cried, "Hey, that's not nice!"

Peter made shushing gestures.

"Oh, now we're correcting other people's manners, are we? I do not need this sort of criticism! You could just wait a few months and say any damn thing you want about me without worrying about hurting my feelings, but no! You have to insult me to my face, while I'm still alive."

"I—"

Gwen started to cry.

Everything was turning out awful. "We're not far from the mall. Do you want me to get out here?"

"Maybe you'd *best*."

When the limo stopped, Peter got out with Jane and gave her an awkward hug. Lowering his voice he said, "She'll get over it. We'll go dancing in a little bit, and then we'll go to my place and . . . Well. Don't let her upset you. She'll be herself again come morning."

He smiled a sad, haunted smile.

———◆———

So she did go to the mall after all.

She found Hebog and Salome on a bench by the miniature golf course. It was a temporary attraction, all astroturf and cheesy plywood windmills, presided over by a bored ogre half-dozing into his cupped hands. Nobody was playing. Her two friends sat side by side, a sweater draped casually over their laps.

When Jane approached, Hebog's hand darted suddenly up to scratch his chin. Salome, coloring, began folding up the sweater. To her flat-out amazement Jane realized that they'd been secretly holding hands under its cover. "Hi, guys."

Salome favored her with an aloof nod.

"Hiya, Maggie," Hebog said.

"That's what Ratsnickle calls me. I prefer Jane."

"What's with you two?" Hebog asked curiously. "Aren't you going out together any more?"

With all the self-control she could muster, Jane said, "Ratsnickle and I never went out together—not in any way, shape, or form. We were once friends, but we are friends no longer. The Lady willing, we shall never again be friends of any sort in any possible or foreseeable future."

"Yeah, he said you were having a spat."

Before Jane could frame an adequate response, Salome said, "Hey, have you seen Trotter-and-Stinch lately? They've got like three-point-five eyes between them now. The middle one has got two irises, one brown and the other blue. Gross."

They traded gossip for a bit, and then Jane said, "I'm looking for something to get Gwen. She's really down in the dumps and I thought a present might help."

"You mean like a sweater?" Hebog said. Salome punched his ribs.

"No, something special. Like jewelry maybe. Gwen loves jewelry."

"Cold weather's coming in. A sweater would be more practical."

"Try the House of Oberon," Salome said. "If you're looking for something really nice." She glanced quickly at an empty wrist. "Oh, hey, lookit the time. We gotta go."

One couldn't just cruise into the House of Oberon dressed as Jane was dressed. First she had to steal herself a better blouse. She finally settled on peach-colored watered silk. The chinos would be okay if the shoes were right, but since she was wearing a ratty old pair of sneakers and it was next to impossible to steal shoes that fit really well, she chose to lift an expensive pair of jeans instead. She needed a handbag, too, good makeup, and a scarf that would look overpriced even considering the work that went into it. Cheap jewelry and a drop-dead pair of sunglasses completed the look. One glance at the rotting sneex and plastic baubles arrogantly accessorizing top of the line designer fashions and even the most perceptive merchant would think: Elf-brat.

What with one thing and another it took her three subjective days to assemble everything. She had to periodically to lie low to avoid attracting attention from security. She had to steal food. Goddess only knew how many trips to the public toilets it took to complete the transformation.

But it was worth it. When she entered the H of O, an orend almost broke a leg to get at her before one of the other salesclerks did. They discussed what Jane was after, and then she was ushered to the third most impressive jewelry case in the store. The orend unlocked the glass lid and swung it back so she could examine the contents more intimately.

Jane ran a bored forefinger down a line of brooches, and stopped.

At first glance the brooch seemed a silver moon at quarter phase, pocked and cratered on the bright crescent, metamorphosing into anodized circuitry in the dark. But on closer examination, the printed circuit revealed itself to be a complexly etched and scored maze at the heart of which a single tiny emerald, like a green tear, slid freely. Jane touched it with her one unbitten fingernail and watched it trace a difficult path through the winding blackness. "Gwen would love this," she breathed.

The salesclerk mentioned a price.

"Ah," Jane said regretfully. "No. Not this week. Mother would have a cow." As the orend started to close the case, Jane turned away and said, "What about that black coral number, the necklace? Is it any cheaper?"

As the clerk looked up to follow her pointing finger, Jane

reached behind her to the memorized position of the brooch and snatched it up. The descending lid brushed against her knuckles, a blow from a moth's wings, and then she was stuffing her catch into the back of her jeans.

"Oh, considerably cheaper."

"Then I don't think I'm interested." Jane let the orend guide her through two more cases and then politely, firmly, called it a day.

At the holy well, Jane pitched a copper penny for luck, and took a good long look around to make sure nobody was watching. Then she dug the trinket from her pants.

A hand closed about hers, crushing the brooch into her palm so hard that the pin pricked her flesh.

"Gotcha," Strawwe said.

"Ow!" Jane drew her hand free, and sucked on the puncture wound. "You asshole, I'm bleeding!"

"Won't work." He stared at her in that pop-eyed way of his. "We've known about your thieving ways for some time now. Grunt told you we'd be watching. We've been watching."

Jane said nothing.

"I didn't need to catch you to turn you in. All I *had* to do was say I'd seen you nick something. They would have believed me." He took her chin in his hand and forced her to meet his gaze. "Do you doubt me?"

She knocked his hand away. "So why are we talking?"

"I'm going to make you an offer, and I want you to understand that I'm serious."

"What kind of an offer?"

"You and I are two of a kind." Strawwe was silent for so long that Jane began to wonder if maybe what he'd said made some kind of sense and she was simply too stupid to get it. "I don't—" she began, and "We're both outlaw powers," he said. "We're not like the rest of them. There are things we can do that the rest of them never can. You know that, don't you?"

She shook her head in bafflement.

Strawwe's eyes were as round as marbles. They bulged from his face. A faint whiff of nutmeg rose from his armpits. "There's things better than theft," he said. "I'll teach you." He leaned close to her and inhaled deeply. "You know what I'm suggesting. I can smell that you do."

He wasn't lying. Jane could see that. "You want me to become a . . . to be like you."

"A snitch, yes. Here's the deal: I don't report you for stealing. You get that scholarship you want. I'll be your mentor. You'll do whatever I tell you." He met Jane's horrified look with equanimity. "It's easy. You'll turn in Salome and the dwarf, tell the secretary what they've been doing. I'll tell them that you've changed. Reformed your ways. They'll believe it. They believe anything I say."

"I could never do that to my friends!"

"If you don't, I will."

Again, Jane could see he wasn't lying. Hebog and Salome were going to suffer no matter what she did. If she cooperated, on the other hand, there was a chance to salvage something out of the wreckage.

"And to seal the deal, you'll tell me your true name, and I'll tell you mine."

"But that's—" Impossible, she was going to say.

"—permanent. Yes, I know." He stared at her, bug-eyed and unblinking. His arms hung straight down by his sides. "You can go to University, if you want. I'll follow you. Wherever you go, there I'll be, closer than the closest friend you ever had. We'll read the same books. We'll eat out of the same bowl. We'll share the same bed."

All in a flash Jane realized how lonely Strawwe must be, scorned and feared by his peers, tolerated but despised by the administration, so isolated from normal interaction that he no longer even knew how to talk to her, threatening where he should be persuasive, harsh when he ought to smile. Which meant that his offer was sincere.

"I won't!" she said wildly.

He looked her up and down. She was trembling. He sniffed at the top of her hair, at her knees, at—she jumped away from him—her crotch. "You're not sure what you're going to do," he said. "I'll give you until tomorrow morning. Make up your mind. I'll smell your decision on the way in." He held up the moon brooch—she had almost forgotten it existed—and added, "I'll keep this as a token."

He put the brooch in his mouth, turned, and departed.

———◦◉◦———

"Kill him," she said. "That'd be easy enough for you."

Melanchthon said nothing.

Outside, actinic lights limned the meryons' defense perimeters and machines moved in the shadows. The dragon stared blindly down at the ground, but underneath his willful refusal to speak, Jane felt currents of power eddying, swirling resonances of electromagnetic anger. She had his name. She could master him; having done it once she felt sure of that. But sooner or later she would have to leave the cabin, and then he would be free to turn the force of his rage on her. She was safe only so long as his need for her overbalanced his anger.

"Look. He wants to have sex with me. You made me promise no sex, remember? It alters the aura's charge, you said, I couldn't make repairs on your electronics, they'd go haywire. Remember? Hah?"

It was useless. Jane piled her schoolbooks back onto the pilot's couch, and changed into her nightgown. She unfolded the futon and put on the sheets and a light blanket, with a heavier wool coverlet folded down at the foot just in case. The nights had been getting cooler lately. It was the season.

She lay down to sleep.

Eyes closed, slumber would not come. Instead she chased the old puzzle of the dragon's silence around and around in circles. Perhaps he was ashamed at being mastered by one of human blood, and this was petty revenge—he would act on her behalf, but in no other way acknowledge her existence. Then again, dragons were subtle. Perhaps he was trying to goad her into some rash act. Perhaps a situation would come in which, fearing to trust him, she would instead act as he required her to, in some baroque plan of his own devising. Perhaps he was manipulating her every move, thought, emotion within some conspiratorial maze too vast for her to even see it.

Perhaps he had gone senile.

———— ◈ ————

The school was organized in concentric circles of terror centering on the Principal's office. The worst pedagogical monsters walked in fear of that room, with its door forever closed, and the agonized screams of its captive horror sounding at random intervals from within.

The secretary's office was located immediately beside the Principal's. She listened, eyes blazing, while proctor Strawwe made his report. Each word seemed to inflate Grunt another puff of indignation. Jane could barely stand, she was so afraid.

Strawwe finished.

"Well!" The secretary tucked a bony knee under her arm and stood on one leg. "In all the years I have been here, this is the most outrageous and brazen episode that has come to my ears. Can there be any doubt of her punishment?"

She looked to Grunt. He cleared his throat and looked away. She looked to Strawwe. He met her gaze. "Very well," she said at last. "Throw this wretched child to the basilisk!"

With eyes averted, Grunt and Strawwe dragged her out into the hall. They flung open the door to the dire office and thrust her inside. The door slammed shut behind her. She looked up and saw the Principal's creature preening itself atop a blotter befouled with green droppings.

The basilisk clutched at the corner of the desk with clawlike fingers. It was a featherless biped, pale as chicken flesh, with a long neck and undersized appendages that were less wings than stumps. The round alembic of its belly was taut as a drum, where the rest of its body had the disorganized looseness of butchered meat.

But it was the creature's face that inspired dread, eyeless, all but headless, tiny human ears framing enormous soft lips that glistened with mucous surfaces. It had no nose, so that its every breath was a liquid gasp of pain.

Seeing this horror, Jane involuntarily found herself imagining what it must be like to be trapped within such flesh. It would be a fate even more repulsive than the creature itself. She wanted to look away and could not.

It flapped its stubby, goosefleshed wings.

Suddenly it craned its pale neck forward and down, and stretched wide its rubbery lips, revealing even white teeth and a wet pink tongue. Jane flinched away from its blind scream.

Everything went blank. For a timeless, airless instant she stood nowhere, dimensionless, unthinking. In a state of perfect negation. Then she staggered as she found herself back in the Principal's office, staring horrified at the basilisk, mouth closing, lips wet with spittle.

She had not heard the least fraction of the basilisk's black scream, yet its effects echoed in her body. She wanted to run for the nearest toilet so she could vomit up bile and foulness. She felt unclean, filth encrusting her tongue and digestive passages all the way down to her anus.

Then for the first time Jane managed to drag her gaze away

from the basilisk, and up to the Principal. He sat unmoving behind the desk, dressed in waistcoat, rep tie, and jacket. His hands rested inert in his lap. His eyes studied her with a reptilian alertness that was totally without emotion.

It was the Baldwynn.

A little choking cry rose up in the back of Jane's throat. She had been found! Melanchthon had promised he would shield her from detection, from search, from the hounds of persecution. It was yet another lie. She experienced now such a despair and sense of betrayal as she had never felt before.

But the Baldwynn, though his eyes tracked her every movement, said nothing, and made no move to stop her when she edged toward the door.

Jane's hand was on the knob when her eye was caught by the folder in the Baldwynn's lap. It was a pale manila rectangle, held lightly in both hands, and something about it told her it was significant.

This is crazy, she thought. But, cringing a little, she forced herself back to the Baldwynn.

His eyes followed her hand down to his lap. There were age spots on the backs of his pale hands. Cautiously she took the folder between thumb and forefinger, and tugged. It came free of his hands. His eyes followed the folder up. She looked at the name on its label.

Peter of the Hillside.

In a frenzy she opened the folder. It held a single flimsy square of paper, and nothing more. The lettering on it was gray and blurred; she could not possibly read it here. Not in the state she was in. Jane folded it in quarters and slipped it inside her blouse.

The Baldwynn did not move, even when she put the folder back in his spotted hands.

The halls were empty. Slowly, she stepped into them. A teacher starting out his doorway saw her emerge and ducked back in again. He clearly did not want to know.

Feeling dizzy and unreal, she floated down the hall.

As she passed the secretary's office, Grunt and Strawwe seized her by the arms and hauled her backwards into the room. "What did he say to you?" the secretary demanded. "What did he say?"

Jane had been holding herself tightly under control. Now she broke down, crying uncontrollably, from fear and disgust intermingled. "She's hysterical," the secretary said. She cocked her arm back and slapped Jane so hard her face rang. Spittle flying, she screamed, *"What did he say?"*

Some cold calculating aspect of Jane, lurking unsuspected deep within her, saw the chance then and took over. They none of them had a clue. They were so fearful of the Principal that they dared not confront him in person. They had no more idea what he really wanted than Dame Moon herself. "He said I should be an alchemist!" she sobbed. "He said you should get me a full scholarship."

The three traded looks of perfect bafflement. They could not believe what they heard, no more than they could imagine someone being able to lie after an encounter with the basilisk. It was an incredible statement, and at the same time undeniable.

But in the end there was nothing they could do about it.

The secretary began typing up the forms.

# ─── TEN ───

The dragonfly girls stood in a knot by the side door, smoking. Because their bodies remained neotonous well into sexual maturity, they looked like perverse children. Jane saw them every day, gossiping together, their wings buzzing with excitement, sharp-hipped and all but breastless in their designer jeans and sheer silk blouses, flicking lipstick-stained cigarette butts into the yard.

She picked out one who looked marginally less aloof than the others, and waited for her to separate herself from the group. "Excuse me," Jane said.

The dragonfly girl walked right by her, then stopped and glanced scornfully over a shoulder. "It's the thief," she said to nobody.

"Look." Jane dipped into her handbag and pulled out a silver amulet. It was a delicate thing, a hammered flower-of-life, and worth a pretty bit of change. She had cut classes this morning to lift it, and if she'd been caught, there would have been bad trouble. It was a chance she'd had to take, though, because the masses of cold iron in the dragon meant she could never take jewelry home; inevitably it always sickened and died. The silver sang in the sunlight, and the dragonfly girl's eyes widened at the sight of it. "It's for you."

"Gra'mercy." She extended an anorexically thin arm.

Jane jerked the amulet back. "There's a price."

Those dark eyes went lightless and cruel, lips parting slightly to reveal small, pearly fangs. Jane bulled ahead anyway. "Where can I get good information on birth control?"

Blank astonishment. Then: "Birth control? *You?*" The dragon-fly girl threw her head back in savage elven laughter.

"Do you want it or not?"

"Hand it over."

The instant the amulet hit the dragonfly girl's palm it disappeared. She spun and strode away. But in the air behind her floated the words, "Peg o' the Landfill. She'll want silver."

———◉———

It took Jane weeks to build up her courage. But on a cold and rainy morning early in the Matron's Moon, she stood shivering in a too-thin windbreaker before Peg's place. It was a rundown red-brick row house, one of those that backed onto the landfill. A corroded tin plaque with a double-headed ax on it was all that indicated a witch dwelt within. A crack ran crazily up the front wall, skewing the bricks to either side off true, and plastic sheets had been stapled over the insides of all the windows. The shades were drawn.

Jane stared at the doorway, unable to approach. Save for that desperate night when they had escaped the dragon works, she had never defied Melanchthon, not really, not on anything important. Certainly nothing like this! Coming here was an implicit breach of faith, for virginity was a *sine qua non* of hands-on engineering magick. She didn't know the technological reasons for this; but she knew that all the big corporations neutered their engineers before trusting them with any important work.

She took from her pocket the scrap of paper she had stolen from the Baldwynn. It was folded tightly in four, the edges frayed and gray from repeated handling. She opened it, read it through. It still said what it said.

Take a deep breath, she told herself. Walk up the steps. Go to the door. Knock.

She did.

A long silence, a creak, and then more silence. The door opened. "Yeah? Waddayou want?"

Peg was a fat old crone, heavily made up, with a cigarette jutting from her mouth. She wore a terry cloth robe and a worn brown pair of flip-flops. There were circles under her eyes and a mug of coffee in her hand.

"I can come back later, if you'd like," Jane babbled. "I didn't mean to wake you up or anything."

One penciled eyebrow lifted. Red lips twisted scornfully. "In or out, just don't stand in the doorway. I'm freezing my ass off out here." Peg held the door open and Jane squeezed by her, brushing against that soft belly, those enormous breasts. A stale odor, compounded of nicotine and incense, rose from her robe.

A television was flickering in the fireplace, news footage of refugees fleeing the violence in Carcassonne. Peg snapped her fingers irritably and it died. The sitting room was small and stuffy and impossibly cluttered with escritoires, end tables and chairs, a dwarven anvil, etchings of flayed horses, an ebony apothecary's cabinet, a homunculus preserved in brine. In effect it was like a collage of images torn from different magazines; the eye could assemble it into no coherent whole.

"Sit," Peg said. "I'll get some clothes on." She pushed through a curtained doorway, setting the rings to rattling.

Jane rested her hands on her knees and waited. An electric heater in the center of the room buzzed and clattered. It made her hot on one side and cold on the other. The homunculus stared at her with those dead, astonished eyes, as if to say, What an ugly creature you are.

She looked away. In a bell jar on the mantelpiece was an ormolu clock. She could see the agonized second-by-second twitch of its hand, but because all the air had been pumped out, the mechanism made no sound. It wasn't long before she found herself staring again at the pickled imp atop the ebony cabinet. I hate you, its frozen expression said, because you can move and I cannot, because you have a freedom I can never hope for and yet you do nothing with it.

Jane shifted in her chair.

Against one wall was a set of glass shelves lit by hidden bulbs so that they shone with a cold and unfriendly brightness. Arrayed on them in even rows were eggs, an insane variety of them, all of a size and carved from gem malachite and snowflake obsidian, green onyx and pink onyx, golden rutilated quartz and blue argonite fire opal, or else crystal glass with miniature scenes within, cities and mountainscapes, children at play, manlike fleas with baskets full of eggs and within those eggs smaller fleas carrying baskets of yet smaller eggs.

Jane couldn't imagine why the sight of the eggs should fill her with distress, but it did. She felt nauseous just looking at them. Twisting back around she found herself once again facing the homunculus's petulant mouth, its goggly eyes.

You're stupid, too.

Jane blinked. "Hello?" she said tentatively.

Well, it's about time. You're something of a dim bulb, aren't you? Developmentally challenged. Not exactly the first horse out the gate.

This was too rude to be fugitive thoughts. Wonderingly, Jane approached the bottle, touched its side. The little man within was white and bloated, a puffball about to explode into spores. "Are you alive?"

Are you?

Jane retreated from the bottle. She knew she should say something, but for the life of her could not imagine what.

Ask me what I want, the manikin suggested. That's always good for a laugh.

"What do you want?"

I want to die. I want the witch stuffed into this bottle alive so she can suffer as I have. I want to know what that is standing behind you.

Jane whirled. Nothing. When she turned back to the homunculus it wryly observed, Well of course it's not going to be there when you *look*. It's that sort of creature. Look there on the anvil. Do you see that maul? Of course you do.

A twenty-pound hammer lay atop the anvil, not an arm's length from the homunculus and situated where it was constantly in his sight.

"Yes."

Go to it. Touch the hammer, that's all I ask. Doesn't it feel fine? So strong and heavy.

From a window a weak bar of silvery light slanted down to stab the corner of Jane's eye. It dazzled her and when she moved away tiny suns danced in her vision. The heater's buzz was a constant. She felt weak, dizzy, unreal. "I . . . guess so."

Run your hand along the shaft. So smooth. Lift it a little. Feel the heft of it. Feel how your muscles shift and move. Such a fine sensation, a luxury really, you'd have to be paralyzed like me to fully appreciate it. Lift it a little higher. Swing it back and forth. Feel the force of momentum, the way you have to strain to handle it.

"You're right." Jane had never consciously paid much attention to the workings of her body before; it was an interesting sensation. The room seemed to fade away, drawn into the loudening hum of the electric heater. "It's kind of fun."

Now raise the hammer up over your head. Feel how your arms tremble from the weight. The head is yearning for the ground. It wants to overbalance you and soar curving downward. Can you feel it?

"Yes."

Then swing it down—now! Smash the bottle!

For a giddy instant Jane started to obey. "No!" She yanked the hammer to the side and it fell clangorously onto the anvil. She retreated to her chair. "Why did you do that?"

Oh, don't stop when we've come so close. Release me. Grant me oblivion. You can tell the witch I told you to.

She didn't move from the chair. "Yeah, oh fine, and what's she going to do when she finds I've smashed her thing? Her bottle. She's sure to be unhappy. She might even punish me."

What do I care what happens to you? She torments me. She weighs too much. She eats live mice. She deliberately clips her toenails too short. She smokes unfiltered cigarettes, drinks the oil off the top of her whiskey and holds a match to her mouth just to feel her lips burn. Her shoes are tight.

"Those don't sound like things she does to you, though. They sound like things she does to herself."

Have you never heard of a sin-eater?

Jane shook her head.

Hush. Here she comes.

Peg strode into the room, threw a cloth over the bottle holding the homunculus, and sat down heavily in an upholstered chair. "Payment first."

From her purse Jane drew out a handful of silver moon dollars and a single gold sequin stamped with a laughing sun. Peg flicked the sequin back in with one long, purple nail, and pocketed the rest. "So what is it? Got knocked up, did you?" She squinted. "No? Boyfriend trouble, then."

Jane nodded.

"What are you after, poison or sorcery? Poison's surer, but sorcery works from a distance and with poison it helps to be on good terms with your intended."

"I just need to learn about birth control."

"Fine." Peg stubbed out her cigarette in an ashtray and lit a new one with a disposable lighter. "Well, birth control's easy. The first thing you have to know is that it doesn't work."

"What?"

"Not consistently. No matter how careful you are, every time you play hide-the-salami with the boys, you're running the risk of ending up with a belly full of consequences."

"But—"

"Contraceptive spells are never entirely reliable. That's because their power comes from the Mother, and the Mother wants children. Each cantrip has its loophole, every fetish its flaw. Ultimately, contraception is just a way of luring you into playing her game."

"You mean that sooner or later it's going to fail me?"

"That's not what I said. It works well enough for enough of us that the rest will take their chances. But the odds are never going to be as good as you'd like them to be. There are no guarantees."

"I'd like to learn anyway."

"Of course you would. You're that age." Peg pushed herself up from the chair. She removed a black rubber item from the apothecary cabinet and thrust it at Jane. "This is an exact model of an erect prick. Not necessarily to scale, worse luck." Jane accepted it gingerly, and the witch dropped a foil packet in her lap. "And this is a condom. What you kids call a scumbag."

Peg might be crude, but she knew her business and she was thorough. Hours passed as Jane learned about condoms and IUDs and contraceptive jelly, how to build a windowsill altar and how many doves to sacrifice on it a month. She learned Dame Moon's seven secret names, where to get fitted for a diaphragm, and the medical consequences of getting her tubes tied. Finally, Peg handed her a small stone figurine and said, "This is the two-faced aspect of the Goddess."

Jane turned the figurine over in her hand. It had two fronts. "She's pregnant on one side and not on the other."

"Exactly. It's an especially useful tool in that it can also be used to encourage fertility."

She taught Jane a clapping rhyme and the gestures that went with it, then watched critically as Jane, grateful the homunculus could no longer see her, sang and danced in place in the middle of the room.

> *Hollow bone, crack-a-bone*
> *zaccary zan*
> *my right hand*
> *my left hand*
> *touch the one*
> *who understands*

*touch my knee*
*touch the ground*
*spin, span, muskidan*
*and whirl her*
*twirl and*
*swirl her a-*
*round!*

It was a spell for regularizing her period. The figurine got turned around two, three, or five times, depending on the number of days it had been since first blood. On days when it ended Maiden-side up, she could do anything she wished. When the Mother was up-most, she must remain chaste. It was reliable, Peg assured her, so long as she made no mistakes in counting, remembered to chant the spell every morning without exception, and never got so drunk or besotted she forgot which side was up.

"That's all," Peg said at last. "Now if you're at all typical, you've got a head full of nonsense and a mouth full of hideously misinformed questions to ask. Well?"

"I want to know . . . well, this is more witchcraft than contraception, I guess." Jane blushed. "But I want to know when I start getting in touch with my female wisdom."

"Female wisdom? No such animal." Peg lit a fresh cigarette.

"In school they taught us that everything is divided between male and female principles. They said that action arises from the male principle and wisdom from the female. They said that's why girls are discouraged from going into politics."

Peg snorted. "What a typically *male* thing to say! That's all a load of horseshit, young lady. There's nothing special about you just because you possess a cunt. She's a pretty little thing and if you treat her well, she'll be a good friend to you, but as a source of wisdom—? Bah! Her needs are simple and few. You learn here"—she touched Jane's forehead—"and here"—she touched Jane's heart. "Boys have heads and hearts too, you know. Not that they ever use them."

Confused, Jane said, "Well, thank you. Thank you very much."

"No more questions?"

"No," Jane said. Then, "Yes. Yes, there's just one more. I want to know about that thing in the bottle."

Peg's eyes darkened and she smiled. "He used to be my lover. But he dwindled." She reached over to the bottle and whipped off the cloth. "You'll want to be in on this, dearheart. It's your story, after all."

The homunculus's flat gaze said nothing.

"When first we met he was a great whiskery, yellow-toothed ogre. Big as a mountain, with shoulders out to there. What a magnificent creature he was! Even his faults were large faults. The smell from his armpits would choke a goat. His farts were like thunderclaps. He'd pork anything that held still for him.

"Our courtship was rough, but I liked it rough, and when I caught him slipping it up the bottom of some dollymop or curligig, I'd thrash her bloody while he laughed and yanked his pud. We never had a stick of furniture for my smashing it over his thick head. Ah, but what did we care? We were young and in love.

"But then one night the Tylwyth Teg came looking for him. I forget what it was about—he'd eaten somebody's dog, I think. Must've been somebody important to get the Tegs involved. We were living in an efficiency over a bar then, and the window had burglar bars. No time to rip 'em out. He had no choice but to hide in the closet.

"They were a pair, the Tylwyth Teg were, fever-eyed and hound-lean. Cheekbones you could slice bread with. One of them raised his head and sniffed the air. He's here, he said. I can smell him.

"'Course you can, said I, pointing to the rumpled bed. We haven't changed the sheets in a month.

"The smell's stronger than that, he said.

"It's not him you're smelling then, I said, and gave him a look.

"They exchanged glances, and one of them smirked. Are you trying to bribe us with your body? said the other.

"I looked him in the eye and said, Well I sure as hell ain't gonna give you money!

"So in the end I double-featured them right there on our unmade bed, and it still reeking of their quarry's scent. Eminently corruptible, the Tylwyth Teg are."

Peg scowled. "You look like you've eaten a green lemon, my lass. But I assure you they were glad to have me. I'm not half so bad-looking as you make me out to be."

"Oh, no," Jane said quickly. "It's not like that at all." And it wasn't. It was the story itself that horrified her. For all that she'd had no great expectations for it, sex was turning out to be even more squalid, tawdry, and cynical than she had suspected it would.

"Mmmph. Where was—oh, yeah. We pounded away on that bed for an hour-some, and for me the cream of the jest was that all the time the one they hunted was not three strides distant, watching through the crack in the door, and doubtless with his trousers down around his ankles and playing with himself. How he'd laugh when they were gone, I thought. How he'd roar.

"But when they left and I opened the closet door he did not laugh. No, not at all.

"What did you do that for? he asked me. I said, If you didn't like it, why didn't you stop it? Said he, How could I? I'd've been caught.

"What is it you're telling me, I asked—that you let them do what they wanted with me because you were afraid?

"He looked away. Well, we'll forget it ever happened, he said.

"But forget it I could not. For he was not so large in my sight as he had been a moment before. He had shrunk a little.

"In my eyes he had fallen from grace, you see. So many things happened. I'll tell you just one more, the time I came home to find all my pharmaceuticals gone and half of my clothing. So I grabbed up the baseball bat we kept by the door for intruders and went looking for him.

"He was down by the incinerator in a crap game with a crowd of trolls and a red dwarf. He was as drunk as three boiled owls. The dwarf was wearing my best black lace brassiere as a scarf.

"I screamed and ran at them. They scattered like pigeons, all but him, snatching up bets and bottles as they went. I never saw that bra again. But when I brought that bat down on him, he flinched. He *flinched*. That was what I found unforgivable."

"Why?"

"When you've had a few men under your belt, you'll understand. Well, he grabbed the bat and we fought for it. Neither of us could take it away from the other. He had dwindled down to my own size.

"It went quickly after that. He became furtive, slipping around to Koboldtown to see a mountain ape of a lass with knuckles that brushed the ground where once he would've had her in our very bed while I slept. He began sneaking money from my purse where once when I told him I'd nothing to give, he threatened to put me out on the street to earn it. He lied, he sniveled, he would not meet my eye. I'd've thrown him out, but we had shared our true names and had no choice but to see this thing through to its end. Day by day and month by month, he withered away in my esteem, smaller and smaller, until he was a thing no larger than a hedgehog. Finally I had no choice but to put him in that bottle. And there he remains."

She leaned low over the homunculus and crooned, "Don't you worry, little snugglebunny. Someday your fairy princess will come. She'll be young and beautiful and she'll look you in the eye. You won't have to beg, she'll know what you want. She'll lift the hammer from the anvil and swing it through the air faster than mortal sense can follow. You'll be dazzled, astounded, unable to think. The hammer will descend like a thunderbolt to shatter your narrow little world into a million shards and set you free." She straightened and glanced at Jane.

"But not today."

———— ◉ ————

By the third day in a row that Salome didn't show up for school, it was obvious to all that something was up. In homeroom Grunt announced that she'd had a dirt bike accident and was hospitalized. He said this proved how dangerous unsupervised fun could be and suggested they all think long and hard on this lesson.

But word in the corridors was different. Between classes, Trotteranstinch came lurching up to Jane with their stiff, three-legged walk. Their middle eye was all but swallowed up in flesh now and had a haunted look to it. They grinned cockily. "Heard about Salome?"

"No," she said. "Only what they've told us."

"She's pregnant. They sent her away to a baby farm, and she's never coming back. And guess who's to blame—none other than Hebog!"

"How do you know all this?"

"It's no big secret—Strawwe's been blabbing it to anyone who'll listen."

That afternoon Jane found Hebog standing out behind the school, off by the soccer field. He'd picked up little bits of gravel from the walk and placed them in a neatly spaced line. Holding an old stick as if it were a golf club, he was one by one knocking them into the air. He told her he'd been summoned to appear before the Low Court.

"What will they do to you?"

Hebog shrugged, addressed another bit of gravel and went into the backswing. He knocked it up and away. "I don't know. Probably indenture me to a factory. It's a serious offense, consorting with you tall buggers is. No offense intended."

"Hebog, listen, I want you to know—"

"I don't want to hear it. Fuck your sympathy. This is real and I don't want anybody mucking it over with cheap sentiment, okay?"

So Jane went home and patched herself into the dragon. She had given up trying to get him to talk, but she still liked to watch the meryons at work.

The meryon civilization had fallen on hard times. With the onset of cold weather food was no longer easy to obtain, and with no farms of their own they had grown reliant on raiding their neighbors for provisions. They had no granaries or warehouses to speak of. Their armies had scoured the surrounding land halfway to the schoolhouse. Their supply lines were thus overextended, their patrols more vulnerable to guerrilla action. Their sorties were far less productive than previously.

With the collapse of their economy had come a corresponding physical deterioration. Snug tin houses had become shanties. Starving meryons wandered aimlessly in the streets. Military police in armored cars were everywhere, tense soldiers sitting behind cunningly small machine guns. Jane saw a riot in miniature, followed by a house-by-house sweep of the slum neighborhoods in which hundreds of tiny enemies of the state were hauled out of doors and executed.

Jane watched them for a long time, pondering the random cruelties of life.

---

Samhain was not long distant when Gwen caught Jane between classes and pressed two pasteboard tickets into her hand. "Hot off the presses. They're front row seats right on the forty-yard line, two of them," she gushed happily. "I really believe you should take a date, Jane, you're old enough. I know you're a little shy, but it really is all right to invite a boy out. Just to get things started."

"Yeah, well, that's very nice of you, but—"

"You could invite Ratsnickle. I know he likes you."

Jane's body went cold. It felt exactly like the prickly sensation that sweeps through the flesh an instant after being stung by a wasp, just before the pain registers. "I don't want your damned tickets!" She thrust them back into Gwen's hands and stormed away.

Gwen caught up to her, seized an arm, and when Jane shook it off, grabbed her by the shoulders and swung her into an empty classroom. She kicked the door shut behind her. "All right, what's all this about?"

"You know what it's about."

"No, I do not."

"Well, you ought!" Jane began to cry.

This melted Gwen. With a gentle, shushing noise, she tried to take Jane into her arms. Jane wrenched herself away violently, and Gwen retreated, baffled. "Well, I don't know what's gotten into you, I really don't."

It was raining outside, a gray drenching rain driven by winds that rattled the windows and covered the glass with sheets of water. The inside of the classroom, almost silenced by soundproofing spells and lit with fluorescent fixtures, seemed a raft of bright unreality in a universe of storm. All of its own accord Jane's hand dipped into her blouse pocket. She removed the piece of paper she had been carrying with her ever since her encounter with the Principal and unfolded it.

" 'Peter of the Hillside,' " she read aloud, " 'has been examined by the undersigned practitioners of hermeneutic medicine on this Day of the Toad, Axe Moon, in the one hundred seventy-third year of the Descent of the Turbine, and found to be and is hereby certified as a virgin, innocent of carnal knowledge and a fit sacrifice to the glory of the Goddess and for the aversion of Her dread disapproval and wrathful desire.' " Eyes blazing, she said, "A virgin!"

"Where did you get that?"

"What does it matter where I got it? It says that Peter's a virgin."

"Well, Jane, you have to understand that the Goddess doesn't want—"

A bolt of lightning struck a distant tree on the far horizon, and Gwen gasped. Jane, though, didn't even flinch. She felt the storm's energy flow through her veins like wrath, buoying her up, filling her with power. Every hair on her body tingled. Gwen seemed smaller now, and she shrank from Jane like a shadow bending away from the light.

Thunder filled the room.

She shook the paper in Gwen's face. "All I want to know is, if you don't sleep with him, what do you do?"

"He's my consort."

"Yes, but what does that mean?"

"Peter . . . eases my pain. He makes things easier for me."

With a thunderclap of shock, Jane felt half a dozen scrips and scraps of information fall together into a single blinding insight. "He's a sin-eater, isn't he?"

Gwen hesitated just long enough that she couldn't convincingly deny a thing. "Well, what if he is?"

"Oh, you—viper! I thought you were brave, I thought you were strong. But you didn't have to be, did you? You haven't felt a thing. You haven't suffered at all. It's Peter who's suffered. It's Peter whose feet hurt when yours blistered, Peter who suffered your hangovers and your cocaine jags. It's Peter who's paid for all your pleasures, isn't it? Tell me something. When you mistreat him, who feels the guilt? Hah? It isn't you, is it?"

The lightning was coming closer. Against the greenish afternoon darkness the artificial lighting made Gwen's face look overwhite, skin too taut, like a skull. "That's what a consort's for. Maybe nobody talks about it, but everybody knows. I haven't done anything that hasn't been done every year in every community since time began. So what's the big deal? What are you so upset about?"

"You've had the free ride, but it was Peter who paid the freight."

"I'm *entitled!*" she shrieked.

A wrathful calm came over Jane. She said nothing. She was the focus of the storm, its eye of power. All its bleak strength poured into her. She stared at Gwen with godlike disdain.

With a small cry Gwen broke away from her gaze and spun to the door. She seized the knob and thus anchored turned back into the room for an instant before fleeing. "Anyway, it doesn't matter what you think, Miss High-and-Mighty Jane Alderberry! I'm still the wicker queen, and Peter is still my consort. That's who we are and what our relationship is. You may not like it, but so what? That's just the way things are and there's nothing you can do about it. Nothing!"

The door slammed behind her.

Jane was left alone in a roomful of huddled fiberglass desk chairs, twoscore identical creatures like children with blank, empty faces. They waited patiently for her to speak.

Not necessarily, Jane said, but silently and to herself.

# ━━◦◉◦━━ ELEVEN ━◦◉◦━━

It was only when she went to empty out her locker that Jane realized how overgrown it had become. Orchids and jungle vines filled most of the space within and a hummingbird fled into the corridor when she banged open the door.

"I don't understand," Strawwe said. "Do you want your papers forwarded to the University early, is that it?"

A mulch of corrected assignments, old tests, and mimeographed syllabuses, had formed at the bottom and sprouted mushrooms and ferns. Some of her books were too moldy for retrieval. A tiny animal scurried away when she reached for her hairbrush, rattling the bamboo like a xylophone.

"You can have these examination books if you want. I won't be needing them."

Strawwe danced anxiously from foot to foot, trying to engage her attention more fully. It was pathetic how anxious he was to please. With her reversal of fortunes she had become to him an object of fear and mystery. "It's a little late in the year for a normal transfer, but it might be possible to get you in under Special Status."

"Do what you like."

A white rectangle of paper lay atop her things on the book ledge. Somebody had slipped a note through the air vents. Jane opened it:

> I know your mad at me. But I still think we make a pretty good couple. I cant be happy without you. Let's give it another try. Why not kiss and make up?

It was not signed, but only Ratsnickle could have concocted such a thing. Jane felt an involuntary surge of anger, but forced herself to smile coldly and murmur to her own ears only, "Dream on."

"The secretary thought we should have a little ceremony. Nothing fancy, maybe an afternoon tea. Just you, me, her, and a few teachers who've been significant mentors to you. I could have a parchment scroll made up, with calligraphy. Or a plaque."

"We'll see." She closed the locker for the last time ever.

"That's what I'll do," he called after her. "Okay?"

On the way out she ran into Trinch, grinning his eighty-tooth grin. He had only two eyes now, though their colors didn't match, and his middle leg had dwindled to such a degree that he had to keep it coiled up in his jeans. His metamorphosis all but complete, he was as frog-ugly as ever. By his satisfied demeanor, though, that was what he'd intended.

"Jane! Fancy running into you." He put an arm around her shoulder and she knocked it away.

"None of that! I'm wise to your tricks."

He took the rebuff with good grace. "Hey, I was just up by your digs, watching the exterminators lay down bait. There's little yellow warning flags all over the place."

"That so?" Jane wasn't particularly interested.

"Yeah, I talked with one of them and he said there was a really nasty infestation of meryons thereabouts. Said that if they didn't take to the baits, he'd be coming back in a day or two to flood their burrows with poison gas."

It made Jane feel queasy to think of the little fellows being gassed. But everyone had their problems, and she had more immediate things to think about. "Thank you for sharing that with me," she said. "I'll be especially careful not to eat anything I find on the ground in the next few days."

Then she was outside in the crisp autumn air, with an armful of things to take home to the dragon, and the school at her back. *I'm never coming back here again*, she thought to herself. *Never*. But she felt nothing, and there was no time to force sentiment on herself.

She still had preparations to make for this evening.

———— ◦◉◦ ————

Jane knocked on Peter's door.

"Come in," he said.

Because it was Samhain Eve and the last possible day to make alterations, Peter was wearing his gold lamé suit, double-checking the fit. Gwen was off to the celebratory banquet in the city. Everybody was talking about it. There would be champagne and speeches and a suite had been reserved for the orgy afterwards. So Peter was alone.

Jane's heart went out to him, he looked so pale and ascetic, like a weary, ill-used child. A hand sickle rested on the dresser top. She looked away from it. "I brought some wine. I thought maybe a glass or two would make tonight easier on you."

"Thanks," he said distractedly. "That's really nice of you."

"*De nada.*"

She set the jug on the floor and her purse beside it. The purse contained the minimum she was going to need if things worked out: a toothbrush, the stone Mother, and a change of underwear. "Where are your glasses?"

Peter went into the bathroom and emerged a minute later without his jacket and holding two jelly-jar tumblers. "Will these do?"

"They're perfect," she assured him.

Jane waited until Peter's glass was almost gone then refilled it for him. Her stomach hurt, but she had to ask. "Peter," she said, "are you really a virgin?" Thinking maybe there was some horrible mistake, some misunderstanding on her part.

He nodded. "The Goddess doesn't want used goods." He took a long swallow. "You haven't been around much lately."

"Gwen and I had kind of a falling-out. I, uh, found out she was using you as a sin-eater." His face hardened and turned more intensely white and she hurriedly added, "She didn't tell me; it was something I figured out for myself."

"Well, I'd appreciate it if it didn't get around, okay?"

She touched his shoulder. "Hey. You know I wouldn't do anything like that." His head swung around to look at her and then away, and nodded shaggily. She filled his glass again. "Peter? Can I ask you something personal? See, I don't really . . . I mean, it's not like . . ." She flushed. "Just what does a sin-eater *do?*"

Peter's head whipped around again and she stared into the shocked, unreadable eyes of a forest animal. For an instant he was still. Then sudden laughter exploded from him, knocking him flat on his back on the bed. He howled and howled for so long that Jane began to worry about him. But eventually he gathered himself together and sat up again. All the tension was gone from him. "You know how sometimes when you've been badly treated, you can kick a dog, say, and you'll feel better?"

"No."

Peter ducked his head. "Well, tell you the truth, neither do I. But that's the way it is, apparently. That's kind of what Gwen does to me. There's this special ceremonial knife they gave her, and a booklet with the various runes. But mostly she just uses a razor blade."

"Peter!"

"No, really—it wouldn't work without blood. Here, I'll show you the scars." He began to undo his shirt. His coordination was not too good by now, and Jane moved to help him. Because she'd been drinking heavily too, there was some confusion. Finally, laughing, they pulled it off. Peter turned away and she saw that his back was covered with razor-slashed sigils, row upon row of them, a book of pain. Some were new and scabbed; the rest were white and fine. Jane recognized Gwen's neat hand.

Wonderingly she touched the silvery marks. His skin was hot. She traced the runes with her fingertips. She could not stop stroking them, could not stop touching him. "Poor, poor Peter."

He straightened and stared unseeing at a poster of Gwen tacked to the wall. Her gaze was direct, mocking, enigmatic. "You want to know what's the worst part? I mean, worse than all this, what do I care if my back itches a little? It's how much I want her. I can't stand her, but I want her so bad." He wiped his hand on the side of his pants, hard. "I want her and I hate her. When I think of her I feel like puking. What a sick relationship."

Jane bent to brush her lips lightly against Peter's shoulder. He turned to her and suddenly they were kissing. His arms were about her, his hands running up and down the back of her blouse. She clutched him to her and stuck one hand under his waistband. It only went down to the second knuckle; his belt was too tight to go any farther.

There were all these clothes in the way! They went on kissing and kissing, and making no progress.

Finally Jane drew back and began to pull at his belt, tugging the strap first one way and then the other. She yanked the zipper down. A little button went flying. Meanwhile, Peter was unbuttoning her blouse, fumbling at the catch on her brassiere.

She couldn't believe he was giving in this easily.

⸺⸻◆⸻⸺

There was so much to think about, so much to do, that the act itself barely registered on Jane. It was uncomfortable at first, but then it got better. They were both awkward; Jane was sure that sex wasn't supposed to be so anxious and uncoordinated, so inelegant. But this first time, the fact was all that mattered. They could get it right later, when there wasn't so much riding on it.

Some indeterminate amount of time later Peter's motions grew more hurried, and his face turned red and puffy. He made a small cry, like a lake bird at twilight, and collapsed atop her.

She guessed that they were done.

Peter slipped out of her and rolled over. For a long, still moment he did not move. Then his eyes opened. He smiled at her.

"We're a number now."

"I suppose we are."

His eyes were palest blue and beautiful beyond description. Jane felt herself drowning in them. Peter took her in his arms again, this time for simple affection, and it was the nicest sensation imaginable. A great joy filled her, like the sun rising at midnight. She asked, "Are you sorry?"

He shook his head. He was drunk—they both were—and his eyes had a tendency to cross, but his sincerity was unmistakable. "Jane. I think maybe this was supposed to happen. You know? I feel a connection with you. Something deep. Like . . . you know how if you take a coin and break it in a vise and throw half in the ocean and keep the other in a dresser drawer, they'll yearn after each other? One day you're taking out a pair of socks and you knock the drawer-half onto the floor without noticing. Somebody kicks it toward the door. A week later, it's half a block away. And the other half meanwhile, a fish swallows it and is caught and gutted and the entrails thrown into the trash, half-coin and all. So that maybe a couple of months later, it might take a century, you'll find the two lying in the sand at the verge of some nothing-special stretch of country road, nestled together.

"That's kind of how I think we are."

A thrill of recognition went through Jane. Something within her responded to what he said. Was it possible? Could it be that Gwen had been nothing but glamour and misdirection, a distraction from what had *really* been going on? With all her self and soul she willed it to be true. "Yes," she said. "Yeah, I think that's it. I think that's how it is."

"Don't go home tonight," Peter said. "Don't ever go home. Move in with me." He suddenly noticed the poster of Gwen and got out of bed to tear it down, ball it up, throw it in the trash. It was the first time she'd had the leisure to study his naked body, and looking at it embarrassed and elated her. "Live with me forever."

"Oh, Peter, I couldn't ask that of you."

"No," he said with drunken artlessness. "Look, I think we ought to share names. You know, to make it official." He took a deep breath. "My true name is Tetigis—"

Before he could finish saying it, Jane flung herself on him and stopped his mouth with hers. She thrust her tongue inside him, something she hadn't dared do earlier. It felt strange, impossibly strange, to be acting this way.

Peter pulled his mouth away from her. "It means needle."

Jane closed her eyes, flooded with memories of Rooster, poor doomed and mutilated Rooster, whose true name had also meant needle. Tetigistus. They two shared a single true name, and she did not know what this meant, but it frightened her to the very core of her being. "Yes," she said miserably. "Yes, I know."

---

The next day around noon they were wakened by a loud banging on the door. Before Jane could pull herself entirely awake it burst open and the room filled with elves. There seemed to be dozens of them, all in stern suits and unforgiving shoes. They stared down at the bed with expressions of disgust.

"We'll need another sacrifice," one said at last.

"Where can we get another sacrifice at this late date?"

"Maybe they haven't—"

A handsome woman with the tail and ears of a jackass emerged from the bathroom holding the gold lamé jacket on a hanger and said, "Oh, be sensible. Of course they have—just look at them. What a shambles."

"What a fucking mess."

Jane pulled the sheet up over her chin. Her stomach rumbled and her bowels felt loose. The ache in her head was worse than anything she'd ever imagined possible. A chalk white elf sniffed at her and said, "It's always the cheap little dime-a-dozen sluts that bring them down."

"Hey, wait just a minute!" Peter sat up, fists balled, eyes blazing.

Without even looking, the elf knocked him back in the bed with a backhanded slap in the mouth. Jane squealed.

"There's that tomte kid down to the Reaches. We can get the

medical tests run and have him fitted and ready by tonight if we move fast." In a swirl of suits, silks, and briefcases, they were gone. They took the sickle with them.

Peter sat up and buried his head in his hands.

"What'll I do?" he moaned. "What can I do?"

Jane was too hung over to be of much use. She had to go to the bathroom and she suspected she was going to throw up. But she did as best as she could. "Look," she said. "What's done is done. Last night is history, and there's no turning back. We'll just have to make the best of things, right?"

"Oh, Jane, I'm so sorry I got you into this fix. What a jerk I've been. It's all my fault," he said dolorously. It would've been funny if it weren't so serious.

"Hey, look on the bright side. At least you get to keep your"— she almost said "prick" but managed to veer the sentence to one side—"self intact. Now you don't have to go through life as a sacred eunuch. That's worth a little temporary unhappiness, isn't it?"

"Yeah," Peter said unconvincingly. "Sure."

———❖———

The afternoon was endless and gray. Peter, who had been through countless of Gwen's hangovers, gave Jane some vitamins and made sure she drank a lot of water. He was depressed and uncommunicative and Jane knew she ought to be cheering him up and coddling him, but the truth was she was feeling kind of bitchy herself. It was something of a triumph that she managed not to make things worse.

To keep herself busy, she set to cleaning the apartment of all traces of its previous visitor. It wasn't easy. Gwen had left a surprising number of her possessions behind, and they all hated Jane. Bobby pins fled from her grasping fingers. A hair dryer sparked and snapped whenever she came near it. The silk scarf she had stolen so long ago whipped itself around her neck and had to be torn away. Fortunately it was weak, for it really had wanted to strangle her. She disposed of them all in the dumpster out back in the alley.

At one point, when Peter was in the shower, she took out the Mother and ran through the clapping rhyme. Every day, Peg had said, without exception. By evening they both had recovered enough to eat some microwave food, and Jane volunteered to go out for wine.

Hurrying back to the apartment with the new jug, Jane was caught by the repeated image of Gwen burning in a bank of television sets in an appliance store window: Gwen upon Gwen upon Gwen twisting in unison in the flames. It seemed to be something that was happening in another world. The empty street, the cement sidewalk, the plate glass window all denied Gwen's reality.

Jane was transfixed. The television screens dissolved in her swimming sight, rising like slim blue tapers and then breaking up into triads of red-green-blue motes. Briefly, the air swarmed with phosphor dots. She felt herself dizzily falling into the broadcast.

She blinked away the tears.

The screens fell back into resolution. Gwen's fire seethed with subliminal scenes of horror, flickering glimpses of prisoners in boxcars, mutilated bodies, children aflame, as if suffering were a universal constant, a flat statement of existence and nothing more.

Hands tied behind her, Gwen writhed, as if trying to shed the chrysalis of her body. Her shoulders moved frantically. Her mouth was open in an unending scream. A small blue flame burned on her tongue. Smoke rose about her like wings.

Something bubbled out of her nostrils.

Horrified, Jane stumbled forward, feeling dried grass scratch underfoot. The telecast was all but silent. All she could hear was the fire itself, the snapping of sparks and roar of heated air. Gwen herself made not a sound. Jane was grateful for that—the images, the sweet smell of flesh like burning pork, and the awful taste in the back of her mouth were bad enough.

The crowd too was uncannily mute. She could feel their thronged bloodlust in the bleachers behind her and to either side, like the menacing regard of so many thousand-headed monsters. But she did not turn to look. She could not. She was unable to tear her gaze from her friend's torment.

Gwen's dress was burned away entirely, its charred remains indistinguishable from her skin, and still she lived. Black specks rose up from her. A flake of greasy soot came drifting down upon Jane and stung her hand. She slapped it away. Her foot felt wrong. She looked down and saw that she'd stepped on a discarded mass of pink cotton candy. Reflexively, she bent down to pull it from her shoe by its flattened paper cone.

When she looked up, Gwen was staring straight at her.

Most of the wicker cage had burned through and fallen away but she was held upright by the armature of high-performance alloys that underwired the structure. The fire had burned her unrecognizable, a thing of agony and black bone. Only her eyes were alive. They stared from the heart of pain and it seemed they knew something awful and simple and true that they wished to share with her.

They stared straight into the core of Jane's being.

"No!" Jane threw her arm up before her eyes and fetched a nasty rap on her knuckles when they struck the plate glass window. She found herself clutching the jug of wine to her chest with one arm. Gwen had finally ceased moving.

When Jane looked away, the air was dark. A light had gone out of the world.

<hr />

Back at the apartment she found Peter had turned on the TV and was staring, unblinking, at a small figure in gold lamé. The sickle flashed to a roar of applause, and he flung something small and dark into the embers. Hands reached out to seize his falling body.

Jane snapped off the television.

"Have some wine," she said. "It'll make you feel better."

After they'd had a bit to drink, they began to make a few tentative plans. Peter had a standing offer from a local garage for a mechanic's position. Jane could get a job at the mall. It would mean giving up shoplifting, but that was a sacrifice she was prepared to make. The apartment was good enough for now, but when they had a little money saved, they'd want to move to someplace nicer.

"I'm not sorry all this happened," Peter said. "I think we'll be good for each other." He lifted her hands, and lightly kissed the knuckles one by one.

Later they made love for the second time. Jane didn't really enjoy it much because, despite all the water she'd drunk, she was still a little hung over. But she figured it was like the wine, something she could acquire a taste for.

They sat up in bed afterward, fantasizing their future together and drinking more wine. "Now we always have to tell each other everything," Jane said. "Our thoughts, our innermost feelings, everything. We always have to tell each other the strictest truth. Because that's what being in love is, right?"

"Yeah," Peter said. "That's right."

Jane was careful not to get drunk as she had the night before. But eventually weariness caught up with her. Her eyes grew heavy and she drifted off.

When she awoke it was dark. The jug was empty and Peter was gone.

———⊙———

Peter wasn't at the school. Jane walked twice around the ashes on the football field, then went around behind the bleachers and called quietly for him. The shadows stirred.

She thought briefly that she'd found him when she discovered that the door by the loading docks into the shop was unlocked. But when she went inside, he wasn't there. She was sure he had passed that way, though, for the repair bay was empty—he had taken Ragwort. "Follow the road out of town," a voice whispered.

She whirled. "Who's there?"

Nobody answered.

"Who's there!"

Her words echoed from the far wall.

In the end she had no choice but to do as the voice suggested, following the main road away from the school, past the miracle mile and into the dark hills at the outskirts of town.

An hour later, she found Ragwort.

He lay in the mud of a ditch, one leg broken, his frame obviously bent. There was a dying light in the eye he turned her way. His battery was failing. "Girlie?"

"Oh, Ragwort." She hugged his neck and began to cry. All the uncertainty and fear for Peter and herself both came out in those tears as well, her guilty feelings for Gwen, all the muddled emotions that were her life.

"Aw, don't go on like that," Ragwort croaked. "I'm just an old hack, without nothing much left to look forward to." He laughed a rusty, choking laugh. "Never honestly thought I'd get out of that fucking repair bay again—that boy Peter did proud by me, he did. Took me out and let me run."

"We'll get you patched up," she promised.

"Bullshit. I'm fucking scrap metal now. But it was one hell of a ride, girlie, one hell of a ride. We was all over the road. I ain't got no regrets. Shit."

A better person, Jane was sure, would have been able to restrain herself, to spare the time to soothe an old friend into death before returning to her own affairs. But try though she might she could not. Feeling awful, she asked, "Where's Peter?"

Ragwort chuckled. It sounded like sheet metal tearing. "Last I saw him, the boy was headed upslope." He called after her, "Give him a kiss for me, girlie. He's earned it."

---

Peter had hanged himself.

His slim body hung from a low branch of an elm tree near the top of the slope. It was hard to see at first, but as she climbed the hillside the ground, trees, and sky resolved themselves into three separate shades of gray, with Peter's corpse suspended at their center. A faint breeze moved it ever so slightly—any less and the motion would be undetectable. His feet were a slowly turning compass, quartering out the night.

Jane stayed midway up the slope through the darkest part of the night, unwilling to leave and unable to bear coming any closer. Caught between conflicting urges, she could give in to neither and in the end she simply didn't move.

Around midnight the moon rose and shortly thereafter there was a slight stirring at the center of Peter's forehead. Slowly, a slim black crack appeared and widened there. His face broke open like brittle paper.

Something dark crawled from the crack. It spread damp wings, pulsed, and then flew away. More dark specks emerged from Peter's skull, one and then three and five at a time, pausing briefly and then taking wing. A thin stream formed, thickened, moved away.

It was a swarm of hornets.

"Come." A small hand—a child's hand—took hers and led her away.

---

She was far down the road before she thought to look to her side and see who was leading her. Then, when she did, what she saw was so unexpected she found it hard to credit her own numbed senses.

It was the shadow-boy.

Too much had happened; she could not respond. They walked,

saying nothing. Miles passed. At the schoolyard the shadow-boy released her and said, "I came to say good-bye." He smiled sadly. "I can't help you any more. They've given up on finding you and the child catcher has been recalled. I'll be going back to the factory now."

"The factory," Jane said. It was hard to think of the factory. She tried to come up with something appropriate to say. "How is everybody doing there?"

"Everything is the same there. Nothing ever changes." The shadow-boy's voice was wistful. "It can't." He shifted and was gone.

"Wait!" Jane cried. "It was . . . you in the shadows all this time?"

From behind her, the shadow-boy said, "The child catcher brought me to help find you. Like a bloodhound, you know." She whirled and caught a fraction of his shy smile. "He has less control over me than he thought. I wasn't able to do much. But I gave you what protection I could. On Midsummer's Day, the bonfire? It was me who fetched your teacher when you were attacked. Things like that."

"You did that? Why would you go to all that trouble for me?"

"I'm your friend." A gentle, papery touch of his hand. "Friends help friends."

She turned to return his touch with a hug but there was nothing there. The sense of phantom presence that had haunted her all these past months was gone.

Slowly, wearily, Jane headed back up to the landfill.

———※※———

The dragon was gone.

Unbelieving, Jane wandered across the space where he had been. The low moon provided just enough light to show that there was nothing there but churned-up earth.

The meryons were gone as well, their buildings lightless and abandoned. Jane stumbled across their perimeters and was not challenged. A Quonset hut crumpled underfoot and she was not attacked. She came upon a neat pile of blankets and clothing, rolled-up posters, schoolbooks, brushes and combs, the total accumulation of wealth she had managed to amass since fleeing the factory. She screamed.

"My *stuff!* You just left all my stuff out in the open!"

Not caring what happened, she called on Melanchthon with all her will, howling his true name across the landfill and shouting out the catalog codes she had memorized so long ago for anyone to hear.

A voice answered from within the ground.

*Go away. You are no longer needed.*

His voice was more powerful than it had ever been before. It made her skull vibrate and rattled her teeth. "We cut a deal," she reminded him. "You're supposed to protect me."

*And who broke the compact first? Eh, little virgin?*

His scorn scorched her face and left small blisters on her nose and cheeks. She cried out in pain. But she could no longer control herself. "You bastard! You planned all this, you arranged all this, it's all your doing, I know it! I'm going to rip your wiring out—I'll take you apart with my bare hands!"

A pipe thrust out of the soil, right at her feet, and ratcheted upward, skewing crazily into the sky. Jane danced back from it. To her side, a steel tower erupted from the ground, rocketing toward the moon, shedding dirt. "Stop!" Jane shouted. But metal structures wcre sprouting everywhere about her, in sheets and chrome walls, slamming and clashing against one another, blocking the horizon and hiding the stars and clouds. An iron bulwark curved overhead, clanging into a slotted wall, and then all motion stopped.

Jane was enclosed in a city of steel, with no windows or doors. "Where am I?" she cried in horror.

"Location is an illusion." The voice came from a corridor to her side. She spun about and saw a warrior approaching, elf-handsome in camouflage fatigues, a pistol within a buckled holster at his belt. "That is one of the first things that Melanchthon taught us." The warrior's mouth moved, but nothing else. His eyes were beads of jet. It might as well have been a mask talking.

"You know his name," Jane said flatly.

"A dragon is not like most creatures. Knowing his true name gives you no power over him unless you also stand at his controls."

It was true. Jane knew it was true by how bitter it tasted. "Who are you?" she asked.

"We are your replacements."

She looked more closely at him. She knew now that they were meeting not on a physical level but in some virtual dreamspace of Melanchthon's devising. She studied the simplified planes of the warrior's face, his flat, emotionless expression. Her apprehension of scale did a sudden flip-flop, and she realized that rather than standing within a roofed passageway in an enormous city, she had been reduced in stature and set down among the pistons and workings of the dragon's interior. "You're a meryon."

"Yes. We are. Melanchthon still needs work, and with your virginity you have lost your neutrality of power. Your hands are no longer pH-neutral. His circuitry would burn at your touch. You could not so much as open an access hatch without disturbing the balance of charges within. We, however, reproduce asexually. We have dismantled our industries and moved them within the dragon's thorax, so that we might devote ourselves to his repair and maintenance." He gestured down one long corridor where minuscule service lights gleamed on surfaces of copper, steel, molybdenum. Tiny figures moved purposefully in the distance. "See what work we have done already."

"What do you get out of this arrangement?"

"Shelter," said the meryon. "And enough wheat to see us through the winter."

"You wouldn't need his shelter or his wheat if he hadn't arranged it. He's messed with your culture, tricked you into not growing enough food to feed yourselves, and made you dependent on coal and conquest for survival, when he knew all along that it would lead you to the brink of starvation."

"The strong abuse the weak," said the meryon. "Why should this bother anybody? It's a system."

Jane saw it then. No longer needing her help, Melanchthon had led and manipulated her into losing her virginity. That done, their compact was broken, and he was thus freed from the necessity even of going back on his word. "I could still fight him, you know." She felt weary and useless. "Right here, right now. I know his wiring inside out—I could do him serious damage."

"Yes, but could you win?"

They both knew the answer to that.

The metal walls dissolved, and with them the meryon as well. The smell of the landfill filled Jane's nostrils again, and she was standing beside the pile of her clothes. She squatted to scoop up an armful of the best. She was so tired. There had to be someplace she could find shelter.

Jane slept that night in a wooden crate at the edge of the landfill. In the morning she crawled outside, sore and aching. She stood and looked around.

Above the trees, to the west, faerie towers melted into a gray sky. The skyscrapers had merged together into a single silhouetted wall. A magickal smog hung over the City.

It looked sick with possibility.

# TWELVE

Sirin's experiments always worked.

That's what bugged Jane. They could construct identical assemblages of retorts and glass tubing, heat them with Bunsen burners feeding off the same petcock, flames tuned to the same height and color, measure out portions of sal ammoniac and exsanguinated toad's liver from the same carboys, their weights identical to the gram, and come morning Sirin's alembic would contain an azure essential oil with a spirit of light dancing in its depths and Jane's would be black with carbonized gunk. She had to pay for any glassware rendered unreusable, so there would follow a good fifteen minutes' sincere and futile brushwork at the sink before the thing would finally and mercifully burst in her hands. It seemed her fingers were always stained and bandaged, where Sirin's were long and slim and white as milk.

It wasn't fair.

Frustrated, she stepped out of the Alk-200 lab and let the thronging students sweep her away. The hall echoed with the clicking of hooves and heels. Everyone was in hurry, walking rapidly, turning suddenly to step into a classroom, appearing abruptly from side corridors no wider than a doorway. They seemed to be constantly popping in and out of existence. Jane's half of the traffic suddenly poured down a wide marble staircase, and she was carried along with them. Three floors she descended, and made it to the dissecting theater just as the bell rang.

Monkey was in a benevolent mood and had saved her a seat by the railing. Jane nodded thanks as Monkey lifted her stack of books away. Comparative and Speculative Anatomy was one of

Jane's favorite classes. She looked forward to next semester, when she'd get to do some dissecting herself.

"Are we still on the centaur?" she whispered.

"No, I think he finally rotted." Monkey giggled, slipped a foot out of its shoe, and tugged at one of her own braids. "By the look of the control, I'd guess we're finally going to get to see something cute cut up."

"About time."

In the narrow horseshoe balcony, students were settling themselves in, a bright ripple of beaks and batwings, horns, jackal's-heads, bandannas, and horsehair plumes. Below, the control stood by the linen-covered dissecting table. He was a well-made young fey in an olive dressing gown provided by the Department. He had sleek black hair and a scornful eye—he was scanning the audience dispassionately—and when his gaze met Jane's she shivered involuntarily, as if somebody had touched ice to the nape of her neck.

The Chirurgeon strode into the amphitheater. With a muffled clatter everyone rose. Solemn and imposing in black, she brooded over the corpse, hands folded, like a priestess at the altar. When the class had reseated themselves, she nodded to either side. A teaching assistant whipped the linen cover away. The control put the gown aside and stood naked beside the dissecting table.

Monkey's eyes narrowed. She wrote a large "7" on the top of her yellow tablet. A nixie to her other side reached over to scrawl "6.5 at most!" beneath the 7 and underlined the most! three times.

Monkey dipped her head to stifle her laughter.

"—the incidence and frequency of the minor organs," the Chirurgeon was saying, "the gallbladder, suprarenal glands and kidneys in particular." She gestured down at the corpse, a gray twin of the young fey beside her. "The abdominal cavity has already been partially opened by a transverse and a lower vertical incision. Now I shall continue the operation by making a second vertical incision and opening the peritoneal cavity."

Hands the color of bone china floated delicately down to make the first cut. They flicked an invisible bit of tissue onto the floor as an offering to the Goddess.

An elbow dug into Jane's ribs. Glancing to the side, she saw that Monkey had filled her tablet page with a careful rendering of the control's genitalia. Jane scowled and shook her head.

This was serious, damn it.

By the end of class Jane's hand was cramped and aching from taking notes, and Monkey's drawing was surrounded by a woven wreath of lesser penises in varying states of erection. The Chirurgeon laid down her scalpel and with the slightest hint of a bow removed herself from the amphitheater. The air brightened. The students began to stand, chatter, gather up their books. The control put on his gown. "Oh, hey," Jane said. "Are you done with my *Shearer's*?"

"The dissection manual?" Monkey asked airily. "I ate it."

"You what?"

"I ate it. Why else would I want it? I was hungry and I ate it."

"But I need it for class."

"Then you shouldn't have given it to me." Monkey's beady eyes glittered strangely, maliciously, in her round face. "Really, Jane, you can be so dim at times." With a sudden standing backflip she disappeared through the doorway.

Jane's hands clenched. But really it was no more than she had learned to expect. Roommates were forever eating your books, having anxiety attacks, adopting rats and carnivorous slimes which they then expected you to feed, getting drunk and throwing up on your best dress, moving into the closet and refusing to come out for months on end, threatening suicide the night before Finals, leaving piles of rotting leaves in the middle of the floor, entertaining boyfriends in your bed because it was made and theirs not, evolving into large bloodsucking insects. Monkey was actually good of her kind.

Well, she could always pick up a new manual.

She took an express elevator eight floors up to the University bookstore. Over the past year Jane had come to know the layout well, the nature and locations of its antitheft systems and the identity of the part-time plainclothes dick. Security was tight up front by the cash registers. But there was an emergency exit at the back of the store, hidden from the cameras by the overstocked back shelves. Opening it would automatically trip an alarm, but that shouldn't be too big a problem.

Jane gathered up a new *Shearer's* and traced an indirect path toward the exit. Luckily, she'd had the foresight to case the back halls recently and break the lock on a nearby stairwell door. She was pretty sure she could be down a flight before the detective reached the door, and around a corner by the time he got to the stairs. There was an element of risk, but it was a method she'd never used and was eager to try out.

She took a deep breath and put a hand on the push bar.

A sudden sense of dark unease swept through her, a heavy wash of *gravitas* that unsettled her stomach and left a bitter taste in her mouth.

Iron talons seized her shoulder. "Miss Alderberry."

It was Doctor Nemesis.

"Ma'am!" Stricken, she looked up into her adviser's face. The doctor's eyeglasses rode low on her beak, two luminous disks under a painfully weak pair of watery pink eyes. The effect was like being stared at by two separate creatures, one of which you pitied and the other feared.

"I have been going over your laboratory reports, Miss Alderberry." Dr. Nemesis put an arm through hers, and walked her toward the front. "They are, if I may confide in you, disappointing, most disappointing in a student of your potential."

"I've been having trouble with the sophic—"

"Exactly so." They strolled out the front entrance. Distractedly, Jane realized that, cloaked within the magnetic field of Dr. Nemesis's dignity, she had effortlessly bypassed security. What would have taken calculation, daring, and risk on her part, her adviser had accomplished without even noticing.

She walked Jane to a faculty elevator and unlocked the controls. It was snug as a nut within, walnut panels polished to a glassy smoothness. The doors closed noiselessly. Silently, they ascended. Jane could dimly see her own reflection in the wood with her adviser looming beside her like a storm cloud.

"You must surely realize why I am concerned for you."

"Well . . ." Jane didn't really, but that double glare bored into her, waiting for an intelligent response. "I'm here on a merit scholarship, so I suppose—"

"No!" Dr. Nemesis stamped her foot impatiently. As if in response the elevator door slid open. She steered Jane outside. They were on an office level now. The walls were decorated with large unframed oils of umbrellas and sides of beef. The runners on the hall floors smelled new. "I am not talking about mere money, but about your very *survival!* This is a Teind year, surely you must know that." Jane nodded, meaning no. "The department heads are even now assembling the list of those ten percent of the students who are . . . expendable. Your name, Miss Alderberry, is going to be on that list unless you straighten up and fly right." She glared at her: weakly, sternly.

"There's something I'm missing," Jane said rapidly. "It must surely be something elementary, something basic. If I could only understand it, if only I could see what it was, I'm certain I could keep up."

"I feel it may help, Miss Alderberry, were I to admit to you that at one time I was myself but an indifferent researcher. Oh, yes. Even I." Dr. Nemesis smiled vainly. "Lazy, unorganized, insolent—all the virtues a teaching assistant can have, I lacked."

"I was wondering could it maybe be the pontic water—"

"What set me straight was one particular incident. My adviser, none other than the wizard Bongay himself mind you, had obtained grant money from the Horned Man Foundation to create a divinatory engine in the form of a brazen head. This was, you will understand, very early in the history of cybernetics. It was all done with vacuum tubes then."

"It couldn't be my technique. I was ever so careful."

"We had taken over an unused handball court and fitted it with our equipment. There we spent most of a year, flirting with glory and never winning her. The final month of our funding—the Foundation had harsh penalties for failure—we literally moved into the lab. For three weeks straight we built, unbuilt, and rebuilt that monstrosity. Up all night, every night, and far into the dawn. We slept on cots and lived on take-out, eating cold pizza for breakfast, egg rolls and chocolate doughnuts at midnight. I lost count of the times we booted the creature up, got it to open its eyes, and coaxed it into moving its mouth, but to no purpose. It would not speak.

"After one particularly exasperating failure, Bongay declared himself in great need of sleep and staggered off to his cot. He left me awake, though, with stern warnings to watch the head and wake him immediately should it come to life.

"I was dull with fatigue myself, but I stayed up resoldering some circuits. Vacuum tubes were fussy things. You'd be surprised how often a problem could be resolved simply by ripping out a demonstrably complete circuit and replacing it with its twin.

"Not half an hour later, the head's eyes snapped open.

"*Time is*, he said.

"I put down my soldering iron. To tell you the truth, I was not sure it had actually spoken, for the eyes clicked shut as soon as it was done and that noble brass face was as still as the tomb. It might have been a waking dream. But I had my orders and I went to the wizard Bongay and put my hand on his shoulder to waken him. Only then he rolled over and the blanket slipped from him and I saw how fearsomely aroused he was in his sleep.

"Bongay had the habit, you see, of gratifying his impulses as they arose. To sharpen his wits, you see. I was the first female laboratory assistant he had ever employed but I knew from experience that he would exact from me certain favors which he had grown accustomed to receiving from young male graduate students." She raised an eyebrow significantly.

"You mean—?" said Jane, not sure what she meant.

"Exactly. My hemorrhoids were in bloom. The thought of accommodating him was intolerable. So I decided I must have been mistaken. An hour passed. The head's eyes again opened. Again, he spoke:

"*Time was.*

"This time I was sure the head had spoken. But now—in addition to my perfectly understandable reluctance to arouse the wizard—I knew that I had committed a grievous error in not awakening him the first time. If I awoke him now, he must surely punish me for not awakening him sooner. I was in a quandary. I dithered for a good hour. At the end of which, the head spoke for a third and final time.

"*Time is past*, he said.

"His eyes rolled up and there was a burning smell. Heat radiated from the brazen head, greater and ever greater, until the metal did actually glow. I screamed and Bongay awoke.

"Is he aware? Bongay demanded. I must speak to him. There are things I must explain before—

"Then he saw how the head glowed and how the solder ran in little rivulets from the seams in its neck and with it the gold and silver of its circuitry. Then did the wizard Bongay himself scream, in such fury that I fled for fear of his wrath."

She laughed. "He lost tenure over that incident, and his life as well. That happened near the end of the fiscal year, and the University had been relying on that grant money. Everybody involved with that fiasco was executed by order of the Bursar."

"How did you survive?"

"They needed somebody to write the final report. *The Wizard Bongay, His Brazen Head and Fearsome Doom: Some Early Lessons Learned.* You may well have read it. But that was the incident that taught me. Never again was I so behindhand in my duties.

Vigilance, Ms Alderberry! That must ever be our watchword—vigilance!"

"I'm sure I could catch up. If only I had a little *hint* what I'm doing wrong."

"Good, good," Nemesis said. "I knew our little chat would help. Only remember that we all have quotas to keep. We can show no favoritism. In order to retain you, we must let some other deserving student go. Surviving the Teind, however good a scholar you may be, is a privilege, not a right." They had come to her office. She unlocked the door, stepped inside, and turned. "And remember also, that my door is always open."

She closed it in Jane's face.

⸻⸻◈⸻⸻

The undergraduate elevator from the classroom levels to the three floors collectively designated the Lady Habundia Residence for Female Scholars was crowded with several dozen chattering undergraduates, half of them with bicycles. Jane felt simultaneously inferior and superior to them. They were an unserious lot, most of them, and squandering their educations where she was studiously making the most of hers. On the other hand, there was no denying that they had fun and she largely did not.

A boom box came on. Riders began dancing to the skirl of elf-pipes and synthesizer. Two froudlings with greyhound-lean faces, theater majors as like as not, went into a choreographed sword fight, spinning and kicking, leaping and parrying blows from imaginary sabers. Off in a corner several willies had formed a study group. Notebooks passed from hand to hand.

The elevator operator was a potato woman, her brown face so bulgy and lopsided that her scowl was lost in its hilly contours. She opened the doors onto the dorm lobby, and the Habundians surged forward, giggling. The two duelists crouched in their midst, trying to sneak in.

The potato woman was having none of it, though. She snatched up a broom and drove into the crowd, laying about her right and left, smashing the boys on their heads and arms until blood flew. She was a whirlwind, cursing and forcing the two back into the elevator. With a triumphant cackle she clanged the gates shut.

Jane went to her room and dropped her books on her bed. Monkey was out as usual, but at this time of evening there was always a gathering of girls out on the balcony, playing cards and gossiping. Jane sat down at her desk, resolved to put in an hour's study before joining them.

She opened her Petrus Bonus and read: "Something closely analogous to the generation of alchemy is observed in the animal, vegetable, mineral, and elementary world. Nature generates frogs in the clouds, or by means of putrefaction in dust moistened with rain, by the ultimate disposition of kindred substances. Avicenna tells us—" She yawned, lost her place, found it again. "—tells us that a calf was generated in the clouds amid thunder, and reached the earth in a stupefied condition. The decomposition of a basilisk generates scorpions." Most of this was mere example-mongering, the establishment of authority by largesse of data. But there was no telling when a key concept might be dropped in the middle of a pageful of dross, so she had to read it all. "In the dead body of a calf are generated bees, wasps in the carcase of an ass, beetles in the flesh of a horse, and locusts in that of a mule." She skimmed over several more exemplars. "The same law holds good in the mineral world, though not to quite so great an extent."

Jane slammed shut the book and pushed back from her desk. This was too boring for words. She couldn't concentrate. Her stone was two weeks overdue, and she didn't think she could get another extension. Worse, somewhere along the line she was sure she had missed some basic concept, because with every class she could feel her understanding slipping steadily and inevitably behind. If she couldn't catch up fast, she was never going to catch up at all.

She needed a drink.

———◦◦◦———

A glorious sunset was smeared across the horizon, visible in the thin slits between the buildings of the Great Gray City, reflecting gold from the windows to the east. Sirin was there, feet up on the balustrade, showing off her fine long legs, and Raven, Nant, and Jenny Greenteeth as well with a near-full case of Frog City at their feet.

Jenny was throwing beer to the gryphons. She cocked her arm and flung an unopened can as far as she could. It caught the sun and glittered as it spun toward the unseen street.

Shrieking desperately, three gryphons plunged after the can.

The victor snapped it up in its beak. With a screech of tearing metal the can popped open. Beer gushed and fizzed. The gryphon hovered, wings working mightily, as it chewed and swallowed.

Gryphons, though they loved it dearly, had small tolerance for alcohol. Several of the creatures were plastered already, weaving erratically in the canyons between soaring stone high rises. One narrowly missed slamming into a walkway bridging two University buildings. Jane gasped.

Jenny laughed and belched and threw another can.

"Pull up a chair," Sirin said genially. "We were talking about things."

Jane leaned against the balustrade, staring into the endless stepped towers with their rounded shoulders, like so many termite mounds enchanted to monstrous size. Skywalks linked them in a complex web of relationships. Here and there specks of green marked balconies and rooftop gardens. The buildings were sufficient to the needs of their dwellers, with theaters and shops, hospitals and restaurants ringing their atria. It was possible— especially if you were a student—to go for weeks without ever seeing the street. Staring into the endless rows of windows, Jane felt a sense not of anonymity but of being one among millions, singular in a galaxy of singularities. She felt comfortable here, as she had no place else in her life. "What sort of things?"

"Anarchy and social justice."

"Gryphons' eggs."

"Boys."

Jane popped a beer, letting a little slop over onto the floor. She plopped down in an empty chair. Raven thrust a bowl of beetle crisps her way, but she shook her head. "I'm having trouble making a sophic hydrolith. I don't know what it is, maybe the pontic water isn't pure." The hydrolith was one-third of her final grade, but she carefully kept her tone of voice light. "Any of you guys know what I should do?"

"You're too tense," Sirin said airily. "Too serious. Too academic. You should go out and get laid more often."

"The world's got enough hydroliths anyway," Nant added. She was a black dwarf, and insanely politicized. "What it *needs* is a system of governance that's not simply the strong telling the weak what to do." She made the sign of the hammer with crossed forearms, not at all self-mockingly.

"That's not helpful, either of you."

"Oh well." Sirin stared upward and announced to the general

universe, "Chrysoberyl told me that Billy Bugaboo has three balls."

"What?!"

"As if she'd know."

"He does not! Does he?"

"Well, I'm going to find out soon," Sirin said. "Chrys promised to set me up with a date." She raised a butterfly chip from a cellophane bag in her lap and closed her perfect mouth about it.

"Watch this!" Jenny Greenteeth flung a can into a space precisely equidistant between two of the circling gryphons. In their eagerness, they crashed into each other, feathers flying. While they were fighting, yet another gryphon swooped down and snagged it with his talons. He sailed away, shaking his leg in a futile effort to free it from the can.

They all, Jane included, hooted with laughter.

Nant wanted to play canasta but Raven insisted on pinochle, so they eventually settled on hearts. Sirin won heavily. Jane got stuck with the black virgin and a short run of hearts three times running. "It's not your day," Sirin observed.

"No. It's not."

"Well, I don't know about you but I'm going to check out the action off-campus. There's a new place over in Senauden. Anybody coming with me?"

Nant nodded. Raven scowled and shook her head. Jenny Greenteeth impulsively threw the deck over the edge of the balcony. The wind caught the cards, spread them, and swept them away.

"Count me in," Jane said.

━━━◈━━━

The skywalk to Senauden Tower was located eighteen floors below Habundia. They crossed over and rode up another thirty-four floors to a new club Sirin had heard of called The Drowned Man. It was situated by the central elevator banks and the enamel gray steelplate walls trembled when the larger cars passed by. "It looks like a submarine," Jane said, eyeing the painted water pipes and exposed ducting overhead.

"Submarines aren't this crowded."

"Don't gawk," Sirin said. "We don't want anybody to think we're students."

Banks of televisions over the bar multiplied the aftermath of a bombing in Cockaigne. The images flickered in eerie sync with the toothache throb of the house band. They got a table and had a few drinks. A dwarf named Red Gwalch dropped by to make a perfunctory pass at Sirin and stayed to argue with Nant.

"I'm a hierarchist myself. It comes from being a dwarf— we're all conservative at heart." He stuck a cigarette in his mouth. "Some of us try to pretend otherwise. Not me."

"Oh, don't get her started," Sirin said.

But Nant rose to the bait. "More fool you, then! Hierarchies only work to the benefit of those on the top. If you're high, you'll get by. If you're low, out you go! That's how it is."

"So?" A match flared. A grin floated in the darkness. "What's your pain to me?"

"Sirin?" Jane reached forward to squeeze her friend's hand. "You've got to tell me what's wrong with my experimental set-up."

Sirin looked embarrassed. "Jane, it's something you're supposed to figure out for yourself. Working it out is part of the learning experience."

"But—"

"It's better this way. It really is."

"It's your pain too, or ought to be. Unless you're planning to be tall and elvish when you grow up?"

"Very cute. I've met your kind before."

"What kind is that?"

"Sirin—"

"I won't talk about it. I won't!"

"The kind who talks about dwarven history for hours, but wouldn't dream of dating one of her own kind."

"Don't let it bother you, little man. I'm sure you'll find somebody who'll overlook your . . . shortcomings."

"You're really a bitch, aren't you?" Red Gwalch dropped his cigarette on the floor, and ground it under one shiny Italian shoe. "I like that in a woman." He held out a hand and Nant accepted it. They walked out onto the dance floor and disappeared in the crush of bodies.

"That's the last we'll see of—" Sirin began.

The air crackled with premonition, and an elf in a tufted-silk suit materialized by their table. "Ladies." He had the sort of cultivated good looks that seemed striking face on and less pleasant the instant you looked away. "May I join you?" He slid into a chair, extended an arm. "Galiagante."

"Sirin."

"Jane."

When she touched his hand, Galiagante seized her fingertips and turned her hand over. He bowed low over it, lightly kissing her palm. Sirin hid a smile.

They hadn't been talking long when Nant came back to reclaim her purse. Red Gwalch waited for her by the door. She glanced nervously at him over her shoulder. "I'm going back to the dorm now."

"Sure you are," Sirin said kindly.

They all three watched her leave. "She didn't get much dancing in," Jane commented.

"I cannot blame her. This style of music is not made for dancing." When Galiagante smiled, his cheekbones shifted, as if something were crawling around under the skin. His eyes were feverishly bright. "Too young. However, I know a place where the music is soft and the dancing slow. If you don't mind a touch of travel . . ."

He slid a hand under Sirin's elbow and helped her to her feet.

———◈———

"Hey," Jane said. "This isn't the way to the elevators."

Galiagante smiled patiently. "The public cars are so crowded, aren't they? I'm sure we can do better than that." He led them to a small, tiled alcove, where a bank of unmarked elevators stood, and pushed the call button.

When a car arrived, its interior was small and dark, with black leather seats. A stolid dwarf in chauffeur's livery and cap stood at the controls. They piled in.

"Lac sans Oiseaux," Galiagante said.

Without even nodding, the dwarf slammed the doors shut. Jane's stomach lurched as the car fell. Galiagante shot a sleeve back to check the time and placed his arm across the seat behind Sirin's back, not quite touching. Sirin shifted slightly, accepting the arm, moving into it. His hand closed on her shoulder.

Jane was captivated. It was like a little dance between diplomats, an exchange of formalities ending in entente. The dwarf faced forward, watching the floors rise through a slit of glass. Galiagante's other arm reached out to encompass Jane as well, and this she did not like nearly so well.

"So," she said brightly. "What do you do? For a living, I mean."

"Do?" Galiagante sounded politely baffled. "I do nothing. I suppose that in the sense you mean rather than doing things I am things."

"Like what?"

"Oh, an investor, perhaps. An inheritor. Many, many stockholders. And you, Jane, just what is it that you—do?"

"Right now I'm trying to figure out why my experiments never work."

"You are a researcher?"

"We're students." She ignored Sirin's scowl. "Alchemy majors."

"Ahhh. I have interests in an alchemical firm or two. Perhaps I can help."

The elevator was going deep, deep, and yet it was still accelerating. The cables whined and sang in the background. They must surely have passed ground level long ago, and be speeding into the roots of the world. Jane described her problems with the sophic stone.

"We have a phenomenon very like that in industry," Galiagante said when she was done. "It's called green thumb syndrome. It sometimes occurs when a new plant establishes a complicated but known procedure for the first time. Your people set it up perfectly but nothing happens. The oxides won't reduce, the catalysts won't . . . cattle. Punishing the technicians accomplishes nothing. The reaction simply refuses to run. Eventually management will fly in somebody who's worked on the procedure before and have her run through it once. For *her* it will work. Then, ever afterward, it will work for the new plant. But that first time it must be run by somebody who is sure it will work, who knows it in the core of her being. It has something to do with quantum uncertainty events, I believe, though I wouldn't swear to it."

"Then I'm screwed. How can I make myself believe in an experiment I've seen fail five times in a row?" Sirin's attention was fixed on Galiagante; she never once looked at Jane.

"You can't. But surely there must be some way to outthink the set-up. Let's say that next time you run the experiment, you borrow glassware that's already been used for that purpose. Make sure you assemble it in the proper order—I doubt that identical glass tubes would be interchangeable—and it ought to work fine. You must have friends who'd be glad to lend you what you need. Perhaps you could trade new equipment for used."

"We're slowing to a stop," Sirin said.

In the foyer an ogre in a tuxedo barred their way, saying, "This is a closed floor, sir." Galiagante offhandedly flashed a gold card, and they were let by.

The first thing Jane realized about Lac sans Oiseaux was that while Sirin might be appropriately attired for the club—casually, but in keeping with the rest—she herself was not. It was a rich crowd, Teggish and better, and not a one of them was wearing jeans. Just being among them made her stomach hurt. When Galiagante got a table, Jane slumped down in her chair, trying to look inconspicuous.

Behind the bar was an enormous glass tank, lit by harsh fluorescents, where the rest of the club was bathed in red and purple. A horse was drowning in the tank. Legs churned up clouds of bubbles. Eyes bloodshot and wild, it craned its neck to lift agonized nostrils above the thrashing surface. It was excruciating to watch. The music was slow and romantic, but just loud enough that the horse struggled in silence.

Jane shifted her chair so she wouldn't have to see. Galiagante looked amused. A kobold brought them brandies and was dismissed. "Would you like some coke?"

"Of course we would," Jane said quickly, cutting off Sirin while she was still shaking her head.

Mirror women glided through the crowd, bearing trays. Because their surfaces reflected whatever was before them, Jane couldn't tell whether they were entirely naked or merely mostly so. They were angular singularities, warping reality with their passage, leaving it unchanged in their wake. Galiagante snapped his fingers, and one bent low over their table.

Light flashed from one chrome nipple as she offered the tray. Neat lines of powder were laid out ready to use. Galiagante laid his wallet on the table, and bent to snort up two, one per nostril. Sirin and Jane followed his example. He left several bills on the tray.

"Dance?"

Sirin accepted his arm and they moved out onto the floor.

The wallet had been left behind on the table. It sat in a pool of light, almost breathing it was so imbued with life. The leather was decorated with a skull-and-rose tattoo. This small gesture, leaving the wallet behind, impressed Jane greatly. It implied much about Galiagante's resources.

Casually, she glanced inside.

Elves were volatile. It would be madness to rip one off. It would take a suicidal amount of nerve. She sipped her drink. Sirin danced beautifully, of course, and Galiagante held her close, murmuring in her ear. Her features were fine and aristocratic, and seeing her among her own kind Jane realized for the first time that Sirin was surely one of the Tylwyth Teg herself.

The music was slow and, propelled by it, the two dancers were preternaturally graceful, like ice swans aglide on a pond. By degrees, though, Sirin's placid mood changed to distress. Her step faltered. She seemed to struggle against Galiagante's implacable grip.

Jane watched them thoughtfully.

When the dance ended, Sirin returned to the table and seized her purse. "I'm going to the power room. Are you coming, Jane?" There was a touch of demand in her last sentence.

"We won't be long," she threw over her shoulder.

Galiagante did not respond. He sat staring at the drowning horse, a small smile flickering like flame on his lips.

---

"Hold this for me." Sirin thrust her purse at Jane, and slammed into a toilet stall.

Jane leaned back against a sink, studying the line of stalls. From one came the sounds of somebody puking. Ruby heels showed in the space beneath the door. Jane went into the next stall and slid shut the bolt.

On the tiles by the vomiting elf-lady's knees was a beaded handbag. Slowly, carefully, Jane drew it closer with the toe of her shoe. Its owner was too involved in being sick to notice.

There was a lot of money in the handbag. Jane took it all, and returned the bag to the floor. Sirin's purse had considerably less, but what there was she took. She tore Sirin's public elevator pass into shreds. The pieces floated for a moment in the toilet bowl. She flushed them away.

When she emerged, Sirin was repairing her makeup in the mirror. Her face was ashen. She clutched Jane's arm fiercely.

"We've got to get out of here. Now."

"What are you talking about?"

"Galiagante. Jane, all the time we were dancing, he was talking to me, telling me things. Things that. Jane, you know me. I'm not a prude. But some of the things he said. About fishhooks and . . ." She stopped. "We've got to get out," she insisted.

"Of course we will. We'll leave right now."

———※———

They burst through the club's double doors and ran to the elevator bank. Sirin pushed the call button. She looked anxiously over her shoulder. Galiagante had not yet noticed that they were late returning from the john.

"There's a car coming. I can hear the cables."

"It can't come any too soon for me." Sirin took out her wallet and opened it. Her face twisted in dismay. "I don't have any money! We'll have to use the public—" She rummaged in her purse with growing panic. "Where's my *elevator pass?*"

"Take it easy, Sirin."

"We're trapped. Jane, you don't know what he wants me to do—what he wants both of us to do!"

"It's okay, Sirin. Really it is."

"You can't imagine. It's so . . ."

The elevator arrived, and a dwarf in livery—not the same one as earlier—scowled up at them. Jane shoved Sirin within, and snapped, "Skywalk level to Bellegarde. Step on it." To Sirin she said, "It's okay, I've got enough money to cover it. My treat."

Sirin collapsed, weeping, on her shoulder.

———※———

At Jane's insistence they didn't go directly back to the dorm but went to the Pub instead. The Pub was a student bar not many floors beneath Habundia. It was crowded and noisy and safe. Jane ordered a pitcher of beer, and Sirin knocked back three mugs one after the other.

Beer always made Sirin maudlin. "I'm so grateful to you. For the elevator, for getting me out of there. Jane, you can't imagine what you saved me from, what kinds of things he wanted to do."

"Don't even think of it. It's nothing."

"No, really. What would I have done without you? I'm in your debt. Anything you want, if I can do it—it's yours." She fell silent a moment and then a small, fey smile floated up to the surface. "Not that I wouldn't like to . . . someday. Only I don't think I was ready for it just yet."

Jane stared down into her mug, at the bubbles rising up through the beer, slowly at first and then with gathering speed. They shone like tiny galaxies, each bubble its own universe. She tipped the mug back and drank deep. I am become death, she thought, the destroyer of worlds. Aloud, she said, "That line of bullshit Galiagante gave me about green thumb syndrome won't work, will it? That was just so much noise."

"Well, it could work, I suppose. It just wouldn't be very practical."

"Then what's the secret?"

"Oh, Jane, I've given you enough hints. Please don't make me—"

"You said anything I want, right? I saved you, remember?"

"Yes, but I didn't know you'd ask me something like *this*. It's simply not permitted. It's—"

"Hush." Jane stroked Sirin's hand, touched her knees under the table with her own. Gazing deep into those unfocused eyes, she murmured, "You're very beautiful."

"What?"

Jane was hardly drunk at all and she understood that to communicate with somebody who was required broad gestures, ruthless simplification, bright primary colors. Touching foreheads, she whispered, "Come on, Sirin, I'd do it for you. I'm your friend, aren't I? You can trust me. Give."

Sirin blushed and stared down at their mingled hands. "I cheat. I cook the results."

Jane continued caressing her fingers. She felt a little dirty doing this, but it wasn't as if she had any other options. "Tell me how."

Sirin's eyes blurred and turned a milky white, the pupils and irises breaking into tiny motes and dissolving to nothing. In a husky voice that was not her own, she said, "Do you know the distinction between exoteric and esoteric alchemy?" Jane shook her head. "Everything you've been doing, all the lab work, all the p-alk and organic alike, is exoteric—concerned with the transmutation of matter. It is the outer tradition. Are you following this?"

"Yes."

"Esoteric alchemy is the inner tradition. It's the other side of the coin. There aren't any classes for esoteric alchemy, but a researcher must necessarily learn it on her own. Esoteric alchemy is concerned with the transmutation of the spirit. This can be accomplished in many ways—through pain or terror or monastic discipline, for example—but is most easily achieved through the measured application of sex."

"Tell me how it works. The practical side of it."

Sirin's voice had by degrees hardened and deepened. It was no longer a female voice. "The procedure has two parts."

"Two parts."

"The first part is esoteric. It involves sex. While you're fucking, you must visualize the experiment, start to finish, step by step. If your familiar comes before you're done, you must start over again."

She could not free herself from Sirin's cold hands. A numbing energy flowed up her arms and down her spine, returning to Sirin where their knees touched. It was mesmerizing. The table faded away underneath her, and the chair she was sitting on. There was nothing in all the universe but the voice and the resonant circuit of Sirin and herself.

"The second part is exoteric. When you assemble the experiment and as you run it, picture what you were doing as you imaged it in the first part. Where you held your familiar, how you felt. This will create a feedback loop. You will find yourself growing aroused. For purely social reasons it will be best if you hide this aspect of your work.

"Creation of the sophic stone is entry-level sex magick. As you advance in exoteric learning you will need to acquire more sophisticated esoteric skills. But for now your simple animal drives will suffice."

Out of nowhere, it seemed, a window had been opened into Jane's world, and the alien landscapes it revealed made no sense to her at all. How could it be, she wondered. How could the one affect the other? Where and by what mechanism did they connect?

She recalled a bright summer day, cloudless and without shadow, so immediate that the air felt like a membrane stretched over the yolk of an egg, full to bursting. One prick of a fork and the other side would come spilling out to fill all the world. She was sure then that the seen world was only surface, that deeper and darker things lurked beneath the surfaces, whales sounding under the sidewalks, faces larger than worlds mugging behind the sky.

Jane felt close to something basic, so close that she could almost touch it, taste it, feel it. She was trying to frame a question when the power behind Sirin's words spoke again.

"You've been flirting with great mysteries. Watch that they do not crush you." Sirin's eyes fluttered open and in her normal voice she said, "I feel sick."

Like a tide ebbing the alien presence withdrew. Once again the bar closed about her, as real as a packing crate and as confining.

Jane refilled her mug. When it was empty, she poured another. At some point she looked up and Sirin was gone. There was a pleasant-faced nondescript talking to her. She vaguely recalled him introducing himself as Jake Shake-stick. He was telling a joke. She couldn't follow it, but she was pretty sure she'd be able to guess when she was supposed to laugh. It looked as if she were on her own, to make whatever decision she would.

There was a hopeful smirk in the corner of Jake's mouth.

Well, she thought, as well him as another. Anyway, she'd been chanting the birth control spell faithfully every day without fail for over a year.

It seemed a pity to let it go to waste.

Two days later she ran the experiment again. This time it worked perfectly.

# THIRTEEN

Jane caught Billy Bugaboo's last spurt of semen on a watch glass, then drew up a measured amount in a Sahli pipette. "Ahhh." She diluted it with saline solution and rocked the pipette to mix the two. Then she let a drop fall into the chamber of a cytometer, slapped on a cover slip, and clipped it onto the microscope stage. "Let's see what the omens are."

Billy rolled over and watched as she pulled up her jeans and panties and bent over the microscope. The sheets rustled mournfully.

"I can't figure you out."

"You're not supposed to."

Without removing her eye from the microscope, Jane groped for her brassiere. She snapped it around her stomach then twisted it right side around, straightening momentarily to fit herself into it. Her blouse was draped across the same chairback as the brassiere had been. "Make yourself useful and button me up," she said. Billy obeyed.

"I know you've got other guys. Are you like this with them too, or is it just me?"

"My roommate's due back from class any minute now," Jane said coldly. "Time you got dressed, stud-muffin."

With a sigh, Billy groped under the bed for his trousers. One at a time, he folded and unfolded his legs like a stork to fit them in. He was of a rarefied type, rawboned and spindle-shanked as a scarecrow. Sitting, his head reached almost to the ceiling. Standing, he stooped.

The door rattled in its frame, then boomed as it was struck by angry fists. "That's probably her now. Get the dead bolt, why don't you?"

Before Billy could reach the door, though, the transom pushed open. Monkey came clambering through. Impulsively, he seized her under the arms and, swinging her around like a doll, set her atop her own desk. She stood there, face darkening like a fireplace coal. Billy grinned a snaggle-toothed welcome at her that curled around either side of his face. It was at times like this, when he was at his most amiable, that he looked the most grotesque. Monkey scowled past him at Jane.

"What the fuck do you think you're doing, locking me out of my own fucking room?"

The signifiers in the slide were not good. Then again, Teind year omens never were. If you tested a sample—a clipping of hair, urine, horn scrapings, anything—in a spectrophotometer, the resulting spectrum inevitably showed a thick black bar marking the Teind's approach. Even if you survived the winnowing yourself, odds were you'd lose somebody close to you. "I was preparing a slide," she muttered distractedly. Billy buckled his belt and hastily buttoned his shirt. "Couldn't have you bursting in, right in the middle of things, now could I?" Technically, she wasn't supposed to be applying esoteric techniques to Intermediate Scrying, but doing so would save her countless hours staring into a pool of ink or poring over goat entrails.

"You've been getting mighty pushy lately, Miss Do-What-I-Will Alderberry." Monkey hopped down from the table. "I don't recall giving you permission to use my room for any fucking private assignations."

"Uh, listen, I gotta go now, I'm kind of late. For a class." Billy bundled his shoes and socks under one arm. Bobbing awkwardly, he backed out of the room, a leaf before a storm. " 'Bye."

The secret to successful scrying was to realize that the future was not fixed and there was no way of predicting it. None. All one could do was to identify what already existed unacknowledged. Lovers pledged themselves to each other long before their first kiss. Murder was implicit in friendship. A carcinoma that looked like a speck of dust on the X-ray spelled death. So much of what appeared to be random event was simply the working out of consequences. Jane began jotting down her observations in her lab book.

Monkey snatched the pencil from her hand and snapped it in two.

Jane closed her eyes and traced the sigil of Baphomet with her inner vision. When she was calm again, she slid open a drawer.

"All right." There was a pair of latex gloves within. "I wasn't going to do this." She pulled them on. "But you don't exactly give me much choice, do you?"

Credit where credit is due, Monkey didn't back down. There was a touch of the trickster in her heritage, and the trickster gene was a dominant. She licked her lips nervously as Jane pretended to lift an invisible box from the drawer. "You don't scare me."

"Good." Jane swung a hinged lid back and reached within. "It works best if you don't believe." She removed an equally imaginary scalpel and held it up between thumb and forefinger, admiringly turning it one way and the other.

"What are you going to do with that?"

Jane smiled. *"This!"*

She slammed her fist into Monkey's stomach. The small goblin doubled over in pain and Jane was on top of her, ignoring her shrieks and forcing her down on the floor. She yanked Monkey's blouse up over her head and removed from a pocket a small bladder she had prepared for just this occasion. "A little higher," she said, jabbing stiff forefingers into the exposed abdomen. "There!"

She crushed the bladder.

Blood gushed. A dark crimson stain spread over Monkey's crotch and belly. Jane stepped back, the broken bladder in her hand. It looked for all the world like a scrap of body tissue. Monkey struggled up, tugging down her blouse, just as Jane popped it in her mouth. Jane chewed and swallowed.

It was done.

With swift efficiency then, Jane put away the scalpel in its box and returned both to the drawer and oblivion. She stripped off the gloves and threw them in the wastebasket. She was done. Leaning back against her desk, she waited to see if her roommate had bought it.

Monkey came to her feet. "What the fuck did you just do?"

"Hopefully, I bought myself a little peace and quiet."

"You don't fool me—that was just sleight of hand."

"Believe what you will."

Picking up a heavy stapler, Monkey advanced on her. "Suppose I hit you over the head with this, huh? I'll bet you anything it would hurt you more than it would me."

"There's only one way to find out."

Monkey chewed her lip indecisively. Then, with disgust, she

threw the stapler to the floor and herself into a chair. "Shit." She was all fists-and-eyes with rage. Then, abruptly, all tension left her body and she chuckled to herself. With elaborate casualness she said, "I met an old friend of yours today."

"Now that," Jane said, "is what I call a truly stunning non sequitur." Rubbing a speck of blood from her chin, she went back to her microscope. But try as she would, she could not ignore Monkey's remark. It niggled in her brain. Finally she sighed and added, "Who was it?"

"That's for me to know and you to find out."

Monkey's voice was gleeful, mocking, triumphant. Without taking her eyes from Jane, she lifted one corner of her blood-stained blouse and began to suck on the cloth.

━━●━━

Jane spent a long hour staring at the flimsy before she set out. The yellow paper was already fading at the creases where she'd folded it. Bad news always came on the cheap, in gray print with the proper names and specifics badly typed in third-generation carbon capital letters that floated slightly above the line. She'd read and reread the thing a dozen times since receiving it yesterday.

To: Magister/Mistress ALDERBRERY
From: Office of Penitence and Truth, Division of Financial Assistance

In these times of fiscal austerity, it is necessary that we all do what we can to reduce or eliminate all such expenses as will not adversely affect the quality of your education. Thus, as a cost-cutting measure, we are eliminating such portions of your MERIT SCHOLARSHIP as are covered by this office. We know that you join with us in wishing the University a swift recovery from its temporary financial woes, and strongly encourage you to investigate the many means open to you of financing your education through the private sector. A schedule of your obligations will be posted to you in THREE WEEKS.

Jane's anger was long gone. She read the flimsy only to drain it of power, to purge herself of the last traces of emotionality, to ensure that she did what she had to calmly and alertly. Then it was time.

The University library opened its doors at midnight and closed at dawn. The rationale given for such extraordinary hours was that they discouraged dilettantes and idlers from wasting the library's facilities. Jane suspected darker motives were at work, but this once she was just as glad for the privacy of its empty halls and echoing rooms. By side passages and wrought iron spiral stairways, she traced a labyrinthine path to the more obscure reaches of the collected lore.

To make the most of limited floor area, the older stacks were fitted with electric bookshelves. Only one pair in ten had an aisle's worth of space between them; the others were all pushed together like old furniture in a storage room. Jane walked alongside them, reading the placards, until she came to the one she wanted and flicked a switch on the side of the shelf. A hidden motor hummed to life. Slowly, clumsily, the other shelves huddled away from Jane's, closing the existing aisle and making a new one where she wanted it.

The books were all old and browning. Some were held together with string or with rubber bands so ancient they broke when they were touched but did not fall away for they had over the decades melted onto the book covers. The more valuable were preserved in folded acid-free cardboard containers carefully cinched with ribbons. Even these, though, were rotting at the core, falling away in flakes, inexorably oxidizing, as were all the books, in a process so pervasive that Jane could smell it, an autumnal haze that clung to the stacks like smoke from a distant grass fire. They were all, without exception, dying by degrees.

So it was with no sense of violation whatsoever that Jane used a razor blade to slice the security strip from the spine of one particular volume.

———◈———

Her contact met her by the main elevator bank. He was wearing a shabby brown leather flight jacket with patches from the Broceliande campaign, old jeans, and older boots. "Puck Aleshire," he said. "You got the thing?"

"In my purse."

"Then let's go."

Puck, as it turned out, was the control from Jane's Comp-and-Spec class. His eyes were dark, overserious, all but unblinking. To make him smile, Jane said, "The last time I saw you, you were naked and standing next to a corpse."

He looked at her, said nothing.

In silence they went up ten floors and across a skywalk to Hindfell, where they caught a clanky public elevator down to street level. "Why couldn't we just go down to the ground floor and out from our own lobby?" Jane wondered.

"That's Crip territory. You really don't know anything if you want to hit Crip turf at night."

"Oh."

Hindfell's lobby was bleak and vacant. The store windows had been emptied for the night and a lone dwarf in doorman's red stood yawning and oblivious to their passage. A sheet of newspaper spread its wings and leaped at Jane when Puck opened the door, but was caught by a crosswind and flew sideways into a wall. She clutched her parka tighter about her.

They stepped out into a dark and fearsome emptiness. Streetlights struggled in vain to reach the ground. Neon reflected blurrily from the rain-slicked asphalt. The air echoed with the growls of unseen behemoths and the ugly yak-yakking laughter of streetcorner gnomes in a nearby bar. Somewhere a door swung open, releasing a snatch of music, then, closing again, swallowed it back. Nobody was out on the street.

Jane had to scurry to keep up with Puck's long stride. "You're a rude one," she remarked.

"And you're a rich bitch."

"What?"

"You heard me. I know your kind, with your prep school attitudes and your down-filled quilted parkas. Laughing at the likes of me because the arms of my jacket are pulling apart at the seams and I have to take whatever work comes to hand. Well, let me tell you something. There are worse ways to make money than by standing naked next to a corpse, as you so charmingly put it. And what money I *do* make goes to pay for my education, not because I want a little extra pixie dust to shove up my nose."

"I never—"

"Sure, sure." Puck's anger burned down as quickly as it had flared up. He hunkered his head. "Forget I said anything. No business of mine anyway." The signs glowed bright over the stores they passed—AMBROSIUS, GRANDFATHER TROUT, GNOMOLOGICA, THREE SILK SHOES—but the shops themselves were all dark as caves behind their locked security grates. "Here we are."

Their destination was a stone mansion with gabled roofs and terra-cotta trim. It was squeezed between two skyscrapers, a lone revenant of a bygone era. Graffiti disfigured the first floor. Five empty beer bottles huddled in the shelter of the steps. "She's expecting us," Puck said. He knocked.

The door opened.

Within was one vast room, cold and unlit. The interior walls had all been ripped out. In the dim light from the street Jane glimpsed distant brick, scorch marks, a rotting mattress, and a sarsen stone twice her height. The stone stood not far from a tiled fireplace.

The door closed, immersing them in blackness.

With a sudden spasm of panic, Jane realized just how thoroughly she was at Puck's mercy. Anything could happen to her here. She wondered how she could have been fool enough to put herself in this position.

"It's not usually this bad," Puck muttered. "Shit." A soda bottle rattled and rolled away from his boot tip. "*Hey*, you old dingbat! We're here—turn on the fucking lights!"

The lightlessness intensified odors, the rots and mildews from mattress and wallpaper, the smell of charred wood, and beneath them all a pervasive ophidian stench. Could there be snakes living in this ruin? Jane fervently hoped not.

"One second, please."

The flat, sexless voice came from the heart of the living darkness. There was a metallic clank, the smell of kerosene, the *skritch* of a sulfur match. Light flared, dazzled, resolved into a lantern. It hung in midair, suspended from a scrawny brown hand. The sarsen stone's shadow leaned toward them and then away.

"You may advance now into our presence."

Behind the lantern, where Jane had to squint to see, floated the ghost of a face. Parchment skin stretched over a fleshless skull. It was the mask of a crone, high forehead, heavy lids housing shadow. Aeons of weariness nested in the corners of those eyes. She wore a black turtleneck so that her upper body could only be inferred and not seen; of her body below the waist Jane could make out nothing. A lipless mouth moved, said: "Where is it?"

The expression that spread across that face as Jane removed the book from her purse was as lean and hungry as a candle flame.

She stretched out a hand.

Jane put the offering in it.

The creature raised the book to her nose and sniffed. She riffled it open, tore out three pages, and stuffed them in her mouth. Sourly, she chewed. Skipping forward, she hesitated over another page, then decisively tore it out and ate it as well. Finally she ripped a page from the index. When her mouth was empty again, she returned the book to Jane. "The rest is of no interest to me." The brown hand disappeared, reappeared with an envelope. "Here is your quittance. I trust it is sufficient."

Jane stuffed the envelope unopened into her purse. She hesitated, then asked, "Why are you doing this?"

"Those pages contained a name. One I wish forgotten."

"But why did you eat them?"

"I am destroying my past."

"But why?"

With a dry rustle, as of silks on marble, the face floated nearer her. The mouth hung open in a parody of despair, tightened into a determination that was truly frightening. "I smell iron, cold iron, hard fate, and betrayal." She jerked the lantern into Jane's face. "You are not one of my children! What are you doing here?"

Jane shrugged, frightened.

The lantern withdrew. "It does not matter. Sit down by the hearth, and I will tell you all."

Shadows leaped as she thrust the lantern into the empty fireplace. From nowhere she produced two small chairs. "Fucking waste of time," Puck grumbled as he and Jane settled uncomfortably down on them. A cold breeze gusted from the chimney's throat without throwing up any soot. It had been a long time since fire had dwelt therein.

Their hostess did not sit.

"Things are not as they were," she said. "I ask you to picture an age when there were no dwellings taller than a long spear, no machines more complex than a loom, no calendars but the Moon herself. It was a time when all women lived in harmony."

Puck snorted.

"What about the men?" Jane asked.

"There were no men. We had not invented them yet." The face twisted toward the sarsen stone. The stone reflected no light but drank it all in, a looming darkness within the darkness. "That was my sin, in fact, the separation of women into male and female. It was the first sin and the most hideous, for it was that which set the Wheel in motion."

A cabinet door clicked open and she removed a cut glass decanter and poured herself a drink. She tonged ice from a bucket, then replaced its lid. Gracefully she glided to the sarsen stone and with a slithering sound circled it three times. Each time her face and hands reappeared, they had risen higher in the gloom. "I was powerful then, yes, and beautiful beyond your imagining, as fair and pale as Lady Death. We had no rulers in that long ago age, nor any authority other than the honor of old age, but my standing was great among the mighty, and for my accomplishments the Council of Seven made me their Lamia."

She waited until Jane said, "I don't know what a lamia is."

A rustle like dried newspapers. The face rose yet higher. "It was a very great title, child. And a great responsibility. For we controlled such sorceries then as this sad and disenchanted age cannot even remember. With these two hands"—she held them palms upward—"I could command the mountains to open and the seas to part. I summoned stars to the surface of the earth, that I might walk and converse with them and so learn.

"Nobody died in those days. There was no need for it."

With a rattle and a sizzle, an electric heater came on by Jane's feet. Startled, she stared down at it. The heating elements glowed in red circles, casting a dull crimson light upon the wall. A stain in the wallpaper shrank away to nothing. She had missed a few words.

"—did not listen to it at first. It was just an idle fancy, a voice in the back of my head."

One side of Jane's body was cold and the other overly warm. The smell of kerosene was overwhelming. The lantern flickered and the sarsen stone seemed to flare, as if it were sprouting gray butterfly wings. In Jane's swimming vision it wavered between two irreconcilable forms, between monolith and two-bladed ax head.

A great weariness settled over Jane. "It seemed impossible to me that evil should come of so simple an idea," the Lamia said. Jane was finding it hard to follow the meaning of what was being said. She yawned, pinched the corners of her eyes, shook her head. By slow degrees the quietly monotonous voice lulled her into a half-dreaming state where it seemed to her that all the room dissolved to nothing, leaving only the sarsen stone unchanged.

In her imaginings, Jane was standing on a bright plain, and the Lamia had grown young again. From the waist down she was a serpent. Her coils wrapped three times around the stone. But so beautiful was she, so innocently naked and sweet smelling, that Jane was not at all frightened. The scales were bright as jade. They glittered in the sun. Her eyes were green and unblinking.

"Where am I?" Jane asked.

From above the Lamia said, "This is the Omphalos, the un-turning pivot. All the world revolves about it. The farther from the center you go, the faster and less tolerable the motion becomes. The easier it is to fall. Look about you."

Jane looked. To every side the world fell away from the sarsen stone. She could see to its very end. Highways ran like threads to cities laid out in perfect miniature, and beyond them were mountains, oceans, and ice. It was just like the plaster-and-lichen tableaux the sophomore geomancers put together every year to illustrate such themes as Electricity in the Service of Industry or Allegory Enlightening the Masses. "It's round!" she cried. "The world is round!"

"It is round because it is only an illusion. The world does not exist—not in any important sense—and so it takes on the shape of change." Now the disk was turning, slowly but visibly spinning under the cloud-studded bowl of the sky. "This is change made visible—what the wise call the Wheel. You are seeing existence now as the Goddess herself sees it." Jane was beginning to feel dizzy. Quickly she shifted her vision down from the horizon. Still her stomach felt queasy.

The Lamia's voice grew wild and visionary. "It was I who set the Wheel in motion, through my pride and folly, and so I was punished, condemned that my children should walk on two legs, condemned to be scorned and disbelieved by my descendants, condemned cruelest of all to immortality, so that I might see the consequences of my deed." The lands spun faster. Jane staggered, caught her balance. "As a mercy only slightly less cruel than the punishment itself, I have been promised that some day, when I have destroyed the last trace of my existence, I shall be granted surcease. But that day is long, long in coming."

Winds shrieked up from the spinning lands. "Meanwhile, the Wheel turns. The humble are exalted and the mighty are humbled. The best are inevitably defeated, and the scum always rises to the top. Here is the source of all the world's pain, that restless turning, ever accelerating, always bringing us around again to where we were before, but older, changed, scarred, and sorrowful. Had I only known the identity of the whisperer, I would never have listened. The Wheel would not have been set in motion."

Jane squeezed tight her eyes. Her head whirled. She staggered a step closer to the stone and sank to her knees to keep from falling. "Whose was the voice?" she cried. "Who tempted you?"

"Who indeed? Who was it who punished me for listening to her? Who determined to set the Wheel in motion and decided the guilt for it should be mine? They are one and the same."

"Who?"

The Lamia's voice grew very calm.

"Why, the Goddess, of course. Who else would dare?"

Jane reached out to steady herself against the stone. The instant her fingers touched it, the swirling stopped. Her dizziness was gone. Her eyes snapped open, and she stared up at the Lamia. Up past the perfect geometries of her coils. Past the languid swell and curve of her abdomen. The coral halos surrounding her nipples. Into the universe of her irises, the black holes of her pupils.

The Lamia smiled. It was a warm and confident smile, one that burned from the very center of her being. "You want me."

"Yes," Jane said wonderingly. She had never felt particularly drawn to her own sex before this. Boys had always seemed more interesting. But there was a compellingly androgynous quality to the Lamia, as if she were all that Jane found attractive in the male sex and feminine as well.

"Then kiss me."

The Lamia lowered her mouth toward Jane. Her lips parted moistly to reveal a pink glimpse of tongue. Heart fluttering like a bird between two hands, Jane yearned helplessly upward toward it.

*"None of that, douchebag!"*

Puck seized Jane by the shoulders and pulled. She stumbled over an ottoman and fell backward onto the floor.

The Lamia had grown old again, old and repulsive. A look of mild regret flickered on the mask of her face for the briefest instant and was gone. She folded her arms, making her hands disappear.

"We're leaving," Puck said firmly.

"I'll turn on the lights for you."

"Don't bother yourself."

Puck hauled Jane to her feet and steered her out of the room. While she dreamed, the mansion had healed itself. The interior walls had been restored, and were covered with flocked paper. They passed through rooms that were genteelly carpeted and comfortably furnished. In the hall, frosted glass sconces gently lit their way. The beer bottles were gone from the stoop when they emerged. The graffiti had been reabsorbed into the stone.

"She's crazy as shit," Puck said when they were back on the street. "All those nutty stories. This stunt tops them all, though. If I didn't need the money so bad I'd—" He made a disgusted noise. Without slowing his pace, he shook open and donned a pair of aviator glasses. Neon rainbows slid across their black glass surfaces. They made him look sinister, insectoid. He should have been blind in them this late at night, but his step was sure and unfaltering.

"What was she trying to do?" Jane asked hesitantly. She was still a little dazed, unsure which was real—the world as she saw it now or as it had been revealed to her in the Lamia's vision.

It was late enough that the grigs and gaunts were out in force, rising up from the subway vents, service tunnels, and storm sewers, forming small cliques by the lampposts, watching the action from doorways. A wolf-boy stared at Jane, chewing on a finger. He spat out a knucklebone as they went past. "You don't know?" Puck said. "She was going to—"

"Hey, college boy!" A behemoth slowed to a stop beside them and a grizzled old troll leaned his head out of the cab. He leered down at them, revealing brown teeth and hideous gums. "How come they ain't kicked you out yet?" He looked at Jane. "See ya got a new girlfriend."

"Wicked Tom." Puck's grin was wary, insincere. "What's the good word?"

They slapped hands and Jane caught a glimpse of a small plastic-wrapped package before it disappeared into her escort's pocket. The troll ran a hand over his brown-spotted head and in a lowered voice said, "Rumor is the bane has hit the street."

Puck took a step back from the curb. "Oh no. I'm not touching that shit."

"Nobody's asking ya to touch nothing," Wicked Tom said irritably.

"Just find yourself somebody else."

"Okay, okay."

"I'm not in that business."

"No? Well, too bad. There's good money in it."

The behemoth snorted impatiently, and Wicked Tom disengaged the clutch and revved the engine to keep it in line. He winked at Jane. "Gotta go now—keep in touch, hear?"

When the behemoth was gone, Jane asked, "What's the bane?"

"Bad news. Don't get involved with it."

In silence they returned to Hindfell and across the skywalk to Bellegarde. As Puck was turning away at the elevator banks, Jane said, "There's something I want to make clear. I am not a rich bitch, as *you* so charmingly put it."

It took Puck a second to remember his earlier comment. When he did, he scowled. "Hey, I said I was sorry."

"You listen to me! I'm here on scholarship, okay? I don't have any other source of income. No patrons, no job, no savings, no nothing. Only my scholarship, and the University just took that away. So what ebbs, must flow. The money's got to come from *some*where."

"But your clothes—"

"I stole them. These clothes are nice because if you're going to steal something, you might as well make it the best, right? So I just wanted you to know. I'm not rich or anything. I'm just doing my best to get by."

"Hey, me too." Puck sounded amazed. "I mean, I'm not necessarily scholarship material, but my education means a lot to me. I'm going to the College of Pharmacology. I'm only going through all this crap to pay for it."

"So okay. We understand each other now." Jane started to turn away. She was trembling a little, though whether from anger or the aftershock of fear, she did not know.

But Puck lingered. "Um, listen. Maybe you'd like to go out sometime? We could go dancing, maybe." He saw her begin to shake her head, and lightly rapped his forehead with his knuckles. "What an idiot—I haven't charmed you yet." He dug about in his pockets, slapping his jeans, thrusting hands deep into his jacket. "You'll love this, it's as close to a foolproof charm as was ever made. If I can only—Ah. Here it is." From his jacket he removed the ghost of a rose. The petals were a red deeper than blood, with purple highlights. It was faintly but noticeably transparent.

Bowing deeply, he presented it to her.

When her fingers closed about the stem, the rose faded to nothing. And Puck was right. Jane was charmed.

"So how about it?"

He pocketed his shades and stared deep into her eyes. There was no mistaking his sincerity. Against her better judgment, Jane found herself liking Puck. There was solid stuff beneath his rough exterior. More than that, she felt enormously drawn to him. Something within her vibrated to his presence.

"No," she said.

Jane was still a little stoned when she got back to her room from Jenny Greenteeth's study party. The radiator hissed and rattled, blowing little spit-bubbles from the air vent.

It was a cold autumn afternoon. The City looked dull and inert through the window. Off in the distance, iron-dark anvil heads billowed. Black specks moved before them, storm hags in flight. A few leathery oak leaves, lofted high by who knew what winds, stuck wetly to the glass.

Jane ratcheted the curtains shut and in the subdued light undressed herself. Monkey was away on a field trip and would not return until late tomorrow. She lay down on her bed and began to touch herself, unhurriedly caressing her breasts, running her palm down her belly. At first she thought about Puck, and then she thought about nothing at all.

She lazily stared down between her breasts, past the swelling plain of her belly. Luxuriant hair grew thickly upon the round hill of her pubic mound. Sometimes she liked to imagine it was a forest and she the most diminutive of explorers, wandering through it. Her fingers slipped down to the opening of her labyrinth, felt moistness, and lingered. It was an enchanted forest, and silent. Not even birds sang in the branches. She wandered it, gazing about in wonder. Her fingers moved a little more quickly. Everything was hushed, expectant, waiting. Her fingers slowed. They began to tease out her clitoris. Far ahead there was a rise. In no hurry at all, by roundabout forest paths, she approached it.

Simultaneous with her fantasy, Jane was aware of the dorm room about her, of the bed beneath and the ceiling above. As she played with her button, she felt as though she were rising, the bed shooting up under her with gathering speed, rocketing straight into the sky. The room fell away, the University and the City and all its buildings crumbling and falling down, farther and farther.

The ceiling throbbed and spread out, thinning and attenuating. The first stars of evening appeared through its vanishing haze. They multiplied and thickened. Jane gasped and writhed on the bed. The sheets were bunching up underneath her. Faster now. The sky purpled.

She was soaring.

With a heightened sense of expectation, she began running up the slope. Trees flew by to either side. Faster and faster, in time to the urgent movement of her fingers, she ran, one with the Jane who, worlds away, was rocketing into the sky. She topped the rise and stared in wonder and disbelief.

There was a cottage below.

It was a low house, white, and alien in design, and though surely she could never have seen such a building, it was as familiar to her as a recurrent dream. An outbuilding abutted it, windowless but with a door that filled one wall. A short road, wide as it was, led to that door. On the roof was what must have been a television antenna, for it lacked the warding hexes a lightning rod would have had.

Entranced, Jane followed a slow, winding path to the back door. It opened with a push, and she stepped into the kitchen. Heartbreakingly familiar smells wrapped themselves around her.

A woman was there, and while reason said she must be a total stranger, yet something leaped up happily within Jane at the sight of her. She sat at a Formicatopped table, hunched despondently, head down. A bottle of whiskey and a half-filled glass stood by one elbow, an ashtray by the other.

Jane tiptoed inside, afraid to speak, compelled to draw closer. The woman—her hair was dark, cut midlength and curly—did not hear.

Jane touched her elbow. "Mom?"

With a little shriek, her mother looked up.

# FOURTEEN

Monkey had gotten into Jane's secret cache. She kept it in a cardboard box under her bed with a layer of old pantyhose on top as camouflage. Monkey had hauled it out, dumped its contents on the floor, and pawed through them. Furious, Jane began to pick them up. There was the book she had stolen for the Lamia and which she intended to return to the library someday soon, the bundle of credit cards and ID she'd lifted from Galiagante's wallet, the pipe, hashish, and baby oil she kept in reserve for when she had the time and privacy for them, and a few cherished oddments from her days with Peter and Gwen. Nothing was missing. Monkey had been snooping for information.

There was nothing in the box that would reveal its secrets to Monkey. Jane kept her things hidden not because she feared their discovery but because they had meaning for her and she didn't want anybody running their grubby mitts over them.

Even in her anger, though, Jane felt uneasy. Something was up. Monkey was planning mischief. Jane knew how her roommate's mind worked—this was a message.

There was a burst of laughter in the hall. The other Habundians were decorating their doors with kteis-wreaths in honor of the season. Later they would tear a hog's carcass apart and sprinkle its blood on all the lintels. Jane wasn't going to join them. Her mood was too dark these days for such simple pleasures. The dark and the cold had sunk their talons deep into her spirit. She had never known a winter to last so long.

She drew the shade, shucked her clothes, poured the baby oil down her front, and smeared it about. On her third match she managed to fire up the hash pipe. In her distracted state it took almost an hour before she could transport herself Elsewhere.

———◉———

"Tell me something about yourself." Jane caught up with her mother walking along a river bank at dusk. She clasped her hands awkwardly behind her back. Her mother strode along with her arms folded. Neither dared to reach for the other.

"Well . . . I'm a beautician. Frank and I finally broke up seven years ago. Now I mostly live alone." She laughed raggedly. "It doesn't sound like much when it's put that way, does it? I do some volunteer work at the hospital."

"Oh, Mom." She stared down at the stones passing underfoot, at the lines of driftwood and crack vials and plastic drink containers that marked the limits of the gentle upriver tides. She wanted to ask her mother so many things: How did you feel when I disappeared? What did you think happened? Did you search for me, and where did you search, and when did you finally give up? Somehow, though, she wasn't able to ask any of these things. They just never seemed to connect.

"Is that a new blouse?" her mother asked suddenly.

"What's wrong with it?"

"Nothing's wrong with it. Why does something always have to be wrong? Only, don't you think it's a little plain? You could look so nice if you only took a little more care with your dress and your makeup. You have the bone structure for it."

"Look, I have plenty of boyfriends, I'm not exactly lacking for attention, okay? So let's not get started on the makeup again."

A sharp tone entered her mother's voice. "You aren't letting them take advantage of you, are you? That's the one thing I regret, that I didn't save myself for my wedding night. Don't you look at me like that. If you let them do what they want with you, they don't respect you afterward. Even your father. I'm convinced that if only—well, never you mind."

A tanker, mysterious in the dim light, was off-loading oil across the river. They stopped to look at it. "Mom, I've been thinking. Maybe you shouldn't drink so much."

Her mother stared at the ship, said nothing.

"Listen, Mom. I don't think I'm going to be able to see you for a while. Exams are coming up. I'm going to be awfully busy. I might not be able to visit again until the winter's over. Sometime in the spring."

Her mother shook her head, still not listening. "These dreams are so comforting to me," she said. "You have no idea. Even though I know they're not real, still I somehow feel that on some level they are. I'm afraid I'm not making myself very clear."

"They're not dreams, Mom."

"Hush, Jane."

"Someday I'll be here for real. I'm working on it now, learning all I can. Someday I'll be coming home."

"Don't." Softly, Jane's mother began to cry. "Don't, oh, don't. Don't do this to me."

Jane felt an indescribable outwelling of love and guilt gush up within her then. Without thinking, she reached for her mother and knocked over the bottle of baby oil. The cap went flying across the room, and the oil made such a mess that it took her hours to clean it all up.

———※◎※———

"Get up, old stone!"

Dr. Nemesis slashed an ash-wood wand down on a gray chunk of rock. The wand broke into splinters. Her seminar students leaned over the counter, holding their breaths.

The stone stirred and flowed upward, its outline shifting. Halfway to its feet it froze into inertia again, a half-formed thing that might suggest to the discerning eye a bias toward the anthropomorphous but nothing more.

Brushing the ash-wand fragments to the floor, Dr. Nemesis said, "What have we proved?" Her fierce gaze swept through the students. None of them met it. "Miss Greenteeth. Answer immediately."

"That stone is stronger than wood," Jenny replied, taking a chance. Often enough, Dr. Nemesis would accept a tautology, if it was delivered wittily enough.

"That certainly does not apply to ebony and pumice," Dr. Nemesis snapped. Her students cringed as they were struck by the rotting-meat smell of her displeasure. "Miss Alderberry. Don't stop to think about it."

"We've demonstrated that everything is alive." Dr. Nemesis frowned and Jane quickly emended her answer to, "That life is implicit in all matter. Even those things which seem inert to us are not so, but merely sleeping."

"Embellish your thesis with an exemplar."

"Uh, well, the *vis plastica*, for example. It's compounded of envivifying influences, so that mares and ewes standing in the leas with their backs to it are impregnated with new life. When it passes over the face of a cliff, the surface rock stirs with yearning for complex form and gathers into the images of uncouth beasts, of skulls and bones and coiled serpents that the ignorant take for archaic life ensorcelled into stone. Then the wind passes and with its enlivening influence gone, the normally low metabolism of stone returns and it falls into slumber again."

"How does this prove your case?"

"Because we know that nothing can be invested with qualities it does not possess. Purple light passing through a red lens can be made red through the removal of its blue component, but that same beam will not pass through a yellow lens, for yellow is not implicit to it. So life must be implicit in the stone if it can be made, even temporarily, to move and live."

Dr. Nemesis rounded on a finch-girl. "Miss Peck-a-Bit. Supposing that the *vis plastica* did not turn away from the cliff, but instead blew over it for days on end, what familiar life-forms would it generate?"

"Gargoyles and stonecrawlers."

"Defend your thesis."

"As was just said, things act in accord with their natures. The new life would retain its stony body and habits of mind. Which would include a fondness for vertical surfaces, a certain slowness of process and . . ."

The seminar room was small and its radiators were set too high. They clattered and moaned in operation, throwing off so much heat that the windows steamed and wept. The air was stuffy too. Jane waited until Dr. Nemesis was looking the other way and lifted a hand to her mouth to stifle a yawn.

Alerted by who knew what inner sense, Dr. Nemesis stiffened. She cast a sudden stern look over her shoulder at Jane. Those watery, pink-rimmed eyes hardened.

"Excuse me, I—" Jane began.

She stopped. The room was empty. Its warmth had fled. Gone was the pale winter light slanting through the windows, replaced by too large and dark a vista of entirely too many rooftops. It was, in fact, a different room altogether. She was in the graduate lounge on the top floor of Bellegarde. The embers of an industrial sunset burned low on the horizon.

It was night.

Numbly, Jane put her hand out to touch the plate glass window before her. It was reassuringly cool and solid. Pull it together, she told herself. What am I doing here?

"Jane?" somebody said. "Are you all right?"

A pale reflection swam up in the window beside her own. It rippled and resolved first into a skull and then into a face, slim and lovely, the sockets dark under the ceiling fluorescents. Jane's vision jerked back from the distance to focus on it.

It was Gwen.

With a gasp, Jane whirled. But behind her stood not Gwen at all but Sirin. She looked back at the window and could no longer make out Gwen's face in Sirin's image. "My dear!" Sirin took her arm. "Whatever is the matter with you?"

"I—" With her back to the window, Jane could see past empty couches into the hallway, where a murmurous flow of teachers and students was pouring through the doors of the Erlkönig Memorial Graduate Lecture Hall. "Dr. Nemesis tossed me out of her seminar. I can't remember anything since. I must have lost over half a day."

The consequences of Dr. Nemesis's fit of pique struck her then with the force of outrage. Everything she had done since that instant—most of a day's classes, all her studying, encounters with friends—had been stolen away from her. "That bitch," she muttered. Then, angrier, "Well, fuck her! Fuck her three ways from midnight."

"That's the spirit." Sirin draped a scholar's hood, the duplicate of her own, over Jane's head and steered her into the crowd. "Look pompous. I doubt anybody's expecting gate-crashers but . . ." She laughed. "Did you ever see so much tweed in your life?"

"It's not as if it were deliberate." They passed through the mahogany doorway without incident. "I tried to—hey. Where are we going, anyway?"

Jane favored seats near the top of the auditorium and to the side, where they were least likely to attract attention, but Sirin marched them down to row five left in the shadow of the podium, immediately behind four rows of faculty. Behind and to one side of the lectern the deans of the University sat patiently on folding chairs, like so many crows on a rail. "It's the Deep Grammar lecture, silly. I told you all about it at lunchtime, don't you remember?"

Jane shook her head. Unheeding, Sirin said, "They only give this lecture once every ten years. The rest of the time they keep the speaker stored in the catacombs, sealed in a jar of olive oil."

"Oh, they do not."

"Seriously. I know a teaching assistant who helped decant him."

A goat-headed administrator took the lectern. He cleared his throat. "There are too few heroes in Natural Philosophy. Yet tonight I present you not merely a hero but a warrior, indeed an academic berserker, one who has made a direct assault on the Goddess's most privy secrets. When he and his companions set out to assail her fastness and force her to surrender knowledge to them, they knew that this attempt might destroy not only they themselves, but the upper and lower worlds as well. But this did not deter them for an instant. For they had the courage of their convictions. They had intellectual honesty.

"Only one of that glorious company returned. He stands before us now. Is there anyone who less needs an introduction than my distinguished colleague? Let me present to you the most exalted of scholars, a living intellectual treasure, and the finest specimen in our collections—" Sirin nudged Jane with her elbow. "Professor Tarapple."

In the ensuing applause he gracefully retreated to an empty chair and a wizened figure climbed up on the dais.

Even for the School of Grammarie, which was widely held to have pushed the concept of liberal arts to an extreme, Professor Tarapple was grotesque. A burnt and crisped cinder of a creature was he, blackened and small, his limbs charred sticks, his torso rendered, reduced, and carbonized. His mouth hung open and his step was slow and painful. He seemed a catalog of the infirmities of age.

He felt for the microphone. His hand closed about it with a soft *boom*, then retreated. The charred sockets of his eyes rose toward the ceiling. Jane realized that he was blind.

"Gentles," he said, "scholars, and powers." His voice was weak and reedy, but the amplification system carried it throughout the auditorium. From below, his head seemed huge atop those scrawny shoulders, a melon balanced on a fence post and in danger of falling. He clutched the lectern with both hands. "The world may be perceived in three states, which states may often seem to be at cross-purposes with each other. They are—" He faltered, almost stalled, and struggled to continue. "They are—are—are first of all the unquestioned state. That which a child sees, in which bread is bread and wine is wine.

"The second state is—" He swayed slightly. "—is consensus reality, that set of conventions by which we agree that bread is a meal and wine is camaraderie." There was a small, polite laugh. "The third is the examined state, that with which our colleagues in the Schools of Sorcery deal, the interplay of forces which they hold to be the ultimate reality." A louder, more robust laugh. "Yet let us ask ourselves, what lies beyond them all? What is the true state of what we might call hyperreality?"

A long silence. "First slide, please."

The lights went down and from the projection booth in the rear came a distinct *click*. On the wall behind him appeared a bright vision of what might be some monstrous bleached seashell, large as a mountain, hanging over a limitless ocean. The audience was totally silent.

Professor Tarapple groped for a laser pointer, leaving sooty handprints on the lectern top. He directed the pointer toward the slide with motions as jerky and unconvincing as a rod puppet's. The red dot of light jiggled off to the side of the screen. "This is—" The head wobbled. "This is—is Spiral Castle itself." Nobody so much as breathed. "No one but I myself has ever delved so deep into the Goddess's mysteries. The Ocean above which it is suspended is Time itself, and so far as could be determined with our limited instrumentation extends to infinity in all directions. Next slide."

*Click.* A drawing of a ribbon twisted in a figure eight, afloat in the void. "This is a Möbius strip with one kink."

*Click.* A more complex figure. "With two."

*Click.* Another. "With sixteen."

*Click.* A glass retort, something like an alembic with its beak curving into itself then emerging at the far end so that its inside became its outside. Though again there was no background, it was as bright with reflected colors as a soap bubble. "This is the three-dimensional equivalent of the first slide."

*Click.* Another soap bubble, infinitely more complex. "The six-dimensional equivalent of the second slide."

*Click.* A third bubble that was worse than the first two combined. "The twelve-dimensional equivalent of the third slide."

*Click.* "Spiral Castle again." This time its physical configuration was clearly that of a higher-order solid in the line of progression suggested by the earlier slides. Its curves were involute and dizzying to follow. "You will note how it folds in upon itself. This recursive complexity extends through at least thirteen dimensions. A visitor following the simple curve of a single passage might be physically inverted so that he entered right-handed and departed left-handed. Following that same passage backwards, however, would not necessarily undo the damage; it might, rather, perform a second inversion so that one's exterior was internalized, leaving the skin on the inside and the guts, so to speak, on the outside.

"But what—what—what does this mean practically?

"Here we must make a brief digression into metempsychosis—I'll spare you the actual math, I promise!" He paused for a laugh that did not come. "Not all who enter Spiral Castle leave it again. But those who do may be reborn again as easily in the past as in the future. It has—has been demonstrated that as many as six avatars of an individual may exist at any given moment. Though it would not be advisable for them to meet." Two or three of the senior faculty chuckled, as if at an abstruse joke.

Jane was having a hard time following the lecture. The harsh white image of Spiral Castle was like a magnesium flare. It swelled and dwindled in her vision, as if softly breathing. Her eyes pulsed, aching when she tried to follow the logic of its involutions. She had to look away.

In the pale reflected light of the slide, all faces were gray and composed, as if their possessors were entranced. Jane found herself staring at the side of Sirin's face. She could intuit the shape of the skull beneath the skin, and it seemed to her that the similarity to Gwen was stronger than ever.

Could she indeed *be* Gwen?

It was an alarming and tantalizing thought. But not a new one. Jane had suspected as much for some time. If what Professor Tarapple said was true, it was entirely possible that Gwen had been reborn in Sirin. In which case the charged polarities of their opposed fates would inevitably bring them together in common orbit about a shared doom.

Jane liked Sirin a lot. She was open and generous and, no doubt about it, Jane's intellectual superior. Sirin had the makings of a crackerjack alchemist in her. There was a lot Jane could learn from her. But Jane dared not involve herself in Sirin's life if it meant a possible replay of the earlier tragedy.

Then again, if Sirin weren't Gwen reborn, there was no need to avoid her. The problem was that there was simply no way of knowing.

Puck, though, was another matter altogether.

*"Toadswivers!* Curly-mounted bobtail jades! Codheaded pig-fuck bastards!"

With a start, Jane came to herself. Throughout the auditorium, the audience members were rousing themselves. A Teggish professor directly before Jane's seat straightened with a lurch and a snort. A gnome to her left passed a hand over his mushroom-spotted pate.

Professor Tarapple had abandoned his lecture in a rage. He was berating his audience. "Only one being—one! me!—has ever delved so far into the Goddess's secrets and returned to talk of them. By cannon-fire, holy water, and bells, listen to me! I risked more than life and sanity to bring you these photographs. I—I—I was once young and tall and handsome. I had friends who died in this expedition and will never be reborn. We were caught and punished and punished again. I alone escaped. Look at me! See the price that I paid! So many times I have tried to tell you! Why do you never listen?"

He was weeping now. "Woe!" he cried. "Alas for those who seek after Truth, for such is the Goddess's most hoarded treasure. Ah, she is cruel and unfathomable, and bitter, bitter is her vengeance."

The lights came gently up. The applause was thunderous.

———◉———

Jane knew what to do now.

The only light in the p-alk lab came from the equipment storage room, whose door Jane had left open. Overhead, the stuffed crocodile turned slowly in otherwise undetectable currents of air. Charged and buoyed by the plan engendered by the Deep Grammar lecture, Jane had managed to steal all the keys, equipment, and time she needed to run the experiment in only three days.

She set out the argon ion laser on the lab bench to her left and the sample chamber to the right. The chamber had a monochromometer mated to a photon counter at the far end. Those two and an optical mirror were the principal components of her experiment. What she had in mind was elegantly simple.

The door rattled. A lank, big-headed, and unreasonably tall figure could be dimly seen through the frosted glass.

She unlocked the door.

"I got the thing you wanted." Billy Bugaboo slouched in apologetically, smelling of cheap soap, imported cigarettes, and limp hope. He opened his hand. A rumpled Seaborne First Leviathan patch lay within. The last time Jane had seen that patch it had been on Puck's jacket shoulder. She remembered noticing that it was coming loose.

"Thanks." Jane picked a few threads from the patch and stuffed them into a sample tube.

"How come you know Puck?" Billy asked.

"How come you do?"

"Sirin introduced us."

Jane slowly poured aqua regia over the threads and capped the tube. Royal water was supposed to be used only as a solvent for gold and platinum, but it really did a number on the threads. She shook the tube and watched them break up into a cloudy swirl of particles. "How come Sirin knows Puck then?"

"He's just one of those people everybody knows." Billy shrugged. "She might've bought some sacred mushrooms from him. He could've done some work on her bicycle. He's a hustler. He gets around."

She aimed the laser so the mirror would bounce its beam into the sample chamber. Getting out hoses, she hooked up the connections to the cool hood and the laser's water jacket. When she was sure of them, she twisted the spigots open. "Well, that's how it was with me too."

She snapped a saline control into the sample clips and shut the chamber.

"Oh." Billy sounded baffled. "Hey, I lucked into a couple of tickets to an evisceration. I thought maybe you and I could—"

"No." Everything was in place. She popped the button on the laser and checked the photon counter. The readings were way off. Disappointment sharpened her answer. "Even if I wanted to witness such a thing—and I don't—I wouldn't, because you'd be wanting to go to bed with me afterward. And I don't want to have sex with you any more because that only encourages you."

Billy shuffled his feet behind her, said nothing.

"Why don't you ask Linnet? She's a cunning little stunt, from all reports." Was it possible she was getting the wrong amperage from the laser? She fussed with the fittings, looking for a short, hoping it was something simple. If the flash tube was malfunctioning, she was up the creek. "I'll tell her you have three balls."

Billy flushed with embarrassment. She didn't need to look. "There's no need to be crude," he said in his stuffiest voice.

"Oh, but all the girls—" Turning, she saw his expression, and stopped. Those guileless eyes of his welled with hurt and loneliness. Abruptly she felt ashamed of herself. Only the knowledge that he wouldn't let it stop there, kept her from reaching out to him. "Okay, I'm sorry for teasing you. Pax, all right? Let's be friends again."

"Yah." Billy nodded shaggily, and Jane returned to her work.

If the problem was in the chromometer, on the other hand, there wasn't much she could do about it. The thing was factory-sealed and sold as a unit. But she'd seen Lampblack using this exact same piece of equipment only yesterday, and it had functioned perfectly then. What was she overlooking?

The mirror!

Sure enough, when she looked the mirror was subtly corroded and scattering a vital fraction of the beam. Jane set up a new one. She jiggled the power feed to check its seating. Pop. This time the numbers fit. She yanked the control, clipped in the sample from Puck's jacket, and left the control chamber open. She donned a pair of laser goggles. With the device tuned to 514 angstroms, the goggles would filter out everything but the *raman* from the sample and she'd be able to look on it direct.

"About that evisceration," Billy said.

The excitation of free ions in the solution brought to life a tiny orange sprite. It floated in the watery green of Jane's vision like a weed lashed by undersea currents. The life span of such creatures was fleetingly brief; in the excitation of the laser light they were born and died thousands of times per second. The being she saw now as one was actually many, its movements an illusion of continuity similar to the generation of repeated images on a television screen. It was so delicate she hardly dared breathe. "What about it?"

"I thought maybe now that you've had the time to think it over, you might—you know."

Jane sighed, but did not look up. "Go away, Billy."

He stood for a while sadly jingling the coins in his pocket. Finally, he left.

Through a simple transform of contagion, the *raman* spirit would eventually take on the form of the being most intimately associated with the particles of thread from the patch. Jane waited while the sprite evolved through slow incremental changes, growing ever more familiar. Finally a minuscule Puck leered up into her goggled eyes, licked its lips, and grabbed its crotch. It was too much to expect subtlety from such a primitive creature.

Now that she had come to the point, Jane found that she was afraid. The laser was rigged to provide a carrier beam. She jacked a microphone into its side. She cleared her throat nervously. It had been a long time since she had used Rooster's true name.

"*Tetigistus!*" she cried.

The sprite leaped, as if a lash had been laid across its back. With a loud crack the flash tube burned out. The stench of burning plastic rose from the plug. Jane fell back with a cry as the laser shorted out, her arm flung out to cover her goggles.

But the damage was done. Clear and bright in the back of her brain shone the residual triune image of Rooster-Peter-Puck. Their eyes were clear and their skin like ivory. They lay wrapped in linen and their expressions were composed, assured, immaculate.

They were all dead.

---

So it was true. Rooster was Peter was Puck.

It was late and the express elevators were closed for the night. Jane took a forty-five minute stand-up local home. All the way she did not so much think as grieve. She had believed that finally knowing one way or the other about Puck would set her free. Only now that he was denied to her could she acknowledge how badly she wanted him.

She was dead weary when she finally got back to her room. It had been a long day and all she wanted to do now was go to sleep.

Light spilled from the transom and seeped through the crack under the door. Voices sounded from within. Monkey was back. And she had a friend with her. It doesn't matter, Jane thought. Nothing can hurt me now. You could hit me in the face with a brick and I wouldn't feel a thing.

She opened the door.

An ungainly figure with red eyes and hair like straw was sitting on her bed. He looked up and grinned nastily. "How ya doin', Maggie?"

It was Ratsnickle.

# FIFTEEN

The winter proceeded at a slowness of pace that was entirely without precedent. The Lords of the City declared a third December, so that Black December passed into Ice December with the possibility of a fourth December at the back of every mind. Meanwhile, it was the Wolf Moon, and the Goddess had taken on her most hostile aspect. Sometimes it seemed the Teind would never arrive.

One week after Ratsnickle's reappearance, Jane went out window-shopping with him and Monkey. She trailed after them, anxious and unwilling, through the upscale stores of Gladsheim and Carbonek, elegant places like Horn Fair, Fata Padourii, and Maleficium, where Jane looked and felt hopelessly out of place. Ratsnickle stood back, jingling the keys in his pockets, a satisfied smile on his puffy lips, when some bright trinket caught Monkey's avaricious eye.

"Oh, look," she said then, "isn't it lovely?"

"Yes," Ratsnickle replied, looking steadily at Jane. "Isn't it?"

They wound up the evening at The Cave. It was open mike night, and every would-be bard and minstrel *manqué* for miles around was on hand with a sheaf of bad poetry. They sat around tables made from telephone cable spools, sipping espresso and waiting their turns. Undergrads in jeans and black turtlenecks brought fresh mugs and cleared away empties.

"Oh the gloves, the faun-skin gloves," Monkey enthused. "I'm doing all my shopping at la jettatura from now on." Reaching up to trace the line of Ratsnickle's jaw with a fingertip she purred, "Think how . . . sooofft they'd feel."

Up on the tiny stage, a poet who looked like he spent daytimes sleeping under haystacks recited:

> *The lady no longer crouched at his side,*
> *But stood before him glorified,*

Ratsnickle rolled his eyes. Then, picking up an earlier train of rhetoric, he said, "Sex is all about power. Mastery and surrender, that's the game in a nutshell."

"That's not how it is with us," Monkey said. "Is it, sweetie?"

He patted her hand indulgently. "Somebody has to take and somebody give. That's just the nature of things. The male is a natural aggressor. The female is passive and nurturing. Inevitably, love in action is a clash of hard and soft, seizing and yielding, a war in miniature. Everything else—courtship, estrangement, reconciliation—is but refinement and sublimation of these primal forces."

"You're a brute." Monkey pouted. Then, in a wheedling tone she said, "But, honeypie, nobody likes to be ordered around *all* the time."

"In a threesome, of course," Ratsnickle said thoughtfully, "things are different. It can go either way, but most commonly you end up with two people on top. To maintain balance, whoever winds up on the bottom has to accept twice the dominance. She has to learn to grovel. To crawl. She has to be made to cherish her own humiliation."

Monkey looked quickly at Jane. Her eyes were hard and bright, like jet buttons, and her nostrils flared. Then she shook her head and turned away. "That's perverse."

"Oh yes," Ratsnickle agreed. "But then, so many things are."

Jane stared hard into the candle sconce. Watching the flame vanish and reappear in the thick red glass. Like a moth struggling to escape. "You said you had something to tell me."

> *Shining and tall and fair and straight*
> *As the Pillar that stood by the Beautiful Gate,—*

"Ah? So I did. You left in such a flurry of strange events—" Ratsnickle drew an envelope from an inside coat pocket, placed it on the table by his mug. Jane reached for the envelope and he drew it back. "Strange events, strange indeed. You left so abruptly you didn't even bother to say good-bye to your old friends. After all we meant to each other. It roused my curiosity. I decided to do a little poking around."

Sharply, Monkey said, "You went out together?"

"No."

"It was nothing—a folly of youth." Ratsnickle waved a hand airily. "I convinced Strawwe to put in an inquiry to the Office of the Child Catcher." He tapped the envelope meaningfully. "Aren't you curious what they said?"

> *Herself the Gate wherby love can*
> *Enter the temple . . .*

The poet's voice was high, nasal, and hesitant, a bouquet of unpleasant qualities.

"Do we have to listen to this crap? No, I'm not curious. What business is it of mine?"

"What indeed?" Ratsnickle returned the envelope to his pocket and abruptly changed the subject. "I hope you enjoyed tonight, Monkey, my sweet. Strolling about the City, window-shopping, our pleasant conversations."

She hugged him. "You know I did, Rattikins."

"If you could have only one item of all those we looked at tonight, what would it be?"

"Oh, the faun gloves. Without question, the gloves."

Ratsnickle turned to Jane. "You heard the lady." He snapped his fingers, as if she had perforce to obey.

Too horrified to sort and order her indignation, Jane cried, "But they wouldn't even let me through the door. La jettatura is right out of my league. It's too swank."

"We have faith in you." Ratsnickle stood, and Monkey after him. He closed a proprietorial hand over her behind to steer her away. "Our little Maggie is capable of a lot more than she thinks she is." Over his shoulder he mouthed a kiss at her.

As the two swept out, a smattering of applause rose from the floor. The poet was done reading. He stepped down from the stage, and was replaced by another as like to him as two cigarettes in a pack. The replacement cleared his throat into the microphone and began:

> *Oh, what can ail thee, knight-at-arms,*
> *Alone and palely loitering?*

Instead of dithering over whether or not la jettatura was beyond her talents, Jane should have challenged Ratsnickle directly. She should have told him she would never steal for him again. Should have said there was nothing in his envelope that could possibly affect her academic standing. That she wasn't afraid of him, not any more.

There were so many things she should have said.

———◦()◦———

The booksellers in Old Regents Hall served all the City. But since most of Senauden was taken up by the University, many specialized in secondhand texts, works of obscure scholarship, and other books of special interest to students.

The bookstalls were two and three stories high, but so narrow within that two customers could not slide by one another without discomfort. Long ago, plumbing had been retrofitted into the space below the indigo-and-gold-star vaulted ceiling. Steam hissed gently, unrelentingly, from the joints of one set of pipes and water condensed on the undersides of another. A steady drizzle fell onto the green roofs of the stalls and the tiled street between.

"Why are you so anxious to get an orchid book? Can't you think of a name without?" Sirin took an umbrella from the rack by the west door and shook it open. Jane took another.

"Maybe. It's kind of tough, though. It's such a personal thing, you know? I'd hate to decide too quickly and get stuck with something like Lady Fatima." Umbrellas up, Jane and Sirin linked arms. The passage between the stalls was thick with pedestrians.

"Jenny Greenteeth named hers Miss Primsey's Garden."

"Too flowery. That's almost as bad as what Eleanor named hers."

"What? Tell me."

"Bossy."

"Oh, vile! 'Tis the name of a cow! Do you know the bwca down the hall from you? She swears she's decided on Siege Perilous."

"That's a good name."

"And yet not one likely to draw in much traffic." Sirin giggled. "Raven says she's thinking of naming hers the Ineluctable Cavern of Despair."

"She's just sulking over being dumped for a blood-may. You've heard what Nant named hers?"

"What?"

"Trouble." They were both laughing now. "What about you?"

"The Meat-grinder."

"Oh, don't! Really?"

"No, of course not. I named her Courage. Wasn't that a—"

"Quick!" Jane seized her friend's arm and swung her into the nearest bookstall. Gilt lettering over the door proclaimed it to be INGLESOOT'S. "In here!"

Astonished, Sirin craned and gaped out into the passage. "Jane! Whatever can be the—" Puck Aleshire strode by the doorway, grim of face and bareheaded to the rain, looking neither to the right nor left. The bobbing umbrellas swallowed him up. Sirin made an exasperated noise. "Oh, Puck. This thing between you and him is getting out of hand."

Jane's heart skipped. "What thing? What has he been saying about me?"

"He doesn't say anything about you, and do you know *why?* Because you ignore him, you avoid him, you won't have anything to do with him. He can't want what he doesn't know exists."

Jane began poking through a tray of remaindered dream books, crosswords collections, and herbals. "He has the stench of death about him. You can tell at a glance that he's not going to survive the Teind."

"That only makes him the more delightful. It ought to pander to everything that's depraved in you." An angry light danced in Sirin's eyes. "Come on, Jane, it's perfect. You can do anything you want with him and he's not going to come sniffing around to remind you of it next semester. Any normal girl would kill for that kind of opportunity."

"Well, I've been through all that before, thank you. Never again."

Sirin stamped her foot. "Church bells and holy water! You're just fucking impossible. I don't know why I put up with you."

"But I—"

"Forget it! See if I ever—ever!—try to do any more favors for you."

White with fury, Sirin slammed out of the shop. She disappeared into the swirling currents of the crowd.

Jane was stunned. It made no sense at all. One instant Sirin was laughing, and the next in a rage. Her merry mood had evaporated as quickly as the light on a meadow when a cloud passes over the sun. Nothing Jane had said could possibly account for this transformation.

She sighed, turned to the shelves, and put her hand on exactly what she was looking for. It was a slim volume bound in tooled leather and titled *The Name of the Orchid*. Jane flipped through it. There were a dozen hand-colored plates and a dictionary of several hundred names defined, derived, and argued by merit and deficiency. To hold it was to desire it.

She looked up and down the stall. It was empty. She peered upward. The shelves seemed to dwindle and recede toward infinity. A long, slender ladder stretched beyond the hanging electric lights, into faraway realms where the endless ranks of books were lost in obscurity. "Hello?" she called. "Is anybody up there? Master—" What was the name out front? "—Inglesoot?"

There was no reply. She shrugged and made for the door.

The ladder rattled irritably. A cobbly scrambled headfirst down from above. When he reached the eighth rung he leaped off to flip and land at her feet with a thump. "Not for sale." He plucked the book from Jane's hand.

"What?" She stepped back.

"Not for sale, not for sale! Are you feebleminded? Not for sale means you can't buy it." Master Inglesoot stood as high as her waist and his gold half-rims were bright semicircles against his grizzled black face. "Get out. There's nothing for you here."

"Um . . . this *is* a bookstall, isn't it?"

"Well, and what of it?"

"Most bookstalls sell books."

"Don't chop logic with me." Inglesoot passed the orchid book from hand to foot and stuffed it into the bottommost shelf without even looking at it. Intentionally or not, he was standing between Jane and the door. Otherwise she would simply have left. "I'm wise to your thievish little schemes. These books are mine, d'ye hear? Mine! I'll defend them to the death, and that's no idle boast."

Jane found herself trembling. "This is the craziest store I've ever been in."

"Crazy?" He rounded on her, all angles and motion, and shook a finger under her nose. "I know your type and your pathetic delusions. Oh, yes, I do. You think of a library as being like the mind of a great and noble Scholar—catholic, universally educated, and precisely organized. Every opinion balanced against its opposite, every fact quickly retrievable. The only biases those that exist in the knowledge itself. If a gap exists in the collective omniscience, a horde of servants will scurry to patch it with the best available volumes, each weighed and tasted to make sure the quality and flavor of information is suitably rich. And this puerile construct, this mock-loremaster, you think is a good thing. Get a life, why don't you!"

"If you'll just back up a step or two, I'll leave."

"You sneer at my bookstall because it's more like your mind as it really is—erratically educated, stocked with whatever unexamined assertions chance to pass within reach, crammed with dubious and contradictory information. The volume you need is here somewhere, but misplaced and out of date. Trash and treasure are thoroughly intermingled with no way to easily distinguish which is which." He yanked a volume at random and read the spine. "*Scribbledehob.* Musings on fireplaces? The picaresque adventures of a young demon? The demented scrawls of a disordered maniac? Who is to say?" He put it back, pulled out another. "*Infangthief and Outfangthief*, the merry pranks, doubtless, of a pair of witty and lovable rogues, filed alongside that useful reference work *Unspeakable Cults*. And to serve and order and replenish them? Only I, myself."

"It's okay. I don't want to buy anything. I changed my mind."

"Yet think! Use your head, for once. It is not commonality that we value in others but eccentricity. It is our differences that individuate us. Were you to meet your vaunted Scholar astride down this very corridor, with his perfect features and flawless diction, you would think him knowledgeable but strangely dull, a farrago of facts and citations and nothing more.

"Compare this with the wit and variety, the eternal surprise of my sweet, sweet mistress." Blindly, lovingly, he stroked the books with his piebald old hand. "And would you wish to see her mutilated, reduced—aye, and lobotomized? Oh vile, vile, ten thousand times vile!"

"It was only one book!"

"Excuse me." A mild-faced lizard woman poked her head in the door. "I'll show the young lady out. I think she meant to come into my stall in the first place. Sit you down, gaffer. Take your ease."

"Eh?" Inglesoot started, and swiveled halfway toward the door. A puzzled expression spread over his face. Then his knees bent and in slow collapse he sank down onto a cardboard box overspilling with maps, pamphlets, and commercial throwaways. He put his head in his hands. "Gone, all gone forever," he grieved.

This was Jane's chance. She accepted the lizard woman's hand and delicately stepped over the unheeding cobbly. The way out was clear now.

At the doorway, she opened her umbrella and quietly asked, "What was that all about?"

"It's an occupational hazard." The lizard woman shrugged. She was heavy bodied and her motions were suitably torpid. "You start by reading books, and you end by loving them."

"But all that wild talk! About death and mutilation and lobotomies."

"The notices came three days ago." She fished a yellow flimsy from an apron pocket, unfolded it, looked at it, refolded it, and put it back in. "The authorities will be collecting a tithe of our stock for the Teind-fires. Inglesoot was functioning well enough until then. But when he tried to weed out the redundant books, he found he could not. A few of us came over with cardboard boxes to get him started, dropping into them duplicates, inferior texts, things that would never sell. He scrabbled after us, squeaking, and snatching them back. By the end of the day we had but one carton with a single coverless paperback romance at its bottom, and that he set aside for further consideration. So we gave up."

"What will happen to him?"

"They'll seize all his books, of course, and him with them."

"That's awful. Can't you stop him?"

"Child, what good is a bookseller who won't sell books? It sounds harsh, but he's exactly the sort of misfit the Teind is meant to clear away. We're best off without him." The lizard woman smiled sadly, and ducked into the next door stall.

Jane stood in the rain, hesitating. At last she stepped back inside. "Master Inglesoot."

Without looking up, he said, "Who are you?"

"Nobody. A friend. Listen to me. The City only wants a tenth of your inventory. Consider how many hundreds and thousands of books you have—you can't possibly read them all!"

Master Inglesoot looked up and in his eyes she saw the gnarled toughness of old roots, a fanatical determination that might be killed but never weakened. "It's better this way. Better we should burn together than for me to survive and inhabit the corpse of my beloved, surrounded constantly by reminders of her former beauty."

"Your collection is not a woman. That's only a metaphor—an abstraction! You'll be dying for nothing, for a principle that nobody else can even comprehend."

As she spoke, Jane became convinced that she herself would never willingly die for a principle. She might feel guilty about it, but she'd smile and lie, knuckle under, pretend, anything, in order to survive. It made her feel a little sad to realize this, but also, at the same time, very adult.

"It's not the principles that kill you in the end." Inglesoot hugged an almanac to his chest with both arms. His voice was fading as his interest in her waned. "It's the books."

⊰⊱

Entering la jettatura was like walking into a dream. The quietly intrusive background music of the mall stores was replaced by textured layers of quiet. When she squeezed past the pine-tall coat trees, her cheek was brushed by the imperial softness of vicuna. Here was the quiet gleam of brass, there the gentle cry of a hand-held bell. Everything conspired to soothe the senses. Yet the air quivered with tension, as if an elf-lord were just about to enter the room.

From her observations of the customers, Jane had assembled an outfit that might let her pass. She'd ripped her best jeans at the knees and three places up the thighs, fraying the threads so that they stood out white and defiant. Over a black lace bra she wore a sheer silk blouse with a string of pearls in a setting dowdy enough to suggest they were inherited. To top it off she had borrowed from Raven an embroidered jacket acquired for a fraction of its value on an independent study trip to the mountain country of Lyonesse.

A touch of makeup finished the look. Examining the results in the mirror Jane decided that she was the visual embodiment of a Teggish girl with money trying to pass for an elf-brat with an attitude.

The faun gloves were to the front. Jane passed them by without a glance, as was her usual technique. She lingered over a display of spiderweb shifts that clung to her fingertips when she touched them, then followed a long, winding aisle past autumn shawls and handbags the rich brown hue of dried oak leaves. She startled a squirrel, and it scampered away to disappear among the woolen skirts.

Everywhere Jane felt the pressure of small, bright eyes on her. Yet whenever she turned the sales personnel were discreetly distant, heads turned away, fading already into obscurity. Their attentiveness was perfection itself.

This would definitely have to be a snatch-and-run.

Across the cobbled hallway from la jettatura was a cul-de-sac lined with professional offices. She could burst through the insurance adjustor's and out its back door, skip around a corner, and disappear into the ladies' room there in no time flat. Into a stall, climb atop the toilet, and up into the drop ceiling. From there she could emerge in any of a dozen locales. She'd already moved an acoustic panel aside and checked the space within for trolls. All it would take were nerve and speed.

She took a long, slow breath to calm herself.

"Young miss." A slim and deferential fey in impeccably anonymous clothes touched her hand. "I'd like to have a word with you."

"I really don't think—" Jane started to turn away, then gasped in pain as his hand closed about her wrist.

His apologetic smile did not extend into his eyes. "Over there would be convenient."

In the shadow of a sea-green marble pillar were two gray plush chairs. Her captor released Jane so she could sit. He then sat down himself, tugging lightly at the knees of his trousers so they wouldn't wrinkle. He adjusted his chair so that it faced her slightly. They must've looked like old friends having a confidential chat. "My name is Ferret. Store security. I couldn't help noticing that you were thinking of stealing some of our merchandise."

Jane filled her voice with indignation. "You can't tell any such thing just by looking at me."

"No? We all of us reveal more about ourselves than we suspect. Let's see what subtle signals there are to be seen on you. Don't bother to deny anything. This is just an exercise." He looked at her steadily for a moment. His lids sank low over eyes as white as his teeth. "You're human, a changeling, and a student at the University. Majoring in the sorcerous rather than the liberal arts. That much is obvious. You're not stealing for your own sake." He made a regretful *tsk*ing noise. "Somebody gets a kick out of forcing you to do this. That is unfortunate, but more common than you'd think.

"You're not so ordinary as you seem, though. A shadow clings to you, and a whiff of cold iron. There's a factory somewhere that would like you back, young miss."

She started to stand. But Ferret's hand tapped her knee and stopped her. "Please. Our clientele require a serene and gracious surround. If you're not going to cooperate . . . well. You *are* going to be cooperative, aren't you?"

She sat. Ferret raised a prompting eyebrow and she nodded miserably. "Yes. Yes, I'll cooperate."

"Good. I want to remind you that we're just having a pleasant chat, nothing more." He took a silver case from an inside pocket and tapped out a throat lozenge. He did not offer her one. A slate gray junco perched atop a rack of Italian scarves took wing and flew away. "You're an extremely lonesome child," Ferret said. "Tell me. Do you know what the penalties are for shoplifting?"

When Jane shook her head, Ferret pursed his lips. "Let me tell you, then. For stealing a pair of gloves—gloves of the quality we sell, at any rate—the punishment is flogging, public humiliation, and possible loss of one hand."

Jane felt sick. It must've shown on her face, for Ferret kindly reminded her, "You haven't stolen anything yet.

"But allow me to pursue this line of thought a little farther. Suppose you were to break into somebody's apartment, armed, let us further stipulate, with a knife. We'll say you've chosen well. You might expect to take away with you gold bars, jewelry, perhaps a few items of artistic value. An armful of silverware, at any rate. Burglary takes little more ingenuity than shoplifting, does it? And the rewards are potentially so much greater than a pair of faun-skin gloves. Now what do you suppose the punishment for this crime would be? Flogging, public humiliation, and possible loss of one hand."

Jane waited, but Ferret said no more. She could not guess at the meaning of what he had said. It was like one of those stories that the oracle told on your name day, dense with portent and yet at the same time so smooth and cryptic that the mind could not get a grip on it.

He stood and offered her a hand. She took it.

"I want you to think long and seriously about what I've said."

"I will," Jane said.

"Excellent."

Ferret led her to the shop's front. At the door he released her and, bowing politely, said, "It's been a pleasure chatting with you.

Let me, if I may, remind you that, should you come into money, la jettatura stands ready to serve you."

━━◍━━

"I've been looking for you," Puck Aleshire said.

Jane whirled. She'd stashed her bike in a public locker two floors down from the store. She was unlocking it when Puck suddenly loomed at her shoulder.

His hand closed about something and stuffed it into a jeans pocket. "Listen," he said. "I hear you're having a little trouble with Monkey's new boyfriend."

"I don't see where that's any of your business."

He stood silent for a moment, head down, one thumb hooked into his belt. Bicycles whizzed by, their riders rattling angry bells at him. He paid them no mind. "Yeah, well, see, I have some friends on the street. If you want, I could arrange for them to have a word with Ratsnickle. Some of these guys can be pretty persuasive."

Jane lifted her bike off the hook and eased its back tire to the ground. "If I needed your help, I'm sure I'd be grateful for it."

"Look," Puck said. "I know his type. They think they're tough but they're not. They're just nasty. Drop you down an air shaft for fun, that kind will, if they think they can get away with it. But break just one finger—the little finger, mind you!" He held up his own. "—and they fold. You'll never see him again, I promise."

Lips thin, Jane shook her head. She would not meet his eye.

"You don't have to know anything about it. Just tell me you wouldn't mind."

She ducked her head into her helmet and pulled the cinch snug. "I'm not going to tell you anything of the kind. Maybe I'm happy with what's going on. Maybe I *like* Ratsnickle. Maybe my problem isn't with him, but with you. Did you ever think of that?" Stooping, she donned her clips. Straightening, she gripped the handlebars so hard her hands turned white. "So get out of my face, okay? Get out of my life. Just . . . lay off!"

Puck wasn't buying a word of it. His eyes blazed with anger. Tightly, quietly, he said, "Just keep it in mind."

Jane climbed onto her bike, leaned on the pedal, and fled.

But his eyes stayed with her, the puzzled concern in his voice, and the smell of his leather jacket. He saw deeper into her than anybody else, and she knew not so much from his words as by the tone and timbre of his voice that he cared.

Slowly his eyes faded, and then the memory of his voice. It was the smell of leather that stayed with her, through the day and deep into the night.

# SIXTEEN

Raven had been talking of getting a few friends together and organizing an orgy for the naming. Jane liked orgies well enough, but she didn't relish the thought of making a big event out of it. Something quiet and meaningful was more her speed.

So the last day before winter break she had a few words with Jimmy Jump-up in the hall after class. Jimmy was a decent sort, if a bit stolid. He contrived to smuggle her into his dorm room without being seen. It was a cold day and sleet was gathering in the corners of his window. He clattered down the blinds and carefully remade the bed.

They necked for a while, and then they took off each other's clothes.

"Where's that booklet?" Jimmy asked. Jane handed it to him and sat back on her heels at the head of his bed, knees wide apart. He lit a joss stick, then bowed down low before her cunt.

"Small beauty, flower of life," he began.

Already his cock was stiff. Because he was nearsighted, Jimmy had kept his glasses on. He held the missal out to one side, face solemn as he read the liturgy praising her cunt's every quality and appointment, her colors, texture, shape, and scent. To Jane this was irresistibly comic. She had to struggle not to laugh.

"May all visitors show you proper respect." He let a drop of the red chrism fall from its bottle onto her belly. The oil tickled slightly as it crept downward. The air was chill. It hardened Jane's nipples and raised gooseflesh on the backs of her arms.

"May you never want." He unstoppered the bottle of gold chrism.

With each prayer he bowed lower, and his mouth came closer. She could feel his warm breath on her thighs, stirring the hairs of her crotch, soft as a thought on her cunt. His rumbling words went right through her flesh and still he did not touch her. By slow degrees Jane had lost her impulse to laugh. She ached with desire. But it was important to wait.

At last Jimmy straightened and put down the booklet. "What name have you chosen for her?"

"Little Jane."

"So be it."

Jimmy Jump-up poured the clear chrism. Then he put his glasses aside and, mingling the oils, worshiped Little Jane with his hands. After a while he worshiped her with his mouth. And finally Jane grabbed him by the hair and pulled his mouth up to hers, and he worshiped her with everything he had.

Technically the ceremony was over. But as a practical matter, what came next was vastly important. The purpose of naming Little Jane was to render her cooperative and pliant, to make of her a friend and an ally for life. Her future conduct would be greatly influenced by the quality of her first postnaming experience.

For a while Jane concentrated on making it a good experience. Then she got distracted. Time passed. Jimmy's face turned red and he began making chuffing noises, like a malfunctioning steam engine. Jane wrapped her legs tight around his waist and hugged him to her as hard as she could.

She came then, and the room filled with butterflies.

Jimmy looked up, astonished. His face was blank and gaping. Then he began to laugh. There were bright wings everywhere. Flakes of red-orange-cobalt blue winked in and out of existence, in fleeting patterns that could be glimpsed but not grasped before dissolving into new forms. It was like being inside a kaleidoscope. Jimmy inhaled a tiny swallowtail and almost choked, and by the time Jane had done pounding him on his back they were both laughing helplessly.

They hurriedly pulled their clothes on and, waving towels, shooed the majority of the insects out into the hall. The hall monitor came out from his room just as they shut the door, and went roaring up and down the hall, trying to find out who was responsible. Jane had to lie facedown on the bed, biting a pillow to stifle her giggles. Her sides ached. At one point the monitor came right to their door and stood listening and they were almost discovered.

It seemed an auspicious beginning.

———— ‖◎‖ ————

The next day was unseasonably warm and Jane went out on the Campanile with only a windbreaker. The Campanile had never rung that Jane could recall. Perhaps there was no money for it. But on a good day it was a fine place to hang out with a few friends, catch some sun, and maybe get stoned.

An erratic breeze whipped Jane's hair back. She stuck her hands in her hip pockets and leaned into it. From the top of Tintagel she could see the three other University buildings and beyond them the clustered ranks of buildings great and small that made up the Great Gray City. They were an army of stone, marching to a battle somewhere beyond the horizon. Gray and hazy they looked against a sky that was as white as a blank sheet of paper.

Sirin wasn't here yet, but Jane rolled herself a smoke anyway. It took three matches to light. She drew in, closed her eyes, exhaled slowly. Leaning back against one of the Campanile's support beams, she stared up at the black bronze bells, streaked white with pigeon droppings.

A kind of bleak exhilaration filled her then. Somehow she was going to survive, raise the money to complete her education, and make a place for herself in the world. The blind, clifflike surfaces of the City convinced her of it. Surely there must be niches enough in so vast and anonymous a habitat for one as small and insignificant as she to get by.

"Bitch of a view, ain't it?"

She turned. The speaker crouched on the lip of the stone railing. He was monkey-browed, chinless, squint-eyed, loose-lipped, pugnosed, batwinged, potbellied, goat-horned, hunchbacked, sphinx-haunched, and altogether charming. A thuggish light gleamed in his slitted eyes. A gargoyle.

"Yes," she said. "Yes, it is."

"You going to hold onto that thing all day?"

Jane looked down at her hand, then up at the gargoyle. She dug through her knapsack looking for something the right weight. Then she put the joint down on the rail and anchored it with a compact. "Want a drag?"

"Don't mind if I do." The gargoyle shuffled closer and extended a long, apish arm. His blunt fingers closed about the cigarette. He took a slow, careful drag, then offered it back at arm's length. Jane shook her head. She knew something about gargoyles' hunting strategies.

"What's your name?" the gargoyle asked.

"Jane."

He made a brusque, clumsy, almost comical bow. "Sordido di Orgulous, at your service. Come here to sort things out, did you?"

"No, there's somebody I'm hoping to meet." Jane was looking for Sirin and Nant had told her that she liked to hang out here about this time of day.

"Me too."

Jane stared out into the City, enjoying its complexity, its size, its silence. Finally, more to be polite than because she actually cared, she said, "Another gargoyle?"

Sordido guffawed. "Haw! We rock people are too territorial for that. I got the south face, top fifteen floors. North face, top, belongs to Lordo di Branstock. Down below you got Sozzo di Tintagel. A local boy. One of those sleazebags sets foot on my turf, and I'll teach him a little lesson in how to fall.

"No, I got a regular little clientele comes out to talk things over with me. I'm a good listener. Comes of having such a slow metabolism. I don't get bored easily."

"What sorts of things do they talk about?"

"You'd be surprised. Shit they wouldn't tell their best friends. Most of 'em are just having a little flirt with danger. Others have got a serious self-destructive streak. They talk. I listen. They ask my advice. I give it. Every so often I manage to sweet-talk one over the edge. Then I eat. Nine times out of ten, that's what they were really after from the beginning. I got good hopes for the one who likes to come around here about this time."

A dark suspicion seized Jane. "You wouldn't know her name, would you?"

"Naw."

"Tall, good legs, long hair?"

"No offense, missy, but I have a hard time telling you guys apart."

"I see." Jane lapsed into silence.

For a time, they shared the view without speaking.

"So how about that Teind?" Sordido said suddenly. "You looking forward to it?"

Jane looked at him. "If that's the word for it. You figure it's bound to get somebody you know, maybe even a lot of them. So I'm not exactly anxious for it to happen. But then again, once it's over, it'll be over. You can get on with things. So maybe it'd be best if it happened and were done with." She paused. "What do you care about the Teind, anyway? I thought you guys were immune."

"It's the only time we get to eat our fill."

"Oh." She looked away.

"Oh," Sordido mimicked. "Oh dear. How terribly vulgar." Angrily, he reared up on his haunches and ponderously unfolded his wings. They were enormous. "Look at me. How much energy do you think it takes to get something this heavy up into the air?"

"Well—"

"A *lot*, that's how much. I'll tell you something else you don't know about the rock people. We only mate on the wing. Got that? So once every ten years you fill your streets with carrion and we get to climb down and eat our fill. It ain't pretty, I'll grant you that, but whose fault is that? We eat all we can. Then we start to climb again, back up the sides of whatever building is closest.

"It's a bitch of a climb. It takes hours. We've been at our business all day, so probably it's sunset. Them blood-gorged skies are as shiny bright as Hell Gate itself then. Clouds as purple as a bruise. We climb. Everything grows dark and the stars come out. By the time we get to the top, it's night.

"You've maybe noticed that the rock people ain't got many females. So when our ladies come into heat, there's a lot of competition for their favors. The moon comes up. We wait. Finally one begins to sing." He shivered. "Nekhbet! You don't know how beautiful their voices are. So sweet you want to fling yourself right off the building."

The door to Tintagel quietly opened and shut. Sirin walked out into the Campanile. When she saw Jane, she looked startled. But after an instant's hesitation, she sat down beside her on the railing. Together they listened to the gargoyle.

". . . by one, the gents raise their voices in answer. Deep and low. We don't sound so lovely, maybe, but it's profound. Like thunder after larksong.

"Dunno how long the singing lasts. You kind of lose track. But at last she stretches out and looks around. Kind of teasing-like. She spreads her wings. She leaps. She flies. She soars high up into the sky, and she's still singing.

"That's when we totally lose control. We scrabble over the edge, and instinct takes over. Maybe twenty-thirty-forty of us will form up into a flock and fly after her. We're all feeling our oats, laughing and joking. She's only going to mate with one of us. So it gets rough up there. That's how I got this kink in my leg. That's how I lost two of these." He spread his claws, retracted them again.

"Now, it's the ladies who perpetuate the race. They got to raise the cubs, keep 'em fed, and kick 'em off the ledge when they get big enough to start killing each other. So natch, they're a lot stronger than the gents. Only the best of us can keep up. The flock dwindles. And of course there are ways of convincing the competition that it's maybe time to go home.

"Finally, there's just you and her. She's still ahead of you, but she ain't trying to get away. Fact is, maybe she slows down a bit. Maybe she glances back, kind of flirty, to see what you're like. She tilts a wing, and the moonlight is pale on her flank. Ahhhh, but she's long and as tawny-lean as a lioness. Her talons are like black glass daggers. Her breasts are two white skulls, and there's hunger in her eyes.

"She spirals upward, and you follow. The City falls away. The air is cold and clear. Your every muscle aches like fire, but you're getting closer. Her wings obliterate the sky. She reaches out her slender arms to you, and she's as beautiful and tender as Death herself. The smell of her musk is maddening. She wants you—she can't hide it—as bad as you want her."

Sirin was breathing shallowly. "It sounds lovely," she whispered.

"So the ladies tell us." Sordido heaved a long, deep sigh. "Then again, that's what they would say, innit? It's not as if the gent ever got to voice an opinion on the subject afterwards."

"I beg your pardon?" Jane said.

"Well, we don't survive it, do we? The lady's had a long night, and pretty soon she's incubating a brood of maybe a dozen cubs, she's going to need her energy. She's got to eat *some*thing."

"That's grotesque!" Jane said.

Sirin said nothing.

"Yeah, well, from your point of view, maybe so. But you can't blame them for it—the ladies. That's just our biology. They got no say over it." For a moment Sordido sank in on himself in gloom. Then, with visible effort, he straightened. A slow shrug. "Well. Look, I'm sorry if I'm depressing you. It's just that the subject is kind of—you know."

"I understand."

"No hard feelings?" He held out his hand.

"No hard—"

"*Jane!*" Sirin grabbed Jane and yanked her back as she reached out to take the gargoyle's hand. The stone fingers closed about empty air.

Sordido chuckled. "Damn."

———————

Sirin led Jane from the Campanile. The granite corridors and marble halls of Tintagel closed about them with a faint exhalation of stale air. Jane felt tense and weak with aftershock. But she didn't thank Sirin for saving her life. So long as she didn't thank her, Jane knew, so long as the tension between them held, Sirin couldn't break free. And there were things that needed to be said.

They walked blindly down a passage whose ceiling was so low that Jane cringed whenever they passed under an air duct. Electrical cables were stapled to the gray walls in twos and threes, looping over the doorways to redundant classrooms converted to long-term storage. Cardboard boxes of outdated course guides and commencement addresses waited wearily by doors that would never open for them.

The passage dead-ended into a stairwell and they sat down on the top step. Voices arose from below, and the occasional clatter of hurrying feet, but nobody appeared. Above them, a dusty stuffed crocodile twisted slowly in otherwise undetectable currents of air. Gray stuffing oozed out where its seams were parting.

"Sirin, what in the world are you doing, meeting with that creature?"

Sirin stared at her knees, shook her head.

Jane took her friend's hands. They were like ice. Sirin had lost weight; her cheekbones were sharper, her eyes glittery-cold. She looked beautiful and doomed. "I know it's none of my business. But you've been missing a lot of classes lately. The girls are beginning to talk. They say that if your grade point average goes any lower, you'll be facing automatic expulsion."

"Expulsion. That's a laugh."

"That's exactly the attitude I'm talking about! Sirin, look, I've got problems of my own, I don't dare get too deeply involved in yours. Understand? If I try to help, it'll just drag us both down together. But I'm your friend. At the very least I can warn you of what everyone but you can see coming down."

Still as a pillar Sirin sat. Her face was white as salt. "I'm marked," she said. "For the Teind."

You don't know that, Jane almost said. But something in Sirin's expression convinced her otherwise. "How can you be sure?"

"I scryed it. Three times. Once in a virgin speculum. Once in a pool of ink. Once in a cupped double-handful of my own blood."

"You can't be certain! Prediction is an imprecise science, after all."

"Three times? That's pretty damn sure."

Now at last Jane began to cry. She couldn't help it. "Oh, Sirin, how could you? You know as well as I do how dangerous scrying the future can be. Half the time what it shows you wouldn't happen if you hadn't foreseen it." She released Sirin's hands, intending to hug and reassure her. But her feelings welled up and instead she punched her in the shoulder, just as hard as she could. It was all too awful. "Damn you! Why?"

Emotionlessly, Sirin said, "I didn't have any reasons. I've never had any reasons to do anything. Maybe other people have reasons. But when I look inside myself it's like there was an emptiness inside where something ought to be but isn't. Why? I don't know. Why not?"

The crocodile leered down at them both. An ironic sparkle glinted in one dull glass eye and a silent chuckle threatened to stretch his grin so wide all his gray cotton stuffing would fall out. Mastering herself, Jane wiped her eyes against her sleeve. "You can still take steps to protect yourself."

"I've already done everything. I even looked into buying an exemption, that's how desperate I was."

"You could—"

"But since I'm not going to, what would be the point?" Suddenly Sirin laughed, shook her hair, and said, "Not another word. Let's go hang out in the student center. We'll have a soda, play a few hands of cards, dish a little gossip. That would be fun. But with so little time left to me, I don't want to waste any of it just talking and talking and talking about this thing."

Jane bit her lip and nodded. Together they started down the stairs. The crocodile dwindled above them. She could feel its scornful regard shrink to a hot point source of emotion and then wink out.

"Sirin? What you said about an exemption. You mean I could buy my way out of the Teind?"

"Forget I said anything. It's more money than you've got anyway."

⸺◉⸺

As it turned out, the money an exemption from the Teind would cost was exorbitant and then some. Jane stopped by Dr. Nemesis's office for information, though she doubted she could hack the cost. She had the brochure in her purse the afternoon when Ratsnickle came by to ask after the gloves.

He caught her as she was leaving her dissection lab. The metal door clicked softly shut behind her, closing away the chill rows of cadavers on chrome gurneys. The refrigerator rooms were at the bottom of an obscure culde-sac, and so late in the day there was very little traffic. The halls were quiet.

Ahead, where the corridor turned, Monkey wheeled her bike into view, blocking the way. Ratsnickle strolled alongside her.

Jane stopped.

Leaving Monkey behind, Ratsnickle approached Jane. She waited, ready for anything he might have to say.

"Have you heard?" he asked. "Sirin's on the bane."

"What? I don't believe you." Flustered, because it fit so well, Jane said, "She wouldn't. Sirin's not like that."

A shrug. "Believe what you will." Down the hall, Monkey leaned against her bicycle, eyes two burning smudges of hatred. "You and I have things to talk about."

"I'm not going to steal for you. Not now, not again, not ever."

"There are ways and ways to make us even."

"I don't owe you a thing."

"Oh?" Ratsnickle's eyebrows rose. He held out his palm. "Give me the faun-skin gloves and I'll call it quits. I'll walk out of your life and you'll never see me again."

Jane said nothing. There was nothing she could say.

Ratsnickle glanced over his shoulder to determine that nobody but she and Monkey were about. Then slowly he unbuttoned his trousers in what he obviously thought a seductive manner, and hauled out his penis.

Jane felt an involuntary thrill of revulsion. Penises had never exactly impressed her as things of beauty, but Ratsnickle's was particularly ugly and faintly green as well, doubtless because his standards of cleanliness had allowed some mold or microscopic moss to establish itself there.

He watched her avidly, an electric grin splitting his face. Down below, his penis was hardening in small jerks, like some ludicrous rubber toy being inflated by a hand pump.

"Better put it away before it starts to draw flies," Jane said.

Ratsnickle's face twisted with anger. "You hypocrite! I was watching—you liked what you saw. You couldn't get enough of it. You wanted to go down on me right then and there." But he scooped it back into his trousers and rebuttoned them anyway.

"Funny. I could have sworn what I was thinking was that there's never a pair of pruning shears around when you need one."

Ratsnickle drew himself up and for an instant she thought he was going to hit her. But instead he seized her hand in both of his and kissed her knuckles. "*Touché*, sweet lady. But one touch is not a duel, nor does a single skirmish determine the battle. We shall meet again on the field of combat—dearest enemy."

He swaggered away, without even looking back to see if Monkey would follow.

---

As soon as he was gone, Jane ducked into the nearest bathroom to wash her hands.

The bathroom was tiled and painted a glossy black. Graffiti were painstakingly carved into the paint. Several generations of angular runes were visible through successive coats, palimpsests of anger and flip obscenity. Curved mirrors leaned over the sinks, so that Jane had to stare up into a distorted image of herself to check on her makeup.

The bathroom door slammed. A ballooning and deflating Monkey swam toward her in the mirror.

Monkey was in a state, her face red and her fists clenched. Her hair was a mess. "You bitch! You cat! You get your fucking claws out of my sweetie!"

"You can have him. I don't want any part of him." Jane went on washing her hands. "Goddess knows, the two of you deserve each other."

"Cute. Very cute. I know your devious little ways." Monkey began to cry. "I've done things for him that you never would. Not in a million years. I *degraded* myself for him."

Jane finished rinsing her hands. She cranked a paper towel from the dispenser. "Well, good for you."

"Don't give me any of your lip. Don't you fucking dare. I'm

warning you." Suddenly Monkey staggered and lurched. She grabbed the edge of the sink to steady herself.

"Are you okay?" Jane asked cautiously.

"I thought for a second I was having a—" Monkey shook her head. It was obvious she'd lost the thread of what she was saying. She shivered convulsively. Then from a jacket pocket she removed a tissue-wrapped bundle. "Look at this." She peeled away the tissues to reveal a blown-glass unicorn. She set it down on the cosmetics shelf. "Ratsnickle bought me this on our first date." The sad little trinket caught the light and made it dance. "What did he ever buy for you?"

"Nothing."

"Damn straight, nothing!" Triumphantly, Monkey picked up the unicorn.

It shattered in her hand.

Jane stepped back, startled. Monkey stood as if transfixed, arm extended. Blood ran down her fingertips and dripped to the floor. "That's one small step for man," she said, "one giant leap for—" She gagged, and a spume of fish eyes poured from her mouth. They spilled down the front of her blouse.

"Monkey?"

"The surface is fine and powdery, it adheres in fine layers, like powdered charcoal, to the soles and sides of my foot." The voice that came from Monkey's mouth was unlike anything Jane had ever heard, harsh and broken by static, as if she were speaking from somewhere hundreds of thousands of miles away. "I can see the footprints of my boots and the treads in the fine, sandy particles."

With the onset of the *awen* her pupils had clenched, sucking in the irises, and disappeared, leaving her eyes a hard milky white. She did not resist when Jane, mastering her horror, guided her to a sink and ran cold water over her bleeding hand. "It's a very soft surface," she said. There was a clean handkerchief in Jane's purse; she used it to bandage up Monkey's palm, hoping there weren't any slivers of glass in the cuts. "But here and there, where I probe with the contingency sample collector, I run into very hard surface."

"Hard surface," Jane repeated. She moistened a paper towel and wiped the vomit from the corners of Monkey's mouth. A toilet flushed and a rusalka emerged from a stall. She gave the two of them an odd look and left without washing her hands. Jane realized that she had to decide whether to leave her roommate here for the night or not. She started for the door, came back to the small figure slumped on the floor, started for the door again. She could not leave.

Finally she sighed. "I'm taking you home, Monkey."

Her roommate nodded dreamily. "This certainly has to be the most historic phone call ever made."

———※◎※———

Monkey's bicycle was leaning against the wall outside, and Jane's was in a locker not far away. Monkey was in no shape to ride, but luckily there was a conversion kit in her saddlebags. Jane got out a wrench and deftly connected the two with crossbars, matched gears and slaved the pedals, and shipped one set of handlebars. Before long she had a four-wheeler with a sling seat low in the rear and the driver's seat high at the front. Her roommate reclining in deathlike languor behind her, Jane started off.

Two changes of elevator later, they were back in Habundia. When they got to their room, Monkey climbed weakly from the tandem, stumbled, and almost fell. Jane unlocked the door, seized Monkey by the nape of her blouse, and guided her toward her bed. One shove and she tumbled facedown on top of the counterpane.

Jane swung Monkey's legs onto the bed and rolled her over on her back. Monkey's face was gray, but when Jane laid a finger under her nostrils, there was a warm touch of breath. She yanked off Monkey's shoes and began to undo her clothes. Then she thought better of it. There were limits.

It took ten minutes to disengage the bicycles and put them away. When she was done, Jane found herself too worked up even to think of studying. Sitting on the edge of her bed, she stared at her roommate with loathing.

There was a knock on the door.

"Won't this stupid day *ever* end?" Jane strode to the door and flung it open. "What!"

A buxom little spunkie grinned up at her. "Billy Bugaboo's waiting for you in the lobby. He's got a banana in his pocket that I think he wants to give you."

"Yeah, well, you can tell him—"

"He said to tell you that he got the thing you wanted."

"Oh."

"So what should I tell him?"

"Shit." Jane was tired. She was feeling ill-used and angry and distinctly antisocial. The timing was pure Billy Bugaboo. "Tell him I'll be down as soon as I can put together a change of underwear."

———◈———

"Do you want me to wear this?"

"No, I will." She laid her blouse aside, turned her back to Billy. "Help me with this bra, will you?" While he fumbled with the little hooks, she asked, "Did you have any trouble stealing it?"

"What does it matter? I got the fucking thing."

"Why, Billy," she said in surprise. "That doesn't sound a bit like you."

"I'm sorry, it's just—I don't know." Confused and embarrassed, Billy busied himself undoing the buttons of his shirt. Briefly, he had loomed larger in Jane's sight. Now he dwindled to his former stature. "I just kind of wish it didn't have to be like this."

"That was the deal, remember?" Jane looked at him with mingled guilt and scorn. What a wet, hopeless thing he was! But she was careful not to let it show. Gently, she said, "Sometimes people want things they shouldn't. I'm *trusting* you, Billy." Then, when he did not reply, "It'll be nice. I promise."

She kicked free of her jeans. Billy folded his and put them on the dresser. They were both naked now. "Give it to me," she said.

Billy's was a box of a room, as sparely arranged as a stage setting. No rugs on the floor. No posters on the wall. It had a bed, a dresser, a chair, and a lamp—one of each. A short stack of textbooks rested on the dresser beside the lamp. With the curtain drawn and the overhead dimmed, it felt like the hushed moment before a performance begins.

Billy went to his closet and brought out the jacket.

It was the right one for sure—she recognized the patches and the worn and frayed places as well. This was Puck Aleshire's own jacket. The smell of it was unmistakable.

She draped it over her shoulders. It was heavier than she'd expected, and she liked that. It felt hot against her flesh, and the fact of being partially covered made the rest of her seem exposed and vulnerable. The mingled scents of Puck and leather wrapped themselves about her. She closed her eyes. "C'mere," she said.

Billy bent, slid his arms under the jacket, and hugged her close. Jane raised her mouth to his. She stood on her tiptoes, so that Little Jane rubbed against his cock. She could feel his veins hammering. He was ready to pop already, and rather than try to nurse that first anxious orgasm along, she decided to see how quickly she could bring him off.

Drawing back, she cupped a hand about Billy's stones, squeezing them slightly, balancing two against one. She licked his nipples, sucked them hard, teased them with small bites. Billy's hands clutched her head, and he made a low noise at the back of his throat, like some marsh beast calling across the night for its mate.

Jane slid her hand upward and squeezed. The jacket started to slip from her shoulders, and she reached around quickly to lift it back. She began moving her hand, long hard strokes up and down. "You like that?"

"Yess."

"Good." She kept stroking. Up and down. Faster.

With a small cry of dismay, he spurted. Warm sperm gushed over both their bellies and down the side of her hand.

Jane hooked a leg behind him and toppled him over on the bed. She crawled after him. "What a mess," she murmured. "What a sticky, sticky mess." Seizing hold of his softening member, she shifted herself around so that her crotch was level with Billy's mouth. Then she began to lick his belly clean.

By the time she had worked her tongue all the way down that long, long torso, Billy was hard again. Without her having to tell him to, he began to lick her abdomen, performing the same service for her that she had for him.

"I left a pair of aviator glasses on the chair with my blouse," Jane said after a while. "Be a sweet and get them for me, will you?"

Obeying, Billy grumbled, "I like looking into your eyes."

"It's three-quarters of my final grade," Jane lied. "You don't want to see me flunk out, do you?" She fit them on. "Can you see anything?"

"Of course I can't," he said. "If I stare real hard I can see that your eyes are shut."

"Then don't. Now you have to promise not to say another word until we're done." Forestalling his protest, she added, "This is for my thesis, remember? I'm not asking much. And tonight, anything you want, I'll do. Whatever you want, wherever you want it—go right ahead. But you can't speak. That's just the way the esoteric arts work."

The truth was that esoterica was strictly brew-your-own, irre-producible, a set of techniques and skills without recipes, rituals, or road maps. Half its power came from discovery, from meeting and overcoming one's embarrassment, fear, and even disgust. But some of the things Jane had in mind to do tonight, she could only enjoy if she pretended Billy B were somebody else.

She rubbed the side of her face against his cock and thought, how smooth and silky. So hard, she thought, so big. She closed her mouth about its tip and thought, how salty my Puck tastes!

Time melted away.

Through most of the journey she was like the navigator of a small ship, moving surely with the currents, trimming the canvas to catch more wind, running before the squall. She was skimming over the surface at fantastic speed, the water hissing, the sails creaking with the strain. Then suddenly, all the oceans united to surge up beneath her, and she lost control. Billy was on top of her when it happened. She began to struggle wildly.

Alarmed, Billy started to pull back, but she grabbed him and slammed him back down on top of her. Puck wouldn't pull back. He'd be *relentless*. He was pounding away at her—"Faster!" she muttered—like a wild animal in rut. She raked his back with her nails, hard enough to draw blood. It only made him hotter. He was mad with lust. His passion was so great now that he'd lost all track of her identity. He no longer cared that it was her beneath him. It could have been anybody. The fury of his need obliterated all thought.

She was close to it now. Jane wriggled down inside the jacket so she could bury her face in the collar. She breathed in the smell of leather. Puck's scent imbued the jacket. It rose most strongly from the armpits but the tang of him was everywhere. She was slippery with sweat herself. Their smells mingled and rose in an alchemical marriage, forming something rich and wild. She took the jacket between her teeth and bit down hard. She was going to come.

Sex energy was most accessible at the moment of orgasm. This was why adepts were usually female. Where a witch might have a string, a series, an archipelago of orgasms to work with, the warlock was (usually) limited to one. Males tended to gravitate to the necromantic arts, it taking no special talent to kill things. Jane knew, though, she'd have to work with the one. Inexperienced as she was, it was first time or never.

Marshaling her resources, she concentrated on identifying,

isolating and distancing herself from the power rising within. Her mind closed about it like two hands trapping a thrush. A perfect and universal stillness seized her. Briefly, she was free of all bounds.

Forcing herself—this was the hardest part—to expect nothing, she opened her eyes.

She was sitting on a stool in a crowded lunch counter. Her mother looked up, startled, from a cup of light brown coffee. One of her mother's elbows brushed against an ashtray, knocking it off the counter. Butts and ashes went flying. Heads swiveled.

Jane held the fluttering source captive in her mind. This must surely be what it felt like to be a sorceress! The exultant power filled her entire being, like light in a crystal figurine. It struggled to escape. It was a bird, a force, a sphere of light. She willed it up from within and down along her arm. Her hand tingled with fierce power. It was growing more intensely real, as solid as anything in the room.

Now!

She slapped her hand down on the countertop. The coffee cup jumped, and she snatched up what lay beside it. Her mother's mouth was opening to form the beginning of a question.

Before anything could be said, the power outflowed and dispersed. The instant ended. The restaurant and her mother both were gone. Jane was back in Billy's bed again. He was lying motionless atop her. She reached up and, wincing, untangled the shades from her ears. "I can't breathe," she said.

With a slow groan, he rolled off.

Jane stared at the spoon in her hand.

It was there and it was real. Jane ran her thumb over it and over it. It was made of unplated steel. A simple string of stamped circles bounded by two thin lines looped around the edges of the handle for decoration. She turned it over and read the inscription on its back:

**IKEA**
**stainless**
**Made In Korea**

Strange runes, and perfectly meaningless to her. But full of hope. Their larger portent reassured Jane. They were tangible proof that her power was growing. Anything was possible. All it would take was luck and lore. She could raise the money for her tuition and enough to buy an exemption from the Teind as well. And one for Sirin while she was at it—why not?—and another for Puck Aleshire.

Her life was a complete mess, true, but it could be straightened out. All it would take was money. Money could straighten out anything, if you had enough of it.

She knew where to get that money, but until tonight she hadn't the nerve to try. Now she had proved herself. It was time.

"Wow," Billy said.

"Oh, shut up."

# SEVENTEEN

To make a hand of glory required first of all a hand cut from the corpse of someone who had died violently. The shock of sudden death was necessary because it flooded the flesh with endorphins and endorphins were essential to the spell's puissance. Luckily, Jane had access to the anatomy morgue. She smuggled the hand out in her purse and pickled it in a solution of salt and nitre in a jar at the back of her closet. Drying it in the sun would have taken weeks, so she flash-froze it and sublimed the ice in a vacuum chamber.

The City was bright and hard through the windows and radiated cold into the lab. The last pale lights of a dead sunset flickered like corpsefire on the horizon. Jane sat cross-legged atop a high stool, lashing candle stubs between the fingers of the hand. She hadn't turned on the lights for fear of discovery. But in what light there was, she could see that the hand was coarsely proportioned and that its former owner had been a nail-biter.

The blue hour was the best time for this sort of work, for the influences of sun and moon were roughly equal then and would distort the results least. The candles firm, Jane took out a penknife. Carefully she carved runes between the second and third joints of every other finger, a *sfwa* on the thumb, *ya* on the middle finger and *sig* on the pinkie, so that together they spelled out the hidden name of the Goddess in her aspect as Assigner of Dreams.

All that remained, then, was to rubber-band one of Galiagante's credit cards to the palm.

When the work was done, Jane dumped the ball of twine into her equipment drawer and hopped down from the stool. The hand of glory she dropped into her knapsack along with the pry bar, the suede gloves, and the flashlight.

She'd chosen her clothes for indistinction: black hightops, black denim jeans, and Puck's leather jacket to top it off. Her knapsack was by good luck a dingy gray. She slung it over her shoulder and pulled on a wool watch cap. It was not so striking an outfit as to draw attention to itself; in it she would be as close to undetectable as made no difference.

Her mother's teaspoon she had drilled a hole in and hung on a cord around her neck. Now she drew it from under her blouse and kissed it for luck.

Time to hit the street.

It was a bitter cold night. A sharp wind picked up bits of trash and made them dance in circles. No one was about. She hurried down streets that were empty and silent, past Branstock, Pentecost, and Lonazep, ducking briefly into Anowre's lobby to warm up her cheeks and ears and the fronts of her thighs, where the cold denim stung them, then trotting quickly by Cadbury and Sewingshields, Lombard, Worm, Altaripa, and Melvales. The occasional dwarf or night-gaunt that she saw was huddled and anxious to get back inside, as much in a hurry as she herself. At last she came to her destination.

Caer Gwydion.

She stared up at its bright glass walls, its smoothly gleaming surfaces rising up forever into the night, and for an instant her spirit quailed. It was a citadel, unassailable. She was so small and insignificant before it! Then, squaring her shoulders, she ducked into an alleyway and went around to the rear.

The back of the building was totally unlike the front, a stained cinder block wall with loading dock, dumpster, and an incinerator gently smoldering. It was as if an enchantment had been removed from Caer Gwydion, revealing it as it really was. Jane lit a cigarette and faded back into the shadows, watching.

Time passed. An ogre emerged from a service door, lugging a trash can. He emptied the can into the incinerator and scuttled back inside. The door swung to after him.

Jane lit another cigarette to give the custodian time to find work elsewhere. She smoked it slowly, savoring its warmth, and ditched the butt with regret. Then she pulled on the gray suede gloves and got out the hand of glory. Holding it by the wrist, a disposable lighter ready in her other hand, she went to the service door. She pushed it open. Barrels, brooms, cleaning supplies. Old rags. The custodian was nowhere to be seen. From the gloom, a black iron monster of a furnace hissed at her. "Hello?" she said. "Is this where I'm supposed to come to see about work?"

No one answered.

Jane let the door close behind her. Her heart was racing. Fighting an absurd urge to slink, she advanced into the room. It was warm inside. Her cheeks and the lobes of her ears tingled painfully. Somewhere, a television set murmured. Ahead, a freight elevator waited for her, doors open. She got in.

According to the contents of Galiagante's wallet, he dwelt in the penthouse. Shifting the hand and lighter temporarily back to the knapsack, Jane closed the doors and seized the controls. A gleeful exultation filled her. She was pulling it off! This was brilliant, better than drugs, better than sex, better than anything she'd ever experienced before. Everything seemed preternaturally clear and vivid, as if newly dipped in cool liquid glass. It was a fantastic high.

She ran the freight elevator up as far as it would go.

———◦《◉》◦———

The walls slid by, doorways opening and closing like bright mouths. She had brief, disconnected glimpses into the passing hallways and work spaces. Occasionally she drifted past voices—arguments, sardonic laughter—but she saw no one, and drew no attention. She felt invisible.

The elevator came to a final stop. She stepped out into a darkened kitchen.

The silence was absolute.

Holding the hand of glory before her like a shield, Jane investigated the connecting rooms. It didn't take much exploration to determine that the entire floor was given over to housekeeping functions and that the staff had been dismissed for the night. Still, she held the lighter cocked and ready.

A private lift just off the kitchen doubtless led where she needed to go. But an odd aura infused it, a cold feel of menace that radiated from the emblematic vulture-heads adorning the panels of its bronze doors. It had to be wired to an alarm. She would have to find another way up.

She thought. Where food was prepared at a distance from the dining room, serving time was paramount. Hand-carried to the lift and then up, it would be already beginning to cool by the time it reached the table. There had to be some faster way to transport it. A dumbwaiter.

Once she knew what to look for, finding it was no big trick. The dumbwaiter was in the kitchen across from the ovens.

She climbed in.

It was a snug fit. She put her knapsack in first, then folded herself about it. Drawing knees to chin, she managed to wriggle in. The hand of glory bumped against her nose.

When she pulled the door shut, the dark closed about her like a fist. She could see nothing. Taking a deep breath, Jane seized the rope. She began to pull herself upward, slowly, so the pulleys wouldn't creak.

Hand over hand, the dumbwaiter inched into the dark.

It was a long way up.

Later, Jane would learn that Galiagante's apartment took up four floors, the lowest for the servants, the upper three for himself and the occasional guest. But in the slow, blind oven of the dumbwaiter, it felt like twenty floors at least. The journey seemed to take forever. Though she tried not to dwell on it, the fancy grew that she was trapped in a box crawling through the infinite space between the stars.

Her shoulders began to ache, and then her arms as well.

Sweat rolled from her armpits and down her sides. Her blouse was soaked through. Jane cursed herself for not having removed Puck's jacket before getting in. She was sweltering in it. She was going to broil in this thing.

The cart was padded with leather. The studs dug into her ass. She shifted slightly, but to no avail. Hand over hand, the rope slid by. Her stomach cramped and one leg went to sleep. It was all pins and needles. She stopped, wrapping the rope around one arm to anchor the cart, and tried to massage some life back into it. All the time she was listening for voices, for footfalls, for the sound of someone stirring. She'd risen a long way by now. If she slipped, the fall would surely kill her.

Her palms were sweaty. One by one she wiped them against her jeans. She started up again.

Up and up, through darkness.

At last a crack of light descended, came even with Jane's eyes, sank down to her feet. Her hands slowed to a stop on the rope. She held her breath and listened.

Somebody was moving around out there.

Clumsily twisting the rope about one leg so the cart wouldn't slide down, she took up the hand of glory. The need for silence made every motion excruciatingly slow. She squeezed the lighter from her pocket.

She kicked open the door.

A dwarf in Galiagante's house livery looked up, startled. "Hey!" he cried, "What are—?" She touched lighter to wick. A flame was born.

The dwarf's eyes caught the flare of the candle and widened. A tiny point of light danced at the black center of each.

Jane lit the second candle. "Where is Galiagante?" she asked. The dwarf was holding a silver tray. On it were two wineglasses, napkins, and an empty syringe.

They stood at one end of the dining room. An impossibly long table studded with great silver candlesticks tried but failed to reach to the far end. The dwarf half-turned and gestured with his chin toward a distant door. "In the master bedchamber," he said thickly. "With a friend."

She lit the third candle. "Is there anyone else anywhere in the apartment?"

"No. Just him. Me. The other." A fourth flame kindled. Eight smaller cousins burned in his eyes.

"I think you want to go and lie down for a bit."

"Yes." Dazedly, the dwarf walked past her and into a hallway. The lift recognized him and opened its doors. He vanished.

There wasn't much time. Once lit, the hand couldn't be rekindled. It would last her about twenty minutes.

Jane set to work.

———◦◉◦———

It was harder finding something worth stealing than she would've ever imagined. Avoiding the master bedchamber, Jane prowled quickly through the other rooms. They were all large, well-appointed, and useless for her purposes. She passed by tiger maple escritoires and wonderfully carved mahogany highboys. Crystal vases held sprays of albino tulips or pale, night-blooming fungi. Her feet trod rugs that had devoured lifetimes in the weaving. The credit card rubber-banded to the hand of glory was supposed to guide her to Galiagante's wealth; but the hand was drawn toward whatever she turned it to. It was maddening. Everything here was expensive and nothing pawnable.

Six minutes gone. Fourteen left.

Swiftly, silently, she prowled through room upon room. On the salon walls were paintings of screaming wrestlers in glass boxes and elegant lords leaning heavily over white porcelain sinks. Nothing but the best for Galiagante.

Nine minutes left. Jane found herself dead-ended in a windowless dressing room. The hand of glory turned icy cold and twisted in her grip. She opened the closet, shoved silks and tweeds aside, and unveiled a wall safe. It was a little tricky, but at last the safe recognized Galiagante's credit card and opened for her. Inside was a stack of bank notes—she riffled through them; enough here to pay for all her needs—as well as a selection of legal papers and a minor hoard of jewelry.

At last! Jane slipped the knapsack from her shoulder and crammed in the bank notes. The papers she left behind. Rings, pins, diamond bracelets she stuffed into the pockets of her jacket.

Four minutes left.

She was passing through the dining room on her way out, when her eye was caught by the candlesticks. They were heavy and had the soft gleam of silver. Almost as an afterthought, she reached out to grab one.

A shock of electricity shot up her arm. Her gloved hand clenched on the candlestick and would not let go. Her muscles had spasmed. *"Master!"* the stick screamed, *"A thief! Master!"*

"Let go!" Jane cried. The candlestick could not be moved. It seemed to be anchored to the table. And all the while it continued to shout. *"A thief! A thief!"*

"What's going on out here?" A door slammed open.

Jane twisted about and saw Galiagante in the doorway. He wore a silk robe hastily cinched at the waist. Behind him was a half-canopied bed. Its frame was white and its pedestals carved in the likeness of two whippets reared on their hind legs and holding the ends of a sheet in their teeth, so that the upper line of the sheet formed the top curve of the base. On the cushions was a ball of white light, elongated into a sort of cocoon. Something could be glimpsed within it, half-dissolved, writhing. A nymph.

The door closed. Galiagante strode angrily forward. His eyes were terrible, and he stood revealed as a Power. A wind rose up from the elf-lord. It battered against Jane, driving her hair back in a lashing fury. She held forward the hand of glory. Its flames fluttered, guttered, and went out.

Jane tried to back away, but the damnable candlestick held her prisoner. *"Master! Save me!"* She could hardly think for its noise.

"I know you." Galiagante stood frowning down at her. "The . . . alchemy major, are you not?" He snapped his fingers and the candlestick fell silent. The wind sank down.

With surprising delicacy, he took the knapsack from her back and rummaged through it. The bank notes he neatened into a stack and placed aside. Leaving the sack on the table, he reached into her pockets twice and removed the jewelry. Jane didn't try to resist. She was caught.

"This is an opportunity, I think." A strange little smile flickered like fire on his lips. He was looking her up and down. "But what kind?" he went on musingly. "Whatever shall I do with you?"

Involuntarily, tears welled in Jane's eyes. "Let me go," she whispered.

Galiagante had picked up the hand of glory and was studying it. He made a clucking sound with his tongue. "Don't spoil the good impression you've made so far," he said with a touch of asperity. He put down the hand and reached out to unzip Puck's leather jacket. The smell of rancid sweat came off her like a wave when he held it open. "What's this?"

He undid the top two buttons of her blouse and lifted the Ikea spoon from around her neck. "Oh, my!" His amusement was manifest. He dangled the spoon from his fingertip. "I imagine that I shall have to—"

The bedchamber door clicked open and a naked and disheveled figure appeared there. "When are you—" She stopped, and in a bewildered voice said, "Jane?"

⸺◈⸺

Galiagante stiffened. Without looking, he snapped, "Wait for me in the bedchamber. Shut the door after yourself."

She obeyed.

"That was Sirin," Jane said.

"Forget about her." Galiagante's face grew distant, faintly irresolute, as if he hesitated on the verge of a decision. "Her doom is hers. Think to your own fate." Then, abruptly, he laughed. "I'm going to let you go."

"Thank you," she said humbly.

"And I'm going to make you an offer."

Jane shivered, said nothing.

"Should you survive the Teind—and by the looks of you that's a very big if—come by my office and talk to my people. I'll have employment for you. Profitable employment. Even pleasant, by some standards."

He snapped his fingers again and the candlestick released her. She backed away a step, rubbing her elbow. Her arm felt stunned and painful.

Galiagante returned her knapsack, but kept the spoon. He gestured toward the elevator. "You may leave now. *Not* by the dumbwaiter, if you please."

Then he hoisted the candlestick and tossed it to Jane. Reflexively, she caught it. "Here. Take this. As earnest token of my sincerity."

Even before the elevator arrived, he had returned to the bedchamber. She watched the door close behind him and then she went home.

———— ◎ ————

Jane sleepwalked through her classes the next day. The midwinter thaw had arrived at last, and everywhere students had forced open windows, so that cold, fresh air breezed in and chilled the thermostats, driving the radiators into steamy frenzies of effort to compensate. Small thermals fluttered papers and sent dust spinning in little devils down the halls.

It would have been pleasant, if she hadn't felt so disconnected. Everything was dreamily distant, as if she were a ghost wandering a world whose importance to her she was rapidly forgetting. This couldn't go on. Something would have to break soon. Maybe tonight the Teind would arrive at last and put an end to this provisional, waiting sort of half-life. In the meantime, everything was so awful she just couldn't bring herself to care.

Even when Ratsnickle came up behind her in the line at the lunch counter in the Student Center and mimed a big, sloppy kiss she merely shrugged and turned away. She had a glimpse of his face turning nasty when she did so, and knew this ought to worry her. Nothing she could have done was more calculated to enrage him.

Still, what was she supposed to do? There came a point where it all became just more of the same.

She carried her tray to a plastic table under a potted thorn tree and sat down. A shrike was fussing about in the thorny depths, hopping from twig to twig. There were four chairs about the table.

Ratsnickle took the one directly opposite hers. She looked down at her salad. "You're not welcome here, you know."

Ratsnickle plunged a fork into the greasy sausage on his plate and waved it in her face. "You're going to get sick eating all that green shit. You need to put some meat in your mouth." He bit off the end and, chewing open-mouthed, continued, "Tell you what. Why don't you join Monkey and me for a little midnight snack tonight? We'll put some meat on your bones. Get a little protein into you."

Jane put her fork down. "If you can't—"

Abruptly, Sirin slid into the chair at Jane's side. Without preamble she said, "I've got to explain to you about last night. Just so you don't get any wrong ideas."

Her hair was pulled back into a tight ponytail today, and she wore just a touch of white lipstick and matching eye shadow. A black turtleneck sweater. On her it looked good.

"I think I understand it well enough."

Ratsnickle cleared his throat. "It's good to see you too, Sirin," he said loudly.

"Lo, 'snickle." Her glance at him was so fleeting as to be almost nonexistent. "You don't know what it's like to have appetites that—well, maybe they're not exactly respectable. But they're mine. You can see that, can't you? They're a part of me—I can't deny them."

Embarrassed, because Ratsnickle was hanging on their every word, Jane said, "You don't have to explain to me why you like Galiagante. Different folks like different things. I can appreciate that."

"Like Galiagante!" Sirin loosed a silvery burst of astonished laughter. "Wherever did you get a notion like that? Galiagante has nothing to do with it."

"It's not the individual so much as the Idea of the domineering male," Ratsnickle volunteered. "All those pheromones we put out."

Sirin waved off his remark with a little flip of her hand. It was marvelous how Ratsnickle's barbs glanced off her. "I like the way he treats me. I like the way he makes me feel. If I could find somebody more convenient to do that for me, he'd be history. But you can bet the new guy wouldn't be any improvement on him. That kind of guy never is."

"You won't know until you've tried me. Maybe I will."

"Sirin, why are you telling me all this?" It was unimaginable to

Jane being this open, telling one's secrets in front of everyone—in front of Ratsnickle!—as if it didn't matter at all what other people knew. As if they wouldn't take advantage of what they heard.

"I had a dream. About my doom." Sirin's face was drawn and tense. "I dreamed that Galiagante. That he. Oh, I can't tell you how nasty it was. It woke me up and all I could think was: *Not like that.* Jane, you're always so sure of yourself, so strong."

"I am?" Jane said, astonished. Ratsnickle's grin was lewd and calculating. She could almost see the gears turning.

"I thought maybe you could move in with me for a few days. You know, just talking and hanging out and things. Just to make sure I don't do anything foolish." Sirin's voice sank. "I know it's not much of a plan."

Stiffly, Jane said, "I told you. I feel bad for you and I wish I could help. But there's nothing I can do."

"But I'm asking for so little."

Just then Billy Bugaboo appeared behind the only empty chair that remained, tray in hand. "Is this seat taken?"

"Oh, for—!" Jane stood. "Take it! Have my lunch! I don't care! What have I done to deserve *you* on top of everything else that's happening to me?"

He stared at her, stricken. She fled the room.

———— ··◍·· ————

That evening, rather than chance encountering anybody in the cafeteria or one of the usual student hangouts, Jane went out into the City and ate supper in a diner in Orgulous. She had meat loaf and mashed potatoes. A dwarf tried to hit on her and when she began shouting at him the management asked her to leave.

The evening was soft and pleasant. The traffic sounds were muted and the air was almost warm. Jane strode along hunched into herself, hands deep in pockets, scowling. How long, she asked herself, how long?

Jane had traveled to Orgulous by way of Senauden and on impulse hired a private car to the street. When she stepped into Bellegarde's lobby, she suddenly realized that, what with one thing and another, it was the first time she'd been there in months. She also realized that she'd left her elevator pass in her purse back in the room. "Shit!"

It made no sense to waste good money on something she'd already paid for, so she took the back corridors into the service areas in search of a freight elevator. It wasn't permitted, but students used them all the time.

Almost immediately, she became lost. A stairway drew her down into the basement and when she tried to retrace her steps she couldn't find it again. So she went on, through a series of ever-darkening storage rooms that smelled of turpentine, pitch, vinegar, and moldering books. She was just beginning to panic when she saw a green-painted steel door beside a coal bin. She stopped.

For no reason she could name, an overwhelming intuition filled her that what she was looking for was right behind that door.

She opened it.

Great masses of black iron loomed in the darkness. She sniffed grease and oil in the air. The light of a single bare bulb glinted on an enormous construction of steel and malice, one that was as familiar to her as the back reaches of her own soul. It was No. 7332—Melanchthon.

The dragon grinned.

"Are you surprised to see me again, little changeling?" The heat of his derision was like a blast furnace opening in her face. The door dissolved in Jane's hand and the darkness about her intensified. In all the universe nothing existed save for the dragon and her. Melanchthon's cabin opened soundlessly. "Come in. We have a lot to talk about."

There was nothing else to be done. Jane climbed in.

The pilot's couch looked newer than she remembered it being. But when she sat down, it settled about her in a way that was intimately knowing. Soft lights gleamed from the instruments. Things crawled in the blackness at the corners of her eyes. Somewhere, a meryon screamed and was silenced.

"You abandoned me," she said.

"Now I'm back."

Jane's hands clenched the armrests. One twist and the needles would slide into her wrists. The wraparounds would descend to plunge her into the dragon's sensorium. She did not twist the grips. "You're looking prosperous."

As intended, this offended him. "You are as dull and slow-witted as ever," Melanchthon said scornfully. Deep within his thorax an engine roared to life. Its vibrations shook the cabin. "I have come to bring you death, blood, vengeance, and a small share in the greatest adventure since the first act of murder—and you offer me pleasantries."

"Pleasantries are all we have to say to one another."

"Talk all you want," the dragon said with furious impatience. "Taint as much air as you like with your stale and vapid words, words, words. But you and I have lived within one another. We have shared essences, and we can neither of us be free of the other ever in this lifetime." In the silence that ensued, Jane felt a sickening conviction that he was right.

When the dragon spoke again at last, he had mastered his passions. His tone was cool and dismissive. "How can you have lived so long and experienced so much without ever once asking yourself who was the author of your misfortunes?"

"I know my enemy well enough. Down to the op codes I know him."

"Me?" the dragon said mockingly. "I am at most a symptom. Was it me who created the world and involved you in it? Me who said you must live and love and lose and grow old and die? Who poisoned your every friendship and drove you away from those you most desired? Who said that you must learn only by making mistakes and that the lessons you learned must then do you no good? That was not I. You are caught in a pattern spun by a greater power than mine."

"I know your enemy, for she is mine as well. Compared to my hatred for her, our enmity is like a candle held up to the sun. Understand me well: You are within my grasp, and it would give me great joy to play with you, even as a cat does with a captive vole. Yet I will let you walk free, for we have common cause. You also must set aside all lesser emotions. Focus on your true foe. Hate her with all your might. Fear her, even as do I."

Jane had always thought that blood could not run cold, that those who said theirs had were employed in wordplay and metaphor. Now she knew better. "Who are you talking about?"

Was it mere theatricality or something deeper, a savoring of his own blasphemy, that made Melanchthon hesitate? With quiet satisfaction, he said, "The Goddess."

"No!"

"Come now. You never suspected? Deep in the sleepless night you never saw that life itself is proof that the Goddess does not love you? That her regard is malevolent at best, and that your pain must surely amuse her, for what other purpose does it serve? You cannot shirk your doom. You have a small part to play in her destruction. You should feel proud."

"You're mad," Jane whispered. "Nobody can destroy the Goddess."

"Nobody has ever tried." Melanchthon's voice was smooth and plausible, the antithesis of madness. "Our time apart has not been wasted, I promise you. I have seized control of my own evolution and made myself mighty beyond the normal range of my kind. I have the destructive power, never doubt it. But there is no future for a renegade dragon, oath-broken and lordless. The skies are closed to me. I can either crawl forever about the roots and cellars of the world or enjoy one last fatal flight. I'll not catch the defenders of the Law napping again. Well, so be it. I will make a fourth flight through Hell Gate. I will assail Spiral Castle itself, and obliterate it, and drag the Goddess from its shattered ruins.

"And by all that is unseely, I swear I'll kill the Bitch."

"It's impossible," Jane said weakly.

"You are still infested with hope. You think there is a life worth living somewhere, and that some combination of action, restraint, knowledge, and luck will save you, if only you can get the mix right. Well, I've got news for you. Right here, right now—this is as good as it gets."

"Things will get better!"

"Have they ever?" The dragon's contempt was palpable. The cabin hatch hissed open. "Go. Return to your dormitory room and enjoy your present. Come back when you've grown large enough to look upon futility without flinching. Come back when you've despaired and moved beyond despair to vengefulness. Come back when you've decided to stop lying to yourself."

"What present?"

The lights dimmed. Melanchthon did not speak.

"Enjoy my present, you said. What present?"

Nothing.

"I've been through all this before. I'm not going to play any more of your stupid fucking mind games!"

Silence.

Jane struggled to fight down her anger, her fear, her outraged sense of impotence. It took some time. But finally, she climbed down out of the cabin, just as Melanchthon had desired.

As usual, it was the only thing she could do.

⸻◈⸻

Somehow she made it back home to Lady Habundia. As her hand touched the door, an icy spear of premonition pierced her. She hesitated, unable to turn the knob.

This was silly. There was nothing inside—there couldn't be anything inside—any worse than what she had just faced in the cellars of Bellegarde. It was just Melanchthon, out of simple spite, twisting the knife. She threw open the door.

Monkey and Ratsnickle lay dead on the floor.

A small, inarticulate noise came out of Jane's throat. This was surely Melanchthon's idea of a joke. Or maybe it was just his grotesque version of what Galiagante had called an "earnest token," a courteously intended removal of two petty annoyances from her life.

The lights were on. That's what made it so awful. If there had been a touch of shadow anywhere, her eyes might have fled thither and sought refuge in it. But in the cruel, flat lamplight, her vision was pinned. There was no looking away. There was no denying what lay before her.

In death, Monkey's face had turned gray and Ratsnickle's a ghastly white with blue highlights. Their irises had dissolved completely, leaving behind featureless crescents under purple lids. Their mouths were slack and open. A moist trail of drool ran down Ratsnickle's chin and a single drop clung to its underside, maddeningly refusing to fall. It was as if time had come to a halt.

The needle was still in Ratsnickle's arm. He must've shot up Monkey first and then turned away to inject himself, not seeing her slump back against the bed. Then, as the bane reached his heart, he had simply sagged to one side. His head pointed toward the door. Even in death, he leaned away from poor Monkey.

Jane stood frozen in horror.

In the distance a siren raised its voice. A second joined it and then a third. Soon all the City was a symphony of horns and alarms.

The Teind had begun.

# EIGHTEEN

It was the worst possible thing she could have done. On the mimeographed sheets that the University had distributed to all undergrads, the very first item, in big, sweet-smelling purple letters, had been 1. STAY IN YOUR ROOM.

Jane knew that was good advice.

But blind panic drove her out of her room, out of Habundia, out of Bellegarde altogether, and onto the street. She had no conscious say in it. One moment she was staring down at the two bodies on her floor and the next she was trembling, bewildered, in an unfamiliar part of town.

A boar-headed fey shambled by, crying. His elbows pumped higher than his head, and tears ran down his curling tusks. He was paced by a dozen or so wolf-boys, jeering and laughing. A stick jabbed into his side, he stumbled, and then he was up and gone.

There was the sound of breaking glass.

She had to get back to Bellegarde! They'd be closing the riot gates at midnight. But if she could slip in before then, she might yet find refuge in Sirin's room or maybe Linnet's, high above ground level where the worst was sure to go down.

The street turned and narrowed. Blind walls rose to either side, making of it a trough or chute. Down the block, a crowd of feys was dancing about a bonfire to the throb and boom of a ghetto box. Others had broken into a textile warehouse and were throwing bolts of muslin, calico, worsted poplin, and watered silk from five floors of windows. Unspooling, they showered down to the pavement. Grigs and dunters darted into the crash zone to drag material to the fire.

Jane drew back, but suddenly the street behind her filled with grotesques, chanting

> "Vervaine, Johnswort, Cinquefoil, Hate,
> Burn the Cit-y,
> Smash the State!"

They were playing bells and horns and waving advertising banners back and forth over their bobbing heads. Lanterns hung from high poles. Bat-eared, antlered, and stork-legged, they looked like nothing so much as carnival revelers.

> "Burn the Cit-y,
> Smash the State!"

Too fearful to run, Jane was overtaken by the mob, swept up, and carried along. Abruptly she was one of them, not their target but safe within their merry number, cushioned and upheld by the crush of bodies. Everyone was laughing and red-faced and ugly. A red dwarf handed her a can of beer. To calm herself, she popped it open and drank deeply. It was so cold it stung her tongue.

> "Burn the Cit-y,
> Smash the State!"

A strange, electric mix of fear and excitement filled her.

The mob came to the bonfire. The two groups merged and eddied.

"Having fun?"

Jane whirled, astounded. "Linnet! What are you doing here?"

Her classmate shrugged. "Same thing you are—enjoying myself."

"Linnet, we've got to get back to the dorm. Do you have any idea how far away it is? If it's not too distant, we can still make it to Habundia before they lock it up."

"Fuck that shit!" Linnet hugged herself fiercely, bony shoulders standing up like a second pair of wings. "I'm not giving this up to sit in my room and stare at the wall. Crack a book. Maybe get out the electric coil and brew some camomile tea. Habundia is a million light-years away. Don't you understand? Tonight, nothing is forbidden. You want something—take it! You like somebody—go ahead and do it! You can sit on the curb and eat your own boogers for all the world to see, if that's what turns you on. Nobody's going to stop you. Nobody's keeping score."

She stuck a battered hemp cigarette in her mouth and snapped her fingers beneath it. A spark, a flame, a puff of smoke. She didn't offer to share. The gleeful light of abandon in her face was so intense that Jane ducked her head in embarrassment.

With a roar the crowd surged forward again. Jane was shoved to one side and then the other. She had to trot to keep from falling. "Where are we going?" she cried.

"Who cares?!"

They sped by a row of shops. Plate glass windows shattered in their wake. Scattered individuals darted in to snatch up a purse or a handful of cuff links, but the mob as a whole did not slacken pace. The sound of exploding glass went on and on. "This is awful!" Jane shouted.

"This is nothing." Linnet's eyes were incandescent. Her grin was so wide it had to hurt. "Just wait."

The mob contracted. Shoulders, elbows, and bony chins pushed against Jane from all sides, threatening to crack her ribs. Bodies shifted. Like a grapefruit seed squeezed between thumb and forefinger, Linnet was squirted out of sight.

Jane's helplessness was perfect. Caught in the crush, pressed tight, she was unable even to fall—the mob upheld her. Briefly she was lifted off her feet and carried along. When the road widened, her feet touched pavement and she had to run to keep from falling and being trampled under.

Another roar. The front edge of the mob had found something. It was, Jane discovered when she pushed close enough to see, a behemoth. They had trapped it in a cul-de-sac and were rocking it back and forth. It toppled over with a bellow of frustrated rage, and its conquerors swarmed up over its hindquarters. They sprang the hood and driver-side door and began yanking out its guts. Seats, cables, spark plugs, a plastic dashboard statue of the Great Mother were thrown out into the crowd. "Bastards!" the behemoth roared. "I kill you! Crush you! I stomp you flat!" It was terrifying that so great a beast, so mighty a machine, could be mastered so easily.

Terrifying and just a little magnificent.

The front of a tavern had been ripped away and its bar broken up. Bottles were being handed out to whoever passed by. Jane found herself clutching a pint of peppermint schnapps. It tasted dreadful. But after a while she got used to it.

Smashing and looting, the mob flowed forward until something up ahead—a dead end, a split in the road—made it pause in indecision. Slowed to a walk, Jane again spotted Linnet. She was arm in arm with an enormous, misshapen wight. Jane tapped her shoulder.

Linnet looked up blankly. "What are *you* doing here?" Without waiting for an answer, she released her companion's arm. "This is Bone Head."

Bone Head certainly looked the part. His skull was enormously thick, lopsided, and deathly white under close-cropped hair. Blackwork sun wheels were tattooed onto his forehead and cheeks. His eyes were lifeless, pits of ash.

He grinned loutishly and fingered his balls.

Desperately ignoring him, Jane said, "Do you have any idea where we are? You don't have to come with me. Just point me in the right direction and I'll find my own way home."

With withering scorn, Linnet said, "You don't get it, do you? You just don't get it." Wings flapping, she pulled her sweater over her head. She wore nothing underneath. Her breasts weren't particularly large, but her nipples were enormous, as large as plums and the color of apricots. At the sight of them, a cheer went up.

Linnet flung the sweater into the air. A hunchbacked musician bent to stick his head between her legs, then stood again. She rose up on his shoulders, a figurehead for the mob.

"The Barrows!" somebody shouted. Linnet waved her arms, urging them onward. "The Barrows!" she screamed. With the hunchback playing his flute beneath her, she led them away.

They moved at a fast stride, almost a trot. The intoxicating smell of their sweat surrounded Jane, like rotting fruit. The mob was not chanting now, but making an extraordinary noise, a surf of voices with occasional high cries lifting up from the surface in sonic spikes, and a bass rumble that vibrated in the pit of her stomach and never stopped. It buzzed and crackled in her head like an amphetamine high, constant, unchanging, and yet complexly varied, a symphony to chaos.

Jane ran a hand through her hair. It crackled. She no longer wanted to get away. What was happening was too exciting, too vital in an awful way, to relinquish. She had to see what came next. Weightless, a charged particle in the current of the mob, she let it carry her away, offering not the least resistance to its will.

Abruptly Jane was inside an appliance store. Everywhere dim

forms were snatching up camcorders, CD players, minifridges. A box was dumped into her arms. Bewildered, she took it.

A soot black imp jumped from the shadows and cheerily shouted, "Fire! Fear! Fire! Get out! Get out!"

Flames leaped up behind him.

Everyone tried to squeeze out the front at once. For a fearful instant Jane thought she was going to be crushed and feared for her life. She was blocks down the road before she thought to look down and see what she had.

A microwave oven.

It really was a remarkable bit of luck. She had a serious need for a microwave back in her room, and because there was no way she could ever shoplift anything so large, she decided to keep it.

———※◇※———

Lugging the oven, though, Jane found she could not keep up. By degrees she lagged behind, steadily slipping to the rear of the mob. Until finally, arms and shoulders aching, she had to sit down on some steel-and-concrete steps by an old industrial canal. She felt exhausted.

The last of the mob flowed away. The air chilled. The roar of voices sank to a mutter, one that rose sporadically from different parts of the City, as if the mob were a monster that could exist in several places at once. She stared down at her feet, at the litter of rusty metal scrap, plastic crack vials, and cigarette butts. Her head was still buzzing.

The mob had sucked up all vitality from the streets and buildings as it passed. In its train paint blistered, popped, and released spores of rust in tiny puffs. Asphalt buckled. Stucco fell away from brick in patches. Trash multiplied by the curbs and bobbed in the oily waters of the canal. Walls crumbled.

From the interiors of gutted buildings, weeds sprouted with necromantic speed. As Jane watched, a vine pushed its way from a crack at the base of a concrete bridge pier, and grew into a labyrinthine tangle of thorns. Deep in its heart roses bloomed whose attar, like spoiled milk, drew in some species of winged sprites no larger than her fist.

With a tinkling of small bells the sprites sped over the canal. They traveled in pairs, hauling equally diminutive prisoners at the ends of twin ropes no thicker than threads. Headlong they plunged into the gloomy thicket.

Tiny screams pierced the night.

As an alchemist-to-be, Jane understood natural processes. Balance had been destroyed; it had to be restored. But she didn't have to watch. She had caught her breath. It was time to go. She stood, leaving the microwave on the steps. She didn't really want the damned thing after all.

A gout of vomit splashed the road. She danced back, but still flecks of it spattered her shoes.

Three hyena-headed creatures leaned over the rail of an overpass above her. "Hey, watch it!" she shouted.

One, the sick one, appeared not even to notice her. A second brayed at her distress. The third stepped up on the rail, unbuttoned his fly and shook his prick at her. "Bite on this, honey!"

"Shitheads!" she yelled.

"This bitch," the prick-waggler said coldly, "needs to be taught a lesson." His friend was already casting about for a way down. "Over there!" he cried. Leaving their drunken comrade clutching the rail, they ran toward a stairway on the far side of the bridge. Terrified, Jane ducked into a doorway and discovered that it was the entrance to a less obvious stairway up to the street they had just vacated.

At the top she paused as first a dozen and then a hundred misshapen creatures raced by. Her tormenters had been front-runners of one arm of the mob. It was not the same group she had left— she recognized no one, and there were faces among these she would have remembered. But it didn't matter. She stepped into their hurrying number.

Safe again.

* * *

Jane had not run far when an enormous roar exploded up ahead. Abruptly the street opened into a great five-sided square. Like gas molecules escaping from compression the mob sped up and spread out to fill the new space. With a thrill of fear, Jane realized where they were.

This was Oberon Square. On four sides were taverns, record outlets, hardware stores, haberdasheries, and the like. On the fifth the massive obsidian front of the single most infamous penitentiary in all the Great Gray City jutted over the plaza like the massive prow of an ominous black freighter.

The Long Barrows.

Confronted with the place itself, the mob proved oddly reluctant to attack. It broke into smaller groups on the other four sides, ignoring the obvious target. The storefronts were covered with security grates and blast screens but there were unprotected windows higher up. The mob pelted them with stones and brickbats.

On an impulse too swift for apprehension, Jane picked up an empty beer bottle, cocked her arm, and threw. Her window shattered. She tossed her head and crowed. A troll patted her back, making her stagger.

It felt great.

The madness of the fairy host engaged her fully then, wrapping about her like a pair of gauze wings. She took a deep breath, drawing the swirling, effervescent feeling deep into her lungs and abdomen. Once done, it was inevitable. She was one of them now, body and soul, a citizen of the mob.

A drunk stumbled against her and she shoved him hard with both hands. "Out of my way, you fucking yob!"

And that felt great too.

When they had shattered all the windows, peeled the grates from the shops, looted the interiors, and torched two of the stores, there was a pause. Several burly dwarves tried to smash the hinges of the great gate of the penitentiary. But for all their strength and cunning, they had to step down in disgrace.

The mob almost stalled out then. To keep up momentum some of its number turned to a boutique winery that had heretofore escaped their attention. Leather chairs and spider plants flew into the street. Oils of naked ogres crouching on toilets were thrown into the flames. Then three gargantuan casks rumbled onto the paving stones, pushed by straining lamies. One leaped atop the lead hogshead and waved his feathered cap in the air. "Goodfellows!" he cried. Derisive laughter. He hoisted an ax. "Our beloved masters, the Lords of the City, have imprisoned—for its own good!—this lawless and defiant liquor. Many a long and festering year has it been confined within these oaken walls, maturing, mellowing, losing its harsh edges, aspiring to become a clement and obedient drink, fit for the noble gullets of our most worthy owners." He was the center of all eyes. The lamie puffed out his chest, mugged, and shouted, "Has it matured?"

"*No!!!*"

"Has it learned its lesson?"

"*No!!!*"

"Has it mended its unruly ways?"

"*No!!!*"

"Fair spoken. 'Tis clearly recalcitrant and no suitable glug for the likes of our betters." He brought the ax down on the cask's bunghole. Wine gushed across the square. Laughing grotesques rushed to the gutters to kneel and drink.

A pump was liberated from the hardware store and used to fill an empty fountain at the center of the plaza. Revelers—Linnet was one—splashed naked in it, drinking from cupped hands and pouring bloody liquid over one another. The burning buildings and mercury-vapor streetlamps combined to cast a cheerless orange light over them all.

There was a shout from the outskirts of the crowd.

A construction giant lurched slowly into the square, directed by a grinning devil of a boggart who sat on his shoulder, whispering in his ear. They stopped at the prison gates and the giant lifted his massive fist. Three times he smashed the iron-clad doors. They splintered and held. Then on the fourth blow the gate gave way and crashed down.

A cheer went up that shook the stars.

Jane surged forward with everyone else. She found herself running down a dark and narrow corridor with Bone Head at her side. He seized her arm and hauled her to a stop before a cell door. "Hold this!" He thrust his jacket at her and spat a stream of yellow phlegm between his shoes. Then he rammed a pry bar between lock and jamb. Muscles bulged under his sweat-dampened T-shirt.

The door popped open.

Rotting teeth in a rotting mouth. A face that seemed to be twisted sideways. The creature stepped out of its cell and pinched Jane's cheek with fingers that stung like ice. "Is this for me?" it rasped, then chuckled at her dismay and hobbled away.

Bone Head snapped open a second lock. Something dark, like gritty shadow, flowed free. It glanced at Jane in passing. She had a brief impression of hate-filled eyes, like the tips of a thousand scorpion claws. Her heart leaped with fear.

"Don't just stand there!" Bone Head cuffed Jane's ear. "We got work to do."

But Jane did just stand there. Too involved to notice, Bone Head worked his way down the corridor, springing door after door, releasing horrors the like of which she had never seen.

She dropped the jacket and backed away.

Outside, a grinning pixie handed Jane a bottle of whiskey. She drank. A hytersprite was passing out pills. She popped five dry.

Too impatient to wait, arsonists had already started several blazes within. Rioters and prisoners emerged choking and gagging, drunk and giggling. Only the nearer cellblocks had been emptied. In no time at all the farther reaches were enveloped in flames hotter than any oven.

Escaping convicts issued screaming from the gate, running in frantic circles, their arms flapping and their heads ablaze. They were greeted with laughter.

Ash fell like snow. The flakes were as large as Jane's hand. She stared up, blinking.

As was commonplace in prison architecture, the gate was topped by a short bridge atop which was a small guard tower. The guards were long fled and the gates thrown down, but it yet bridged the gap over the space where they had been.

The bridge was black against the flames and on the short tower at its center feys capered, singing and pissing into the flames. They took no regard for their danger. This went beyond the merely suicidal. It was terrifying.

Suddenly the feys on the gate tower shouted. One pointed to a far street.

Elven warriors in black glass helmets marched into the square.

As if prearranged, blankets appeared at the foot of the wall, held taut at the corners. One by one the lookouts jumped, bounced on the blankets, and were down.

The mob grew curiously quiet.

The elven warriors formed up to one end of the square. They stood in tense ranks with riot clubs drawn and plexy shields slung over one arm. All wore the badge of the winged ronyon on their tunics.

Their captain rode a chrome destrier polished to so fine a gloss it was difficult to make out. Reflections of the mob, the warriors, the burning walls of the Long Barrows, swam silently over its cool surfaces, bulging up as the destrier paced forward, then being swallowed back into mystery as it shifted slightly to one side.

The ashes continued to softly fall.

The elf-captain stood in his stirrups and in a high clear voice cried, "This rabble is assembled against the conventions of the Teind. Your presence here is unseely and forbidden. You have two minutes to clear the square."

They jeered, but weakly. The mob was uncertain, hesitant. At its edges, some few of the fickler wights were beginning to slip away. Had the elven warriors stepped forward then, they could have swept the square clear with little effort. But their captain gave no order. A cruel smile played on his face.

The jeering grew louder. A rock flew and then a bottle. It exploded. At the sound a shock ran through the mob, a ripple of apprehension that crossed the square in less time than a shout. Jane trembled involuntarily. All about her, bodies tensed. "Oh shit," muttered a dwarf. They were actually going to do it. They were really going to go up against the elves.

The dwarf grabbed Jane's elbow and pointed. Heads swiveled. In a side street more warriors appeared. Then in another. They were blocking all the exits. Here was the reason why their captain had hesitated. He wanted the mob enclosed and unable to escape.

"If you don't disperse, force may be used against you." The elf-captain glanced casually at his wristwatch.

The hypocrisy of it steeled Jane's resolve. Her hatred of the high-elven flared to white heat. So they thought they could cow her? It wouldn't work. She might be terrified, but she was no coward. Here I stand, she thought. I will not be moved.

With a shout, the warriors charged.

———— ·(◦)· ————

The clash was all a jumble.

Everyone was pushing and screaming and cursing. There was no order to it that Jane could see. The charge was as brutally simple as the assault of the ocean on the land. But the mob faced it as boldly as the mountains did the sea. Just before the warriors reached the first rioters, their captain raised his club high and spoke a word of power.

All the streetlamps exploded. The square was plunged into a ruddy, firelit murk.

The new conditions favored the elves, who had been trained in night combat and by an ancient blessing of the Goddess would be ever clear-sighted so long as the least sliver of Dame Moon hung in the sky. Clubs flashing, they advanced, and the mob gave way before them. But so eager to get their blows in were the soldiers that the line quickly broke into ragged knots of violence, and much of that advantage was lost.

Jane was shoved one way and then the other. She saw a burly

knocker throw himself on a shield and its warrior fall back with an agonized cry and a broken arm. The crowd swirled and he disappeared. It swung around again and Jane saw three elves clubbing her dwarf. His doublet had been torn off him. His body lay at their feet, bloody, half-naked, and unresisting. The head lolled freely on his neck. It jerked with each blow. His spine had been snapped. Jane stepped forward. Aghast, she realized that she was going to try and help him.

Stupid, stupid, stupid! she raged at herself. What the fuck am I doing here? This is pointless. The dwarf is dead. There's nothing I can do for him. Turn away, run, flee!

Like a sleepwalker she kept on going.

A warrior loomed up before her, helmet lost and his fine blond hair lashing. The battle-light blazed in his face. He raised his club against her. Then his foot fell wrong on a wine-slick paving stone and he stumbled to one knee.

In that instant an ogre was on his back, head down and braced between his shoulder blades, bandy legs scissoring his waist, knobby hands yanking back his chin. There was a sharp *crack*. The elf thrashed, and the light went out in his face. His club clattered to the stones.

Jane snatched it up.

The ashes were falling thicker than ever. Any more and it would be impossible to breathe. The smell of burning vinyl-wood-fabric-plastic from the torched buildings was everywhere; it stung her nose and lingered in the back of her mouth. Jane knew this should be the darkest moment of her life, but in a bizarre and distasteful way it wasn't.

It was fun.

"Get away from me! Get away get away get away!" The club was solid metal and as long as she was, with a short crosspiece on one side to make it amenable to skillful mob control tactics. Untutored, Jane grabbed one end and swung it back and forth like a great two-handed sword. Space opened up before and around her. She could breathe again. "Bastards!" she screamed. "Cocksucking elves!"

A noise like a sigh and then another and then three more, sounds made distinct from the general clamor of battle by their quiet diffidence. Gas canisters clattered onto the paving stones. They exploded, releasing clouds of riot gas.

Those touched by the gas fell back retching. They fought and clawed at one another to escape. But before the warriors could take advantage of their disorder, croppy lads with dampened handkerchiefs wrapped around their mouths and noses dashed forward, grabbed the canisters, and threw them back at the troops.

A touch of wind folded one of the clouds gently over onto the section of crowd where Jane stood.

She couldn't breathe! She couldn't see! Her skin was on fire! She was coughing, choking, crying miserably. Snot ran from her nose. One side of her face felt like it had been wiped with nettles. Stumbling, bent over, she groped for a way out.

And then, miraculously, a hand took hers and led her away. She could feel cool air on her face. Through blinking eyes she got a watery glimpse of open road ahead.

"Come on," her benefactor growled. "There'll be more gas soon."

When they had won free of the square, though, Jane had to stop. She dug in her heels and yanked her hand free. Then she wiped her eyes against one shoulder of her jacket and her nose against the other. Through her tears, she looked back at the riot.

The smoke from a hundred fires had made of the sky a canvas and then painted it a muddy red. Under its somber canopy, dark creatures were hunkered over the bodies of the fallen. Some were stealing wallets. Others were not. She recognized some of them as prisoners she had helped free.

"We ain't got time for sightseeing," her companion insisted. "The Greencoaties are coming." And, indeed, she could hear the cadenced jackboots of fresh elven troops. He gave her a shove and off they ran. It was only then that she thought to look and see who her savior was.

It was Bone Head.

———◦◉◦———

When it was clear that nobody was following, Jane stumbled to a stop. She had to puke. Bone Head steadied her with an arm about her shoulders while she purged herself of the ashes, madness, and blight. When she straightened again she felt surprisingly clearheaded.

"Some brawl, eh?" Bone Head said.

She looked at him.

"I bit this one fucker's finger right off. He had this big old gold ring on, all covered with itty-bitty emeralds and rubies and shit. Got it right here." He patted a bloody shirt pocket gloatingly. "So I got me a nice little profit out of tonight."

Bone Head was as alarmingly ugly as ever. But his eyes had changed. They were green now with flecks of gold, like leaves in early summer. A lively humor shone from them, as if Bone Head were merely a role he was playing, or as if something were using him as a mask and peeking through the sockets of his skull. "You've got something caught in your earring," Jane said.

"Eh?" Bone Head twisted around, hands flying up, as Jane grabbed at his ear. Too late. Her fingers closed about a talisman hanging from its lobe. "Hey, watch that!"

She ripped the talisman away. With a cry of alarm, he wavered and shrank. His face and features changed nature completely. The tattoos vanished, and with them his slack, malevolent expression. He was Bone Head no longer.

He was Puck Aleshire.

Jane glanced at the talisman—amber, bone, a superconducting disk, two bluejay feathers—and tossed it away. It was nothing; she could make one of them herself anytime she wanted to. "What the fuck are you doing here?"

"I was looking for you, okay? Holy pig, that smarts." He winced. Puck was wearing a battered cloth coat that didn't fit him at all well. "Look, I know you didn't ask me to come after you. But here I am anyway. And if you weren't so stoned, you'd be glad. We've got to get out of here. They've taken out their knives. They're not going to put them away when they run out of elves."

He seized her arm and began dragging her away.

Hurrying after, Jane had to admit that Puck looked heroic. His eyes blazed and his jaw was set. Her heart softened briefly. Then she looked down. Something dangled from his pocket, where it had been hastily and incompletely thrust. It was a scrap of black cloth. A pair of panties. The look and weave of them was familiar. "What's this?" Jane snatched them up. They had been worn and not laundered. She held them to her nose and sniffed.

Hers.

"Where did you get this?"

Puck ducked his head, embarrassed, but didn't slacken his pace. "I, uh, swapped something to Billy Bugaboo for it. He said you'd stayed the night at his room once, and forgot to pick it up when you got dressed the next morning."

"That Billy!" Jane said, outraged. "I'll *strangle* him!"

"We didn't think you'd actually mind."

"Well I do mind. I mind very much."

"Anyway, I couldn't've found you without it. Like calls to like, right? That's the law of contagion."

"Contagion?!"

"It's not such a big deal, okay? Billy told me he needed my leather jacket and what did he have that I wanted?" He glanced sideways at her and for the first time took in the sorry mess she had made of his jacket. "Hey. How'd you end up with it anyway?"

She colored.

They walked in silence for a while. Then Puck said, "I guess we've both done things we're not especially proud of. It's not important now. We really do have to get away from here before things turn nasty."

There were bodies in the road.

They were traveling in the wake of one arm of the mob. Periodically they could hear its voice roaring ahead of them. It was spooky, because for blocks at a time they saw not another living being. Just the bodies.

The corpses were mostly small—they were in a tenement neighborhood and various factions of the mob had gone in for a spot of dwarf-bashing. But there were lutins and nisken and goat people as well, though in lesser numbers. Jane was mesmerized by one in particular, a faun whose face was half-flayed. A trophy hunter had stripped the flesh from the lower jaw before something had distracted him from his project, revealing a wildly upturned grin. The one eye that could be seen was wide open and had turned a snowy blue. The resulting expression was knowing, daunting, compelling. Staring into it, Jane found herself close to understanding something important. Oh, what you're in for, that expression said. If only you knew.

"Don't stand there," Puck said. "Are you nuts?" He yanked her away.

The streets swelled and rolled underfoot. Jane had to clutch Puck's arm to keep from falling. "Where are we going?" she asked.

"Well, I'd staked out a space behind a dumpster out back of Bellegarde. But I wasted a lot of time looking for you. We'd never make it back there now. Old Mouldiwarp would take us in, but his digs are over across the river. There's a nest of mimsies I know would give me shelter, but I'm male—they wouldn't take you. We don't have many choices." He sounded like he were not so much running through possibilities as justifying a bad decision.

"Where?" she insisted.

"There." They turned a corner and were on a street bypassed by the mob. Ahead, a cluster of slum buildings huddled under the supporting buttresses of an iron suspension bridge. It could not be far to the wharves; Jane could smell the river. The buildings were all abandoned and their windows had been boarded over. A single unbroken streetlight cast just enough light to read the sign over what had once been a restaurant:

### SISTER MINNIE'S KITCHEN

"It's a shooting gallery," Puck explained. "Wicked Tom runs it. But it'll be as safe as anyplace is tonight. Nothing in it but junkies on the nod. Nothing worth stealing. Nothing worth burning. So long as Tom's not there, we'll be fine. And he won't be there. He'll be out looking for me." He clucked his tongue. "Last place he'd ever look."

"You're sure of that?"

"I wasn't planning to be anywhere *near* the place. He knows me well enough to know that."

A shriek tore the sky. A black hint of wings wrapped them in dread for the briefest instant and then was gone as the terror lifted up for a perch atop the bridge. More dark shapes fell from the cables, screaming. Like nightmare gulls, they fought with the first for something it held in its beak.

Two of the fliers collided, and the morsel tumbled down toward the street. It hit with a sickeningly meaty sound. "Ugh!" Jane cried involuntarily.

"Don't look," Puck commanded. But of course she did. It was the armless and legless torso of a dwarf. It was far from the most horrid thing she had seen that night, but somehow it affected her more. She felt it like a slap in the face.

"Take me inside," she pleaded.

They climbed a single crumbling concrete step. Puck pushed open a splintered door with a loop of string through the hole where the doorknob had been.

It opened onto splendor.

The interior was as elegant as a perfume ad. The floors were a checkerboard of gleaming marble. Slim pillars of semiprecious stone held up a roof too high to be seen. Snowy owls fluttered in the air, appearing and disappearing at random. Silk hangings floated before the walls. Below them godlike youths lounged on enormous throw pillows. A tape of synthesizer music droned in the background.

A wave of dizziness washed over Jane. She put a hand against a porphyry column to steady herself. Chips of dried paint crackled under her fingertips. The marble floor sagged underfoot. It felt slightly spongy.

"It's all glamour." Puck let the door swing shut behind them. "We're catching a kind of contact high." One of the golden dreamers swam languidly toward them. Puck held out a coin but the dreamer waved it away with a toothy grin. "Everything's free tonight." He gestured toward a line of white plates, each with a cone of powder or stack of resin bars at its center. "Take as much as you like. There's enough for all and everything the best." Jane caught a rank whiff of putrefaction. "Our host is paying for it all."

"Leave it to Tom to find a cheap way to pay the Teind."

"He is generosity itself," agreed the youth.

"He's a putrid son of a bitch."

With a shrug and a hint of a salaam, the dreamer returned to his hookah. High over his head an arched and grated window afforded a glimpse into a midsummer afternoon, all flowered vines and songbirds. A touch of breeze carried its scent to Jane and she caught her breath. It was her mother's garden! She'd recognize that smell among a million others.

Puck took Jane's head in his hands and forcibly turned it away. "You don't want to get too involved," he said. "I knew a girl once who fixated on that garden. She kept coming back, trying to find a way in. She was as bad as a crackhead looking for crumbs. She just couldn't stop. She was sure there had to be a door."

"So what happened to her?"

"Nothing happened to her." Puck's face was like stone. "She's around here somewhere."

Jane shivered. "I've never actually seen anybody on the bane before. It's not like I imagined it."

"This crap? This isn't the bane. Just your everyday vein food. Front room stuff. Nothing happening here but dreams and pretty pictures."

"Oh," Jane said. Then, "You seem to know a lot about this stuff."

"Yeah, well, I made a few mistakes when I was young." Puck

glanced about tensely. "I wonder if there's anyplace around here that's clean enough we can sit down."

A curtain shot to in a Moorish arch doorway at the far end of the room. A figure clothed in the light of the sun stepped through it.

"College boy!" Tom grinned madly. "I been waiting for you."

Jane knew then what it was like to enter somebody else's story midway through the plot. Nothing of what happened then made any sense to her. There was no chance to ask questions. She knew they would take hours to explain. And she wasn't in any shape for explanations anyway. It all seemed hopelessly unfair.

"You know where my office is," Tom said. "I got the game all set up and ready for you."

"What is this? What's going on?"

"I made a few mistakes once."

"Aw, don't be so hard on yourself," Wicked Tom said. "Everybody makes mistakes. How else ya going to learn?"

"But I still want to know—" Jane began.

Puck rounded on Tom and grabbed the front of his blouse. "Nothing happens to her! Get that?" he said fiercely. "No matter what happens, she walks free!"

"She ain't done nothing to me. Why should I do anything to her? Not that you've got any say in it."

All the life went out of Puck. "Yeah, yeah." He released Wicked Tom's shirtfront. They passed through the Moorish doorway.

On the far side the silk curtain was a torn and dingy rag. Gray linoleum curled up underfoot. A poorly lit hall led by rooms that went beyond squalid. The doors had been removed and Jane could see thin junkies nodding on piss-damp mattresses. On one wall was a hand-lettered sign reading "Let Us Clean You're Needles 4 U."

Tom glanced shrewdly at Jane. "*That's* the bane. Not like that bullshit up front. No illusions. No dreams. No lies. Nothing but the straight truth."

This last briefly roused Puck from his torpor. "What is truth?" he said bleakly.

"Well, we're gonna find out, ain't we?"

At the end of the hall was a real door. Tom opened it onto a room that was lit only by five television sets scattered about the floor and one atop a metal filing cabinet. They hissed and sputtered noisily. Their screens were all snow. Were they always tuned to dead channels, Jane wondered, or was it just that this one night nobody was transmitting?

A card table had been set up with two rickety chairs. On the tabletop were a pair of leather straps and two loaded syringes. Puck sat down on one of the chairs. His eyes were empty.

The televisions crackled and spat.

How do you talk somebody out of something you don't understand? Jane squeezed Puck's shoulder and whispered, "Please don't do this."

"He ain't got that option, young lady," Tom said, almost regretfully. "All this was established long before you entered the picture." He sat down facing Puck. "Trial by injection all right with you?"

Puck nodded.

They looped the straps around their upper arms. When the straps were yanked tight they clenched and unclenched their hands to pump up the veins. Tom gave Puck his choice of syringes. He picked up the other and studied the milk gray fluid within. "Yer looking at the basis of all our civilization."

"What?" Jane said.

"The piston." He waved it in the air, like a cigarette. "This is the four-stroke engine in its simplest form. Intake. Compression. Ignition. Exhaust. Elegant."

"Just this once," Puck muttered grimly. "Just this fucking one last time, I could do without your line of snappy patter." He thumped his elbow down on the table. Tom chuckled and did likewise. They locked thumbs.

"Ready?"

"Let's get it over with."

They picked up the syringes with their free hands and positioned them delicately against each other's forearms. The needles poised, paused, probed, and finally slid in.

"Puck—"

"Don't," he said. "Don't say a thing."

"But I—"

"*I don't want to hear it!* Okay? I know what I want to believe and the odds are real damn good that's not what you want to say." To Tom he said, "First stroke."

The plungers drew back slightly. A serpent of blood coiled and writhed within each glass cylinder. The noise from the television sets rose up deafeningly. The bluish glare cast pink shadows up over the duelists' faces, demonic brows over their eyes, hard crescents above their chins. Their gazes locked. Jane stood outside their circuit of loathing and desire, excluded.

A shadow passed before her eyes.

A gentle hand touched her shoulder.

"Come," the shadow-boy said. "You can't do anything for him and you know it."

———⟐———

The shadow-boy led Jane away from the frozen tableau. They passed without hindrance through the false oriental splendor of the front room and out onto the street.

They moved through the streets of the City as if charmed. Twice they came upon fragments of the mob, wild and bloody, with trophies Jane didn't like to look upon. Each time the shadow-boy led her away unharassed. So long as he held her hand, it seemed, she could not be detected.

A side door into Bellegarde opened at the shadow-boy's touch. They commandeered an elevator big enough to carry a hundred and rode it empty all the way to the top. Her guide had wanted to take Jane to her room, but she insisted on going to the student lounge instead. "It'll be okay," he assured her. "The administration has already cleared away the bodies. They're very good about that sort of thing."

"No."

The lounge was empty. Jane turned her back on the windows and surveyed the couches. Any one of them would do for a bed. Or else she could always sleep on the floor.

"I have to go now. If I'm not back at the plant soon, well . . ." The shadow-boy shrugged sadly.

"Yeah, sure, the plant." Jane did not release his arm.

"I have to go," he repeated.

"Who are you?"

The shadow-boy looked away. "You know me," he mumbled.

"What are you?"

He did not answer.

"Then suppose I tell you."

"No," he whispered, "don't."

It was a terrible thing that Jane was about to do. But she was drunk and wired and aching and crashing and she no longer gave a shit. She wrapped her arms around his thin, unresisting frame.

He felt so cold and small. She was astonished to discover how much she had grown since leaving the dragon works. He looked up, stricken, into her eyes and trembled. Jane bent her head down and whispered her own name into his ear.

"I did everything I could," he whimpered.

"So did I. It wasn't enough, was it?"

He was shivering convulsively now. He didn't answer.

"If you want to hold a hippogriff captive, you clip its flight primaries. For a faun, you hamstring one leg. But how do you cripple a mortal without lessening her value as a laborer?"

"Please . . . don't." The shadow-boy writhed weakly within her embrace.

"Shush." Jane lowered her mouth to his. She pushed her tongue between his unresisting lips to open them. Then she sucked his tongue into her own mouth. She sucked more of him into her, and more. She went on sucking until there was nothing there.

When she looked up a faint brightness had entered the lounge. The sun was coming up.

The Teind was over.

# — NINETEEN —

It was late afternoon by the time Jane managed to drag herself up from the couch. She was still dressed in yesterday's clothes. They were pretty rank, but not as nasty-smelling as herself. The sky outside was gray and the atmosphere within was oppressive. Her head ached. A crusty sensation had lodged itself in her throat and her bowels felt loose. On top of everything else, she had a hangover.

She needed a shower and a change of clothes. They must surely have removed Monkey's and Ratsnickle's bodies from her room by now. The shadow-boy had been right about that. It was exactly the sort of thing that the administration was good at.

She rolled her head in a circle a couple of times, listening to her vertebrae crackle. Then she dutifully scraped the worst of the grunge from her front teeth with a fingernail.

Then she looked at the time.

"Oh fuck!"

They'd be posting the lists any minute now.

———

Sirin's body had been found in Watling Street by Caer Gwydion. Somebody had thrown her out of a high window. According to the exegesis, the Lords of the University had needed her dental records to make a positive identification.

The notices were hung in locked glass bulletin cases in New Regents Hall. Along with many of the survivors, Jane was there to watch them go up. Her hair was still damp—she'd spent over half an hour in the shower—and her head throbbed. She went carefully down the lists looking for friends and classmates. It took time; for bureaucratic convenience they'd been listed by order of discovery.

Sirin.
Monkey.
Ratsnickle.

There was a slow, almost erotic isolation to the experience. Jane crept down the lists an inch at a time, running her hands over the glass, studying each name intensely. All about her others were doing the same. Nobody spoke. No eyes met. Nobody cared to make contact.

New Regents was an enormous space, barrel-vaulted and indirectly lit by hidden clerestory windows. The walnut paneling gave it an almost natural feel, as if Jane were but an insect creeping along the floor of a hollow log. But emptiness dominated. The scattered students seemed sadly few, the University depopulated.

A dwarf in a three-piece suit and cockatrice shoes briskly scanned the lists, moving down the cases with brusque, businesslike efficiency. It was—Jane tried to remember—Nant's friend, the one she had met that long ago night when she and Sirin first encountered Galiagante. Red Gwalch, that was his name. She wondered if she should say hello. But then he burst into tears and, throwing an arm over his eyes, turned away. So she guessed maybe not.

Nant.
Skambles.
Martha Falsestep.
Jimmy Jump-up.
Loosestrife.
Vinegar Dick.

Most of those on the lists were strangers to her. Others she knew only vaguely, by hearsay and repute. Up and down the hall students lingered over the listings. They were all puffy-eyed and stunned-looking. Some moved their lips as they read. Occasionally one began to sob. Abruptly, another laughed in disbelief. Nobody spoke. They all had their own stories to tell. Nobody was going to tell them.

Linnet.
Barguest Summerduck.
Itch.
The Cauld Lad.
Puck Aleshire.

There it was. Her heart thudded once, as if it had been hit with a brick. Then nothing. She felt no emotion at all. Only an awful gray sense that she really ought to feel something.

Jane discovered then that she had no tears in her to shed. She felt a monster, but there it was. A hogboon to her side shuffled his feet meaningfully and she drifted on to the next case. Automatically she kept on reading. Puck would never have encountered Wicked Tom if he hadn't come looking for her. He had thrown away his life for her sake. And he had died without even knowing how she felt about him. It was incomprehensible that she could not mourn for him.

Punch.
Lampblack.
Billy Bugaboo.
The Whiddler.

She stopped. What was that she had just read? She went back up the listing and found the entry again. She stared at it in disbelief.

Billy Bugaboo was dead. According to the exegesis he had been leading a faction of the mob—impossible to believe!—in an attack on the Stockbrokers' Guild when he was struck down by a Greencoatie bullet. An asterisk and dagger at the end of the citation meant that since he had died heroically, a posthumous degree would be issued.

Because it had never even occurred to her that Billy might be dead, the shock of seeing his name unfroze something within. Like a river breaking through an earthen dam the tears gushed out and overwhelmed her. They ran down her cheeks in sheets and streams.

Jane threw back her head and bawled.

She cried for guilt, for how badly she had treated her friends, and for loss. She cried for the sheer horror of existence. She was crying at first for Billy Bugaboo and the greater pain of Puck behind him. But somehow Linnet and Sirin and Monkey got mixed in there as well. And the shadow-boy too, though intellectually she knew he was only an aspect of herself. She was crying for them all, for the students she knew and those she did not, for all the victims of the Teind, for all the victims of a dangerous and hostile world.

Then, as rapidly as they had come, the tears stopped and she was emptier than before and drained of all emotion. I will never cry again, she thought, and almost immediately proved herself a liar. But these new tears, though violent, didn't last long either. And in their wake she felt flatly emotionless once more. This was how the rest of the day would go, she realized, sometimes rational and sometimes helpless with grief. But never rational and grieving at one time. There was a breach in her that would only be closed by time and sleep.

A taloned hand fell on her shoulder.

"Welcome to adult society," Dr. Nemesis said dryly. "Deserving or no, you are one of our order now."

Jane turned and for the first time actually looked past the repugnant pinches of pink flesh around her adviser's eyes and into the depths of those hard globes themselves. She saw culpability there and the sociable quality of shared guilt. It was repellent that a part of her responded to this with sympathy. "Thank you," she said.

Dr. Nemesis was wearing tinted glasses today with bluebottle lenses so thick they were almost purple. She pushed them up her beak and her eyes disappeared entirely. "I have good news for you. Your financial aid is being reinstated."

"Why?"

"It's customary after the Teind. Mere economics, really. With the abrupt drop in demand for the University's resources, there's enough of everything to go around. For a brief time, money flows freely. In your case it's moot, of course. A formality. But one that will look good on your permanent record."

"Why moot?"

Dr. Nemesis's hand dipped into a vest pocket. It emerged with an envelope held between two iron claws. "As your adviser it is my glad duty to inform you that your application for a sabbatical has been approved." She withdrew a document, examined the seals, and slowly read it over to herself. Then she nodded, replaced it in the envelope, and returned the envelope to her pocket. "Normally sabbaticals are not granted to students. To facilitate your case, we have issued a provisional degree in industrial alchemy and appointed you—contingent upon your successful completion of the program—to the teaching staff. Shockingly irregular." Her beak lifted in what on her passed for a smile. Light flashed darkly on her spectacles. "Fortunately for you, the administration is totally corrupt. Otherwise it would never have been tolerated."

"I didn't apply for a sabbatical."

"You didn't have to. The Fata Incolore applied in your name. The paperwork is done. All we need is your consent."

"Who is the Fata Incolore?"

"A great intimate, I gather, of the Lord Galiagante, who is himself a favored sponsor of many University activities."

"Ahhh," said Jane. "I begin to see."

"Come by my office anytime within the week and we'll get the paperwork out of the way. Your salary is suspended until you actually begin teaching of course. But you will receive a housing allowance and certain small discretionary moneys to cover your incidental expenses."

"Well," Jane said. "I guess this must be my lucky day."

———◦◉◦———

With the aid of a small glass of vodka and a quarter-gram of hashish, Jane finally managed to doze off. She slept dreamlessly through most of the next day, awakening only as the sun set. A quick change of clothing and she left her room never to return again. She did not pack; she could send for anything she might later decide to keep. It was time for a long talk with Melanchthon. They had things to settle.

The dragon had moved from the basements of Bellegarde sometime during the Teind. Jane knew this, though she did not know how she knew. It was a deep knowledge that welled up from within. And she knew that all she had to do was to walk blindly, paying no particular heed to where she was going, and her wandering footsteps would lead her directly to the dragon. He was lurking in the blind interior of her mind. She could feel him back where her thoughts ever turned with the reluctant compulsion of a tongue to a loosened tooth.

He was hers again, as he had been before. This time she knew they would never be free of each other again in this world.

———◦◉◦———

She found the dragon in Termagant, fourteen floors from the very top. It was an extraordinarily posh neighborhood and she got some strange looks just riding up in the elevator. Not that she cared.

Her feet came to a stop midway down a silent and preternaturally clean hallway. The brass plate on one door read 7332. It opened at her touch.

Large rooms, beige walls. Track lighting created textured densities of illumination on gleaming hardwood floors. Through an arch she could see the kitchen, all butcher block and built-in appliances. Everything had been freshly painted. There was no furniture.

"Hello?"

Only a dull echo answered her.

Jane let the door click shut behind her. She stepped forward into what must be the living room. By which logic, the almost equally large space beyond it was surely the master bedroom. Jane walked through the carved double doors. It was there she found the dragon.

Melanchthon waited, silent and grim, a wall of black iron that stretched beyond the limits of the room. He must fill most of this floor, she realized, and half the floor above. Just making the room for him must have been incredibly disruptive. Arranging the repair and furbishing of the apartments about him without alerting the Lords of the City to his presence was a trick worthy of the dragon himself at his most cunning.

The cabin opened into the room, a metal circle in the very center of the wall. Jane climbed the rungs and yanked down the hatch bar. It swung open for her.

"No games," she said. The interior was warm and gently lit. The pilot's couch awaited her. "No lies, no bullshit, no evasions." She sat in it, as she had done so many times before. "I've come to cut a deal with you. If you act cute, I'll walk." The wraparounds closed about her head. Everything was black. She spoke into an infinite void. "You only get the one chance."

No response.

Her hands closed about the grips. This was the point of no return. The rubber pads were dry and hard. Convulsively, she twisted them. The needles stung her wrists.

The darkness about her intensified, taking on a depth and texture it had lacked before. Otherwise nothing happened. Jane waited. She was old enough now to realize that Melanchthon was indeed communicating with her in his way. His silence was more eloquent than any words he might have chosen. It spoke to her of weakness and strength, of her helplessness when held up to his power. It said that their feelings toward one another were unchanged.

There was a gurgle as liquid freon was pumped from one part of the dragon to another.

Jane shifted in the couch. The cabin felt impossibly close. The smell of iron was everywhere. She sighed and scratched an itch on her shoulder with her chin and a spark of light was born within the wraparound. It was pale as a glowworm and small as a mote of dust.

A star.

Without fanfare a second star appeared and then a fourth, more and more until there were billions of suns arranged in galaxies and nebulae, and those arrangements contained in still larger structures. Jane seemed to be standing somewhere aside from Creation, watching dispassionately while everything shrank toward nonexistence. Or else it might be that she was rushing away from everything at unimaginable speed and ever-increasing acceleration. Until finally all the stars and their attendant worlds merged into a single structure whose shape she could hold in her mind.

Jane saw the universe whole then, all of space and time pulled by the totality of gravitational forces into a saddle-shaped solid. Melanchthon rotated the vision through the higher dimensions so that the universe fell in upon itself, growing in complexity from the saddle into a nine-dimensional butterfly and finally into an n-dimensional ziggurat. It was the summation of futility, for the ziggurat was all there was. It had no exterior, no beyond. It was not that there was nothing outside it, but that an "outside" did not and could not exist.

Staring at the radiant involution, Jane realized that here was the perfect and exact model for her life: She was caught in an ascending spiral maze, always coming around to familiar places she had never been before, always returning to dilemmas that in retrospect she should have seen coming. She was moving in diminishing circles, being twisted around in ever more limiting ways, until by some final twist or kink she would arrive at the omega point of inertia, with no options, no directions, no future, no way out.

It was obvious at last how thoroughly, how pitilessly, she was trapped. Everything she tried—trickery, compassion, inaction, patience, ruthlessness—led inevitably to failure. Because that was simply the way things were. That was the way the game was rigged.

The stars had melted together into solidity. The universe burned in Jane's sight like a monstrous white seashell. It was not the first time she had looked upon that shape. With a sickening lurch of revelation, she recognized it and put a name to it.

Jane looked upon Spiral Castle and despaired.

Melanchthon must have been waiting for exactly that, for now at last he spoke. His voice surprisingly gentle, he said, "In the Riphaean Mountains there are still wild trolls, their primitive tribes protected from modern culture and their territories held as vast preserves. They are brutal creatures who lead simple lives. Their males are savagery personified, but the otherwise admirable character of their females is diluted by an inexplicable love of beauty.

"Knowing of this weakness, hunters will leave moonstones alongside the mountain trails. A day goes by, a week, and a troll shambles innocently by. She sees a glimmering in the dust. She stops. She is caught by the subtle interplay of colors. She wants to look away, but cannot. She yearns to snatch the bauble up, but she fears to approach it. Hours pass and her strength wanes. She sinks to her knees before the moonstone. She is helpless, unable to look away even when she hears the approaching feet of the hunters.

"What makes this a sport and not mere slaughter is that there are two breeds of trolls, outwardly indistinguishable. One of the first breed will die with her eyes fixed on the moonstone. Ah, but in the second the love of beauty is overmatched by her strength of hatred. This troll will gouge out her eyes with her own fingers to free herself of the tyranny of the stone. Blind, she could then escape to the lightless caverns of her birth. But she does not. Instead she crouches unmoving for as long as it takes, though it be days, awaiting he who set the trap. She knows she will die. But she is determined to take at least one of the hunters with her.

"Which is why you should never approach a captive troll alone but always in the company of a friend. A friend who does not realize he is a little slower than yourself."

For a long time the dragon did not speak. The air was chill in the cabin; the air-conditioning had been set too high. At last, fiercely, he said, "The time has come for you to choose. What breed of troll are you?"

"Can you really kill the Goddess?" Jane asked.

"You stupid gobbet of flesh! Don't you understand yet? *There is no Goddess.*"

"No!" Jane cried. "You said yourself—"

"I lied," the dragon said with a fearful complacency. "Everyone you have ever met has lied to you. Life exists, and all who live are born to suffer. The best moments are fleeting and bought with the coin of exquisite torment. All attachments end. All loved ones die. All that you value passes away. In such a vexatious existence laughter is madness and joy is folly. Shall we accept that it all happens for no reason, with no cause? That there is nobody to blame but ourselves but that accepting the responsibility is pointless for doing so cannot ease, defer, or deaden the pain? Not likely! It is so much more comforting to erect a straw figure on which to blame it all.

"Some bow down before the Goddess and others curse her every name. There is not a fart's difference between the two approaches. They cling to the fiction of the Goddess because admitting the alternative is unbearable."

"Then what—why—what do you want me for?" To her dismay, tears coursed down Jane's face. Oh how Melanchthon must be enjoying this, she thought. What satisfaction it must give him. "You've toyed with me, made promises, gone through Hell-knows-what machinations to bring me here. Why? What's the point of it?"

"I want your help to destroy the universe."

Jane barked a short, bitter laugh. But Melanchthon neither spoke nor by any other sign indicated annoyance. A cold sizzling sensation ran up her spine. He was serious. In a small voice, she said, "Can you really do it?"

The seashell image burning in the swimming darkness lap-dissolved to a schematic of Spiral Castle, lines diving dizzyingly into one another, swooping in wild curves, always returning to converge upon a central point. "The universe is built upon an instability. A point source of weakness at the beginning of time and the birth of matter. One trembling instant from which all else arrives. A child with a sling could upset that point if he could only reach it. And it is upon the centrality of that instant that the entire system derives its structure. Disturbed, all collapses."

It was unimaginable, and yet hooked into the dragon's systems, Jane could not doubt his sincerity. "What happens then?"

In the iron depths of darkness an engine came on-line. The couch trembled. "You ask a question that cannot be answered without knowing the nature of the primal chaos from which being arose. Is Spiral Castle like a crystal, once shattered, forever destroyed? That is what I prefer to believe. Or is it like a still pond, whose mirrored surface may be shattered and churned, but which will inevitably restore itself as the waves die down? You may believe this if you choose. You can even believe—why not?—that the restored universe will be an improvement on the old. For me, so long as I have my vengeance I care not what comes after."

"And us?"

"We die." An involuntary rise in the dragon's voice, a slight quickening of cadence, told her that she had touched upon some unclean hunger akin to but less seemly than battle-lust. "We die beyond any chance of rebirth. You and I and all we have known will cease to be. The worlds that gave us birth, the creatures that shaped us—all will be unmade. So comprehensive will be their destruction that even their pasts will die with them. It is an extinction beyond death that we court. Though the ages stretch empty and desolate into infinity and beyond, there will be none to remember us, nor any to mourn. Our joys, sorrows, struggles, will never have been.

"And even if there is a universe to come, it will know naught of us."

So all-encompassing was the dragon's nihilistic vision that Jane could not at first speak. It reduced her to inconsequence, made her feel clownish, a triviality, a ridiculous squeak. By slow degrees Melanchthon had shut down his external senses, leaving her afloat in the void, her ears stuffed with silence, her eyes blind and unseeing, her mouth and throat choked with paralysis. There was only his voice and, when it ceased, the reverberations it left behind on the silence.

Then there was nothing.

"All right." Jane took a deep breath. She felt cold and hard as a stone. "All right. Just so long as we understand each other."

# TWENTY

Two dwarves, one red and one black, fought grimly on the balcony. Their bodies were slick with sweat and their knives gleamed in the floodlights. Their feet kicked up puffs of the sawdust that had been strewn over the flagstones to soak up blood. They were both naked.

Jane watched from the roof garden, resting her drink on the rail.

The dwarves circled each other warily, like scorpions, looking for an opening. Suddenly one swung wildly and stumbled. It was an incredible gaffe for a fighter of his quality to make. The second feinted as if about to take advantage of the lapse. But when the first pivoted on a stiff arm and whipped his legs around to knock him off his feet, his opponent was out of reach. With a scream the second dwarf leaped. The first only managed to block his blow at the cost of a finger. Luckily the finger wasn't on his knife hand.

Partygoers thronged the balcony. Jane was not the only one watching from above, but the rail was far from crowded. The serious aficionados all wanted to be close enough to hear the combatants grunt, close enough to smell their rage and fear.

It was an appalling sport. Jane couldn't understand its appeal at all. But the spectators, now—she chewed her lip. She had promised Melanchthon fuel; nearly any of them would do. Which to choose?

She was reaching for her drink when the down on the nape of her neck and the tiny hairs on the backs of her arms and the insides of her thighs stirred and lifted. It was an electric, crackling sensation, akin to the abrupt realization that a millipede is crawling up one's leg. Galiagante was approaching.

Jane waited until he was almost upon her, then turned as the flirtation coaches had trained her: lips parting at the same time that one eyebrow rose ever so slightly and both eyes widened in a way that was subtly mocking and challenging all at the same time. Put together er expression said, Let's see what you've got.

Galiagante was not impressed. "You should be mingling." Flambeaux dotted the banks of an artificial stream. With the torches burning at his back, he looked like one of his own savage ancestors, a harkening back to a time when his kind could not be invoked without forfeiting a geld of blood in one form or another. Jane leaned back against the rail, feigning nonchalance.

Never apologize. That was the first thing they had taught her. "I am mingling." She raised the glass, looked at him over its rim. "Mingling and showing off my costume." Turning, she sat, and lifted a high-heeled boot to the rail beside her in a way that showed off her black leather pants to good advantage. "And very popular both it and I have been, I might add."

She leaned forward, letting her zippered jacket display the truly stunning decolletage that was largely its own creation; the bustier lifted and squeezed her breasts so, she felt as if they rested on a shelf. "Do you like what they've done with my spoon?" She teasingly dandled it at the end of its chain.

Galiagante took the spoon and glanced at both sides. The handle had been twisted into a complex spiral by dwarven crafters to make its allegorical meaning more obvious. The bowl had been hammered flat and worked into a relief of the Goddess, the front all boobs and cellulite, the back all butt and mystery. "You are a cartoon." He let it swing back. "That's not good enough."

"I could do a better job of selling myself if I knew just exactly what you're going to package me *as*."

"You're still under development. The exact details are unimportant."

"But I—"

"If you don't work out," Galiagante said, "I'll put you back where you came from." The emphasis on those last five words was too distinct to be unintended. He snapped his fingers and over his shoulder said, "Show her about. Keep her circulating." Then, like a mountain wrapping itself in fog, he withdrew his presence.

"Fata Jayne," someone said deferentially.

For servants the chin should be lifted in a way that is aloof but not arrogant. Servants, dwarves, and creditors are never important enough to snub. Meet their eyes firmly. Look away before you've finished speaking. Don't treat them like friends unless you have good reason to want to make them squirm.

Jane turned. Her jaw fell. "Ferret!"

"Madame remembers me." The gray-haired fey smiled gravely and dipped his head. With his mouth closed and eyes lowered, he looked not in the least dangerous. "I am honored."

The only time Jane had ever encountered Ferret was the once in la jettatura when he'd caught her shoplifting. She remembered him vividly enough, though, to find his presence alarming. "What are you doing here?"

"Lord Galiagante ran a background check on you. In the course of which he found me. Galiagante likes clever things. He offered me a position on terms I could not refuse. Here I am." Ferret offered his arm. "Have you met Fata Incolore?"

"Not yet. She's Galiagante's inamorata, isn't she?"

"Oh, much more than that."

Chatting amiably, he steered her into the heart of the garden.

———※◆※———

The Fata Incolore stood by a shallow pond made luminous by the skylight beneath it. She was deep in an animated discussion with three Teggish intellectuals. Dark fish darted over the shimmering dancers of the ballroom below. The watery light showed off her fashionably ghoulish pallor. Her clothes made Jane feel like a cartoon.

In Jane's ear, Ferret murmured, "The one in blue is Fata Jouissante, a hot prospect to be the Left Hand Path candidate for senator in the coming elections and an even hotter prospect to replace the Fata Incolore in Galiagante's affections. She'll have to choose soon. She can't have both. Beside her is the Lord Corvo. Corvo is archetypical of his class, aloof but quick to wrath should you engage his dislike. Laugh at *all* his jokes. The lean one in crimson with the plumed hat is a parvenu. Ignore him." He released Jane's arm and faded back.

She approached the group. Intent on their argument, nobody noticed her.

"But surely, Fata Incolore—"

"The experiments with tortured chimeras have proved, you will agree, that—"

"Is it not possible that—"

Fata Incolore shook her head impatiently. "Everyone tries to draw correspondences between the two worlds. They are the lower and we the upper. We the boat and they the anchor. They the reality, we the dream. Ridiculous. The worlds are simply two different levels of physical being, ours existing at energies higher than any that exist in their world and theirs at energies exactly so much lower than our own. The separation is absolute. Nothing of our world can exist in theirs and nothing of theirs in ours. If you stuck your arm into the lower world, it would explode with hideous fury as every atom of it converted instantly to energy. It is possible to pass through Dream Gate, yes, but not to take anything to or from their world."

"There is always the child trade," Fata Jouissante said. The parvenu's face lit up in the sudden smirk of one who enjoys an unexpected obscenity. "You make a brisk profit in changelings for someone who doesn't believe in the possibility of such intercourse."

Anger bloomed on the Incolore's beestung lips. Her eyebrows flared like black flames. But the anger that danced beneath them was laced with amusement. It was as if she were a carnivore that found itself cornered by a foe it did not wholly respect. "There is no physical traffic between the worlds, after all, and that is all that matters. The changelings are a special case, an exemption if you will, that—" She looked up. "Ah. It is our host's new toy."

All eyes turned to Jane.

"Oh, please." Jane affected a pained expression, though all her interest lay in the conversation she had just interrupted. "Not a toy. Say rather, an investment."

"What's the difference?" The parvenu addressed not her but her tits, her boots, the tangled hipful of chains, locks, and keys, that chimed and dangled from her belt.

Glancing sidelong at Fata Jouissante, Jane said, "In my case it means that I can expect Galiagante to give some serious thought before casting me aside."

Fata Incolore snorted, and her rival may have colored faintly. Corvo cleared his throat sternly and stepped between them. "Tell me," he said to Jane, his gray face gathered into an implausible smile. "Is it true, the story they tell? About you and Galiagante."

"He pegged me in his case with a bindle of his silver," Jane admitted. "Not in *this* outfit, obviously—this is just make-believe and fantasy. But I was a professional thief, yeah. That's how Galiagante and I discovered each other."

"I gather that Galiagante is working up a television special based on your exploits."

"A series, *I* heard," threw in the parvenu.

"Actually, I believe that Galiagante is considering giving me the addresses of a few of his friends and having us split the swag."

The parvenu laughed so hard at this that his hat fell off. Even Jane had to look away.

Waiters were passing through the party, indentured children clad for the occasion in such fantastical costumes as flower-petal dresses, bumblebee-fur tunics, fox grape shawls, and acorn caps. Some had white-puffed dandelion stalks slung over their shoulders. Others carried mushrooms big enough to serve as umbrellas. A few were purely decorative; they skipped and twirled in a grotesque pretense of childish play. Most were as solemn as psychopomps.

A girl in a daisy-petal skirt and a boy in spiked brown tights and doublet and a hat shaped like the head of a thistle, came by with a silver platter on which was a flayed horse's head.

Fata Incolore waved the horse's head to her. Taking up knife and spoon she deftly scooped out the eyes. One she placed on a small white plate. "For you." The other she picked up between thumb and forefinger and took for herself. It filled her mouth and bulged out one cheek. Jane watched her chew it, horrified. Then she looked down at the plate in her hand. That hideous eye stared vacantly upward. It inevitably reminded her of Melanchthon's fable of the hunters and their moonstone baits. She felt trapped by it, unable to look away.

"May I?" Corvo produced a knife and with enormous gravity began slicing the eye. Vitreous humor gushed onto the plate. He speared a circlet. "Like so many delicacies, it is an acquired taste." He pointed the knife at her. "Open."

Jane started to shake her head. But at the look that came over Corvo's face she quickly changed her mind. She opened her mouth. He popped it in. "Not bad, eh?"

It was as cold and rubbery as she had imagined it would be. She had not expected, however, that it would be so hotly spiced. Her eyes watered. "Wonderful," she gasped.

"Putting new things in your mouth excites you, then." The parvenu looked pleased with his own wit. The fatas looked bored.

"I'm sure I don't know what you mean," Jane said coldly.

"Sure you do."

"Excuse me." Fata Jouissante brushed the parvenu aside. "That's not how it's done." She peeled a glove from her hand and delicately laid a cool fingertip on the back of Jane's wrist. A hot flash of desire ran through Jane's veins, and she shied like a horse. Her belly tautened and her nipples stood erect. Staring up into the elf-lady's face, she felt open and vulnerable in a way she did not like at all. But she was helpless against it. Had she wanted, the lady could have led her away to her boudoir then and there. And everyone there knew it.

"All right," Jane said hotly. Holding her hands low, she crooked her fingers, as if she were a street fighter beckoning the fata to come at her. "If that's what you want. Right here, right now. On the floor. In front of your friends."

Jouissante bristled.

For a long moment nobody moved. Then Fata Incolore laughed, and the spell was broken. "You two are even now," she said. And then, not unkindly, "But do try not to involve yourself in politics, little one. It is a dangerous game, and one that will break you if you don't take care." She turned her back. The group shifted slightly, and suddenly Jane found herself standing outside it. As was, on the side opposite her, the parvenu.

She slunk away.

The parvenu hurried forward to match paces. "I'm a social leper," he said bitterly. "Did you see how those two quaints treated me?"

"To be brutally honest," Jane said, "no."

"It was the cut direct! That bitch Jouissante cut me off when I was speaking. She brushed me aside—me!—as if I were nobody." In a more confidential tone, he told her breasts, "My house is old, however new our wealth may be. Do not listen to those who say the lineage is assumed. The name is but restored, and our ancestral sword reforged."

"Look," Jane said. "Exactly what must I say to get rid of you?"

"Why, you mustn't." Grinning, he swept off his hat in what amounted to a parody of courtesy. "My dearest Fata Jayne, I am your squire, your lovesick swain, your very slave."

"Good sir." Ferret materialized in their path and bowed. "I do not believe I've had the pleasure?"

The parvenu gaped at him buggishly. "Apollidon," he said at last.

"Charmed." Ferret took Jane's arm. "You'll excuse us, I'm sure."

A stairway curved gracefully out of night and into brightness. They descended. From the heights, the revelers were like flower petals aswirl on flowing water. Gliding with sure ease, they joined in temporary alliances, gyred slowly about, and then were sent spinning apart by breezes too slight to be otherwise detected.

A nixie hurried up the stairs with a tray of fresh drinks. Jane's had gone flat. Ferret took the glass from her hand, plunked it down, and snagged a bubbling replacement without so much as slowing the child's ascent.

Not a drop of alcohol had passed Jane's lips that evening. The *numen* of so many high-elven gathered in one place made the very air sparkle with the giddy charm of their presence; she felt as if she were swimming in champagne. One sip would send her right over the edge.

"You did quite well, by the way," Ferret said.

"I was humiliated."

"That's only to be expected when you match wits with three powers. Nonetheless you diverted both ladies and roused Corvo to at least a token show of protectiveness. They are potential investors, and you've managed to engage their interests."

"I doubt Jouissante was much diverted."

"Oh, but she most certainly was. In her own way." Changing the subject, Ferret said, "Have you been introduced to Rocket yet?"

"No."

"A delightful lad. Don't be deceived by his name—he is no mongrel woods fey. He is of noble birth, brother sanguine to Fata Incolore herself. If he weren't a bastard and half-human to boot, he might expect great honor in House Incolore. Even so, he is somebody to be reckoned with."

"How does the Fata Incolore come to have a mestizo brother?"

"He's a dragon pilot." Ferret lowered his voice. "House Incolore derives its wealth from the trade, you know, and there is . . . an inherited weakness in that direction." They moved silkily through the crowds, with Ferret murmuring here a name, there a title, but mostly dismissing the guests as irrelevant to her. At last he said, "There's Rocket now."

The dragon pilot wore dress blues and had his back to them. He was in light converse with a triad of low-elven nondescripts. From behind he was distinctly attractive. Jane was quite taken by his height, his buns, and the width of his shoulders. Maybe him, she thought. Yes, he'd do quite nicely.

Alerted by some subtle change in the atmosphere, Rocket turned.

Their eyes met. His were the everchanging green-gray of Hyperborean seas. Subtle eyes, trickster eyes, eyes that meant nothing but trouble. Jane's stomach lurched. She knew him. They had never met before, and yet he was as familiar to her as the inside of her own purse.

It was Puck again, Peter again, Rooster again. The externals were superficially different, hair shorter and more disciplined than any of the others', nose thinner, features more regular. He was taller and straighter and had the bearing of a warrior. But inside it was him and nobody else. He burned in her vision like a neon sign. She'd know him anywhere.

Don't let it show.

The defeated dwarf was being carried through the party on the same silver platter that had earlier held the flayed horse's head. It took six straining children to bear him up. Revelers surged about them, vying to dab a sprig of holly in his blood for luck.

Smiling oddly, Rocket took a tentative step her way.

"Get lost," Jane told Ferret. His teeth flashed in a brief, astonished hiss, and then Jane was pushing her way through the merrymakers, through the hot crush of bodies and out onto the balcony.

The air was cool and fresh; it cleared her head wonderfully. Two dwarves in Galiagante's livery were sweeping up, dumping the last dustpanfuls of sawdust over the edge. They took their brooms, nodded curtly, and left.

Jane stared out over the Great Gray City. The buildings were black and mysterious, their lights a message she could not decode in a language she had never learned. She started to put her drink down on the rail, then impulsively cast it away from her. It tumbled and glittered on the way down, a temporary star.

Rocket came out on the balcony, as she had either feared or hoped he would.

"Who are you?" he said. "I know you. Why?"

She favored him with a scornful look. "Perhaps you've had too much to drink."

"I *know* you," he insisted. "Your fate and mine are bound together in some way. If not in this life, then in another."

"Your premonitions and fancies mean nothing to me, sir. Good night."

"I am a dragon pilot. Every day I deal with machines that would eat my soul from the inside if I gave them the chance. I assure you, madam, that I am not one who is prone to whimsy."

"Ah." Jane was not deaf to the boast in his statement. A very macho thing, handling dragons. Strapping those great black iron machines between one's legs and then opening the throttle. Sure to get the young ladies' juices flowing. "You are one of those gentlemen who make their living by enslaving children."

Rocket flushed. "There is more to my job than harvesting changelings," he protested.

"Is there?" Jane felt light as air, conscienceless, amoral. "I should think the one would be quite enough."

His face was taut. But Rocket managed to construct a plausible smile and an apologetic bow. "We seem to have somehow gotten off on the wrong foot. If you would allow me the privilege of starting over again—? My name is Rocket. I would very much enjoy the pleasure of your company."

"Are you witless?" This was wonderful fun. "You have been dismissed, sir."

The dragon pilot made an abortive movement toward her, as if driven by some great emotion. It seemed he must either leave immediately or else strike her. Jane stared at him coolly, feeling an unhealthy excitement, an irresistibly unwise desire to see exactly how far she could provoke him. Then, with a strangled cry, he strode forward and seized her chin. Roughly, he tilted her head back and to the side. "By the holy wolf, you're a changeling!"

Jane wrenched herself free. "Is this how you usually treat ladies? Good *night*, sir."

"I've been through Dream Gate seventeen times. This is nothing I could be mistaken about."

"And just what do you intend to do about it?" Jane demanded. "Will you turn me over to the Hospitalers? I'm old enough for them to start breeding me, aren't I? They ought to be able to get ten or twelve mestizo bastards out of me before my womb collapses."

Had she slapped him, Rocket could not have turned more white. He stepped back from her, hands clenched, eyes afire. He opened his mouth to say something, closed it again.

Still, he did not leave.

"There you are!"

Galiagante strolled out onto the balcony. His entourage followed, shedding glamour and sparks. Jouissante said, "We're going slumming," and Incolore explained, "We're forming up a little group to visit the Goblin Market," and Galiagante himself asked indifferently, "Would you care to come along?"

"Yes," Jane said. Why not? "Yes, I would."

"I'll come too," Rocket said grimly.

———❦———

There were seven in the party: Galiagante, with Jouissante and Incolore in uneasy balance on either arm, Rocket, Jane herself, and two elves from one of the lower houses, Floristan and Esplandian, more functionaries than actual guests. Servants fetched their cloaks. Jane, along with the other fatas, pulled the hood up so that only a slim oval of face showed. They all donned white masks.

They took the elevator down to the street, the functionaries shortened the way, and the entire party strolled easily into the Goblin Market.

"Gents, gents, gents!" a goblin barker cried.

Bad disco music gushed from aging speakers, all fuzz and repetitive bass thump. Galiagante gestured, the goblin stepped aside, and they ducked through a doorway into a lobby with mirrored walls.

Bank notes crinkled and sighed. They were ushered into a small, dark screening room. The linoleum floor was sticky underfoot. On the screen the magnified head of a kobold was noisily chewing food open-mouthed. They stood in the back, watching as beefsteaks, bananas, oysters, chocolate bars, and endless bowls of hot oatmeal disappeared into or fell in moist globs out of that enormous maw. There were only a few patrons in the cramped rows of seats.

Just when Jane's temples were beginning to throb in time to the sound track, Galiagante abruptly strode to the rear and threw open the fire door. They all followed him down a corridor that stank of disinfectant and up a narrow set of stairs. More paper whispered, and another goblin stood away from a turnstile. They passed through.

The room they entered was dominated by a horseshoe curve of doors. Galiagante went through one. Jouissante opened another. One of the functionaries—Esplandian?—dropped several tokens into Jane's hand. She opened her own door.

There was a chair. She sat down. A single dim light revealed a device on one wall with a slot for tokens. She inserted them all.

A window covering slid up. She was looking at a semicircular stage. At its center a troll writhed on a flat couch. He was naked save for a pair of socks and tight-laced brown shoes and the upper half of a gray undershirt. His great hairy belly protruded like a continent rising from an ugly sea of flesh. His eyelids had been sewn shut so long ago the flesh had grown together.

Jane saw Rocket in a window opposite. His mask stared at her.

The troll groaned. He had the most amazing hard-on. It was a raw pink for most of its length, as if the top layers of skin had been abraded away, shading to a bruise-like purple at the tip. From the slow way he twisted about, Jane thought at first that he was masturbating. But then he turned over on his side, and she could see the stump by one shoulder and realized that he had no arms with which to perform that function.

When the tokens ran out, the windows shut again and the party emerged with a clatter of doors.

"I want to arrange a private showing," Galiagante told a goblin with a mustache on his upper lip like a thin line of grease. They conferred briefly. Then the goblin led them two landings downward, through a storage room with leaking pipes, and into a vest-pocket theater.

A weak attempt had been made at glitz. Small tables were scattered about a low stage. Heavy metal played from a boom box, and scattered points of light bounced from a mirror ball to swirl about the theater. They took up chairs.

"This should be good," Jouissante remarked.

"Are you looking at me, sir?" Jane asked.

Rocket shook his head and sullenly stared down at the mask clenched in his hands. "I'm not sure this is my sort of scene at all."

"If you're not here to have fun, then why did you invite yourself along in the first place?"

A nymph wearing not much at all came by their table. "Falernian," Galiagante said, and tucked several bills in her underwear. He removed his mask and laid it down by the ashtray. The room was hot and stuffy, but Jane decided to keep her own mask on anyway.

Shortly, the same troll they had seen earlier was led onstage by two dwarves. They removed his dressing gown; he was dressed exactly as before in undershirt, shoes, and socks. One of the dwarves had a stick and prodded the troll with it.

He crashed to his knees in the center of the stage.

The nymph returned with their wine and baskets of silver coins for each table. The goblin with the grease-pencil mustache plugged a microphone into the boom box, and his voice overrode the music.

"LAYdeezangents," he said in a wash of muzzy sound. "Lordzanfatas, revered patronzovza ardz—"

"Shitheadzandwarves," muttered one of the lesser elves.

"Seekerzafterwizdom," Incolore laughed.

"—welcomdawr show." The lights over the tables came down. Blue and red spots pinned the troll. "TONIGHT weerproudabrezent duhmazing and todally unprezadent Tooooby CLUNCH!"

Jane joined the others in a polite smattering of applause.

The dwarf with the stick cued Toby by slashing him in the throat. The troll shivered, and in a high, clear voice said, "The Cold War is over. We stand at the dawn of a new world order. But many dangers and uncertainties are ahead. You've got to read all the tea leaves and listen to the nuances. I know we're in hard times. Out of the loop. But I never felt kind of—you mean, along like the Rodney Dangerfield kind of thing? Crematoriums of a thousand pointed lights. This is no Johnny-come-lately vicious assault. I put confidence in the American people smart bombs stealth drawing a line in the sand. The vision thing. I put my hand out to those crazy guys." Toby twisted, a conduit for madness, words bubbling out of him faster and faster, voice rising to a shriek. "To sum it up in one word, it's *jobs!*"

Dwarf One silenced him with another slash in the throat.

Dwarf Two grabbed his ears from behind and pulled down. The troll's chin rose and he made an incoherent, gargling noise that might have been protest. Dwarf One tapped his lips with the baton. Slowly, painfully, he forced his mouth yet wider. A creaking noise sounded from the hinges of his jaw. Still he strove to enlarge that impossible gap, forcing it bigger and rounder, until it was a great hole in his head, an immense funnel down his gullet. Something popped. The goblin with the painted mustache pumped up the music.

Galiagante dipped a languid hand into his basket. He cocked his arm and chucked a coin. It flew over the stage and into the troll's mouth-hole.

"Bravo!" cried Jouissante. She threw one herself. Down it went. Incolore threw another. A fourth coin, Jane's, looked about to miss. But Toby, guided by some primitive sense, wrenched his neck to one side and caught it.

Then the air was full of silver, like shooting stars etching white streaks toward the stage. Toby Clunch bobbed and darted comically, desperate to catch them all. It was amazing how many coins the wretched creature managed to snap up.

Jane paused, glancing sidelong at Rocket. He was drumming his fingers on the table. Alone of them all, he had not pitched so much as a single coin. She slapped one down before him. "Join in, 'sieur dragoneur!"

Rocket shoved back from the table so violently it almost tipped over. The chair crashed to the floor.

He strode from the room.

Unaccountably offended, Jane scooped up a handful of coins and threw them all at once, as hard as she could. Toby half-rose from his knees in his eagerness to intercept them. He managed to swallow some, but most bounced from his face and body, leaving small red marks.

Laughing, Fata Jouissante placed a warm hand on Jane's shoulder. "What do you think? Could you catch so many coins if you had to?"

"Oh, I could never get my mouth open so wide."

"I was thinking you could stand on your head and catch them in your *bel chose*." She turned to Galiagante. "How much do you want for her?"

"Straight sale?" Galiagante considered. "Three times investment at a minimum. But I'm not really ready to sell yet. I want to see if I can get a package going, use it to shoehorn my way into television. So much of my money is tied up in the trade. I'd like to see it diversified."

The nymph came by with fresh baskets. Toby Clunch was filling up. Each coin made a harsh clinking noise now as it struck coins already in his throat. "Excuse me," Jane said. She gathered up her purse and stood. The goblin jerked a thumb over his shoulder and she followed it to the ladies' room.

It was filthy. Jane could tell without looking that some of the toilets were stopped up. She stepped around a rancid puddle of water, went to the sinks, and removed her mask. Her mascara was a mess.

The door swung open. Fata Incolore came in. Doffing her mask, she went to the mirror. She peeled up a lip and scraped a bit of something off a canine. Then she took out her compact.

"Toot?" she asked.

"All right."

Incolore laid the compact on the edge of the sink and measured out two lines. She offered a rolled-up bank note. Jane held one end to her nose and bent over the powder.

It hit the back of her throat and the top of her skull almost simultaneously, with an intensely artificial sensation of clean green meadows. It was like a little light going on in a room you hadn't known was there.

Incolore did up the other line, then crumpled the bill and tossed it away. "What's this thing going on between you and Rocket? You've really put a burr under his saddle."

"Have I?" Jane said carelessly. "I guess it must've been something I said."

"Hum." Incolore's hand closed about the compact and pushed it into nonexistence. "First Fata Jouissante, and then my brother. You seem to be at war with the world."

"If I am, it's certainly no business of yours."

"I'll be blunt. My brother is clearly attracted to you. For reasons of my own, it is an alliance I would not mind fostering."

"Dream on." Jane reached for her mask.

Incolore stopped her with a touch. "Galiagante is overextended. This notion of his to expand into the entertainment media—" She shrugged. "Hopeless. He can't even make up his mind what he intends to do with you. Do you follow me? If he can't find funding, he'll have no choice but to try to recoup some fraction of his investment. He'll sell you to Jouissante." Her eyes were dark, serious, glimmering with anger. "I promise you it's a bargain you would learn to regret."

"I'm not for sale," Jane snapped. "Galiagante doesn't own me. Jouissante can't buy me. And you're not even in the game."

"What a strange creature you are." Incolore passed a hand over her mouth and a lit cigarette drooped from her lips. She blew smoke out her nostrils. "I'll tell you what. I have no particular interest in funding any more of Galiagante's follies. But I'll string him along for a week or so, if you'll agree to let me show you something."

"What thing?"

"Nothing you can't live with." She picked the coal off the cigarette and swallowed it live. The rest she dropped on the floor. "Call my secretary, and we'll set up a date."

Galiagante was impatient to go. They followed him down the blind gut of yet another kinked set of stairs. A broomstick jammed between the walls shunted them aside and into a room lined with glass booths from which houris in hot pink bikinis and chrome-studded leather harnesses beckoned. It came to Jane suddenly that the Goblin Market might well have no end. There might be an infinite number of windowless rooms and orgy pits beneath the City, all redolent with incense and ammonia, charged with over-amplified rap music, and tended by uncountable dawdling lowlifes. She was hopelessly lost, hopelessly tired, and hopelessly bored. She stifled a yawn.

"Fata Jayne doesn't seem to be enjoying herself," the one who was probably Floristan observed.

"I'm all right."

"Perhaps our pleasures are too *refined* for her," said maybe-Esplandian.

"Why don't we go to a place Jayne would like?"

"If there *is* such a place."

The lesser elves advanced on Jane, eyes glowing spitefully behind their masks. Backing away from them, she suddenly panicked, whirled, and discovered herself standing before an archway. Over the glass doors, surrounded by blinking lights, was a sign:

### RUN WITH THE APES OF HELL
**\*Dreams Realized \* Addictive Drugs \***
**\*Disgusting Fantasies \***

"I think," Galiagante said, "that we can provide Jayne with what she wants." He held open a door. "In here."

⇒◦《◉》◦⇐

"Yes, certainly, delightful, oh yes." They sat in the anteroom on chintz chairs, listening to a fat, hairless old goblin run through his spiel. He bobbed and bowed restlessly, rubbing his hands together. "Oh, we know," he said. "We know what you want, before you do. Secret things, *private* things, revolting things that you would never admit to another. True love, enemas, eight yards of old lace turned brittle and brown with age. Your heart's desire." He leered at Galiagante. "Fishhooks. Other things."

Galiagante produced a mass of bank notes. "Serve her." The

goblin bounced toward him, hands extended. But Fata Incolore intercepted the wad. She counted out half, and folded the rest back into Galiagante's jacket pocket. "If we're going to be business partners," she said, "we must first institute some financial accountability."

He looked at her with new interest. "Are we going to be business partners, then?"

"Wait and see."

"In through here." The goblin put his hand on an undistinguished-looking door. "Filthy nasty, very nice, oh my yes."

Jane hesitated. She was loath to enter. There was something fearsome inside. She could feel it. Something she knew she would forever regret seeing.

"You're afraid?" Jouissante said.

The two words hung in the air, a challenge.

"No, of course not." Jane went through the door, pulling it firmly shut behind her. Be damned if she was going to let the others see this, whatever it was.

She entered a room the size of a basketball court, and empty. Half a dozen dwarves sat on the floor in one corner, huddled about a portable television set. At her entry, they snapped it off and scattered through several doors. Two returned, wheeling in an old hand-cranked console record player. A third hurried after them with a wax cylinder. He snapped it in, spun the crank, and lowered the needle.

Scratchy waltz music came on.

Ladders slammed up against the walls. Strings of crepe-paper bells were stretched across the hall with dazzling speed. There was a clatter on the stairs as the remaining three dwarves returned.

They led in the Baldwynn.

The Baldwynn was dressed in formal evening wear. His suit was classically expensive, and just worn enough to indicate that it wasn't rented. His step was weak and faltering. His porcelain hands, mottled with brown, hung down motionless. But his head swung slowly from side to side like a turtle's, its gaze disconcertingly unfocused, as if he were staring into another universe.

I'm not afraid, Jane told herself. I won't be afraid.

The Baldwynn's head swiveled toward her. It stopped.

He looked directly at Jane.

Grinning, the dwarves swarmed about her. One removed her mask. Another took her cloak. They tugged her forward, placing her left hand on the Baldwynn's shoulder. One of his dead white hands was put into hers and the other around her waist.

Then they were dancing. The tinny waltz propelled them about the gym. They both moved clumsily, shuffling in response to the pokes and prods of their attendants. Awkwardly they spun around and around.

At first Jane stared fixedly at the Baldwynn's chest. But then a dwarf darted between them and knocked her chin up with his small fist. She looked into his pale gray eyes.

A spark of something glimmered briefly there. His lips trembled, as if he were trying to remember how to perform some long-forgotten task with them. Once. Twice.

The third time was the charm. Slowly he puckered his lips, like a little girl begging for a kiss. He released them with a faint *tchk* noise.

Jane shook her head. "No."

Again his lips puckered. He moved his head down toward hers. She could smell his breath, maggoty and sweet. Life came to his hands. His fingers plucked feebly at her.

"*No!*" Jane pushed back against the Baldwynn's chest with all her might. But she could not break free. It was impossible for one so frail and infirm to hold her, and yet he did. His arms were like metal bands. Slowly, inexorably, they tightened, crushing her against the aged elf-laird. His mouth closed on hers. When she tried to turn away, dwarves held her head in place.

He poked out his tongue and pushed it into her mouth. It entered her like a key gliding into a lock.

She opened at its touch.

At the prodding of his tongue, everything changed. The ballroom, dwarves, even the Baldwynn himself, all warped and melted away like wax in carbolic acid. Jane's stomach lurched. She experienced a bewildering dizziness unlike anything she had ever felt, as if she were being rotated through a dimension impenetrable to her senses. The room resolved into someplace else.

———※———

"Jane?"

She did not turn. She was staring at the window, mesmerized by the horrible thing there. The panes were streaked and filthy, and there were the blown husks of dead houseflies on the sill. The paint on the wood was white and chalky and broke away in sharp flakes if you pushed down on it hard enough with your thumb. Doing that pricked the flesh hard enough to hurt, but never enough to draw blood.

But none of that was the horrible thing.

"I brought you some nice fruit," Sylvia said. "Apples and bananas. And a carton of Salem Menthols, hundreds this time, just like you like. I gave them to the nurse at the station, and I wish there was some way you could tell me how many you actually smoke. I'm sure she's been stealing some."

The sky was low, but it didn't look like it was going to rain. It looked like it was going to stay gray and overcast forever. The view was ugly here, though it was not supposed to be. The rolling grounds existed only to be mowed, every other day it seemed, cropped so close that from up here the dirt could be seen through the stubble. They were afraid, she supposed, lest a blade of grass might briefly rise up and grow freely. To Jane, the lawn was the perfect symbol of oppression. But that wasn't the horrible thing either.

"Sit down on the edge of the bed and I'll do your hair."

Jane turned then to face her mother. How worn Sylvia looked, how unhappy, how old. She had that brave little look she always wore on entering, that reassuring everything-is-okay smile that was more then contradicted by the weary misery of her eyes.

Jane walked to the bed and sat down. Her body felt heavy, lumpish, awkward. It was the starchy diet, the lack of exercise, the fact that there had never been any reason *not* to let herself go.

Sylvia sat down beside her, took out a brush, and began putting Jane's hair in order. How her hands flew! Contemplating them, Jane could imagine how graceful her mother must have been in her youth, how gay and flirty back before Jane had happened to her. "I saw your Aunt Lillian the other day," Sylvia said lightly. "She said that young Albert is going back to his wife again, can you imagine that? That's what—the third time? There's something off about that relationship if you ask me, something more than meets the eye." She paused to light a cigarette, eyed Jane critically. "How would you like it if I braided your hair in cornrows?"

Mom, she tried to say. I want to come home.

But nothing came out.

Nothing ever did.

She raised her head slightly and stared at the window again. Though it was not visible from this angle, in her imagination she could see the horrible thing she had been staring at when her mother entered. It was her own reflection. The round, puffy face, the carelessly applied makeup, the dark, resentful eyes. The cast of expression that said her attention was a million light-years distant.

Suddenly it came to Jane that things weren't going to get any better. She was trapped. She was going to stay in the institution forever, slowly growing older and heavier, draining off the sap of her mother's life a shriveling drop at a time until it was all gone. Then there would be no more visits. She would be alone, decaying, growing ever more silently bitter, creeping toward zero.

She began to cry.

Astonished, her mother dropped the brush. It clattered loudly on the floor.

———————

The Baldwynn's tongue withdrew from Jane's mouth.

He released her.

In a panic she whirled and, dwarves scattering and falling away from her, fled the room. The door resisted her tugging, shuddering in its frame, until she thought to push. It opened onto the front office.

When she emerged, her party was gone.

Only the goblin remained. He waddled toward her, grinning effusively, holding out her mask and cloak. "Nice and filthy—you like, right? Just what you want, disgusting. Come back again."

———————

Elves were fickle. They'd pick you up at a thought and drop you for no reason at all. They weren't to blame, really; it was just their nature. You didn't go out with one unless you were willing to take the chance of suddenly discovering yourself standing alone in a puddle in the dark with a pocket full of dried leaves, abandoned.

Those were the facts. Jane kept reminding herself of them, over and over, for all the long and fearful hour that it took her to make it back to Caer Gwydion. But what she really wanted was to feed the lot of them, with all their cousins and relations, to the mouth of the Teind. If she could have shoved them one and all through Hell Gate, she would have done so gladly.

By the time she got to the party, Jane had largely recovered from her encounter with the Baldwynn. But she was tired and sullen, and in no mood for one more instant's lighthearted revelry. Why am I here? she asked herself. If she hadn't promised Melanchthon he'd feed tonight, she could be home now.

She discarded her mask and surrendered her cloak to a servant. Apollidon materialized in the foyer.

He saw her and headed straight for her boobs. "I'm nobody here," the parvenu said without preamble. "They all treat me like trash. Nobody here respects me for my ancestry."

"Well, they're pretty stuffy I guess," Jane said indifferently. He was still staring at her outfit. She could go home and change into a sweater and jeans, and he'd never recognize her.

"If I disappeared tonight and never showed up again, nobody would even miss me. I must be the most universally loathed individual in all creation."

"Really!" Jane was startled. Was it possible the answer had been staring her in the face all night long?

She resolved to find out.

Touching Apollidon's arm she sent a surge of desire up his nervous system. It was the same trick that Fata Jouissante had played on her earlier, and if she did not use it half so well, still, it was her first time. At any rate, to judge by the parvenu's reaction, she used it well enough. He shuddered and for the first time his eyes looked up and into hers. They connected. His pupils were wide with desire.

Then Apollidon flushed with awareness of what she had done.

"You're perfect," Jane assured him before he could look away. "Come home with me."

# TWENTY-ONE

Cheek flat against Tommy Paddlefoot's thigh, Jane waggled his penis back and forth. It was such a funny, floppy little fellow, she thought affectionately. She liked penises quite a lot, clownish things that they were, the sort of silly dangles that would look equally at home on a jester's cap or scepter.

It was only at times like this, immediately after sex, that Jane ever felt truly at peace anymore. She cherished this still, calm feeling of content, and prolonged it as best she could, wrapping the moment about her like a blanket that could briefly ward off the harsh shocks and chills of the world. She dreaded the rude instant that must inevitably come to end it.

"Hey. As long as you're down there anyway, how's about blowing a little tune on the mouth organ?"

Jane let it drop.

"That won't be necessary." She scraped up a bit of something from the wet spot and, holding the tip of her nail directly over his cock, whispered a summoning. "Stand up, Mister Bumble. Arise and grow larger." With her other hand she formed the mudra of spiritual expansion. And because she knew his organ's name and the proper techniques, it engorged with blood and stood erect for her.

Playtime was over. Back to work.

She sat up, twisted around, and crouched over Tommy's torpid form. With one hand, she guided Mister Bumble into Little Jane.

"You going to do the thing with the scarf again?"

"I'm going to do something better," she promised. "But to do it, I'll need your true name."

"Aw, no," Tommy Paddlefoot mumbled. "I really shouldn't."

"No?" She brushed her breasts lightly over his face, drawing them back from his questing mouth so that he only got the slightest sweet taste of nipple, and then reached a hand behind her to rake her nails lightly up his balls. He drew in his breath. "But you did like the game with the scarf?"

"Well, yeah, but –"

"You'll like this a whole lot better. I promise."

———⋙◉⋘———

There was a pantry cupboard off the kitchenette that Jane had no use for. She opened the door and threw Tommy Paddlefoot's clothes inside. The cupboard had amassed quite a pile of silks, cottons, and leathers. Apollidon's plumed hat must surely be crushed flat. She slammed the door. "Ferret was asking questions today," she said.

"Oh?"

"Is that all you have to say— Oh? Doesn't the thought of Ferret sniffing after your trail even bother you?"

"No."

"It should. He knows there's something wrong about my background. It can only be so long before he finds out what."

An angry hiss of steam rattled the walls. But the dragon's voice was cool and aloof. "So you are being pursued! What a weak and pathetic waif I find myself harnessed to! You don't know the least jot of it. We have been more closely pursued than you can imagine and by powers that would freeze your blood to think upon. Eight times in the last year have we come close to discovery. Even now, all sources of flight-octane fuel are being carefully watched. They know I'm out here and they know how much fuel I took with me. They're sure I'll try for more sooner or later. And so I would, if we hadn't worked out this alternative source of energy."

"What powers? Name them!"

"Save for one, their names would mean nothing to you. And that one you surely would underestimate gravely. If I were to say that for three nights running the Baldwynn had stalked the corridors outside this very apartment, you would—"

"Oh, the Baldwynn," Jane said airily. "Did I mention that I went dancing with him? You'd never guess what he tried to do."

"*Don't let him kiss you!*" In his shock, Melanchthon's voice was a roar that shook the steel frame of Termagant down to its foundations. Jane staggered. In the dining room a candy dish fell and broke.

"Why not?" Jane demanded. "What'll happen if I do?" It did not escape her notice that the dragon had known the Baldwynn wanted to kiss her. Nor that he had assumed that he had not succeeded. Well, she was tougher than Melanchthon realized.

He retreated into silence.

"You're still lying to me, damn you! I don't lie to *you!* We're supposed to be partners, right? Equals. In this together. When are you going to stop your stupid mind games and power trips so we can work in concert?"

Still the dragon said nothing. After a while Jane went to take a shower.

When she emerged twenty minutes later, wrapping a towel around her head, the dragon could not be seen. He had drawn the illusion of off-white walls, draped windows, and hanging baskets of English ivy about himself. But the air sang with tension. It trembled with the malice of his regard.

"Well?" Jane said testily.

For a long moment the silence held. At last, grudgingly, the dragon said, "You are right. We have little time left. We must complete our preparations as soon as possible."

"I know what you want and you can just forget it. Not tonight."

"Tonight," the dragon insisted. "I need more."

"More? I must've given you close to a hundred names by now. Just how fucking many do you need?"

"I'll let you know when it's enough."

Jane had a script to go over and lines to memorize. She'd been up late three nights running and it was beginning to affect her complexion. She'd promised herself she would go to bed early with a mud pack and a trashy paperback. "Cut me some slack. You can spare one night."

"Destruction," said the dragon, "is my all. Your screams would be as meat and drink to me, your torment sweeter than the blood of innocents, your slow death a lifetime of pleasure. Don't think the only sacrifices made have been yours. Do you want the Goddess or not? She's a tricky piece of business, and I won't go against her at anything less than full strength. If you won't cooperate, say so and I'll lower my sights. I may not have the power yet to kill the Lady, but I have more than enough to destroy the City and all that abide in it."

The reek of indignation and cold iron filled the apartment.

Jane sighed and glanced at the clock. She always lost these arguments. Maybe on some unconscious level she wanted to lose them. Maybe, living within the sphere of the dragon's aura, his passions were translated by her body into desire. In any case, Little Jane always silently sided with Melanchthon. And there was no denying that her duties in this phase of the conspiracy were proving far less onerous than she had expected them to be.

"I've got a shoot in the morning," she said. Her handlers needed publicity shots for an image makeover. So far as Jane could tell, her new image was the same thing as her old, only in red leather instead of black. But two weeks' scheduling had been shuffled to make time for a new set of glossies. Still, she could always pop an amphetamine with breakfast. Just so long as she didn't start making a habit of it. "I suppose I could pick up somebody in the bar."

"My little slut," Melanchthon said approvingly.

---

At the end of the shoot, while the photographer's assistants were packing up the equipment, Corinde came over and, putting aside his walking stick, placed an arm around Jane's shoulders. Corinde was the single most anorexic elf Jane had ever met, a stick figure in black, and such a bundle of mannerisms that it was hard to guess at the real personality underneath. Rumor was that he wasn't an elf at all, but some socially elevated variety of nightgaunt, and it was certainly true that Jane had never seen him in natural light. Still, he'd always treated her well enough.

Nattily tucking his cane under one arm Corinde said, "Darling, I have to say this. I've worked with the best—and you know me, I never flatter anyone if I can avoid it—the absolute best, and in all my years I've never seen anything the equal of you today. You were quite simply *dreadful!*"

"I'm sorry, I—"

"Yes, yes, yes. All this sex-drugs-and-glamour. You think I don't understand? You get to go to all the best clubs and take all those pretty young boys home and do whatever you want with them." Jane held herself expressionless. "Believe me, sweetcakes, I understand perfectly. But listen to me. Your wealth and notoriety—they're simply borrowed against expectations. They could vanish in the morning light. You haven't earned them yet. It's like shooting up speed." He raised his eyebrows significantly. "You feel fine and vigorous for ever so long. You look marvelous. You have the time of your life. But sooner or later, you have to crash. And then you will pay the piper, in exact measure according to how much you've drawn on account. Are you following me?"

"Yes, I—I think so," Jane said in a small voice.

"Good. Now go home and get some sleep."

"Oh, Corinde, I *would*, really. But I promised Fata Incolore . . ."

Corinde's eyes flashed. He slammed the floor with the tip of his stick and spun on his heel. Over his shoulder he snapped, "Somebody shorten the way for Fata Jayne. She has an important date uptown."

Under his prickly exterior, Corinde was really very sweet. It was a pity she had offended him. Jane hoped dearly that she hadn't won his enmity. The thought troubled her all the way to Pentecost.

———◈———

The doorway to House Incolore—or, rather, to the physical expression of House Incolore's local nexus—was gray and unassuming. It opened at her touch and closed noiselessly behind her. She walked unsurely through a dimly lit narthex.

The hall Jane stepped into was overwhelming. It seemed to be carven of vaulted and arched shadows that lofted in great curves to the farabove gloom. The gray walls, which turned to granite when touched, were braced by slim white pillars that glowed faintly in the distant gray. At first Jane thought the pillars were marble. But when she brushed against one, it had the warmth and texture of ivory.

Startled, she looked up at the vaulting again, dizzy with recognition. She was standing within the buttressed chest of some enormous monster whose ribs and bones had been polished and reshaped to form the supports of the granite hall. How could such a creature even support itself? Surely its organs would collapse under their own weight. However could it have taken in enough food to keep itself alive? It must have had an incredibly sluggish metabolism. Perhaps its movements had been excruciatingly slow, centuries for a single thought, ages to complete an action.

"There you are."

Fata Incolore strode briskly into the hall, pulling on her gloves. "Shall we go?"

"Uh, yes. Why not?" Jane continued to stare curiously at the ivory columns. She could not help herself. Incolore followed her glance.

"My ancestor."

"Oh." Jane trailed her hostess into an ambulatory beyond the right-hand row of columns. They stepped into an open-work elevator the details of which were invisible in the murk and rose to an upper gallery. A narrow corridor led deeper into the shadows. With every step they moved farther from the entrance.

"I thought we were going out somewhere," Jane said.

"Yes. To that place you agreed to see."

"Aren't you going to have somebody shorten the way?" Incolore was a gray-paper silhouette just before her, in constant danger of fading away to indistinction. Her stride was long and Jane had to hurry to keep from losing her.

"No need. In my house there are doors that lead wherever I want." She paused, one hand extended, and glanced over her shoulder. Her eyes were twin sparks of predatory calm. "Through here."

Jane stepped through the door and was blinded by sunlight.

As her sight returned, a hospital room coalesced about Jane. The antiseptic smell was unmistakable, as were the half-drawn institutional curtains, before which dust motes danced in slanted light as thick and golden as honey. Yet Jane knew for a fact that there was no hospital within miles of Pentecost.

Shoes clicked loudly in the hallway. Incolore walked over and closed the door. Quiet returned. Behind her, the portal through which they had entered shut without a trace. At the center of the room, an IV drip idle by its side, was a glass coffin.

There was a woman sleeping within.

She was thin, drawn and desiccated, and her scalp was pink beneath wispy white hair. Her face was deeply lined. Jane thought at first that she was old and then that she was not so much old as used up. In sleep she had found a kind of sad peace. Her brow and the skin at the corners of her eyes were tense, as if she were peering into a great distance. But the mouth was relaxed and unworried. Hers was no joyous expression, but that of one who had attained after long struggle a hard-won cessation of suffering.

"She's a mortal," Incolore said. "A changeling like you."

"I'm sure I don't know what you're—" Jane began. Then, seeing the indulgent expression that spread itself across Fata Incolore's features, she said, "How could you tell?"

"I'm in the trade, darling child, remember? You could no more hide your nature from me than you could from Rocket." She laughed briefly. "Don't worry, your secret is safe with me. What's one bit of shrinkage when the inventory is so full?"

Jane let some time pass before asking, "What's the matter with her?"

"Sleeping beauty sickness." Fata Incolore ditched her cigarette stub in the water glass and knocked another cigarette from its pack. "It's endemic among changelings of a certain age. They don't really belong here. The world rejects them, or they the world. It's what will happen to you eventually. Does that frighten you?"

"Yes." Jane peered, fascinated, into the face of the woman. Trying to comprehend her, trying to fathom what alien dreams played in the theater of her sleeping brain. "No. I don't know. Who is she?"

"Her name is Elizabeth."

"Elizabeth." Jane tasted the name, savoring its exotic syllables. This was the first full-blooded mortal, herself excepted, she could remember ever encountering. "She looks like she's had a hard life."

"How could it be otherwise?" There was a small table by the window with a vase of browning flowers on it, Incolore's drinking-glass ashtray, and a twisted bonsai pine in a glazed ceramic pot. Incolore picked up the pot and held it in the flat of her hand. "This tree is over a century old. Do you know how it's stunted into the desired shape?"

"You wrap wires around its trunk, right? You restrict its intake of water and you don't give it much soil to grow in. You prune it too."

"Yes. It's only a plant, of course. A serviceable half blood takes ever so much more manipulation. But we have clever gardeners. They begin by transplanting the mestizo boys and their mothers to small huts on a walled estate maintained for this purpose on a Southern island of perpetual summer. It's a lovely place; you'd adore it. Life is pleasant there. The hills ring with laughter and the mothers are encouraged to bond with their sons. Some refuse, and these are weeded out and sent back to the same factories that absorb their daughters. Most, though—well. The Goddess has given them no choice but to love their own. They raise their sons as best they can. They try not to think of the future.

"But there are servants in the garden, storytellers and other attendants with subtle ways of reminding the children of the noble heritage of their fathers. When they are old enough, the boys are dressed in silks and taken to visit their elven half-kindred. In their father's mansions, they are waited on hand and foot. They taste wealth for the first time. They are denied nothing. They are treated by their grand relations with the utmost condescension and disdain.

"Then they are dressed in wool again and returned to the huts.

"By such small means are they shaped. Ambition is encouraged. Envy is unavoidable. With puberty there are cousins who will take them to bed, teach them courtly ways, and snub them in public. Their fathers make it explicit that they are of tainted blood, bastards who will never be acknowledged. It is left to their mortal mothers to wipe away the tears of humiliation. What do you imagine the upshot of this is?"

"They despise their mothers."

"Exactly. Let us skip ahead several years—you can imagine them well enough—to the day when the best and most cunningly warped of the young mestizos are invited to the Academy. To be a dragon pilot is a great thing, beyond any reasonable expectations they might have, and close, very close to their most unreasonable dreams. They have no idea this was intended for them from before their births.

"A messenger presents the invitation in a distant corner of the estate, in a cool wood, by a gate they have never seen open before. The recipient must leave on the instant. He must pass through the gate without going back for food or cloak or farewell. Knowing how she will feel, he must leave his mother without so much as a word of regret. He is told he will never see her again."

"So he betrays her," said Jane.

"He betrays her."

"But what is the point of such an elaborate exercise?"

"Guilt," said Incolore. "So rare a quality, so precious. I confess I don't understand it at all myself, though the fortunes of House Incolore rest upon it. But its workings are simple. Having denied their own kind once, the young warriors understand the pain of betrayal on a very deep level indeed. Their loyalty to that side of their heritage which remains uncompromised is fierce beyond belief. This is a most desirable trait in one who handles creatures as dangerous as dragons and must bathe in their treachery every day."

Gracefully, she put down the potted tree.

Jane studied the woman's face. It loomed in her sight, as large and mysterious as a new continent. She could fall into it if she weren't careful. "What is she looking at?"

"Well—"

The hall door rattled. It opened.

Rocket walked in.

He stopped, flustered, at the sight of her. He had a bouquet of flowers in the crook of his arm. "Excuse me, I wasn't—" he began. Then, puzzled, "What are you doing here?"

"I bid you good den, brother," Incolore said.

"Ahhhh." It was almost a sigh. "So that's it."

Jane frowned. "Would somebody mind telling me just what is going on here?"

"I come here every week. To visit my mother." Rocket turned away and placed the nosegay on the table. He removed the old flowers from the vase, freshened the water, and set about arranging the new blossoms. "My half sister knows this. Doubtless she has her reasons for confronting us with each other."

When he turned back his expression was stiff and formal. Bowing slightly he handed Jane a daisy. "I beg you forgive my family, madam. I recognize you are not a deliberate party to this farce."

Jane looked down at her hands, at the flower clasped in them.

"Oh, don't be so stuffy," Incolore said. "Jayne, take off your blouse and show my brother what nice breasts you have."

Jane felt her face redden. But Rocket only said, "Don't insult the girl, Lesya. You won't manipulate us into each other's affections with such cheap tricks."

Smiling sternly, Lesya Incolore folded her arms. Her long, black nails dug unpleasantly into the flesh of her forearms. "It is most vexing," she said, "to be thwarted."

A touch of humor animated Rocket's expression. "By definition."

"Oh, don't chop words. Here you are, surrounded by reminders of death and mortality and here's Jayne provided with as nice a proof of your blockishly loyal nature as could be wished. You two could save me a lot of trouble by falling madly in lust."

Ignoring his sister, Rocket went to the coffin and laid a hand on its surface. Briefly he stood there. Then he turned back. "With your permission," he said, "I'll leave by that same way which you came." He groped in the air. Something clicked, and a portal opened into shadow. "Fata Jayne," he said meeting her gaze steadily. "I remain your devoted servant."

"His haunch and thighs are dappled," Incolore said. "Like a fawn's."

He slammed through the portal, shivering the air in his wake.

Incolore sighed. "The loyalty of the systematically betrayed. Is there anything sadder?"

"I can think of a few things." Jane put the daisy behind one ear. She patted the stray hairs into place. "Just what the fuck were you trying to do?"

Fata Incolore shrugged angrily. "I was meddling, of course. That's the source and summa of it. Nothing more. I thought you two had the potential to complicate each other's lives enormously. It would have been amusing."

"Amusing? What kind of shit is that? You're a power—don't you have anything better to do with your life?"

"It is important for me to involve myself in the ephemera of your little lives. To convince myself that they matter. To anchor myself—" Incolore stopped. "To—" A spasm passed through her body. One arm trembled uncontrollably.

Suddenly she cried out. Light poured from her eyes, blazed from her open mouth. It was as if a god had seized her by the hair to reveal the nuclear fires burning within. The light splashed against the wall, and nicked Jane's eyes. Wincing, throwing up an arm to shield herself against it, Jane cried, "What's happening? What should I do?"

"I have . . . pills," Incolore gasped. "Back in . . . back in House Incol—" She bit off the words, forcing eyes and mouth tight. When she opened them again, the fires were quenched, and her features once again appeared normal. But they were not the same features she had had an instant before.

"Gwen!"

With a smile of recognition, Gwen placed a finger to her lips and winked. Jane wanted to ask her old friend how she had survived the sacrifice on the football field, how she had come to be reborn in the Incolore. But then Gwen's face slackened and turned gray. Horns sprouted from her forehead. When Jane seized her by the shoulders, she hissed and bent a needle-toothed mouth toward Jane's neck.

Jane jerked away. "None of that now!"

The creature swayed and straightened, thinning, growing taller. For an instant Jane thought she was turning into a serpent. But then her face stabilized into distinctly male features.

"Oh, this is a nuisance," Lord Corvo grumbled. "Tell Incolore that if she can't control herself any better than—" He choked in midsentence, bent over, and became someone else.

Jane waved an arm back and forth in the air, groping for the portal back to House Incolore. But however one found it, whatever the trick might be, it was beyond her. She could not hope to fetch Incolore home by herself.

Then Incolore underwent one final transformation. She hooked a finger under Jane's chin to force up her gaze. With horror, Jane recognized the sharp intelligence of her new features.

"Oh, my!" Jouissante laughed. "This is an opportunity."

She touched velvet fingertips to perfect lips. "Where to start? Shall I trim a bit of this and that from you, little darling, would you like that?" Then, when Jane took a frantic step backward, "Pooh! Of course you would, if I wanted you to. But let's not waste this on such a trifle. We must do something memorable, something truly wonderful."

With a sudden gesture, Fata Jouissante opened the shadow portal.

She seized Jane by the arm and dragged her back through the door into House Incolore.

———⊙———

Straight through the house of shadows Jouissante hauled Jane, and up an endlessly twisting spine of stairs. "We are all bubbles of earth," she said. "Did you know that?"

"Please!" Jane cried. Desperately, silently, she called upon Melanchthon. He could not be invoked. She reached into the primitive depths of her brain, where he normally lurked, quiescent, alert, waiting.

The dragon was not there. He had abandoned her again.

"You are an alchemist and understand that everything is made out of the same component parts. The difference between a tree and a troll is one of organization only." Cold mists blew over the stairway, lit only intermittently by braziers that were smears of silvery light in the harsh sea-fogs, charcoal-smelling with unsteady pinkish hearts where the coals contended with the moisture. "If a tree's understanding of itself were great enough, it could fart and eat meat."

"Why are you telling me this?"

"I should think its applications were obvious." The landings flew by. "Do you never wonder why the powers are so quick to anger, desire, and envy? Why we suffer so many feuds, affairs, and scandals? We have them by choice. Our comprehension of the world and of ourselves is so great that there is no clear distinction between the two. We are in constant danger of dissolving altogether. And Incolore—never doubt it—is great among us. There are those who whisper that—well, never mind. Our flaws are the friction that keeps us from sliding right off the surface of existence."

Jane lost her footing and was dragged up a dozen stairs, struggling like a rebellious rag doll. Jouissante paused at a landing just long enough to let Jane get her legs under her, then plunged upward again. Her heels struck sparks from the stairs.

"But if—if—if you're not really you—" It was hard to think clearly under these conditions. "—if you're really Fata Incolore, then why—why are you behaving as if—?"

"Are you retarded?" Jouissante demanded. "Am I speaking to myself? Identity is a fiction. Surely you can grasp that. The Fatas Incolore and Jouissante are simply games that matter chooses to play. I am no more Lesya Incolore than you are."

They were still climbing. Fata Jouissante's vigor was apparently bottomless. Jane, however, was short of breath. Her head swam dizzily. For a second it seemed as if the ghosts of all her victims thronged about her, plucking at her hair, pinching her with their small, mean fingers, silently demanding the return of their stolen names. She shook her head and they were gone.

"—you may well ask. Occasionally a child is born without a true name. It has no subtle body—you understand? No self. It has eyes, brain, fingers, and organs in the proper place and number. But it is insensate. It knows nothing. It responds to nothing."

Give me back my name said Esmeree. Jane turned and she was not there. I want said Wibble said Apollidon said Gandalac. Give me said Lip back my said Gloam life said Hypallage. There were too many to keep track of and they were none of them there and Jouissante was speaking.

"When this happens the child is claimed for the good of the State. A dragon is sent through Dream Gate to raid the lower world and harvest the subtle bodies—they are there called souls—of mortal children. Nothing material may be returned to the upper world. Ah, but souls—!"

I don't feel guilty, Jane told the phantoms. Go away. They swirled about her, less substantial than the skeletal remains of autumn leaves, rattling angrily against her side, batting against her lips with all the force of a wayward moth. It was astounding that Jouissante couldn't see any of them.

Jouissante glanced back over her shoulder. "If you're not going to pay attention, I shall be forced to gouge out your eyes."

"Please!" Jane gasped.

They came at last to a final landing. Breathless and exhausted, Jane gratefully stumbled to a stop. Jouissante flung open an ivory door. "This is her seat of power—the chancel of the skull."

They stepped within. Cool white light scattered and banished the phantoms.

The walls were lined with ivory chests and the floor had off-white rugs. A low ceiling supported track lighting. A pale wall divided the room into two chambers in such a way that one could look into one chamber or the other, but never both at once. Each chamber had a single straight-backed chair facing the leaded-glass windows that were set into the eye sockets. Jouissante yanked her into the left-hand chamber. "We are standing within the skull of the first Incolore. If you hold very still, you can feel the force of her personality humming deep within the bone."

If so, then Fata Incolore's ancestor had been stranger even than her remains would have led one to think. For an overwhelming sense of the tenuousness of existence throbbed through Jane from all directions. Here, she sensed, nothing very dearly wished to remain itself. It made no matter to the albino maple escritoire whether it held letters or motor oil, stood stock still or burrowed in the earth, screamed for blood in the pouring rain or merely burst into flames. An alabaster crocodile trembled on the brink of flight.

"What—what are you going to do to me?"

"That's what I've been trying to explain to you, small lack-wit. I'm thinking of destroying your gross body and incarnating you in the flesh of a thrush or a wren. With your own wicker cage." She began rummaging through the cupboards. "Or better yet a little pink pig. Incolore could lead you about on a ribbon." She glanced up briefly. "Oh, don't look so! You'd have ever so much more pleasant a life as a pig than a wren. You could be potty-trained, for one thing." Bottles clanked and clattered. "Sit in the chair but don't stare into the window. You wouldn't like what it might choose to show you."

Jane had no choice but to obey, though she did risk one quick glance anyway. The window looked upon an empty room with a lone pair of work boots resting to one side of center. They cast a pale shadow. One lay on its side. Mud clung to its sole. Its laces were filthy. For the life of her, she could not imagine why the window should focus on such a thing. And yet her captor was right. For some indefinable reason, the sight of it filled her with an irrational terror.

"There are two windows in the chancel; one looks upon lies and one on truth. Not even Lesya Incolore knows which is which." Jouissante tipped over a chest. She kicked its spilled contents across the room. "Not here either! Where in the name of Maga Argea can it be?"

Something in the chair or possibly the room itself was conducive to lethargy. Jane stared down at her lap, unable to stand.

"Aha!" Fata Jouissante held up a cordless phone in triumph. Numbers booped. She waited, then said, "This is Fata Incolore. I would like you to send up a pig. Yes. No, the creature must be personable. Sweet, yes. Its disposition is very important to me. No, female."

Listening, Jane knew she ought to be upset. But it was hard to care. The apathy that held her to the chair was spreading through her body. If she didn't do something right away, she'd never do anything again.

In a detached way, Jane's fingers meandered to her hair and combed from it the daisy that Rocket had given her earlier. She looked down at the blossom and closed her fingers about it. Crushing the petals.

"How soon can you have it here? Oh, and a satin pillow too!"

Staring down at her hands, Jane concentrated on Rocket's true name and performed a summoning. She had never tried so powerful a spell before, but she knew the theoretics inside out. Tetigistus, she whispered in the Arctic stillnesses of her hindbrain. Come to me.

Jouissante whirled, phone in hand. "What have you done?" she cried. "You've done something! What have you done?"

Jane smiled vaguely up at her. The summoning had burned up the last of her volition. She was entirely passive now. She lacked even the will to speak.

There was a step on the stair. The door opened and Rocket entered.

He was masterful. Rocket took in the situation at a glance. He acted without hesitation. Striding forward, almost too fast to follow, he struck the telephone from Jouissante's hand. With a cry of dismay, she flew at him, raking her nails across his face, reaching for his eyes. Deftly, though, he seized her wrists, forcing her arms back. She thrust her body forward, striving to reach his jugular with her teeth. This was what he had been waiting for. Briefly, her ear was alongside Rocket's mouth.

"Kunosoura," he murmured in a voice so low that under ordinary conditions Jane could not possibly have heard him. But Jane knew his true name and with it had summoned him. His whispered word went right through her.

Kunosoura. It meant dog's tail.

It was Lesya Incolore's true name.

At the sound, the delusion of Fata Jouissante's persona fled from her face. Features melted one into another, some hardening, others softening, yet others growing sharp and keen. When they were done shifting, Incolore had stabilized as herself once more. Her eyes closed and her limbs went limp. Rocket hoisted her slumping body in his arms.

He gestured with his chin. "Open that door, please."

With the return of Fata Incolore, whatever force had held Jane passive was gone. She sprang from the chair and opened the small door he had indicated.

It took them to a room whose walls were lined with carnival masks. There were no windows. Rocket eased his sister down on a couch. "There's a medicine chest in that cabinet," he said. "When she comes to, we'll give her two of the white pills. That'll be enough."

Jane straightened from checking to see that Incolore was comfortable.

They looked at each other shyly.

"Well," Rocket said at last. "Lucky thing I dropped by."

"Yeah," Jane said. "Lucky."

"I apologize for forcing my presence on you twice in one day, madam. I realize that you don't like me—"

"Look, I like you, okay? I like you fine."

Rocket took a step forward and Jane took a step back. He stopped, looking puzzled. "Then why? If you do indeed like me, why then do you behave as you do? Why do you so consistently seek to put me out of countenance?"

"I don't want you to get caught up in all this shit," Jane said. "That's all. There's stuff going on, and I don't want to hurt you."

"Hurt me." Rocket was the stiffest, most sincere thing she had ever seen. "So long as my honor is unsullied, you may do as you wish with me. Treat me badly if that's what makes you happy. It can't be any worse than the pain of your disregard."

This was getting out of hand. To rein things in, Jane said, in as chill a tone as she could muster, "Your sister's political games have run completely amok, sir. She was going to turn me into a pig." Suddenly the ludicrous nature of it all struck her and she giggled with alarm. "A pig!"

"That was Fata Jouissante," Rocket reminded her. "But you are right to be angry, and if I cannot make amends, I can at least make explanations." He sighed and pinched the bridge of his nose. "The eyes of the chancel are delicate mechanisms. Performing a major transformation beneath one would—what is the word I'm seeking?—distort? no, *obsess* the eye, rendering it unwilling to look at anything but the act itself, over and over. It would diminish Lesya's power incalculably. But many a strange deed is performed under the banner of love."

"Love! For who?"

"Why, Lesya, of course. Poor Jouissante! She lives in dread of that day—and it is coming—when Lesya is raised to the invisible college and becomes a guardian. To be made a guardian is a terrible scandal and as great an honor as one may aspire to. Its prospect arouses everyone involved to extremes of emotion." He shrugged. "Even under the best of conditions, powers play such messy games when they sport at love."

Jane pondered this in long silence. At last she asked, "Is that what the Baldwynn is—a guardian?"

All of Rocket's warmth blew away like mist before a wind. "How do you know of the Baldwynn?" he demanded sternly. "He is one of the Eight. Nobody is supposed to know of the Baldwynn."

Jane touched Rocket's doublet. She undid the top two buttons and slid her hand within. Her fingers stroked his chest. It confused Rocket, addled and silenced him. "Where do you live?" she asked. "I mean the full address."

"Caer Arianrod. North 9743-A Plaza Court D."

She invoked his true name a second time. "Go there," she said. "Forget all that has happened here tonight."

Reluctantly she withdrew her hand.

And Rocket went away.

———◦◉◦———

Fata Incolore shuddered as the pills took hold. Color returned to her face. "It seems I'm in your debt."

"I don't want your gratitude!"

"Yes, so I gather." Long fingernails tapped against the top of the medicine kit, as if it were a small drum. "I suppose if I told you I could arrange for a certain stalwart young dragon pilot to materialize, naked and cooperative, in your bed one of these nights, you'd simply snarl at me again."

Jane folded her arms and said nothing.

"You really are the most amazingly perverse thing. I don't believe I've ever met anybody like you." Lesya laughed lightly. "Well, let's change the subject. Have I ever showed you my collection?" A negligent wave of one hand indicated the masks on the wall. Stern faces looked down on Jane, blank, assured, alluringly soulless.

"No."

"They're quite valuable. And useful as well. What I like about them, though, is that for all the sorcery that went into their making, they're not brute enchantments. They're instruments, dependent on the training and natural talent of whoever wears them."

"I don't follow you."

"Take this one, for example." She lifted a feathered demimask from the wall. The mask swooped up from the eyes in mock wings, covered the brow and nose, and left the mouth free. "Three bullocks were sacrificed just to activate it. Yet most of its power lies in the skill with which it's applied."

Jane shook her head slightly, involuntarily.

"The glamour of the mask is strong enough to confound identification so long as you do not speak. Such a mask can be, and often is, employed for a casual sexual fling, to protect one's reputation. But its true purpose is to be used on someone forbidden to you whom you yet strongly desire.

"You must want him greatly, so passionately that when you couple the extremity of your desire will be obvious to him. You must be shameless in your heart; you must do things you thought you would never do, and you must enjoy them. You must strive to shock your beloved. You must drive him to the limits of his endurance—so that when you rise from his body at the first weak light of dawn, he will not be able to raise a hand to stay your going, though he will want to do so.

"All the time you make love, he will stare into your eyes, whose color, because of the decognitive powers of the mask, he will not be able to remember, and see the fierce love of him burning there. They will be mirrors of his inner self, and they will show him in a far more flattering light than he has ever seen himself, as if he were a being composed of flame.

"He will want to know who you are—*you must not speak.* When he asks do you love him, smile and look aside. He will study the color and proportions of your nipples and try to size your breasts by how well they fill his hands, how much of each he can fit in his mouth. He will memorize your sighs and groans, and tickle you to learn the music of your laughter. He will store in his heart the smell and taste of your every part, the gentle hollow below your neck, the warm spot at the innermost top of your thighs, the flavors of your cunt herself and how they change with each stage of your arousal.

"It is only natural to wonder at the identity of one who so obviously loves you. And thus your intended is left with what at first may only be a mild curiosity. Perhaps he has a few surmises as to who you might be. Casually—at first—he begins to look for you.

"Of course, the only sure evidence of your identity can only be obtained by making love. You must arrange not to be one of the many he takes with him to bed. You will be jealous of them each and all, agonizingly so, but also needlessly. For every time he beds one, he will taste her sweat, lick the back of her knees and the downy line leading from the small of her back to the cleft between her cheeks, and he will be thinking: No. It is not she."

Lesya hung the mask back on the wall, her hands as graceful as butterflies. "What begins as mere curiosity soon burns out of control. Months pass. He is obsessed. Those rivals you had best reason to fear are one by one insulted and driven away by his behavior—for what woman cannot tell when the man she is abed with is thinking of someone else? You remain elusive. Your beloved engages in wild and aberrant behavior. He is ruled by love and desire alone.

"That is your opening gambit."

It was late and if Jane were ever to get back in Corinde's good graces, she needed to be bright and rested in the morning. She would gladly have left then, but Incolore was still wired from whatever was in the pills she had taken and kept her talking for an hour more. They discussed Lord Corvo's difficulties with his inamoratas and Fata Jouissante's chances at the senatorial cape. They talked about the war. They debated the merits of ermine viscera as a catalyst for skin-moisturizing spells and whether the increased efficiency justified the extra expense.

At last, Jane rose to leave. At the door she paused and, as if struck by a sudden notion, said, "That mask—may I borrow it?"

"My dear. Why do you think I showed it to you?"

⎯⎯◦⟨◉⟩◦⎯⎯

Jane meant to go straight home. But somehow her feet took her directly away from Termagant, toward Caer Arianrod. I won't go in, she thought on the way up in the Plaza Court D elevator. I'll just go up to his floor and then straight back down. The elevator doors opened and she stepped out onto the carpet. I'll walk by his door. I won't knock.

She knocked. Fata Incolore's mask was still in her hand, dangling from its cord. Impatiently she stuffed it into her purse.

Rocket opened the door. "Jayne," he said flatly.

"Can I come in?"

# TWENTY-TWO

Jane awoke at dawn. Gently she disentangled herself from the sheets and Rocket's arms.

She dressed quickly, stuffing her underwear into her purse, being careful to collect Incolore's unneeded mask. Rocket snored lightly. She looked down at his sleeping face. His mouth hung open, giving him a distinctly loutish appearance which she found well-nigh irresistible. She would have kissed him, but she was afraid he'd waken and she wanted to slip out without any fuss.

The streets were almost empty. The air was crisp and cool, and the City was awash in early morning light. Jane walked quickly, almost running, swinging her arms to keep warm. After a while she started to sing an old pop song:

> "Did you miss me? Come and kiss me.
> Never mind my bruises . . ."

A raptor girl heard her singing, laughed, leaped into the sky, and was gone, lost amid the golden dazzle of dawn bouncing from a million plate glass windows. Jane shook her hair and raised her voice:

> "Hug me, kiss me, suck my juices
> Squeezed from—"

Her voice bounced from the building sides and mellow brick walls. Oh, she felt fine!

It was a beautiful morning, a perfect morning. Her mood held all the way home to Termagant.

———◦◉◦———

Black smoke poured from the heights of the building. Soot covered its sides in great streaks. The street was choked with evacuees from Termagant. Nixies, orends, and Teggish lawyers milled about in an agitated confusion, while fashion models, powries, and leshiye argued with each other, gesturing wildly upward. Three candymen had brought out a great bell and were tolling the alarum with slow, steady strokes.

She stared. Far above there was a flash of light, followed by a distant rumbling like thunder. Jane felt as if she'd been kicked in the stomach. All joy collapsed within her. It was over. Everything was over.

A Greencoatie rode up, forcing the crowd away from the building with the metal breast of his destrier. "Stand back!" he commanded Jane.

"But I've got to get inside!"

"Nobody gets inside. This is a police matter!" He raised his lance against her, and she was forced to retreat. More Greencoaties moved into place, cordoning off the building.

Something shifted in that dark part of her brain that the dragon had vacated the night before. Melanchthon was back, a wordless and compelling presence. A cold sense of urgency filled Jane. She had to get past the police lines. She pulled out Incolore's mask and critically examined its interior. The outlines of its workings were clear enough to her. She was sure she could jigger up a spell of invisibility with it if she could only get hold of some sal ammoniac, tincture of Redness, and an elder leaf. It would burn out in five minutes, but five minutes would be enough.

There was a pharmacy on the corner. She ran.

———◦◉◦———

The passenger elevators had all been drawn by the heat to the burning floors like moths to a candle. But the freight elevators were simpler creatures, operated manually. Jane commandeered one.

Three times on the shudderingly slow climb to the seventy-third floor there were explosions. At each, she halted the car and waited lest the machinery be injured or the shaft thrown out of true. Jane feared the fire might block her way but her own floor, when she arrived at it, had only a light haze of smoke. It was suddenly silent. She tasted burnt plastic and charred wood at the back of her mouth.

Jane stepped into the canted hallway. Her mask turned hot and she ripped it from her face. Blistered and crisped, it fell to the floor and burst into flame. She left it burning behind her.

The door to 7332 fell off at her touch.

Her apartment had been leveled. Its furnishings were reduced to rubble. The interior walls were all gone. Splays of lathing fanned down here and there from the ceiling. The dragon was exposed, a cliff of black iron.

Ferret was in the center of the room, a short double-edged sword by his side. It was an athalme—Jane recognized it by the black handle and the almost imperceptible tug of its magnetized blade.

He was dead.

Wee bodics littered the floor, black and shriveled. They formed drifts by the walls. The meryons had died here by the thousands. Now at last, their nation was extinct. Loathsome little fascists though they were, Jane found their annihilation affected her horribly.

Without any conscious intent, she knelt by Ferret's side and stroked his short, silvery hair. It was soft, so soft. In death, his face was open, guileless, innocent. Too late, she regretted never having cultivated him. What a friend he could have been! And now he was gone.

"Who would have thought there was so much power in him?" she murmured.

"Not all the destruction was his," Melanchthon growled. "Less than half."

She looked at him.

"Your Master Ferret was a fool. He wanted the pleasure of taking me by himself. But he was not so much of a fool as not to have left word behind him. Others will be here soon, and they will not be fools at all. I would there had been another month to prepare. But we've power enough and more for our needs. It is time to leave. It is time for us to pass through Hell Gate and make our assault on Spiral Castle."

Jane raised her head.

She should have felt devastated. Ferret was dead, the meryons were dead, and there were surely others, caught in the flux of

Melanchthon's battle with Ferret, who had died as well. When they blasted free of Termagant, everyone in the street outside would be caught in the building's collapse. And that would be only the beginning of the general slaughter. They were embarked on a quest of destruction, going up against the greatest Enemy of all, to die and in death seek the obliteration of history. It was the end of all things.

She felt great.

"Do we have enough power?" Jane asked. She was already racing across the rubble, climbing the rungs to the cabin. She threw her windbreaker and blouse out the portal into the living room and slammed the hatch. Her flight jacket was waiting for her. She zipped herself into it.

"It will have to do." Melanchthon's words were mild, but his tone was confident, smug in his strength and destructive potential. One by one his engines were coming up, rattling the walls and causing the soft green instrument lights to flicker. There was a helmet—Jane pulled it on and tucked her hair in. The cabin smelled of leather and lubricating oil. She fit the oxymask over her mouth.

Jane settled herself into the couch, seized the rubber grips, and twisted. The needles stung deep into her flesh. The wraparounds closed about her head. Once again she was resting in the warm center of the dragon's sensorium.

To three sides of Termagant there were too many skyscrapers to plot a safe course through. They would have to fly east, into the rising sun. Already, bits of cornice and brick were falling, shaken loose by vibrations from the dragon's engines. Jane called up his weapons systems, and the controls spread out before her in three tiers, like the keyboards of that great organ on which the Lady had played the very first sunrise.

Everything was in place. "Are you ready?" Jane asked.

"Before I existed, I was ready."

"Then let's do it!"

———※———

Three floors were reduced to dust when they blasted free. Jane glimpsed the pyramid-topped upper section of Termagant falling slowly into the gray cloud, outlines softening as the walls crumbled. Windows shattered for blocks around, filling the air with a sparkling crystal mist that burned red with the reflected glory of their jets. Then they were gone. The Great Gray City spread itself thinner and thinner beneath them, the tight grid of streets and buildings gradually giving way to the exurbs.

They came in low over Whinny Moor, flying at what would have been treetop level had there been any trees. The mud flats and industrial parks, the shanties, oil tanks, and chemical dumps, flashed by beneath them. Light turned the shallow ponds and rivers silver and kicked up rainbows on the oil slicks. Narrow roads whipped and twisted like snakes.

"Up! *Up!*" Jane screamed, and the dragon strained skyward, skimming a string of high-tension power lines, missing them by yards, leaving them lashing furiously in his hot wake. "That was too fucking close! Give us some more altitude, why don't you?"

"We're going under their radar," Melanchthon growled. "You've heard of radar, I trust?"

The dragon works were a smear on the horizon.

Jane brought the two cannons on-line and called up the aiming systems. A sun cross appeared at the center of her vision, floating up and down slightly as they hugged the contours of the ground. "First flyby," Jane said. "We'll be taking out the front gate and the Time Clock, and blasting the Goddess stone to gravel." She felt wild, free, vengeful, obscene—unstoppable. "Serving the Bitch notice." She knew that there was no Goddess, save as a metaphor for what was otherwise inconceivable, that the forces they were going up against were as impersonal as they were vast. But it felt more satisfying this way.

"That won't get her attention," the dragon snarled. He was willing to play along with her; if there was one thing he understood, it was the mechanics of hatred. "Nothing less than a heat-seeker right up the wazoo is going to get her attention."

Jane adjusted the trim a feather's touch, pulling the sun cross down onto the factory walls. "It's what we're going to do."

They passed over the front gate like thunder, low and hard, flying subsonic, and left twin gouts of flame blossoming behind them. Melanchthon twisted right and they flew over the marshaling yards, dropping hellfire and elf-blight.

Dragons screamed behind them, twisting in agony, burning, raging for vengeance over every frequency of the electromagnetic spectrum even as they died. One somehow managed to lift up into the air before a fuel tank ruptured and exploded, sending him tumbling end over end into the side of the orange smithy.

Melanchthon was laughing and Jane was too, cheering and

whooping as they swung around tight for a second run. Black specks were pouring from all the buildings. Flames shot up from the orange smithy. Staticky voices welled up on the radio between the dragons' mad cries, demanding that they identify themselves, calling for help, warning them away, ordering pursuit craft into the air.

Turbulence bounced the cannon fire up and wild, taking out one side of the erection shop. But not before enough fire found its target to blast what remained of the front wall into rubble. Jane thought she saw tiny figures, smaller than ants, glimpsed and gone, darting into the smoke. Taking their chance to escape. Go for it, she thought. They flashed over the marshaling yards, making sure the first overflight had done its job. It was an inferno down there. Through the smoke she spied two dragons locked in blind combat, furious even in their dying moments. Others still writhed in the chemical flames. There was no danger from any of them.

Jane started to loop the dragon around for a third run. Most of the wall was down. "They're coming!" shouted Melanchthon. Radar showed three blips lifting up over the horizon.

"Once more."

The final time over, Jane held the weaponry off-line. She strained to make out Building 5, where her dormitory had been. She fancied she could, but by the time she had picked it out it was gone behind her. It was like something seen by lightning flashes. Run, she commanded the children silently. Don't look back. If Thistle and Dimity were still alive, they'd make it out, she was sure of that. They were opportunists. But some of the others . . .

"I've kept my part of the bargain," Melanchthon said. "See that you keep yours. Hold steady and bank right when I tell you. At their speed they've got a monster turning radius. We can use it to eat up some of their edge."

"Gotcha."

Their pursuers were visible behind her as amazingly fine miniatures, no larger than grains of sand. Jane could hear their voices over the radio, the cool and arrogant young technocrats and their angry machines.

"We have visual. Hawk, keep steady. Anybody got a positive ID?"

"Roger. Adjusting a point. That's our rogue, all right."

"Rip their fucking guts out!"

"Spitfire, you're too wide."

"Lemme shove one up the bastard's rectum!"

"Hawk, Spitfire, ready your AAM. Bring 'em on-line."

Jane felt her face freeze. She knew that voice! It was Rocket! For a giddy instant it seemed impossible—she had left him sleeping, miles away from any interceptor base. Still, he had access to House Incolore, whose many doors, Lesya had said, opened everywhere. How long would it take him to reach his base if he were summoned? Not long at all.

"Now!" Melanchthon shouted. Jane brought them around hard and tight. The interceptors overshot wildly, air brakes out, dwindling with distance. Melanchthon was headed due north now. Jane opened up the throttle.

"Full power," the dragon commanded as he reconfigured for maximum speed. "No more dicking around. We're going straight for Hell Gate."

"Where is it?" The navigational systems were no help. "It's not marked! I can't find it anywhere."

"Where is it? Fool! Hell Gate is not a place—it's a *condition*."

At his direction, Jane lifted Melanchthon's nose straight up. Before he could stall out, she cut in the afterburners. G forces slammed her back into the couch. They flattened her face and narrowed her vision—everything was jumping; she dared only look straight ahead. The dragon seized control of her autonomous functions and pumped blood back into her head to keep her from blacking out.

The pillars of smoke towering above them shrank to nothing.

"Moving into position. Look at them climb."

"Hold back, Spitfire."

"I think I can squeeze off a shot."

"Hold back."

Flyspeck alphanumerics flicked off and on as the dragons spoke, tagging them with their public IDs. 2928: "C'mon down, sweetheart. We want to teach you a little lesson in experimental entelechy."

6613: "Hah!"

8607: "Is your pilot listening? I got a message for him: Spread your cheeks, dipshit, and brace yourself for a shot of ontology in action."

Disgusted, she slapped a masking function on them, leaving only the calm chatter of their pilots.

"Hawk, can you lock on radar?"

"Ah, negatory, Rocket."

"Craziest damn tactics I ever saw. What do you make of it?"

"Looks like a DG maneuver to me."

"That's my reading too. Spitfire, set up your point of inter-cept. Hawk, ditto on the left. I'll sit on his tail and drive him straight at you."

"Roger."

"Double affirmative."

Their pursuers had altitude. Climbing above them used up half the distance Jane had over them. "Cocky bastards," Melanchthon said. "They think they've got us pegged. Bring up the rear guns. If they come anywhere near range, give 'em a burst. Just to dust 'em back."

"O-okay." Jane was being battered and rattled like a die in a giant's gambling cup. It was all she could do to follow his instruc-tions. The instrumentation lights flickered as Melanchthon fired up the two barrel-sized banks of superconductors located just be-neath the ventral hatches of his thorax. "I never did understand what those things are for."

"Watch and learn."

Melanchthon threw 350 degrees of enhanced exteriors onto the wraparound screens. Jane saw electromagnetic fields warping out from his iron body like vast invisible wings. Actinic blue light flared where the fields interacted with air ionized by the dragon's passage.

"There it goes, right on schedule. It's a DG maneuver for damnsure."

"Can't see why they'd want to hit Dream Gate, but nothing else makes any sense at all. Hold position, Spitfire. We'll do this by the book."

"Your call, Rocket."

They shot entirely out of the atmosphere and Melanchthon cut the burners. The blue flares of energy dimmed, became ripples in the structure of space. Briefly, they went ballistic. After the crush-ing forces of acceleration, the sudden weightlessness almost made Jane empty her stomach. She swallowed back the sudden upsurge and ran a quick check of all systems. Everything came up green. "Can you engage our pursuit on an electronic level? I want to have a private word with their flight leader."

"I've been engaged in electronic countermeasures since they came over the horizon," Melanchthon said disdainfully. "Here. You and your paramour can trade endearments on virtual."

Rocket's face appeared on the wraparound. "Jayne!" he cried in astonishment. "What are *you* doing here?"

She couldn't answer.

"You've been abducted," he said flatly.

Rankled, she said, "Fuck that noise! I know what I'm doing." In the background she could hear the indistinct mutter of dragons inadequately squelched, their anger carrying a conviction stronger than any words could express. She couldn't ignore it. It was as if her bones and viscera, her organs and innards had been given voice. "There's no future for me. All my life I've been stuck in a rigged game. The dice are loaded and I was declared a loser before I even began to play. These are not just words! What choice was I ever given? Only this one, right here, right now. I can swallow defeat meekly or I can throw the board up in the air and smash all the pieces. Well, I've been screwed from Day One—I have no intention whatsoever of being a good sport!"

Tensely, Rocket said, "You *can't* go back through Dream Gate. I don't care what your dragon's said, it's a lie. Dragons lie. You don't know what's waiting for you on the other side. If you cross over, you'll be—" His image cut off abruptly. But Jane knew Melanchthon's circuitry too intimately for him to work that trick. She overrode his commands. Rocket reappeared. "—forever. The mundane body you left behind is still alive. Like calls to like. You'll be drawn straight to it."

The streaming electromagnetic fault lines ahead fluttered wildly, as if struggling against a recalcitrant medium. "Yeah, yeah."

"You won't reintegrate." Rocket's dragon said something to him over his headphones and he shook his head impatiently. "You'll be trapped in your old body. No speech, no responses, no communication of any kind with the outside. Maybe no control over your own bowels."

"Stop behaving like an idiot, you asshole." She hadn't meant to speak so harshly, but the dragons' muttering distracted her. Their three streams of rage combined with her own dragon's suddenly rising apprehension to form a fast, jittery chord in her blood. "I just wanted to say—good-bye. I just wanted to say no hard feelings. That's not much. But you just keep on talking!"

"I have to make you listen. You don't know—"

She cut him off. "I know everything. I know the worst. There's nothing bad you can tell me—I've been kissed by the Baldwynn."

Melanchthon roared with fear and relief. This was what he had been trying to hide from her: That if they succeeded, she had a fifty-fifty chance of being thrown back to her original body in the aftermath. If the destruction were anything less than universal, she would spend the rest of her life a prisoner within her own alien flesh. But Jane didn't care. She'd figured that out long ago. Her will was as steady and unwavering as the dragon's own.

"I'm trying to help you, you fool!" Rocket was angry at last. "You're making a terrible mistake."

"Help me? What did you have in mind? If I turn back now, do I get to walk away free? No hard feelings? I can pick up my career where I left off? Maybe you're planning to marry me and carry me off to a clean white marble city on the grassy, windswept plains of Mag Mell. That it?"

Rocket bit his lip. His eyes were two coals.

The e-m fields abruptly steadied, merged, collapsed into a narrowing spear and disappeared altogether.

"We've got our gate," the dragon reported.

Hell Gate blossomed at the far limit of visual, an uncertain blackness against the starry bowl of space. Beyond it were two bright specks, Rocket's comrades moving into position where they expected a different gate entirely to open.

Rocket's voice rose in disbelief. "Damn you, what do you think you're doing? Things are unstable out there—one wrong action could harrow the upper world and the lower alike. You can't go through Hell Gate."

He looked so pale and tormented that Jane wanted to hug him. I love you, she thought. I want you. But something strong and perverse within her wanted not to comfort but to goad and provoke him. She didn't understand this impulse at all, but she was helpless before it. Melanchthon chuckled with disgust.

"Watch me."

"I am a defender," Rocket said in a choked voice. His face was highly colored; his temper barely contained. "Do not presume on my emotions, Lady. I will not throw over my honor for you—I will not!"

"Nobody's asking you to."

Squeezed out of nothingness, Hell Gate was a shimmering lenticular hole in the void. The two lead pilots, anticipating the wrong set of conditions, could not bank sharply enough to follow her in. They peeled away, their dragons bellowing with frustrated combat-lust. But Rocket's mount kept on her tail, hot in pursuit. Desperate with the need to engage and destroy.

"This is the last warning you get!"

"Warn away—you're wasting your breath. I'm beyond all that now."

"*Jayne!*"

Hell Gate exploded in her face.

———«◉»———

They were flying high above a turbulent white ocean. Its surface bubbled and frothed, throwing up spikes half a mile high and as bright to look upon as an electric light bulb. One shot up beneath them and was only barely evaded. Just as it looked about to collapse, the spike was drawn rapidly back down into the ocean and reabsorbed.

"What the fuck is *that?*" Jane asked.

"Quantum uncertainty—chaos—unformed matter—the stuff of creation," Melanchthon said distractedly. "There's no adequate name for what it is. Who gives a shit? Just make good and sure none of it touches us."

Ahead, a white seashell shape that Jane could have covered with her outstretched thumb tumbled slowly in a featureless sky. Spiral Castle!

Rocket loosed an air-to-air missile at them.

It flew with single-minded fury. The dragon's tracking devices translated the missile's hunting song into a rising electronic squeal. Just as it peaked, Jane slammed the dragon left. The missile slipped past one wing. A spike of the primal ocean rose beneath them and she threw them right again. "Cer-fucking-*nunos!* Why can't we get above this crap?"

"Local conditions—this is as high as we'll go. Forget that. Your flyboy is too close. Brush him back."

Belatedly Jane remembered her rear guns and squeezed off a burst. Rocket's dragon slid to one side and back again, losing next to no speed at all. Jane swung around a rising pillar and glimpsed him dipping under a falling loop of primal matter for a fractional gain of distance. He was a crackerjack pilot, there was no denying that.

Two black explosions blossomed in the air beyond Rocket. His fellow warriors appeared in his wake.

"Yo, buddy, you miss us?"

"Hope you left something for us."

They fell into formation. All three were intermittently visible and invisible among the twisting, rising, and falling tentacles of light. Abruptly Rocket's voice rose, clear and surprisingly high, over the radio, singing:

> "I weep for my lady—she is dead!
> Oh weep for my lady! though our tears
> Thaw not the frost which binds so dear a head!"

A swaying starburst slammed up before her, and Jane just barely managed to evade it. "He's crazy!" she said. "What the hell does he think he's doing?"

"Singing your dirge." An odd inflection, almost of regret, entered Melanchthon's voice. "It's a Corps tradition. Ignore it." The deeper-than-bass rumble of 8607 welled up under Rocket's and was joined by the doubled voices of Hawk and his 2928, and of Spitfire and his 6613, all merging into one:

> "Where wert thou, mighty Mother, when she lay,
> Thy daughter lay, pierced by the shaft which flies
> In darkness?"

There was a strange, unworldly beauty to the song. Fleetingly Jane had a shivery glimpse of what it might be like to have Melanchthon subservient to her, broken to her will, undiminished in strength and intelligence but compliant. "Pussies!" Melanchthon roared. "If you had any self-respect, you'd eject those parasites and join with me. Cocksuckers! Slaves!" But the singing went right on, uninterrupted. A forest of chaotic waterspouts separated them from their pursuers, but by slow and steady increments the distance was shrinking.

"I'm not dead yet!" she shouted at them.

Heedless, her pursuers sang the dirge to completion. The song did not distract them from the business at hand but, rather, served to focus their concentration. When it ended, they were closer than they had been when they'd begun.

"Slide aside, Rocket," Hawk drawled, "and I'll loose an AAM."

"No."

"Hey, trust me on this one. I'm that close to a lock."

"No!"

"We're coming up on the turnaround point," Spitfire said. "We've got fuel enough for another two–three minutes if we expect to get back to base intact. Give us our target!"

"No, I've got her." Rocket's dragon hung tantalizingly on the edge of Jane's blind spot, flickering in and out of her peripheral vision. Ironically, his proximity was sheltering her from his comrades' missiles.

"Rocket, get the fuck out of my way!"

"A three-way convergence and release, boss-man. That's how the book calls it."

"I've got her, I tell you."

He was drawing slowly closer, into the hammerlock slot, where no conceivable evasive tactic could dislodge him. Even if Rocket's dragon weren't younger, stronger, faster—and Jane had no reason to doubt that he was—she was no pilot. She had not a fraction of Rocket's fighting skills.

Spiral Castle was getting closer, but slowly, too slowly.

"Here comes the moment of truth," Melanchthon muttered. On the navigationals Jane saw four pinpricks of light creeping up on a curved orange line—the extremes of the dragons' range. None could cross it and hope to return home alive.

Already, Hawk and Spitfire were reining in their frustrated mounts, veering off well short of the line. As their commander failed to follow, they called to him in voices suddenly fearful:

"Heads up, Rocket!"

"Yo, buddy! Turn back."

"Rocket!"

Jane squelched their fading voices. On virtual she saw Rocket's face, his eyes fixed on her own virtual image. In the false-color exteriors, she could make out the curved line of her own contrail, visible in the high UV and low IR frequencies, the superheated ion trace of a hundred true names painstakingly gathered and now being squandered in one prolonged and reckless burst of speed. Rocket's dragon was almost to the orange line.

"Now I'm giving *you* one last warning—turn back!"

"No chance," he said grimly. "We're going down together."

"You wish!" she crowed.

Over the screens Rocket looked like a young god. The battle-light blazed furiously about his face. It snapped and crackled in the cockpit. His fleeing fellow warriors must have said something to him, for his face suddenly twisted. "She's mine!" he yelled. "Nobody nails her but me!"

"Come and get me, loverboy!" Jane jeered. "Anything you can catch, you can have!"

Rocket's dragon crossed the line.

"Shit," Melanchthon muttered in so dark a tone that it cut right through Jane's exultation.

"Shit? What do you mean—shit?"

"Work it out for yourself."

8607 was in Jane's blind spot now, just off to one side of her exhaust, hanging out of range of her guns. But not out of range for his missiles. She slammed her dragon right, left, left again. Rocket hung onto her with effortless grace. He wasn't going to turn back. And Spiral Castle was still far, far away.

"We can't outfly him!" Jane cried in sudden despair. "We're not going to make it."

"Then give me the mestizo's true name."

"What?"

"His true name," Melanchthon growled. "I've got the programming and I know how to use it. Give me his name and I can command him to destroy his mount under himself."

"No!"

"I know you have it. It burns in your brain like a lodestar." The dragon reached dark tendrils into her. She could easily have shut him out by snapping his electrical systems quickly off and on. But at these speeds, they could not afford even the briefest distraction. It would have killed them both.

"Rocket," she cried. "Turn back! Turn!"

The dragon's touch was deliberately foul in a crude and cartoonish way, like a hand dipped in black molasses and dragged across the front of a white cotton blouse. Quick as a wet rat on a garden wall, it scuttled into her hoard of memories.

It was totally irrational, she knew. There was no safe place he could go. "You've got to listen to me!" She heard him chuckle, a low and nasty noise compounded equally of desire and tears. "Rocket!"

The squeal of a second air-to-air being brought on-line sounded on the tracking systems. A sharp beeping as it searched for a radar lock. A glad cry as it found it.

"His name!" The dragon was closing on his prey. Jane resisted, throwing out random snaphot recollections in his way: Ratsnickle standing, prick in hand, sneering at her. Gwen trying on a new necklace. Smidgeon sitting in the shadows behind a scrap iron box, weeping, while Rooster looked on in disgust. Being dragged up the twisting spine of House Incol—Melanchthon snatched greedily at what he saw there.

"Kunosoura!" he cried, just as the missile was launched.

For the space of an eyeblink Jane saw a spherical wave front race away from them at Mach One. There must have been some tangential influence to Rocket's half sister's true name, for at its touch the missile veered crazily, spinning end over end toward the glowing ocean. A rising dome of blistered white touched it and without transition the missile simply ceased to be, melted back into its own potential. Lesya's true name as well collapsed upon its own syllables and ceased to be.

A third missile was being brought up. Jane could hear its voice in her earphones, and Rocket's too. He was crooning quietly to himself in a crazed kind of amalgam of anger, lust, and despair. "Come on, baby. A little closer. Yeah. Yeah, I've got you now. I've got you sweet and nasty." He held 8607 tight and steady behind her, just off-range from her guns. The beeping began. "Ohhh yeah, you're mine now."

"Does your word mean nothing?" Melanchthon demanded. "You've been lying to yourself all along, fantasizing that you could provoke your half-breed leman into stopping you from your actions, rescuing you from their consequences, knocking the dagger aside, sweeping you up in his arms and carrying you away to a pink, warm, satin-coverleted bed where you'll be as safe and comfy as two maggots in an acorn forever. Bullshit! It doesn't matter how he feels or what he wants. He can do nothing now but kill you. The universe has backed you into another corner—you can kill or die. There are no other choices. Doesn't that make you angry? Doesn't it make you want revenge? Or are you going to truckle to Dame Fate one more time, to be crushed and for all I know resurrected to run the maze of torment again and yet again? Stand up on your hind legs for once!"

"I—"

A glad cry arose from the third missile.

*"His name!"*

It was inevitable. There was nothing else she could do.

"Tetigistus," Jane murmured.

Melanchthon roared his triumph as the missile, caught in the act of launching, exploded directly in front of 8607. Rocket's dragon tumbled away in pieces.

Jane couldn't watch. She was crying with rage.

Kill the Bitch, she thought desperately. The spikes were rising wildly about her, hundreds of them, twisting like tornadoes. If I have to die, let these be my last words, my final thought. Kill the fucking Bitch. Her heart was racing. Kill the Bitch kill the Bitch kill the Bitch kill the Bitch. The words ran together in her mind, becoming a scream, a mantra, a kind of hysteric prayer, a last grudging acknowledgment of the Goddess's power.

Spiral Castle grew larger and larger, filling her vision with its chalky white walls. Jane felt like a gnat assaulting a continent. Melanchthon was laughing—*laughing!*—as they flew, all weapons firing, the pure embodiment of madness and destruction. The dragon's iron body shuddered spasmodically as two by two the missiles were launched. I am the shattering stone, Jane thought. I am the arrow in flight. It was her own thought, but it tasted like the dragon's. The cabin was heating up, sweat tickling down Jane's face and pouring from her armpits and down her sides, where her body was already slick and itchy. She didn't give a damn. This was what she had been born for, built for, plotted for tedious years of exile from the skies to attain.

This was the death of everything.

<hr>

But as Spiral Castle continued to swell, filling the universe, and the ocean grew strangely still beneath them, something began to happen to the dragon.

It started as a failing responsiveness at the tips of his wings and spread rapidly. Columns of alphanumeric readouts sank toward zeros. His extremities numbed. All feeling was lost on the skin. Great masses of status data went flat. Wisps of white mist obscured the quantum ocean below. They were flying through a tepid, oxidizing milkiness. Patches of corrosion grew upon the dragon's exterior. Holes appeared in his skin.

The atmosphere was eating away Melanchthon from the outside in.

"What's happening?" Jane cried. "What's happening?"

The controls did not respond.

"Torment and buggery!" the dragon howled. "Damnation, death, and red agony, I say—fuck the elves, fuck the Tegs, fuck the dwarves, kobolds, Nimble Men, and grims. Fuck them all in every rank and degree. I fix on them the eye of death. I call down on them the word of wrath. I curse them with the cry of guilt. Damned be they and all their lords and powers and masters and matriarchs."

"What can I do? Tell me what to do!"

Great chunks of the dragon's substance tore away. Jane was

deafened by the hideous screeching sound of metal being ripped apart. An engine exploded and fell away. She was slammed one way and then the other. Most of the dragon had broken up and what remained was melting away and still he raged, raged against the Goddess, against life, against the very fact of existence.

"Tell me!"

Melanchthon's voice rose in a wordless howl as he unraveled toward nullity.

"I'm sorry," Jane said quietly. "I'm sorry it had to end this way."

No words remained to the dragon. His language systems had been destroyed. But the empathy between him and Jane was great enough that she could still decode the emotion modulating his dying cry: It was satisfaction that she was going to die too and regret that it would be quick.

The scream was the last to go, growing suddenly faint and then rapidly trailing off into a whimper and then silence.

He was no more.

For the briefest instant, Jane continued going without him. Momentum carried her forward with undiminished speed through the lukewarm whiteness. Their destination was growing infinitely larger without getting at all closer; she might fly forever and never reach it. Jane had just time enough to realize that they had never really had a chance at all, that Spiral Castle was by its very nature proof against the very best efforts of women and dragons.

Then she died.

# TWENTY-THREE

Sylvia, wearing a stained white lab smock, was leaning over an electron microscope.

"Mom?" Jane said wonderingly.

"Shhh." Without looking up, Sylvia jabbed a cigarette in the corner of her mouth. "Light this for me, would you, sweetie?"

Jane complied.

"Little buggers." Her mother sucked deep, blew the smoke out her nose. "They really do try, but it's so hard to make the cretinous things understand what I want of them."

The laboratory was alarmingly ordinary-looking: Cinder block walls painted an undistinguished beige, ebony-topped lab benches, no windows. It was inexplicable. The last thing Jane remembered, Melanchthon was falling apart in the white mists above the quantum ocean. And now this. Her head buzzed. She had that same strange, spacey feeling she always got about an hour after dropping acid, just before the rush hit. "Where am I?" she breathed.

"You're in Spiral Castle," said a male voice.

She whirled.

The newcomer was dressed in a pin-striped suit with unfashionably narrow lapels. He wore a dapper black derby whose brim curled up in two short horns. For all that his face was wrinkled and wizened, a lively amusement sat deep in his eyes. His mouth puckered up into a smile.

"Miss Jane," the Baldwynn said. "A pleasure to see you again."

Jane gaped at him.

"If you'll permit me." He took her arm. "It is my honor to be your cicerone."

"My what?"

"Your guide." With a tip of the hat to Sylvia, he began leading Jane toward the door. "Spiral Castle is so very large, after all, and there are parts of it you wouldn't want to stumble into by mistake." His stride was long and vigorous. Jane hurried to keep pace.

———◦◉◦———

"When I was young I had a Trans Am." The Baldwynn's voice was warm and confidential but not particularly strong. Jane had to walk with her head down to hear him. The empty silence after the slam of a screen door echoed in her ears, but she had no memory of hearing the screen door slam.

"That was a very serious muscle car, and I'd put a lot of work into it. I had a gig at the Navy Yard then as a welder, and whenever they laid us off for a few weeks, I'd get a buddy to go in on the gas with me and we'd drive down to Fort Lauderdale on U.S. 1, taking turns at the wheel, with a thermos of black coffee and a pocketful of amphetamine to save us having to spring for a motel. We'd crank the radio up loud and listen to, oh, Queen, T. Rex, maybe a little early Springsteen. Whatever the local deejays were putting out. Zooming along with that wash of electrons singing down on us from the ionosphere, as if the machineries of the night had been given voice. When you've been driving long enough, the highway gets behind your eyes and you feel a kind of floating Zen sensation. You become very still. Only your hands move, and the steering wheel. The world flows by beneath you."

Jane frowned, trying hard to follow his narrative through the tangle of unfamiliar terminology. A branch cracked underfoot. She looked up and saw they were treading a path through a dark wood. The branches of the trees were leafless and ended not in twigs but human body parts. One nearby was all hands, unmoving in the breathless air. A clear fluid gathered under the nails, formed drops on the fingertips, and fell to the loam with a sad, final plop.

"One time, passing through the Carolinas somewhere between 2:00 and 3:00 A.M., Jerry-D and I picked up a white Lotus with two blonds in it. We honked and waved. They gave us the finger and put the pedal to the metal. I did the same, of course, but even with dual carbs it was no contest. We had a muscle car but they had a sex machine. They made us eat their dust."

The land rose to either side of the trail. Jane looked up at the distant, slanting trees and saw no horizon. She raised her sight higher and higher, until finally she saw the woods looping far overhead and down on the other side again. They were walking through an immense tube or tunnel. It twisted dizzyingly, an artery fleeing the dark heart of some unimaginably huge body. The chimeric, half-human trees closed about them.

"Ten–fifteen miles down the road we saw the Lotus in a Roy Rogers lot. We pulled in for some take-out burgers. There they were. We struck up a conversation. When we left, Jerry-D went with the driver of the Lotus. Her friend went with me."

"This wasn't our world, was it?" Jane managed to ask the question only with difficulty. When the Baldwynn was speaking, his words carried her along compulsively; she followed him effortlessly. Otherwise, it was hard for her to concentrate. "Not the upper world, I mean. It must've been in the lower world."

"Oh, you don't believe there's any serious difference between the two, do you? Anyway, there I was, a blond in pink hot pants rubbing up against me. I had my foot to the floor, her tongue in my ear, and her hand down my pants. I pushed up her halter top and squeezed her breasts. The air shimmered with the immanence of revelation. Little Richard was singing 'Tutti-Frutti' on the radio and it somehow seemed significant that what I was hearing had been electromagnetically encoded, transmitted as modulated radiation, reconstructed by the radio as sound, and only reinterpreted as music somewhere within the dark reaches of my head. I felt then that the world was an illusion and a rather shabby one at that, an image projected upon the thinnest of membranes, and that were I to *push* at it just right, I could step out of the world entirely.

"I unbuttoned her shorts. She wriggled a little to help. I slid my hand under her panties. I was thinking that everything was information when I found myself clutching an erect penis.

"I whipped my head around. The blond was grinning wildly into my face. My hand involuntarily tightened about her cock. Her hand tightened about mine. They might have been the same hand. We might have been one person twinned. The car was up to about 100 mph. I wasn't even looking where we were going. I didn't care.

"It was in that instant that I achieved enlightenment."

Something turned underfoot. Jane stumbled and, turning, saw that a hand sprouting from the roots of a nearby tree had seized her shoe.

She gasped and snatched her foot away.

The shoe fell free. The hand pushed it into a mouth that opened in the trunk and began to gnaw it down. Jane made no effort to regain the shoe, but hobbled after the unflappable Baldwynn. "I did my best to stop your coming here," he remarked. "Spiral Castle can be particularly dangerous when you arrive early."

"I don't understand!" she cried. "What does your story mean? Tell me what it means."

"But such things can only be explained by the Goddess," the Baldwynn said in a genially puzzled tone. "Who am I to speak for the Goddess? I am but her consort—and I am far from being the only one, I assure you. You can ask any questions you like when you meet her."

"I thought there wasn't any such thing as the Goddess. I thought she was a metaphor."

"Most certainly the Goddess exists. I am taking you to her now."

A spray of cold babies' fingers brushed against Jane's cheek. She drew away and shuddered. But the trail grew narrower and the trees and bushes closer together. She was crowded and jostled by dark shapes, arms and shoulders bumping against her. There was a whiff of diesel exhaust and then the crowd, Baldwynn and all, poured down a set of stairs. Helpless, she was carried along.

The people about her were silent, unspeaking. Heads down, they rapidly descended several flights of stairs. The only sound was the rush of clicking heels and scuffling soles. The graffiti on the dirty stone walls were oddly shaped and she couldn't read them. Overcoats and shoulder bags pressed against her from all sides.

The stairs turned and swept them past rows of chrome turnstiles that carded the crowd like wool. From the throats of the dark passages beyond came a roaring as of great machines or of rivers plunging down bottomless chasms. Beyond the landing, the stairs deposited her in a dim concourse. The crowd expanded to fill the larger space but did not slow. Everyone was silent, hurried, self-absorbed. "It's not far now," the Baldwynn said. Jane nodded.

Ahead, she saw a bright pool of light around which the crowd flowed and eddied without slowing. As she got closer she saw it was a child, a girl with red roses in her hair. The girl's skin was paler than marble, blanched and bloodless. Her features were exquisite, delicate without the least hint of weakness. She looked up at Jane with eyes the same harsh white as her skin, her dress, her hair. "You!" she cried.

"Me?" Jane stopped, bewildered. Nobody else paid the extraordinary creature the slightest attention. The crowds hurried by.

"You're so stupid!" said the little girl. "How can you be so stupid?"

"I—"

"You haven't understood a thing, have you?" She grabbed Jane's flight jacket and began going through the pockets. "What an idiot you are, what a total loss. You were the cause of Rooster's injuries—why did you dawdle so in Blugg's office? You screwed up Gwen and Peter when I meant you to be a comfort to them. You never even went to bed with Puck! You—I haven't the time to list your failures and treacheries. Where are the things I lent you?"

"What things?" Jane tried to back away, but the girl swarmed over her, a small fury, unstoppable. She ripped open Jane's blouse, reached a hand inside her chest, and pulled out a small leather fetish bag Jane hadn't known was there. She spilled the contents of the bag out on her hand. There was a mummified object about twice the length and thickness of a rabbit's foot, and a thin, bright glint of light.

Jane stared down on them. Her heart raced. Though she had never seen them before in her life, these two objects seemed to her the two most precious things in the universe.

"You wasted them!" The little girl held up the glint of light between thumb and forefinger, so Jane could see it for what it was: a needle. She dropped it back in the bag. She held up the larger object. It was covered with short, wiry hair: an amputated dog's tail. Angry teeth clicked. "I'll bet you don't even know what they were *for!*"

The dog's tail went in after the needle. Horribly white fingers closed about the bag, making a fist. "You weakling! You fool! You conceited, self-centered prig!" With every name, the girl hit Jane in the chest. The blood-red roses rattled with each blow. Finally, sneering disdainfully, the child turned her back. The crowds closed about her, and when they opened again, she was gone.

Jane blinked. She pulled shut and rebuttoned her blouse. Then she zipped up her jacket. She stood at an intersection. The concourse stretched far and indistinct in all directions.

In sudden panic, she realized that the Baldwynn was nowhere in sight.

Her guide was gone.

In a gray haze of despair, Jane wandered by signs reading Bar-B-Q Beef, Discount Vitamins, Deli-Sandwiches, Shoe Repair, Dollar Expres$, Jewelry, and Chinese Fast Wok. Flatly she thought, this is it, then. A pointless wandering through eternity. It was a singularly bland doom and yet one that felt oddly appropriate.

Just as she thought this, though, she chanced to glance within a diner and saw the Baldwynn sitting at the counter, eating a powdered doughnut. She went in.

At her approach, he put down his doughnut on his plate. Dabbed at his thin lips with his napkin. Smiled politely. "Here you are."

"Yes," she said. "But where am I?"

"In the same place you ever were; only your perception of it has shifted." The Baldwynn stood. "Follow me."

He led her behind the counter and opened what she had taken to be the door to a broom closet. They went through.

---

They were in a room, she supposed. Or a space of some kind, or possibly no space at all. It was impossible to tell, for all her attention was sucked up and swallowed by what was before her.

She stood before the Black Stone.

It was enormous, three times higher than herself at a minimum. But as there was nothing to gauge its scale against, it might have been any size, larger than worlds, greater than stars. Its surface was smooth and irregular, almost glassy in places, pitted and whorled like that of a meteorite. Mostly, though, it was black and solid and real. Jane had no doubt whatsoever that it was the Goddess incarnate.

"You may ask anything you want," the Baldwynn said, and left.

Jane looked up at the Black Stone. For a long time she did not speak. Then she cleared her throat and asked, "Why?"

There was no answer.

"Why?" she said again. "Why is life so loathsome? Why is there pain? Why does pain hurt so much? Couldn't you have ordered things differently? Or did you have no more choice than we? Is there no such thing as choice? Are we nothing more than automatons? Why is there love? Did you create us merely so we could be punished? Why are we punished? What was our sin? How could a mother treat her own children so? Don't you love us? Do you hate us? Are we aspects of you? Are you so hungry for

sensation that you incarnate bits of yourself as us in order to experience ignorance, fear, and pain? Is omniscience that bad?
What is death? What becomes of us after death? Do we simply
cease to be? Do mortals have only the one life? Were there other
lives before this one? Did we do something unforgivable in them?
Is that why you hate us? Will there be more lives? Will they be
worse? Can even you die? If you hate us so much, why is there
beauty? Does our misery rely on it? Would we be happier without beauty? Why is there joy? Exactly what do you want?"

There was no answer.

Jane stood before the Black Stone unmoving for what must
have been hours, days, ages, before she finally turned away. The
Baldwynn materialized at her side and, taking her elbow, steered
her away.

———— ·◎· ————

The dark wood held no terrors for her now. Seventeen pairs of
eyes opened suddenly in a nearby tree. They were merely eyes.
Rubbery hands clutched at her. They were only hands. "Do you
feel better now?" the Baldwynn asked.

"Yes."

"The Goddess has directed me to give you whatever you
want."

"Oh."

"What do you want?"

"I want to be punished," Jane said. She had no control over the
words. They came out of her mouth without volition and she was
amazed to hear what she had said. But she didn't want to disavow
them. She knew the truth when she heard it.

For a long time the Baldwynn did not speak. At last he said,
"Will you serve the Goddess now? Knowingly and lovingly, in
sweet obedience and humble acknowledgment of all that she is?"

"No." The word was a pebble in her mouth. She spat it out.
"Not now, not tomorrow, not if I live to be a million. Never."

The Baldwynn stopped and took her hands in his. "Dear
child," he said. "I feared there was no hope for you."

———— ·◎· ————

She was back in the lab again. Jane shook her head and
hopped down from the stool on which she was sitting.

Her mother looked up from the micromanipulator controls. "You're back," she said. "Did you have a pleasant visit?"

Jane couldn't bring herself to speak. She wandered over to the bench and began picking through the sloppy mound of papers there. They were all photocopies of the same circular gene map. Each had scrawls indicating the sequences that had been broken out and replaced, tested, and discarded. For all the hundreds of sheets there were, only a fraction of the possibilities had been worked through. "Lots of work here," she said inanely.

"All of it negative." Her mother twisted up one side of her mouth. "Sometimes you wish you could grab the little bastards by their lapels and *shake* them, they're so obtuse. I tell you, I'd like to dump the lot of them in the autoclave and start all over again in some other line of work. Tending bar, maybe, or selling used cars."

Abruptly it seemed to Jane that her mother wasn't talking about gene sequencing at all, but something at once greater and more personal. Her sudden agitation must've shown, for Sylvia gave her a perfunctory hug. "Oh, don't look so—it's only a passing fancy. I get these whims all the time, and they almost always go away on their own sooner or later." She released her. "It's not really their fault, is it?"

"No."

"It's just the way they're made."

"Yes."

Sylvia stubbed out her cigarette. Jane could tell by a certain horsey restlessness that she was anxious to get back to the electron microscope. "Well, kid, it's been lovely having you here. But right now I really do have work to do. Thanks for coming by, honey."

"Yeah," Jane said. "Okay, sure. You take care, huh?"

She started to turn away.

"Wait," her mother said. "You've got something on you." She reached out and plucked a small black creature, much like a millipede, from Jane's collar. It wriggled furiously in the palm of her hand, twisting about, impotently stinging her again and again.

Briefly it spread black wings. Jane flinched. She looked closer and saw that the mite was No. 7332, the dragon Melanchthon of the line of Melchesiach, of the line of Moloch.

"I don't think you need this anymore," her mother said. In a matter-of-fact fashion, she crushed it between her thumb and forefinger.

Aghast, Jane looked directly into her mother's eyes and saw something vast and alien within them, laughing. She realized then that Sylvia was only a mask for something impossibly huge and in that instant experienced a terror greater than anything she had ever imagined possible. Then a hand seized her by the scruff of her neck. It picked her up and put her down again somewhere else.

## TWENTY-FOUR

On a cold February afternoon Jane was released from the institute. Her mother took the day off from work and drove her home in an old Subaru with a malfunctioning heater. They both smoked all the way. Neither said much.

Jane got a job as a salesclerk in the mall. She took night courses, and within the year had her high school equivalency degree. She read all the chemistry texts she could get her hands on. The following September she was accepted at the local community college, where she could save money by commuting from her mother's house. By then she'd lost her excess weight, taken up tennis, and gotten herself into halfway good shape.

It wasn't easy. There were days when she had trouble even getting out of bed, the prospects of her ever having a normal life looked so bleak. Often she had nightmares. In them she stood before the Black Stone again, demanding to be punished. Hostile intelligences thronged the shadows, snickering, and this time the meaning of the Lady's dread silence was plain. Come dawn, though, she would remember the expression on the Goddess's face in that last instant of their final encounter, just before she found herself alive again and restored to her own world. And she knew it for love.

Surely, then, this was not punishment she had been given.

Within two years she'd managed to absorb everything the department could teach her. After a long conference in late January Dr. Sarnoff began making phone calls on her behalf. By April he'd swung a working scholarship to Carnegie Mellon. Which was where she'd *really* wanted to go all along. They threw a little party for her and drank New York State pink champagne out of Erlenmeyer flasks, and she cried at the thought of leaving all her new friends. But did.

Things really took off then.

She got a combined bachelors and masters from CMU under an accelerated program for promising undergrads. Her doctorate was a lot tougher because her adviser believed that however good a student might be, she ought to be doing better. "If we settle for good," Martha Reilly liked to say, "we only sacrifice the chance for brilliance. But if we settle for brilliant, we're throwing away the chance for a first-rate chemist!" Reilly was a tyrant, but she bullied Jane into doing better work than she'd imagined herself capable of. More and more now, though, she found herself bumping her head against something basic, a place where the language of chemistry and her intuition of how it ought to work just did not come together.

She jotted down a few things to help straighten out her thoughts. Her adviser saw them and suggested she base her thesis on them. So she did.

Reilly made her rewrite it from scratch five times.

The day after her orals, Diane came by to say there was a party in Squirrel Hill. It was the end-of-year blowout for a young physics instructor she knew and there'd be students there from Pitt and Chatham as well, so it wouldn't be just the usual crowd. Jane agreed that there'd probably never be a better time to get drunk and misbehave. She changed into a clean skirt and grabbed her purse.

Diane found a parking space for her Miata that was only slightly closer to Schenley Park than it was to the party. When they got out, the smell of honeysuckle made Jane stop for an instant. It's spring, she thought wonderingly. No, summer. How quickly the time had passed. She closed the car door and the button popped up. She tried again.

"Something's wrong with the mechanism," Diane said. "You have to lock it from the outside. Here, catch!"

Jane tried to snag the keys with her right hand and knocked them to the ground. She was left-handed now; sometimes she forgot.

"How's your mom taking it?" Diane asked when they were under way.

"Well, initially it was 'I don't know how you can even consider working for pigs like Du Pont.' But now that I've decided to turn down their offer and go the academic route it's 'Jane, you can't! All that money.' " Jane shrugged. "Sylvia's okay. We've had our differences, but who hasn't? Where is this place, anyway?"

"Three blocks up." The sidewalk led them past a line of Victorian brownstones. Stained glass numbers over the doors and asparagus ferns in the windows.

Jane looked up and saw Dame Moon floating high in the sky. An abrupt and sourceless melancholy seized her then and she shivered. "I feel like a child in this world," she said quietly.

"Hush! That's a fast ticket back to the institute. Did I tell you what Roger tried to pull last Thursday?" Talking lightly, Diane swept her down the street. By the time they got to their destination, Jane's mood had passed. "Here we are!" Diane cried and, returning to an earlier theme, "It's discouraging. Why is it so hard to find a good man?"

"You think that's difficult? Try giving up smoking."

"Oh, stop!"

Laughing, they clattered up the stairs. Voices poured down on them. "If that's not the right party, it'll do until the real thing comes along," Diane said, and hammered on the door. A very drunk undergrad with a liberal arts haircut opened it and said, "Drinks are over there."

They went in.

The rooms were predictably charming, the usual clever arrangements of space appointed with a tasteful mix of the original hardwood fixtures and postmodern wall hangings. Students were crammed in everywhere. They found their host up in the loft with a braided, rather Nordic-looking piece of jailbait, waved, and got a couple of beers. Diane nudged Jane and pointed her bottle at an expensively framed print on one wall. A Piranesi. Out of the corner of her mouth she said, "Waddaya think—an original?"

Jane trembled.

"Oh, my God." She seized her friend's arm so tightly that Diane laughingly objected, and pointed to a man across the room. "Who is he? You've got to tell me." By chance, or possibly prompted by a comment from someone nearby, he looked up. Their gazes locked. Jane knew Diane must think she was making a fool of herself, but she didn't care, she didn't care, she didn't care.

"His name!" she said. "I've got to know his name."

# SFBC 50th
## ANNIVERSARY COLLECTION